BY
MORNING
LIGHT

—— A NOVEL ——

By Morning Light

— A NOVEL —

RACHEL ANN NUNES

DESERET BOOK

SALT LAKE CITY, UTAH

Several special women were willing to share with me feelings and experiences surrounding the loss of their husbands. Thanks most especially to Deborah, Colleen, Valinda, Shaundra, and Ann, who are all valiant women with the courage to carry on. I appreciate your willingness to open your hearts to make Kerrianne real. I wish you all the best!

© 2006 Rachel Ann Nunes

Visit us at deseretbook.com

This is a work of fiction. Characters described in this book are the products of the author's imagination or are represented fictitiously.

Library of Congress Cataloging-in-Publication Data
Nunes, Rachel Ann, 1966–
  By morning light / Rachel Ann Nunes.
    p. cm.
  ISBN-10 1-59038-616-7 (pbk.)
  ISBN-13 978-1-59038-616-3 (pbk.)
  1. Spouses—Death—Psychological aspects—Fiction.
  2. Bereavement—Fiction. 3. Widowers—Fiction. 4. Domestic fiction. I. Title.
  PS3564.U468B92 2006
  813'.54—dc22   2006009039

Printed in the United States of America
Publishers Printing, Salt Lake City, UT

10   9   8   7   6   5   4   3   2   1

In fond memory of Adam Tolman

For all the years you were my friend
(Since that day we met at stake youth conference!)
For long talks on the phone and your good example
From your bicycle to the famous red Mustang
Our trip to California
Air Supply and Classic Skating with little brothers and sisters
Pizza with Binky
For chocolate and jewelry ads
Letters on our missions
The songs you wrote and played on your guitar
For all the dreams you dreamed . . .
And achieved
You are missed

Chapter One

Kerrianne Price sat on her bed with a heavy sigh. Today had been the second worst day of her life. Funny thing was, it was supposed to have been one of the happiest. Seeing her baby brother sealed to the woman he loved and watching them stare at each other with adoration shining so blatantly in their eyes should have warmed her heart. And it had.

For a time.

Except that after Tyler and Savvy had driven away in their Jeep, decorated generously with shaving cream, streamers, and pop cans, her parents and other siblings had gone to their vehicles with their spouses, discussing the day and exchanging special looks that could only be shared by couples in love. Kerrianne didn't have any special looks cast in her direction.

Normally her big, loud, loving family was the main thing between her and despair. They were good to her, and she certainly didn't begrudge their happiness. Yet why did it hurt so much that when all was said and done, no matter how good they were to her, the space next to her was empty?

Kerrianne went home alone. Well, not exactly alone. Her three children were in the van—all of them falling asleep. When they were back in Pleasant Grove, eight-year-old Misty roused enough to stumble inside to her bed while Kerrianne carried in the little boys, one at a time.

The house was quiet—too quiet—as she knew it would remain in the late evenings for a long time to come. Tyler wouldn't be stopping by so often or staying the night as he had in the past. He was married now, and it was right that he spend most of his time with Savvy. But for Kerrianne that meant more hours of silence and loneliness. Oh, he wouldn't mean to leave her alone, as her other siblings hadn't, but life took over. Despite her family's great love for her, not one of them could really comprehend the complete loneliness she felt.

The feeling was with her always. In church, in the grocery story, at the school where she was active in the PTA. After Adam's death, couples she had once been friends with slowly faded away as though they worried the same loss could touch their own happiness. No longer was she part of a pair but a fifth wheel, not necessarily unwanted but unneeded. But nowhere did she feel as out of place as in her own home in the dead of night when the children were sleeping. In her own big bed where her husband's pillow lay unused except to soak up her many tears.

She loved Adam intensely. Loved the shape of his head, the blue of his eyes, the smile he had reserved only for her. The way she felt safe in his arms . . . and loved. So loved.

On the worst day of her life, her perfect dream was shattered. Adam had died, his compact car crushed like a tin can by an old truck whose youthful driver had lost control. In a few hours it was over. Hours of suffering, of tears.

Next to the silence, Kerrianne most hated being alone. She hated not feeling Adam's touch on her face, watching him brush his teeth in the bathroom mirror, and listening to the love songs he sang for her on his guitar. She hated not being able to lay her head on his chest and listen to the beating of his heart.

"Adam," she whimpered, blinking back tears. Sometimes, if everything was right, she could feel him like a whisper against her skin. A touch of warmth on her senses. Often in the past years, she'd had the distinct impression that he was looking down on her and the kids. But of late these impressions were coming less and less often. As though to make up for the loss, Kerrianne found herself talking to him more than she probably should.

People told her she needed to go on with her life. Nearly four years. Yes, it had been a long time—seemingly a lifetime—but Kerrianne still felt she was living in limbo . . . waiting. For what?

But she knew.

She was waiting for Adam to come home.

Shaking her head, she impatiently wiped away her tears. Adam wouldn't like to see her this way; she hoped he wasn't watching now and seeing how cowardly she was behaving. She knew her lack of faith was showing, too, for she could never deny the comfort she received from the gospel of Jesus Christ. Knowing where Adam was made missing him bearable.

A shadowy movement from the hall caught her attention. She heard feet brush against the carpet. Goose bumps rippled up her spine, and her heart began pounding furiously. Her muscles clenched, ready to defend her family. "Who's there?" she called.

The shadow stepped forward, becoming Benjamin, her six-year-old son. "Mommy, can I sleep with you?" His big eyes were large in his small face, now threatening tears. In the dim light coming from the window, his hair looked blonder than usual, his skin more translucent.

"Did you have a bad dream?"

He shook his head. "I just want you."

Kerrianne wasn't surprised. Since starting first grade, Benjamin had been more clingy and anxious to have her close. During the first few months of school, she had gone every morning before lunch to help in the classroom just so he could see her and feel comforted. Now she only went once or twice a week. "Come on, then." She patted the bed. "You can stay here until you fall asleep. There's plenty of room."

He smiled and climbed up next to her, holding out his arms for a big hug. "I love you, Mommy."

"I love you, too."

Kerrianne was tucking the covers around him when he spoke again. "Mommy, if you found a daddy, then you wouldn't have any room for me here, would you?"

Kerrianne forced a strangled laugh. "Where did that come from?"

"I heard two ladies talking. They said Savvy's dress was too fancy and that you should get married."

"Who were they?"

She felt him shrug. "Don't know."

Kerrianne felt a wave of bitterness, remembering how one woman at Adam's funeral had told her she should get remarried soon, as though a husband were replaceable, like a car part or a pair of jeans. Aloud, she said, "Well, they shouldn't have said anything. It isn't any of their busin—it's really not up to them."

"But I wouldn't mind. I could always bring my blanket and sleep on the floor." That was Benjamin, accommodating to a fault.

"Don't worry, honey. You won't have to sleep on the floor."

He lay on her left arm and snuggled into her side. After a few minutes she could tell he was asleep, but she didn't move, savoring the momentary peace. Kerrianne was so grateful for Benjamin, for all her children. Being their mother was enough . . . wasn't it?

Her right hand stole out to touch Adam's pillow. The fabric was cold. Fighting tears, Kerrianne took her arm out from under Benjamin and hugged the pillow to her chest. It no longer smelled like him—the pillowcase had been washed many times since his smell had first faded—but it comforted her nonetheless.

After an hour of restless tossing, Kerrianne got up and went outside to the garage where she kept a stash of semisweet baking chocolate in her chest freezer. In the dim light from the single overhead bulb, she inched down the cold cement steps, jabbing her toes against Misty's bike tire. Stepping over the bike, she opened the lid. With dismay, she saw that she was down to one smallish slab—more than an inch thick but only about the size of her palm. That meant another trip to the store when she thought she'd bought enough to last two weeks. She couldn't risk being without a stash. Grabbing the chocolate, she let the freezer lid fall and went inside the family room, ripping off the remains of the clear plastic wrapping as she went.

She stopped at the CD player to slip in one of the new CDs her brother Tyler had made of Adam's taped songs. He'd done a great job, undistinguishable from the original, and she was grateful that with the extra copies and the hard drive backup, she would never have to worry about losing at least this part of her husband. His guitar music had been important to him, and so it was important to her.

She sat on the couch, bringing a foot under her and the chocolate to her mouth. The first bite was difficult to work off with her teeth, but the shards of cold chocolate melted quickly in her mouth. By the time she finished the piece, she felt significantly better. *As long as there is chocolate,* she thought, *women will somehow manage to survive.*

When the morning light angled through Kerrianne's blinds to wake her at nearly eight-thirty, she was tempted to stay in bed, to put Adam's pillow over her head and block out the light. After all, everyone deserved to sleep late on Saturday. But if she did that, she wouldn't be able to get the mail. She was one of the first houses on the postal route, and she hated the idea of letting the mail sit in her box unattended. Not that it was in much danger of being stolen. There had been a rash of mail thefts years ago that had started her morning habit, but there hadn't been trouble lately.

There could be again. She pushed herself from bed, knowing it was little more than an excuse. The mail gave her purpose, forcing her out of bed on those days that she wanted only to stay in bed forever and

5

drown in her own tears. Days when even the slabs of bulk chocolate in her freezer failed to make her feel better.

Reaching out, she softly stroked Benjamin's blond hair. She had forgotten to take him to his bed last night, but it really didn't matter. There was plenty of room here. Of all the children, Benjamin took after Adam the most. Sometimes looking at him brought a swell of pride—as it did right now—but at others it brought a bitter despair.

"I'm being brave, Adam," she whispered, though she couldn't feel him near. "I am."

Resolutely, she pulled on a pair of old sweats. It wouldn't do to get the mail in her robe if the mailman was still nearby. Passing the family room, she heard the TV on. Apparently Misty and Caleb were already up watching their allotted hour of Saturday cartoons.

Four-year-old Caleb spied her as she peeked in the room. "Mommy!" Immediately, he left the TV and launched himself across the room and into her arms.

"Good morning, sweetie." She kissed him, enjoying the feel of his plump arms around her neck. His thick hair had darkened to a light brown over the years and was sticking out in all directions as it usually was, unlike Misty, whose hair curled in many ringlets like a porcelain doll, looking beautiful even without a brushing. Or Benjamin's, whose finer strands knew how to lay obediently flat.

"Getting the mail?" he asked.

"Yes."

"I'm coming, but first . . ." He wriggled from her grasp and disappeared up the stairs toward the room he shared with Benjamin.

Smiling, Kerrianne went out onto her porch. The November frost was already melting on the lawn from the rays of the sun. She could see the mail truck down the road and watched the mailman reach from the cab to put letters in the boxes. The truck pulled up at her house, and the mailman hesitated when he glanced up and saw her waiting. Kerrianne smiled, unsure if he could see her response. She was surprised when he climbed from his vehicle and started up the walk.

He had letters in his hand but not a package, nothing that should evoke such treatment.

He was wearing the blue uniform coat, the blue trousers with the dark stripe down the side, and the heavy boots he always wore in the winter. In the summer it was a blue shirt and long shorts that showed remarkably fit and tan legs. Kerrianne blushed at the thought. *Not that I ever look at his legs,* she told herself. Suddenly, she became aware of her stringy hair, unwashed face, and shapeless sweats.

Why would she think about that now?

She shifted her bare feet uncomfortably on the cold welcome mat. The door banged behind her, and Caleb appeared with a large blue ball. He giggled before he threw it at the mailman, who was now only a couple of yards away. Surprised, the man gamely stuck out a hand for the ball, barely missing the catch.

Her son giggled. "You missed!" he sang, dancing from foot to foot on the cold porch.

"Caleb!" Kerrianne scolded, though she couldn't force too much objection behind the words. He was simply too cute.

The mailman grinned. "That's okay."

"I always throw him the ball," Caleb protested.

Kerrianne blinked. She knew her son often watched for the mail truck as she was getting the other children ready for school but had never dreamed Caleb had been throwing balls at the mailman.

"It's really okay." The man bent over for the ball. "I'm just slow this morning. It's a little cold."

"I'll say." Kerrianne shivered.

"Here's your mail. Thought I'd save you the trip to the box." His eyes went to her bare feet, which were becoming quite frozen. He couldn't have possibly seen from the curb that she was barefoot. How did he know? Did people always dash out to the mailbox without their shoes—even in the winter?

"Thank you." Kerrianne accepted the letters, meeting his eyes briefly. They were a dark, intense gray, unreadable in his handsome face. His hair, black and curling slightly, was longer in the back than she generally liked to see in a man, but it suited him well. He wore an extremely short beard, as though he'd let the hair grow for only a few weeks, something she hadn't noticed in all the years he'd been on her route, but it suited him, too.

She felt a strange disappointment when his eyes left hers and went to Caleb. He balanced the ball on the tips of his fingers. "Catch!" He tossed the ball to Caleb in a way that told Kerrianne he had practice with small children. She smiled at the delighted grin on her son's face when he managed to hang onto the ball.

"Again, again!" Caleb chanted.

"Honey, he has to go."

"That's all right. One more time, okay, buddy?" The gray eyes glinted as he said the words.

Caleb tossed the ball and then caught it again. With a smile and a wave the mailman strode toward his Jeep.

"Thank you," Kerrianne called.

He turned without slowing his gait. "I've got a boy his age. I know how they are. Have a good day."

Kerrianne wished he wouldn't go. She wished she could talk to him . . . about the weather, the mail route, politics—anything. She groaned. *What am I thinking?* With a sigh, she opened the door and went inside. Next thing she knew, she'd take up going to fast food restaurants just for some conversation. Or make an extra trip to Macey's to talk to that friendly checker who liked to chat with customers.

How desperate am I? Kerrianne wondered.

"Mommy, are you okay?" Caleb asked, following her inside.

She crouched down next to him. "I'm fine, honey. I'm just missing Uncle Tyler."

"But you saw him yesterday."

"I know. But he's married now, and we won't see him as much."

Caleb frowned. "Oh." Then he brightened. "So we'll go see him whenever we want."

8

"Good idea. Come on, now. Let's make breakfast."

Kerrianne thought longingly of chocolate, but she'd eaten it all. Besides, it wasn't healthy living on chocolate alone, and she also didn't want to fight another acne battle. She didn't care what skin experts said about chocolate not causing blemishes. The only time she ever broke out was after raiding her stash.

Ryan Oakman whistled as he made his way back to his mail truck. He normally hated working Saturdays, as he liked to spend the day with his children, but they were shorthanded today, so he'd come in, even though he'd already put in his five days that week. He was glad it was a slow mail day; he'd be home by four, maybe earlier if he hurried. That would give him plenty of time to be with the kids before the play that evening, and he could use the overtime with Christmas coming up. Tiger wanted a bicycle and Ria was angling for a video game and a new baseball mitt. Not *any* baseball mitt, mind you, but the best money could buy. She was serious about her baseball. She was serious about every sport she played.

Ryan frowned as he thought about his daughter. She was a girl, but she didn't seem to realize it. She dressed like a boy and even cut her hair short. Not like the blonde girl who lived at this house, the one who looked like a dainty porcelain doll. Still, even the blonde girl enjoyed tossing the ball about with her little brothers. He'd usually see her outside several times a week—except this past week when it had become so cold.

Thinking of the boy made him smile. He and Tiger were two of a kind; it was too bad they didn't live near each other so they could play.

Glancing up at the house, he saw Mrs. Price turn to go inside. She was an interesting sort. In all the years he'd been on the route they'd rarely exchanged more than two words. Yet every morning she was there. In warm weather she often sat on the porch waiting, or she would come out as he drove away from her house. He'd occasionally look back and see her sitting on her porch, holding the mail and lifting her face to the sun.

She was an enigma to him. There was something tragic about her face, something intense, but he had no idea what it meant. All he knew was that she waited each morning for the mail, almost as though her life depended on it. At first he had wondered if she was waiting for a certain letter, but over the years her habits had not changed.

He'd been glad to deliver her mail. He made sure to be on time. None of the others on this route seemed to care what time he came, but she did, and that was enough. Even when his own life was in turmoil and he wondered if he could go on another day, he had forced himself to go to work because she'd be waiting. She'd been a reason for him to get out of bed, when there had been so many other reasons to give up.

Laurie, he thought. Two years had passed since his wife's death. The thought of her no longer brought the searing pain, but only the terrible ache of loss. He'd gone on with his life for the sake of the children, as Laurie had urged him to do in the weeks before her death. He'd even started dating this past year, and while it felt strange at first, he'd become accustomed to the company of other women. But lately he'd begun doubting that another woman he could connect with on the same level even existed. Perhaps Laurie had been his one and only chance for love. At least he had the promise of eternity with her.

That morning Mrs. Price wasn't the only one waiting for him on his route. Down two houses, Maxine Madison, a sixty-something widow, was out on her porch and came trotting up to his truck before he even came to a full stop.

Maxine was definitely a striking, noticeable woman. She had a ready smile, piercing eyes that seemed to see everything, and a little bit of attitude. Once she'd told him that she was going to the grave kicking and screaming, and that was why she dyed her hair, exercised every day, and kept her wardrobe updated. "I may be getting up there," she said, "but I'm far from dead yet."

Pushing away the memory, he smiled. "Up early, I see."

She snorted. "Are you kidding? It's almost nine. I've already walked three miles, done all my laundry, answered five e-mails, and read five chapters in my new book. Early, schmurly."

"Wow, I wish you could have done my route for me. That way I could be home sleeping." He covered a yawn with his hand.

"I bet you stayed up late last night because of the play, didn't you?" She paused, but when he didn't reply, she rolled her eyes. "That's a hint in case you didn't recognize it. Goodness, you have to spell out everything for the younger generation these days."

Ryan stifled a smile. Younger generation. He hadn't thought of himself that way for many years. To tell the truth, thirty-four didn't feel all that young. "What are you talking about?"

Maxine's pale brown eyes narrowed. "Did you forget my tickets?"

"Tickets?" he asked innocently.

"Humph!" She folded her arms and glared at him.

He tilted his head back and laughed. "Don't worry, Maxine, I got 'em. I know you've been waiting." He pulled the pair from his coat pocket and handed them to her.

Maxine's face relaxed, and a grin appeared. "You'd better have remembered. I'm taking a friend to your play tonight."

"Oh, is it that gentleman I saw you with last month?"

Maxine gave a little gasp and glanced heavenward. "Then I wouldn't have needed the tickets; he'd have been buying. Our generation isn't like yours at all. The gentleman always pays. No. I'm taking a woman friend with me tonight."

Ryan imagined two little old ladies watching the play together. He grinned. "I'll be sure and put on a good show."

"You always do, dear." She patted his hand that was braced on the side of the truck. "Now where's my mail? Come on, I don't have all day. There's stuff to do, people to see, so let's get a move on. I'm not getting any younger, unfortunately."

Ryan handed her a small bundle, his mouth twitching. "I bet that widower has a hard time keeping up with you."

"Him? Darn right. He's lucky to make it to the end of the walk. But he'll get in shape, you'll see."

"Oh, does that mean I hear wedding bells in the future?"

Maxine looked aghast. "Are you kidding? And have to wash his clothes and make dinner every night? No way. I've paid my dues. If I was younger, maybe I'd feel differently, but I'm enjoying running my own life. No, getting him in shape is purely for my own good. I don't enjoy sitting on the porch sipping juice all day. Now if they let us have coffee, it might be worth it." She looked at him expectantly, but he didn't react. "I'm kidding, for crying out loud. Vile stuff, coffee, but there's no reason we can't make a joke now and again. You have to tell that wife of yours to get you out a bit more. It's plain as the nose on your face that you're working too hard."

Ryan's face froze, though he tried not to let Maxine see. She didn't know him, not really. For all the years she'd chatted with him at the curb, they hadn't gotten that far into his personal life. The only reason she knew of his involvement at the community theater was that she'd spotted him there a few months earlier. She certainly didn't know about Laurie. She didn't know that this job, the theater, and his kids were the entire extent of his life.

"You okay, Ryan?" she asked.

"I'm fine," he managed. "Just fine. And you're right. I'm working too hard. But I won't be tonight. You'll enjoy the play. My little girl's in it, too. Plays a boy, though. She's the skinny one with the cap that follows Robin Hood around. She's hilarious. If you have time, come on back and meet her." His breath was coming easier now, and he was relieved to see the concern leave her face.

"Will do. Bye, now. Thanks for the tickets." With a little wave, Maxine headed up the walkway.

Ryan pushed on the gas, determined not to stop again. Any more delays like that and he might not make it through this day.

Chapter Two

Kerrianne cleaned the house, though it was already spotless. Then she moved on to the laundry and the inside windows. She even organized the boys' closet, which was an amazing feat. After she finished, it was still only six o'clock and the evening stretched out before her like an empty hallway leading into another night filled with bitter loneliness.

She thought about calling her sister, but Amanda was five months into her second pregnancy and had problems with swelling feet and finding the motivation to do anything. Well, anything other than the adoption of the two children she and her husband, Blake, had taken custody of shortly before their marriage almost four years ago. Blake's cousin, the children's mother, had finally agreed to terminate her parental rights, so at last the children were really theirs. This left Amanda and Blake delirious with joy. They hoped to have the children sealed to them by the end of the year.

Tyler, of course, was on his honeymoon with Savvy. Her brother Mitch would be with his wife, Cory, getting ready to present their newest project to their publisher. Their nonfiction book featuring animals in Australia was bound to be a big hit since even Kerrianne's breath had been taken away with Cory's photographs and Mitch's text—and she didn't like reading as much as she should. In addition, Mitch and Cory had their hands full with their adopted daughter, EmJay, and with Lexi, Savvy's teenage half sister. Lexi was staying at their house while Tyler and Savvy, now her guardians, were on their honeymoon.

Even her parents had plans with their friends for the evening. Everyone was busy—except her. Kerrianne couldn't help feeling sorry for herself. How different her life could have been.

If only . . .

"Hey, it's your turn, Caleb!" Misty said. She was playing *Sorry!* with the two boys. Benjamin played well, but Caleb was distracted by everything—this time by a scab on his leg. "Here, I'll move for you."

"No!" Caleb screeched.

"Then hurry!"

Kerrianne lay on the couch and squeezed her eyes shut. She'd have to do something for dinner, but maybe leftovers from Thursday would do. The children liked hash browns with hamburger, and she had frozen broccoli that would cook in a few minutes.

She didn't move, unable to find the motivation. Tears pricked at her eyes. She loved her children, loved watching them and being here for them, but even their presence couldn't stop the loneliness. When they were in bed, it would be much worse.

Adam, she thought, *this isn't fair. How you would feel if I had left you instead?*

She thought about this a lot. Most men remarried within a year of their wife's death. Though some women also married quickly, many waited as long as five years. Some never remarried. For Kerrianne, even the idea of another man in her life seemed impossible, but would Adam have felt the same way? He had been a devoted, loving husband who had needed her a lot. She had always thought he was the strong one, but maybe she was more up for this challenge of single parenting. That didn't make doing it any easier.

I love you, Adam Price—but I should have known from your name that loving you would exact a big price from me.

The doorbell rang and the children immediately lost interest in the game. "I'll get it!" shouted Caleb.

"No, I'll get it." Misty followed behind. "You don't know how to unlock the door."

Only Benjamin stayed by the game, picking up a card and lying down on the floor to study it.

Kerrianne was glad Misty was old enough to reach the extra lock she'd had her father install on the door. Her head ached, and she felt too exhausted to move. "Ask who it is before you answer," she called. "If you know who it is, you can answer, but tell them I'm not feeling well."

"Okay." Misty's voice floated back from the entryway.

Kerrianne shut her eyes, wondering when she had become so lax. There had been a time when she would never have permitted her children to answer the door alone—especially in the evening. If only her head didn't hurt so much.

Voices filtered through the growing pain in her head, but Kerrianne could tell they weren't threatening. She stopped listening so closely. Maybe in a minute she would get up and heat the food. She might even find the energy to make something the kids loved, like homemade pizza. They always enjoyed that, and it had been one of Adam's favorites. A whimper escaped her lips.

"Are you really sick?" came a brash voice.

Kerrianne's eyes flew open. Maxine Madison from two doors down was staring at her skeptically, hands on her hips. Next to her, Misty shrugged her shoulders apologetically and returned to her game with the boys. Kerrianne couldn't exactly blame her for letting Maxine in. The woman never took no for an answer when she wanted something.

Maxine was wearing a pink pantsuit with black trim on the jacket, a black shirt with pink polka dots, and black strappy heels. Her white-blonde hair curled becomingly around her chin. Was she on her way somewhere? It was hard to tell since Maxine always looked dressed to kill.

Kerrianne forced herself to a sitting position. "I've got a terrible headache. I was just lying here thinking what to make for the kids."

"They haven't eaten yet? Well, take some aspirin, for crying out loud." Maxine started toward the kitchen. "Where's your aspirin? I'll get it for you. But I tell you, you're cutting things close. The play starts at seven."

"Play?" Kerrianne staggered after her. "What are you talking—oh, that play. So you got tickets?"

"Yes, and I figured you might forget so that's why I'm a little early— to make sure you have time to get ready." Maxine set her black purse on the counter and reached to open a cupboard. "Are they in here? No? There? Okay, here we go. Now you take this, and tell me what I should heat for the kids while you get ready. Hurry!"

"Look, I'm a mess, I don't have a sitter, and I don't feel well. I'm sorry to disappoint you but—"

The doorbell rang, and Kerrianne could hear Misty and Caleb running toward it.

"That will be your sitter."

"Sitter?" Kerrianne didn't like the sound of that. She was particular about baby-sitters, and only her siblings and parents usually made the cut.

"Yeah, that cute little girl, sister to your brother's new wife."

"Lexi?"

"That's right, Lexi. I talked to her at the reception last night, and she was glad to come over. Your brother—not Tyler, the other one— promised to drop her off. Oh, and she's spending the night."

"But—"

Maxine shook her head. "No buts. You promised me you'd come, and I'm not going to let you get out of it like the last two times. Goodness, I had to take Harold from two streets over last month, and now he thinks we're practically engaged. Imagine that!" She sighed with disgust. Then her eyes narrowed. "Besides, we both know it's an excuse. I bet you'll find your headache disappears once we get there. Go on now. But wear some makeup, for crying out loud. You look all washed out. And don't wear sweats. Wear that bright pink blouse you wore at church last week. That'll help some."

That was Maxine, bluntly honest to a fault. Kerrianne threw up her hands and disappeared up the stairs without telling Maxine about the hash browns. No doubt she would find them herself. She apparently had everything under control.

Though she wanted to feel resentment toward Maxine, Kerrianne had to admit to being secretly glad for the change in her routine. At least there would be some adult conversation. It might be odd conversation but likely fascinating all the same. Most important, Maxine was a widow, who understood what it was like to lose the love of her life. In the past few months since they began team-teaching a Primary class at church together, Kerrianne had found herself drawn toward the older woman. Maxine reminded her a great deal of her mother, only brasher, more outspoken, and in a more compact form. The woman was a veritable fireball, unafraid to voice her opinions and apparently rarely thinking before she spoke. She'd offended half the neighborhood at one time or another but had won them back the same way.

The children were making excited noises by the door, obviously pleased at Lexi's appearance. Even Benjamin had made the effort to come to the entryway. While there had once been a time that Kerrianne wouldn't have dared leave her children with Lexi, the girl had made a lot of changes. Lexi still had challenges, to be sure, but since her baptism last month, the thirteen-year-old had reevaluated her lifestyle. Her many piercings were no longer filled with jewelry, and her revealing shirts and ultra miniskirts had disappeared. Her attitude about what was important in life had seen the most change—a good thing, since Misty adored her and the boys obeyed her every utterance with eagerness.

Upstairs in the bathroom adjoining her room, Kerrianne set the pills Maxine had given her in the mirrored medicine cabinet and looked at herself in despair. It was too late to take a shower, but she could put a few steam rollers in her hair to sit while she applied a bit of makeup. She had some in the drawer that she sometimes used on Sundays.

Kerrianne set her hair quickly and reached for her eye shadow. The makeup had definitely seen better days. In fact, Kerrianne wondered if it was still safe to use; she couldn't remember when she'd purchased it. She dabbed a bit on.

"Kids, come and eat!" she heard Maxine call downstairs.

After the eye shadow, she tried to put on some liner, but the pencil was dull, and she couldn't find a sharpener. Her lipstick was so used that she'd have to scrape it out with a bobby pin. Instead, she smoothed a bit of Vaseline on her lips.

Going to her closet, she quickly discarded several choices. When had her clothes become so big? Nothing seemed to fit except the blouse Maxine had suggested. It had been a gift from her sister months ago, but Kerrianne didn't often wear it because the color was so bright. Happy. As though there were something to celebrate. Kerrianne didn't often feel like celebrating.

She pulled on black pants, and though they were too loose, the fitted top set them off just right. Lastly, she took out the curlers, running her fingers gently through the curls. Her hair looked nice, but it wouldn't last through the play if she didn't use hair spray. She grabbed the bottle only to find the tip was clogged.

"Kerrianne! Are you ready yet?" Maxine called. "Do you need some help? I'm pretty good with makeup, you know."

Kerrianne knew. Maxine sold makeup—an expensive brand that Kerrianne couldn't remember the name of—and she was a walking advertisement. Not that she put on too much; Maxine was tasteful in her makeup choices, as she was with her clothes. Too bad the tendency didn't extend to her word choice.

"I'm ready." Without another glance in the mirror, Kerrianne headed down the stairs. Maxine waited at the bottom, hands on her hips, her lips pursed in disapproval.

"Well, at least you had the good sense to wear the blouse. Don't you have any lipstick? And base? You can't go without base."

"I'm running low on a few things." Kerrianne scowled at her—or tried to. The way Maxine was looking at her made her more nervous than anything.

"That's what I thought. Don't worry, dear—I came prepared with my samples and plenty of disposable applicators. Come here for a minute." Maxine pulled her into the downstairs bathroom, simultaneously flicking on the light.

"Maxine, I don't want any more makeup."

"What color of eye shadow is that anyway?" Maxine squinted at her for a moment before pulling out her reading glasses and sticking them on her face. "Purple? No, with your eyes I'd rather use a shade of blue. Just enough to enhance the color of your eyes. Not for the lid, mind you, just the crease. For the lid we'll use this pale pink. But it has to be the right color . . . Oh, here it is." Maxine was opening a kit as she spoke. Her face was so serious and absorbed—so happy—that Kerrianne decided to let her have her way. What could it hurt?

"Oh, wait. First we should put on base." Maxine shook a bottle and began dabbing the contents on Kerrianne's nose and cheeks. Then she went back to the eye shadow. "We'll use a dark blue eyeliner," Maxine said as she worked. "And you need some pencil for your eyebrows. They're too pale."

Kerrianne endured Maxine's ministrations with good grace. Mascara followed the eyeliner, and then Maxine took out a mini bottle of hair spray and began working on her hair, rising to her tiptoes to back comb the hair on top near the scalp. "Your hair really is a beautiful light brown," she said, "but I'm thinking you might want to get some highlights. I'll give you the name of my hairdresser. She's the best."

Kerrianne had no intention of coloring her hair, but she didn't say so aloud. "My hair isn't light brown," she said. "It's dark blonde."

Maxine snorted. "Same thing."

"It's not the same thing at all." Kerrianne had always been blonde, and she didn't know if she was ready to have brown hair.

"There, all done. See? It only takes two minutes." Maxine turned Kerrianne toward the mirror. Kerrianne stared at the transformation. The eyeliner was thicker than she would have used, and she'd never known her lashes could be so long, but the whole picture was nice. Better than nice. Stunning. But this wasn't her. This woman was a stranger. A familiar stranger, but a stranger nonetheless. This was the woman she had been before the accident. This woman belonged to another life. The perfect life, where wives knew how to keep their husbands from dying and leaving them alone.

"You okay?" Maxine's voice was subdued now, as though she had read Kerrianne's thoughts.

"I—I don't know." Kerrianne felt tears gathering in her eyes.

Maxine put a hand on her arm. "You look fabulous. And I'm not just saying that."

"Thank you." What would Adam say if he could see her now? She bet he'd sweep her up into his arms and kiss her until all the pink lipstick was gone. And she would kiss him right back as hard as she could. She'd never let him go. *Oh, Adam! I miss you.*

Kerrianne swallowed hard. "Maxine?"

"Yes?"

"Do you ever talk to your husband?"

Maxine's face broke into a wide smile. "Are you kidding? I talk to him more now than when he was alive. He wasn't much of a conversationalist. Now I chat and chat and he just listens. Why, only this morning I was cleaning my bedroom and I felt he was there, lying on the bed like he always used to on Saturday mornings. I told him all about how Harold was trying to take his place. I tell you, it was good to get it all out in the open like that. I could really see what I wanted to do—and that's not to let Harold get his way."

"And what did your husband say?"

Maxine's eyes glistened with unshed tears. "Oh, sweetie, he doesn't talk back. He just listens. If they talk back, well, then you have a problem." She paused. "Well, at least if they do it all the time."

"But do you sometimes feel him? Kind of like talking? Here, I mean." Kerrianne held her hand to her heart, which was aching with need for Adam so acutely that she felt that if she moved even so much as an inch she might die.

"Yes. I do. I know what you mean. But I feel it less now than I used to. He's been gone more than five years now, you know."

Kerrianne did know. She also knew that Maxine had been devastated by her husband's death from cancer and that she'd gone to live with one of her daughters for more than a year afterward. She'd still been with her daughter at the time Adam was killed. It comforted Kerrianne to know Maxine still missed her husband, that she talked to him, and that at the same time she somehow managed to be happy without him.

"Anyway," Maxine added, "I think Charles has stuff he's doing. And so do I."

Kerrianne wondered if among all the things to do in heaven Adam had learned to play a harp. He'd always wanted to, but his guitar had taken all his free time.

"Guess that will have to wait until the next life," she'd told him so often it became a joke between them.

"That's a great idea," he'd said. She wasn't so sure anymore. Not since it had taken him away from her.

"Are you ready?" Maxine asked, breaking through her thoughts. "We should go if we want to be on time."

"What is this play anyway?" She was sure Maxine had told her at one point, but she couldn't dredge up the name from her memories.

"*Robin Hood*. Don't you listen to anything I say? Come on, let's go."

Kerrianne followed Maxine from the bathroom. "I just want to say good-bye to the kids."

"Okay, but no kissing them. That lipstick is good, but it isn't kid proof."

"I hope Misty doesn't make a scene about going. She loves plays." Kerrianne hoped Misty's adoration of Lexi would keep her from begging to go with them.

When they spied Kerrianne, the children ran up and hugged her. "You look pretty, Mom," Misty said, her blue eyes wide with admiration.

"Pretty?" Lexi echoed. "She's hot!"

Kerrianne flushed. "Uh, thanks. I think. Now don't let the kids go outside while I'm gone."

"I know—and no neighbors over." Lexi grinned at her. "Don't worry. I promise they'll all be alive and safe when you get home. I won't even let them watch TV."

Kerrianne walked to the front door. "Well, you can put in a video if you need to. But have them brush their teeth and put pajamas on at eight and then bed."

"Aw, Mom," Misty protested. "Can't we stay up a little later? Lexi's here, and we want to have fun."

"Okay, nine—since it's Saturday. But remember, we have church tomorrow."

"Yes!" Misty lifted an arm into the air. The boys copied her, giggling.

"Have a nice time at the play," Lexi called as they went down the porch steps.

"I will. Thanks. Lock the door. And don't answer the phone unless you hear me on the answering machine. I have my cell phone if you need me. I left the number on a piece of paper next to the kitchen phone."

"Okay. But don't worry. We'll be fine!" Lexi shut the door.

Maxine grinned at her. "Whew, I forgot what it's like having little kids. I'm glad you have them when you're young. It's too much effort for old people like me."

Kerrianne blew out air between pursed lips. "You have more energy than anyone I know."

"That's because I exercise. If I didn't do that, I'd really be old. Like Harold. If he doesn't do something soon, he's going to have a heart attack."

"Well, at least then he wouldn't ask you to marry him." Kerrianne grimaced. "I didn't mean it that way. I wouldn't want Harold to . . . I just meant that—"

Maxine laughed, the skin around her eyes wrinkling into a myriad of fine lines. "I know how you meant it. Don't give it another thought. Besides, Harold's too ornery to die. If he did have a heart attack, all that would mean is that the neighborhood would have to come in and take care of him, me included. But I won't do his laundry, I tell you. I'm finished with men's laundry."

Kerrianne smiled and fastened her safety belt. Going with Maxine tonight was a good thing. Her headache was completely gone—and without the benefit of the aspirin tablets that still sat in her upstairs bathroom cupboard.

❋ ❋ ❋

As he helped put finishing touches on the tiny stage, Ryan took a moment to glance between the curtains and peek out at the audience. The community theater at the Pleasant Grove library wasn't large, and on this closing night all the seats would be filled. The audience was a lively group, and people chattered to one another as they found their seats. A grin came to his face as he spied Maxine. True to her word, she had a woman in tow instead of her gentleman friend, but contrary to his expectations, this woman was at least half Maxine's age with hair that looked dark in the dim light and framed her face in becoming waves. At this considerable distance the friend looked attractive, if too slender, but she carried herself with an air of grace and confidence that drew his attention—and seemed oddly familiar. Who was she?

He tried to stifle his interest. She probably had five children and a husband waiting at home, and this was a girls' night out. All the good ones seemed to be taken. By the time they got enough experience to really be interesting, they had already been snatched up.

Or could there be a woman out there for him? One near his own age that he hadn't yet met? Laurie had believed she existed.

"Ryan," Sam hissed. He turned to see the assistant director behind him, her chin-length blonde hair shining around her like a halo. She was beautiful.

Ryan dropped the curtain. "What?"

"Ria's having some sort of problem. You'd better go check it out."

He quickly went to the small backstage dressing room, crammed with actors, and found his nine-year-old daughter in a corner crying about a rip in the seam of her pants. "I can't go onstage with my underwear showing!" she sobbed.

"Hey, I've got some masking tape. Don't worry about it." He set a comforting hand on her shoulder.

"That's what you did the last time, and it doesn't stay! You said you'd sew it! Every time I sit down, it could pop open." Her words rose to a wail. A few cast members glanced in their direction. Ria looked away angrily.

He stood and began rummaging through a box of costume odds and ends, finding a box of safety pins. "How about some pins, then? Hurry, take off your pants behind that chalkboard, and I'll fix it right up."

"Dad, I'm not taking off my pants in here!" She gestured to all the other people, who were immersed in their own last-minute wardrobe and makeup fixes.

"Well, there's no time for me to do anything else. I have to go on stage in a minute. What's the big deal? You can hide under this blanket."

"Oh, Dad, you just don't understand!"

No, he didn't. The Ria he knew wouldn't have minded changing behind the chalkboard, blanket or no blanket, and in fact had done so many times before. What was different now? She'd suddenly turned into a creature he didn't understand. Was this early puberty, or simply the way girls were?

Ria thrust out her hands for the pins. "Just give them to me. I'll get Sam to help me fix it in the bathroom."

"Okay, but hurry. You don't want to miss your cue."

Ria wrapped the blanket around her waist and stomped away.

Ryan sighed. What was he going to do with her? Somehow they had to get through this new phase, but would she still like him when it was over? His understanding was growing thinner each day—and so was hers. Once they'd been best buddies, but now she was drawing away from him, which made him try to hold on tighter. He didn't want to lose her. He'd lost enough already.

What Ria needed was a woman to help her find her way. A woman to soften and buffer their interactions until they found themselves again. But he'd tried to find someone. The only woman who remotely fit the bill was Sam—and that was another story.

Ryan heaved a sigh, pushing these unhappy thoughts from his head. Only a few minutes left to get into character, a few minutes to give himself over to this other identity. It wasn't hard once he concentrated, and leaving his own life for a few hours gave him the respite he so desperately needed from single parenting.

At the same time a fleeting thought came to him. If there was a woman out there for him, she would have to find him or magically appear in his path. Because behind the happy mask, behind the facade of capability, he was mentally and emotionally exhausted. Maybe next week he'd feel differently, but for now he was sick—sick of dating, of hoping, of trying.

Chapter Three

T he play was very good, and the smallness of the theater gave it an air of familiarity that Kerrianne enjoyed. She clapped enthusiastically as the cast came out on the stage for a final bow. Maxine put her fingers to her mouth and let out a loud whistle that made Kerrianne laugh.

"Come on," Maxine told her as most of the audience began filing up the two aisles and out the doors. "I want you to meet someone."

"You know one of the actors?"

Maxine gave her an enigmatic smile. "Yeah, you do too—or should—but we were sitting kind of far back. Let's see if you recognize him up close."

Kerrianne wondered if one of the teens who'd played Robin Hood's Merry Men lived in their neighborhood. Or did Robin Hood look like her home teacher's oldest son, the one who was in college now?

"He was the best actor tonight, I think," Maxine continued. "I'll have to tell him so. He wasn't quite as good in the last play I saw."

Kerrianne followed Maxine to the impossibly narrow backstage where people were packing things away and talking excitedly. She didn't see how they would find anyone in this confusion.

"Ah, there he is." Maxine edged around two teens and walked toward a man hefting a large backdrop, his movements awkward in the confined space. Kerrianne recognized his costume as belonging to the Sheriff of Nottingham. He'd been very good, and now that they were closer, there was something familiar about him. Maxine was already talking to him, and he set down the backdrop and shook her hand. Kerrianne hurried to catch up, knocking over a water bottle someone had set up against the wall. The man looked up, eyes locking onto hers.

Recognition flooded over Kerrianne. She knew him! And yet he looked so different than she'd last seen him that morning in his postal uniform. He was taller than she'd thought, broader too, but the friendly smile was the same one he'd had while throwing the ball with her son. Tonight he was more handsome, more dangerous, though that might have more to do with his costume and his villainous role as the Sheriff of Nottingham than his own personality. His eyes slid over her in appreciation, causing her to flush. She was grateful for the dim lighting—and that he couldn't feel the pounding of her heart.

"You were really great tonight, Ryan," Maxine was saying. "You nailed it just right. Much better than the last play. In that one you were a little flat."

Ryan shifted his gaze from Kerrianne to Maxine. "Well, it's always fun to play the bad guy."

"So does that mean you're going to lose the beard now? And cut your hair?"

He smiled and gave half shrug with one shoulder. "Maybe. I kind of like looking dangerous."

As Maxine laughed, his eyes wandered back to Kerrianne. She felt them burning into her face. Her heart started pounding again, and her breath caught in her throat. What was wrong with her? He was just a man—her mailman, to be exact. A man she'd glimpsed almost every day for the past four years and probably longer. Why was her body acting so strangely?

There was no reason for it, unless . . . With horror, Kerrianne realized she was attracted to him. But how could she possibly be attracted to another man when she was still in love with Adam? The idea was utterly ridiculous. Yet it hadn't been so long that she couldn't remember what attraction felt like.

"Who's your friend, Maxine?" Ryan asked. "A lot better looking than your last date. Better company, too, I'll bet."

He doesn't recognize me. Mortified, Kerrianne wished she hadn't come backstage with Maxine. She knew she'd been rather uncaring about her appearance of late, but how could he not recognize her? Only that morning he'd played ball with her son. She'd even remembered what his legs looked like in the summer. Was she so unremarkable that he didn't remember her at all?

"Well, she didn't fall asleep, that's for sure." Maxine gave Kerrianne a pleased glance. "But you already know her. Look closer. Guess who?"

Kerrianne could have killed Maxine.

"Now that you mention it, she does look kind of famili—"

"Dad!" A young child wearing a cap burst into view. "They're having a cast party over at Dawn's. Can I go? Just for a while? Dawn said to tell you that she'd watch me if you aren't coming."

"Is this your daughter?" Maxine asked.

"Yes, this is Ria." Ryan pulled off her cap, releasing a mass of straight, shiny, black hair that fell to her jaw line. Kerrianne couldn't be sure, but the girl seemed to have a slight olive cast to her skin. *Must be from her mother,* she thought. Her eyes were impossible to put a color to in the dim light, but they were definitely dark.

"Nice job tonight," Maxine said. "I really believed you were a peasant boy. I thought you pretended to mimic Robin Hood very well. I've never seen that version before. You did a great job."

"Thank you. It was fun." Ria gave her a fleeting smile before looking back at Ryan. "Can I go, Dad? Can I?"

"Sure. But only for an hour. I'll be there in a while. We have church early."

"Thanks," the girl said breathlessly. She pulled her cap from her father's fingers, shoving it onto her head.

As she started to turn away, Ryan asked. "Where's your brother?"

Ria paused near Kerrianne. "He's out on the front row, talking to Sam. He'll want to come, too. Can he?"

"Not without me. I'll bring him when I come. But don't take off until the props are put away."

"I know, I know." Ria darted behind Kerrianne and out onto the stage.

Ryan grinned at them, and Kerrianne was angered by the warmth in her stomach. She didn't want to be attracted to this man. Even if he didn't already have a family, she certainly wouldn't be interested.

Jostling past actors in the tight backstage, they began moving back the way they had come. "I'd better check on Tiger," Ryan was saying to Maxine. "Have to see that he's not making a pest of himself."

Kerrianne trailed after them, glad Ryan hadn't recognized her and that she'd been saved further humiliation. At the first opportunity she would disappear up an aisle and wait for Maxine outside by the car. With any luck, she wouldn't have to face his gray stare again or feel that disturbing warmth.

They had managed to squeeze past more actors and were finally free of the backstage area, when Ryan stopped and turned abruptly in her direction. She came within an inch of hitting into him. Up this close she could see each tiny hair of his trim beard and smell the slight odor of maleness that had always lingered after Adam exercised hard—apparently acting was rigorous work. The scent wasn't overwhelming enough to be unpleasant, but it evoked a flood of memories she'd forgotten: Adam riding his bike, his playing ball with the kids, their family camping in the mountains. Tears stung her eyes. *Please don't let him see,* she prayed.

"Hey, I figured it out. You're Mrs. Price—Kerrianne, right? Third house on my route. I play ball with your kids." His eyes traveled over her face and briefly down the length of her. "Only you look different somehow." The admiration was back in his eyes, almost like a gentle caress. Or was she imagining his interest because no man had looked at her in so very long?

"It happens when the sun goes down," she said dryly. "Like becoming a werewolf. Takes me all day to tame the beast." There, that ought to put him in his place.

He gave her a slow smile that did nothing but exacerbate the heat in her stomach and the rapid beating of her heart. "I find that's true with most of the people on my route. All day, I see pajamas, curlers, and"—his grin deepened—"no shoes. After all, nobody will see them, nobody except the mailman. Yep, they all do it. All but Maxine, here, of course. She's always dressed to perfection, no matter when I see her."

Maxine rolled her eyes. "One of these days I'll have to go out to get the mail with curlers in my hair."

Ryan put a hand to his chest and staggered. "What? And cause me a heart attack?"

Maxine shook her head and tried to look bored, but her blue eyes danced with mirth. "In case you hadn't noticed, the play is over. I know acting when I see it."

Chuckling, Ryan did an about-face and made his way to the front row of seats. Kerrianne saw her chance to escape, but with her identity discovered, there was really no point in running away. She watched him bend down to speak to a little boy about Caleb's age. Like his sister, he had black hair and his huge tear-filled eyes were a dark shade of brown. Upon seeing his father, the boy immediately wrapped his arms around his neck. The scene tugged at Kerrianne's heart, while at the same a caustic thought ate its way into her mind. *Adam can't wipe away his children's tears.*

"Hey, what's up, Tiger?" Ryan asked, hefting the boy in his arms.

"I want to go to the party."

"Of course you do. I'll take you as soon as we get the props put away."

Kerrianne noticed the gorgeous blonde woman sitting next to Tiger only when she spoke. "I told him that, but he wanted to go now." She gave a languid stare and crossed her legs, showing well-defined calves beneath her gauzy skirt.

"Thanks, Sam. I appreciate you sitting with him."

Kerrianne wondered who she was to Ryan. She didn't seem to be the child's mother. And where was the mother anyway? Perhaps home taking care of another child?

"Any time." With a graceful movement, Sam came to her feet. She touched the sleeve of Ryan's costume, gliding her fingers briefly along his arm in the way of people who were familiar with each other. "I'll be taking stuff out to my car if you need me." She pivoted on her high heels, her dark eyes flicking over Maxine to linger on Kerrianne briefly and dispassionately, as though measuring her worth and finding her lacking. With a polite smile and a dismissive nod, Sam walked past Maxine and Kerrianne. With great effort, Kerrianne didn't turn to watch her go.

"Aren't you gonna hurry, Dad?" Tiger wiped a tear with the back of his hand.

"It'd go faster if you'd help."

"Why don't *they* help?" Tiger pointed his small finger at Maxine and Kerrianne.

Ryan laughed with an amused chuckle that made Kerrianne smile. "Because they're the audience. You can't ask the audience to help when they've paid money to see your play. Besides, these are two ladies on my mail route. This lady here has a boy your age. I play ball with him and his sister and brother sometimes."

"You have three kids?" Tiger asked.

Kerrianne nodded.

"We only have two."

There went Kerrianne's idea of Ryan's wife sitting home with another child. Maybe she was also an actress and was backstage somewhere. But then why was Sam so proprietary? Or had Kerrianne completely misread the situation?

31

"I'm four," Tiger said. "Is your boy four?" When Kerrianne nodded, he rushed on. "I'm the only boy my age around here. I'm bored all the time. Where do you live? Dad, can I go to his house to play?"

"Whoa, there, Tiger. First things first. Let's get the props into my truck." Ryan looked up at Maxine and Kerrianne. "Some of the props I made were specifically for this play, and we won't be needing them for the next one we do in January. With space being so tight here, I keep the stuff I build at my place. Well, at least the stuff I paid for." He laughed, sending a warm shiver up Kerrianne's spine.

She tugged on Maxine's sleeve, hoping the woman would get her message. Maxine didn't appear to notice. "Well, after the free tickets you gave us, it would be bad manners not to help. Show me where this stuff is. Can't be too heavy or dirty, though. As you can see, I'm in a dress."

"Oh, no, don't worry about it." Ryan shook his head. "Honestly, it won't take but fifteen minutes or so. The others will help."

"Oh, yeah?" Maxine challenged. "Well, I just saw a bunch of teenagers leave—right behind several others in your cast. Now, I won't take no for an answer. Show us what to carry. We have to walk outside anyway."

"But—"

"No buts." Maxine reached out to pat Tiger's hand. "This young man's tired of being here, and that's that."

Tiger stared at her with unconcealed admiration. "I'll show you!" He scrambled from his father's lap and ran up on the stage, motioning for Maxine to follow.

Ryan shook his head, chuckling. "Kids. Aren't they amazing? I mean, they're moody and difficult and sometimes really selfish. But they're also, well, amazing."

His eyes rested on Kerrianne, and she wondered if he was remembering what she looked like that morning. *Not that it matters,* she told herself.

"I know what you mean," she said. Of course her situation and his weren't at all the same. She was home with her children every day, while Ryan only dealt with his kids at night, relieving his wife. Kerrianne had no relief. Everything was up to her—soccer games, dentist appointments, homework, fixing things when the kids broke them. Sometimes the idea of doing everything was so overwhelming that it reduced her to tears. Adam wouldn't be coming home to relieve her— ever. Sadness ate at the bands of her self-control. In her wildest dreams, she'd never imagined she would be raising her children without a father.

"Those kids make me a lucky man." Ryan smiled as Ria emerged from the backstage door, waving at him as she went up the aisle with a friend. "I bet you and your husband feel the same."

Kerrianne tried not to internalize those words and tried instead to ignore them. But she couldn't. She saw Ryan several times a week and would likely have to talk to him more now that they'd been officially introduced. She couldn't have him asking again. She willed all emotion from her voice as she forced herself to recite the ugly words she'd said so many times before. "My husband died four years ago."

His forehead creased with sympathy. "I'm really sorry."

She sighed, twisting the wedding ring she still wore on her finger. Everyone was sorry, but that didn't change Adam's death. It didn't make them able to understand the pain she'd been through, the pain that even now sometimes took control of all her senses until she didn't know which way was up.

"Thank you," she managed.

He continued to look at her with concern, as though wondering what to say to ease her sorrow. Kerrianne steeled her heart for more platitudes about death.

"I have to admit that I wondered," he said finally. "I couldn't help noticing there wasn't a lot of mail for him these past years."

"There hasn't been?" Nearly every week she still received something addressed to Adam, no matter how many letters she wrote to tell people to stop sending him things. She'd developed a new hatred of direct mail ads. Kerrianne dropped her gaze to the ground, praying that she could control her tears. Why had she ever come tonight?

Please don't say anything more, she thought. *Please don't say you know how death feels because your favorite dog died.*

Ryan shifted uncomfortably. His hand reached out to her but stopped before touching her arm. "I know it probably seems like you still get a lot of mail for your husband. It's that way for me, too. My wife died of uterine cancer two years ago."

Shocked, Kerrianne met his eyes. His wife was dead? Well, that certainly explained why she wasn't here supporting him. "I'm sorry," she replied softly, more for her thoughts than for anything else.

He shrugged. "It's okay. I wouldn't have said anything except I wanted you to know that I understand. I really do." He nodded at her and began walking toward the backstage area. Kerrianne stood there, watching him go. Strange how knowing that he really understood her situation gave her such comfort. She'd felt the same type of connection with Maxine. Why did it help to know that someone else had also experienced such misery?

Not knowing what else to do, Kerrianne followed Ryan backstage.

Ryan knew he'd caused her pain. Not so much by her expression but by the feelings in his own heart. He understood that pain intimately. Certain instances always brought it out—like now. He glanced behind and saw her following him. The confidence he'd noted in her earlier was gone, her face drawn into rigid lines of control. He recognized that, too, and he felt a fresh wave of hurt and loss for both of them.

He remembered how she'd been that morning, looking pretty, youthful, and unassuming in her loose sweats and bare feet. He recalled the fierce expression of love in her eyes when she looked at her son. Could it be possible she might give Ryan a second glance? He knew he was fairly good-looking, and compared with most men on the single circuit, he had relatively little baggage. No ex-wife taking up alimony and child support payments, no fighting over custody, no overt hangups that had caused a divorce, no abuse issues or past adultery. But Kerrianne Price was classy, perhaps too classy to look seriously at a down-to-earth man like him. Pulling words from her had been a challenge, but what little she'd said had been delivered with an educated lilt. Did she like him at all? And was she ready to move on? He wanted to ask but couldn't find the right way. There was never a right way for that question.

"What can I help with?" Kerrianne asked. They were alone in the confined space, and her nearness made him forget his earlier decision to give up on women.

He pointed to several props leaning flat against the wall. "Looks like the rest of the cast has taken out most of it already. I'll need to take those. There's one on the stage, but Tiger and Maxine are probably getting that. The rest stays."

She nodded and started for the props without a word.

"So," he said, "you go to plays a lot?"

"Not in a long time."

He took the other side of the prop she'd grabbed. Usually, he carried it himself, but it was too heavy for her alone. "I've always been interested in the theater. I think I got it from my mother. She's a real arts buff. She had me in a lot of plays when I was a child."

Kerrianne nodded and hefted her side.

"What about your family?" he probed.

"My parents and siblings go all the time."

"Did any of them act?" Extracting information from her was worse than getting it from Ria when she was upset. Yet he sensed it wasn't because Kerrianne was upset but rather attempting to protect herself.

"I did—a little." There was a flare of interest in her voice that he noted and put aside for future reference. She glanced behind her. "So where are you parked?"

"Out that way." He gestured with his chin.

Maxine and Tiger were walking off the stage with a tree prop, and they went out to the parking lot together. Others from the cast gathered around a green Chevy truck, lifting in props and several plastic totes.

"Is there much more?" a young man called to Ryan.

"Not much. You guys go ahead. I'll meet you at the party." Ryan's words met approval from the small crowd.

The man jumped down from the truck, and people began dispersing to their cars. Sam sauntered up to Ryan. "Ria left with Dawn already. She said you said it was okay."

"Thanks. I'll be by in a bit."

"You don't want me to wait?"

He hesitated. For some reason he felt Kerrianne and Maxine staring at him, though they seemed to be engrossed in conversation with Tiger. "No, better not. You go on ahead."

Sam sighed, pulling her jacket closed. "You're right." Sudden tears gathered in her eyes, reflecting the light from the moon overhead. "In fact, I think I'll just stay a minute and then swing home. Maybe he'll be there."

Ryan's heart broke for her. "It'll be all right," he said. "I know it doesn't seem that way, but someday things will work out."

"If it weren't for you, I might have given up on Scott already. I just wish he'd agree to counseling."

He wanted to hug her but knew it wasn't a good idea. She was too vulnerable, and no matter how lonely they both were, he wouldn't be the cause of breaking up a marriage. No, whatever decision Sam made about her relationship with her husband, it had nothing to do with him. Nothing at all. Otherwise, he could never live with himself. With a heartbreaking half-smile, Sam left alone in her car.

Ryan turned and gently lifted the prop he was carrying into his truck. Then he stepped closer to the others, taking the tree from Maxine.

"Can I come play at your house?" Tiger was saying to Kerrianne.

She hesitated only briefly. "Sure. That'd be fine—if your father says it's okay. My son would love to play with you. But only after three. I do a preschool before that in the afternoons."

Five whole sentences. She's becoming positively chatty, Ryan thought with a smile. Tiger seemed to have a way with her.

"Can I, Dad?" Tiger asked loudly, bouncing on his toes. "She said he has a real tent in his room with toys in it."

Ryan was torn between taking Kerrianne up on the offer and scolding his son for inviting himself over.

Instead, he opted to avoid the issue. "We'll see."

"Either he can or he can't." Maxine faced him with a stare. "Kerrianne doesn't mind. She loves kids. All the kids always play at her house, don't they, Kerrianne?"

"Actually, yes."

"And you don't have to worry about her being a crazy weirdo, because she's not."

Ryan could see that just looking at her. She was most definitely not crazy, but her life was obviously not simple, either. One could see that as well. She was beautiful, polite, and caring, but also removed, wary, and vulnerable. That might be fine for Tiger, but Ryan wasn't sure the combination was a good thing for his heart.

"Okay, we'll talk later. Maybe on Monday?"

Maxine grunted with disgust. "Sorry, Tiger, that's all you're gonna get, but don't stop bugging him."

"Maxine," Kerrianne protested.

"Fine. Okay, I'll be quiet." Maxine laid a hand on Tiger's shoulder. "At least about that. But tell me, Tiger, where'd you get such an odd name? I mean, what kind of a name is Tiger anyway? Sounds like you were born in the jungle."

The boy laughed. "Oh, that's my sister's fault. She liked golf."

Maxine cast Ryan a confused look.

"Ria's into sports," he explained. "She was going through a golf phase. When we named him Tyson, she was sure we'd meant to name him after Tiger Woods but made a mistake. So she called him Tiger, and that was that."

"I like the name Tiger," Tiger said proudly. "It's tough, like a Jedi knight. Or maybe a wizard, like Harry Potter." He growled and lifted his hands up as though clawing something.

"My, my," Maxine said, adding a few tsks for good measure. "Sounds like you'd better put him in Kerrianne's preschool. Wherever you have him now, he's watching way too much TV."

Ryan chuckled without amusement. "I'll do that," he said, wishing she'd mind her own business. He glanced at Kerrianne. "Got any openings?"

Kerrianne blinked in surprise, and he found he was glad he'd followed the urge. For a moment the closed look was gone.

"Uh, sorry. I don't have any openings. But you never know. Maybe later."

Disappointment that was completely out of proportion to the question made a bitter taste in his mouth. "Maybe." He glanced at his truck. "Guess I'd better go get the rest."

"We'll help," Maxine offered.

"There's only one or two left. They're not big—I can get them in one trip. But thanks. And thanks for coming to the play."

"Thank you for the tickets. Are you doing another play soon?"

"Not until January."

"What is it?"

"I'm not telling." The truth was, they hadn't really decided. The group had voted to take December off this year, since there was so much competition with other productions and activities during the Christmas season.

"Humph." Maxine pursed her lips. "Tiger," she said, "it seems we'll both have to keep bugging your dad."

Tiger lifted his hands in the exaggerated shrug that Ryan had spent hours teaching him for a play he'd been in several months earlier. All the adults laughed.

"Good night." Maxine started for her car.

Kerrianne nodded at him, and Ryan felt a warm tingling shoot through him. At that moment more than anything he wanted to get to know her. He wanted to discover what she was feeling underneath that stiff veneer. He wanted to see if his gut feeling was right about her somehow being important in his life. Or was it just to Tiger's life as a future preschool teacher? The thought made Ryan depressed. He wasn't ready to believe that quite yet. Miraculously, this smart, attractive, funny woman had appeared in his path, and he wasn't the type to turn down what might possibly be destiny.

No, he thought, *we're not through, yet. You wait and see.*

"Good-bye," he called after her. "I'll see you on Monday."

Chapter Four

M axine," Kerrianne said as her friend drove from the parking lot, "was this a set-up? Because if it was, you did a lousy job."

"What? A set-up?" Maxine glanced over momentarily. "What are you talking about?"

"Ryan What's-his-face." Kerrianne tried to remember what name had been listed on the program.

"Ryan Oakman. Actually, S. Ryan Oakman, but I never asked him what the S meant. So what about him? And don't scowl so. It'll give you wrinkles."

"He's a widower. Are you trying to say you didn't know anything about it?"

Maxine's jaw dropped. "Oh, my. For crying out loud. No wonder those children kept coming to him for stuff. I never imagined. The poor guy! Alone all this time. And I had the nerve to hit him up for tickets."

Kerrianne felt her defensiveness fade. "You really didn't know? This wasn't an effort to get us together?"

Maxine made a left turn at the light. "Honey, if I'd known he was single, I would have snatched him up myself."

Kerrianne let out a burst of laughter.

"What?" Maxine asked, in an offended tone. "I mean it. So what if he's a little young?"

"I thought you didn't want to do any man's laundry again. Or cook him dinner."

"I wouldn't have to. He'd do it. That's the beauty of youth; they can be trained."

"Right." Kerrianne rolled her eyes. "He's still a man."

"Well, at least at his age, he's bound to be romantic. Not like poor old Harold, who would have to take vitamins just to get up enough energy to kiss my cheek."

Kerrianne had a brief vision of Ryan's lips coming down on her own. Guilt flooded her and she pushed the unsettling vision away. She loved Adam. She most certainly would not think about kissing Ryan—or any other man. Good thing she'd told Ryan she didn't have any openings in her preschool, though that wasn't strictly true. If she'd really wanted, she could have squeezed in one more student, but interacting with Ryan on a regular basis wasn't something she was prepared to do in light of her attraction to him.

Maxine turned right at the next bend in the road. "Of course, Ryan does have children, and I'm quite beyond that. So I guess you can have him if you want."

"I don't want him!"

"Okay, okay. I thought you did." Her glance was teasing. "Still, you have to admit that it was fun to go out tonight. In fact, I think it's time you got out a little more. I know you're still missing Adam, but he wouldn't begrudge you a little fun."

"I don't want another man."

"I'm not talking about another man. I mean to get out and meet other singles, men and women alike. I tell you, there's a lot of comfort being with people who know what you're going through."

Acid rose in Kerrianne's throat. Was Maxine like all the others who seemed to think everything in her life could be cured with a little understanding? A dash of understanding, a priesthood blessing, and a little fresh air. Voilà, she'd be cured of heartache permanently.

Not in a million years. What they didn't understand is that nothing could bring back Adam. She still had to endure a lifetime without him. She had to raise her children alone. Not even Maxine could understand that kind of heartache.

She was about to protest, to voice at least some of these thoughts, but then she remembered her feelings when Ryan told her about his wife. She *had* felt something at the realization that he understood her feelings, at knowing he lived the same existence she did. Maybe she had everything wrong. Maybe each thing—understanding of others, the blessings, and even fresh air—did lessen her pain until she could actually be happy again. Not just fleetingly, but every day.

"Maybe you're right," she said slowly. "I'll think about it."

Maxine obviously sniffed victory. "Good. There's an activity next Friday night. I'll pick you up at seven."

"An activity? What kind?"

"A gathering. Don't worry about it. You'll enjoy it. I'll be right with you, and if you don't like it, we'll leave."

"What would I wear?"

"Something like you have on tonight." Maxine brought the car to a stop in Kerrianne's driveway and looked her over with a critical eye. "I was going to suggest getting some new pants, but do you think you could put on a little weight instead? Five pounds would do you a world of good. You're a woman, you know, not a scrawny teenager."

Kerrianne sighed. "I'll think about it." She climbed from Maxine's car, feeling drained of all energy. "Thanks, Maxine. It was a really good play."

"You're welcome. Call me if you need me." Maxine always said that as they parted. So far Kerrianne never had taken her up on the offer.

She went to the front door, fumbling with her key. It wasn't late, but the children were likely in bed; she prayed that they were. She didn't want to check teeth or find pajamas tonight. The entryway and the living room were darkened, and Kerrianne followed the light emanating from the family room.

She was surprised to see all the children spread out on the floor. More children than she had left a few hours earlier. They all seemed to be asleep, covered in her extra blankets, except for Lexi, whose eyes were glued to the television. The overhead light had been dimmed with the wall switch to about halfway.

"Lexi, what—" She broke off as a figure on the couch lifted slightly and turned toward her. Kerrianne's heart beat overtime until she realized it was only her sister. "Manda? What are you doing here? Is something wrong?"

"No," Amanda said hurriedly, her green eyes glinting in the half light. "Or nothing too serious, anyway. Benjamin wasn't feeling well and wanted you, but the kids couldn't remember your cell number, so Misty called me. I came over instead of giving them your number so you wouldn't have to miss your play."

"We think Caleb took the number from by the phone." Lexi sat up from her mound of blankets. "He was making a paper plane with it earlier, and I took it from him like three times. Then we couldn't find it— not even he could remember where he put it."

"Where's Benjamin?" Kerrianne mentally berated herself for not realizing he was sick. No wonder he'd come to her bed last night. And come to think of it, he had been rather listless all day.

"He's here, right by me." Amanda gestured.

Kerrianne walked quickly around the couch and saw Benjamin sleeping with his head on a pillow wedged next to the armrest. Even in the dim light his cheeks were rosy with fever.

Amanda stood up to let Kerrianne sit beside Benjamin. "He is hot," Kerrianne said, as she gathered Benjamin's thin body into her arms.

"Blake and your neighbor gave him a blessing, and then Blake went to the store to get some children's pain reliever. I'm out, and I couldn't find yours."

"It's in my vitamin cupboard, clear at the back. You should have called me." Though she was happy her sister had stepped in to take care of things, she felt guilty to be enjoying herself while others did her job.

Amanda grinned. "Not a chance. You don't get out enough as it is."

There it was again—the insinuation that if she got out enough, her life would miraculously change. Kerrianne let the words run over her without stopping them; she'd already lost that argument once tonight. At this point, staying silent was the best way to protect her emotions. Especially with Amanda. Her sister had more than once accused Kerrianne of relishing the pain. "You *like* missing Adam, don't you?" she'd said only last month.

"Well, I'm certainly not celebrating the fact that he's gone," Kerrianne had retorted.

"Yeah, but you don't have to stop living. You can't believe he'd want that."

"I am living!"

"No. You, my dear sister, are only existing."

Kerrianne knew Amanda was right, but she didn't know what to do about it now any more than she did then. Regardless, she didn't want to repeat that particular conversation in a hurry.

"So how was it, anyway?" Amanda asked, oblivious to her thoughts.

"Good. Fine." Kerrianne was too distracted by both her thoughts and her son's fever to dwell on the play. "What about your kids?" She lifted her chin to indicate Amanda's soon-to-be-adopted foster children, Kevin and Mara, who were snoring together under a blanket by the TV, and Amanda's two-year-old son, Blakey, who had his own blanket next to Caleb in the middle of the room. "I'd feel bad if they got sick."

Amanda shrugged. "They were together all day yesterday. If it's contagious, they've already been exposed. But don't worry. I kept them away from Benjamin as much as possible." Amanda sat down on the other end of the couch as she spoke. At five months along, she was in the cute stage of pregnancy when the stomach is big enough to tell the world you really are pregnant and not simply gaining weight, and yet not so large as to be overly uncomfortable. Or at least most people wouldn't normally be so uncomfortable at this stage. The swelling in Amanda's legs had her midwife worried about gestational diabetes.

Kerrianne held tightly to Benjamin. If Adam hadn't died, she would have had another baby two years after Caleb. They might even have a fifth one by now, a newborn, if she'd kept up the two-year spacing. But there were no more babies for her and Adam. She hoped her face didn't show any of her thoughts, not wanting her sister to know how desperately she envied her.

"I'll go get the pain reliever." Amanda came to her feet again, and Kerrianne let her go, though she didn't want to wake Benjamin to give it to him. As long as his fever wasn't too high and he wasn't uncomfortable, she knew by experience that it was better to let him sleep for as long as possible to aid in his healing.

As Amanda returned with the small, childproof bottle, her husband, Blake, arrived from the store. "We'll just keep this for ourselves," Amanda said, taking the small bag from him with a smile. "Kerrianne's already got two bottles, and if this spreads, we'll need it."

Kerrianne groaned. "I'm sorry."

"Don't be." Amanda smiled. "It's not your fault. Kids get sick."

Blake knelt on the carpet and scooped up eight-year-old Kevin, reminding Kerrianne briefly of Ryan, though the two men looked little alike. Blake's brown hair was short, his face clean-shaven, and his eyes brown. Though he was a handsome man, her stomach didn't feel the slightest twinge of warmth at his gaze. *Thank heaven!* she thought, still more unsettled than she liked to admit by her unexpected encounter with Ryan.

"Don't you want to give him the medicine?" Amanda asked.

"Not yet. He'll probably wake up soon."

"Look, why don't we take Lexi home with us? That way Blake can run her back to Mitch's tomorrow and save you the drive to Sandy."

Kerrianne looked at Lexi. "Would you mind?"

"Whatever's best for you," Lexi said. "I'm just sorry he got sick."

"Thanks, Lexi. Here, let me pay you first."

"No, really, it's okay. My dad left me money, when he . . . you know, in his will." Like Kerrianne, she seemed to hate saying the D word.

"Yeah, but that's for your future—college and all. This is for candy and video games, or whatever it is you girls like to buy these days." Kerrianne fished bills from her purse and pressed them into Lexi's hand.

Lexi grinned. "Well, if you put it that way."

Blake had returned from settling Kevin in their van and now picked up four-year-old Mara. Amanda awkwardly lifted little Blakey, curling him against the bulk of her stomach. "If you need us, just call. We're only five minutes away."

"I will."

Amanda's green stare fixed her in the eye. "You mean it?"

"Yes." Kerrianne laid the still-sleeping Benjamin on the couch and walked them to the door, locking it after them.

With her sister's family and Lexi gone, the house had fallen into its customary bleak silence. A silence that was almost loud. Kerrianne lifted Misty and took her upstairs to bed, trying not to think of Adam helping to carry the children as Blake had done for Amanda. Misty opened her eyes briefly but didn't speak or seem to understand that she was being carried. Next, Kerrianne picked up Caleb, who didn't stir in the slightest as she put him in bed and pulled up the covers. Benjamin she placed in her own bed, knowing he would be more comfortable there and that she might be able to doze at least a bit as she watched over him.

"Mom," he moaned.

She smoothed his forehead. "I'm here."

"I wanted you. Caleb lost the number."

"I know. But it's okay. I'm back now."

"I'm hot. I hurt all over." His fingers tightened weakly on her arm.

"You'll be okay. I promise. Here, I have something for you to take. Chew it up quickly, and drink this water."

Benjamin didn't complain as the other children always did when taking pain reliever. He didn't try to spit out the tablets or make horrible faces. He just chewed quickly and drank a sip of the water.

"Try a little more water," Kerrianne urged. "You don't want to get dehydrated."

He gave it a try but choked.

"Good, that's enough. I have it right here if you need more."

"I love you, Mommy."

Tears threatened. "I love you, too, Benjamin."

Between worrying about Benjamin and taking care of him each time he awoke, Kerrianne spent a sleepless night. Half the time she felt pity for Benjamin's pain, and the other half she spent feeling sorry for herself for having to endure the vigil alone.

Overshadowing all was the fear of losing Benjamin the way she'd lost Adam.

Suddenly she was angry at Adam for not being there. Yes, she knew it wasn't his fault, but it was better to be angry at him than feel the bitter loss all over again as though he'd died only yesterday. Four years. Yesterday. It made little difference to the rest of her life.

"I'm so mad at you," she whispered. "We were just beginning. We had our whole lives ahead of us. If you were here, you could have been the one to give him a blessing." She could almost imagine his saying in return, "Ah, but then you'd miss all these growing experiences."

She sobbed aloud. "I don't want to grow without you!"

There was no reply this time, as though not even her imagination had anything left to give.

At four in the morning, Benjamin's fever shot higher still. Kerrianne contemplated taking him to the hospital emergency room. But what would she do with the other children? Any of her neighbors would be willing to help, but she was embarrassed to reach out to them. She was embarrassed to need them at all.

Almost in tears, she called Ask-A-Nurse, and was relieved when, after asking a list of questions, the nurse recommended more pain reliever. Kerrianne followed her advice. Benjamin's fever broke a half hour later and did not return.

Kerrianne lay next to her child, vowing never to leave his side again to go out with Maxine. She couldn't take the chance of losing him. She couldn't.

Or was that only an excuse?

Before she could decide, she fell asleep, holding Benjamin's hand.

Chapter Five

All Sunday morning, Ryan couldn't get Kerrianne out of his mind. How strange that she should be on his route so long but he hadn't realized she was a widow, despite the dwindling mail for her husband. How odd that he hadn't noticed her kind eyes and the fine bones of her face. Her smooth skin.

"Stop it," he told himself, only to think of how she'd looked at him when he told her about his wife. For a moment there had been a connection. An understanding. Or had he imagined it? He'd been searching for someone for so long now, maybe the connection was wishful thinking.

To be truthful, his search hadn't really been that long. Laurie had died only two years ago. But she'd been sick two years before that, when Tiger had been a newborn. They'd had time to plan, to talk about the future. He'd had time to realize that he would have to go on without her.

On some days Laurie had cried about leaving the children. At the time he would have gladly given his life in her place. But now he suspected that he ended up with the harder lot. He hoped so. More than anything, he wanted her to be happy.

"Dad, I'm hungry!" Tiger was staring at him with a scowl on his face and a glare in his brown eyes. He'd said the same thing five times since they'd arrived home from church.

Ryan looked down at the meat he was planning to barbecue on the back patio. Mostly, they ate things they could cook in the microwave, but on Sunday afternoons, he liked to serve a semblance of a healthy meal—or a least a tasty one. Using the barbecue, even in winter, saved him from cleaning a pan.

"Go set the table. It'll be done before you know it."

With a resigned sigh, Tiger grabbed a few plates and headed off to the table.

The phone rang, and Ryan frowned. "Ria, would you get that? My hands are dirty."

A mumbling came from the living room where he knew she had gone with a book. A few seconds later, she came in with a fatalistic look on her face. "It's Grandma. She wants to know why we haven't left yet."

Ryan groaned. He remembered now that his hotshot brother, Willard, was coming in from New York, and Ryan had promised his mother he'd show up for a family meal by two.

"Give me the phone," he said, experiencing a rush of guilt that his mother suspected his reluctance enough to make the call.

"She already hung up. Probably so you couldn't say no. Do we really have to go?" Ria gave him her best puppy-dog look. She knew that was hard for him to resist. She thought it was because the expression was cute, but the real reason was because it made her look so much like her mother. "Can't I be sick? I'm old enough to stay home alone, aren't I?"

He shook his head. "We have to go. I promised."

"You promised! I didn't. So *you* go!"

"Ria!" He slammed the meat into a plastic container, already planning to cook it for family home evening on Monday instead. "We all have to go."

"But I'm hungry!" Tiger whined.

50

"We'll eat there." Ryan squirted dishwashing soap in his palm and began scrubbing his hands at the kitchen sink.

"Her food tastes funny! She always has green beans. And I don't know how to use a knife."

"That's enough, Tiger."

"I hate going there!"

"Your grandmother loves you, you know. It's not so unreasonable that she wants to see you every now and then. You're the only grand-kids she's got."

"But it's boring," Ria put in. "There's nothing to do." Funny how she would say that when his parents' house was easily three times the size of theirs.

"I'm hungry now!" Huge tears swelled up in Tiger's eyes.

"Tiger's got a point, Dad. It's like hours to get there."

"Actually, Ogden's only a little over an hour." Ryan sighed. "But you're right. Hey, I know." He scrambled through the cupboard, filled with half-empty packages and containers of old spices he had no incli-nation or idea how to use. There, under the bag of shredded coconut that had turned an unspeakable shade of brown, was the sack where he'd hidden the chocolate bars he'd bought on sale at Macey's. "Here, take your pick," he said, handing them the sack. He threw the spoiled coconut in the garbage.

Tiger's tears vanished instantly. "Wow, oh, wow!" He picked the biggest and began ripping it open.

Ria touched several, hesitated, and then finally chose one with a contented sigh. That was his Ria, testing and weighing the options before wholeheartedly taking the plunge.

The candy would most likely make the kids hyper, but he didn't figure it would make their visit any worse. Whatever he did, his par-ents wouldn't be happy with him. They hadn't been since he'd chosen to work at the post office. On the other hand, they would practically kiss Willard's feet. He just hoped his brother had washed them.

When they finally arrived in Ogden, Ryan was feeling out of sorts.

Take a deep breath, he told himself. He didn't have to explain his life to his family anymore. He was doing what he wanted and that was enough, wasn't it?

Fleetingly, he wished Laurie were there to help him through the next few hours. But that was selfish. His parents had never really approved of her. She hadn't completed enough education for their liking, and though they never admitted it, the knowledge that Laurie had a grandmother who was Mexican had also worked against her. Laurie's siblings looked as Caucasian as he did, but because Laurie had inherited that certain exotic something, either in the slightly olive cast of her skin or in the lovely sheen of her black hair, his parents had seen fit to treat her with little warmth.

The thought still made Ryan furious if he dwelt on it for long. He'd met Laurie's grandmother before she'd died, and she had been one of the most gracious, honest, hard-working people he'd ever met. He had been only too proud to call her *Abuela.*

All that was behind them now. Or at least behind Laurie.

Fighting the longing for his old life, Ryan marched up the wide, sweeping steps ready to do battle.

"Finally," said his mother, Elizabeth, as she opened the tall door. She wore a green, gauzy outfit with large fluttering sleeves that made her arms look rather like wings. Her short and well-coiffed hair was dyed to its youthful dark brown, which did little to flatter her aging face. She had gained weight, so she must be off her diet again, but at least that meant Tiger might find something to eat. Ryan liked his mother better when she wasn't dieting; she looked younger when she was heavier and her face less pinched with worry.

Her eyes fell over his unshaven face and long hair, a question in her eyes. He'd forgotten about the hair. "It was for a play," he explained.

"Oh, I see." She hugged him, and he felt his heart soften. He really did love her. If it weren't for his father, he'd come to visit more often.

He watched as his mother made a fuss over the children, hugging them and smoothing their black hair. Ria stuck her tongue out at Ryan as she received her hug, and Ryan stuck his out right back. Tiger giggled.

Okay, so maybe this wouldn't be as bad as he had expected.

His thought was quickly squelched as his brother strode into the spacious entryway as though he owned the place. "Ryan, is that you?" he said, with a New York accent that was more affectation than real. "You look positively heathen. Is that what all the postal carriers look like here? It's enough to make you want to carry a gun when you go out to get the mail."

"It's for a play," Elizabeth intervened. Ryan wasn't sure, but he thought he heard a note of pride in her voice. Maybe.

"You're still acting? I thought you would have outgrown that by now. But then if you had, I suppose you wouldn't still be at the post office slaving away."

"Nice to see you, too," Ryan said sarcastically. "Looks like you've gained weight. You know, you might want to get out of the courtroom and exercise more like I do working for the post office." Along with her brown hair and blue eyes, Willard had inherited their mother's tendency to gain weight, and he hated being reminded of that fact.

"Well, I guess I am a little preoccupied with earning a *decent* living," Willard retorted.

"Now, boys," Elizabeth chided. Yet her tone was one of helplessness, as though she knew they wouldn't heed her words.

Ryan bit his tongue to stop the words he wanted to say and forced himself to give his older brother a hug. Willard was taller than he was, but all soft, so it was somewhat like hugging an oversized stuffed bear.

"So these are the kids." Willard stared down at Ria and Tiger, who had removed their jackets and hung them on an elaborate wooden coat rack by the door. "They've sure grown since last Christmas."

Ria stuck out her hand, apparently unwilling to endure another hug. "Hi, Uncle Willard. Where's Aunt Cindy?"

"Ria," Ryan warned. He'd told the kids Aunt Cindy had left Uncle Willard, but Ria must have forgotten. Frankly, he was amazed that

Cindy had put up with her husband's infidelities and neglect for as long as she had. Five long years. Willard's mistreatment and lack of remorse had been so great that even her bishop had finally counseled her to leave. They had no children because Willard couldn't yet bother with that kind of responsibility. He'd wanted to put off having a baby for at least another two years. It had been one more thing to cause Cindy anguish.

"Oh, yeah," Ria said quickly. "I forgot. Too bad, 'cause I really liked her."

Willard's brow furrowed. "Well, good riddance to bad rubbish, I say."

Ryan was about to defend his sister-in-law, but his mother's expression of dismay stopped him. He put an arm around her and walked with her past Willard.

"We're in the dining room," she said.

"Where else?"

His father was already seated at the table, reading the *Wall Street Journal,* which Ryan knew he devoured more avidly than anything else—no matter what day of the week. He looked up as they entered, and Ryan felt the slight shock that he always felt after not seeing his father for several months.

Sterling Oakman was a man of only slightly more than average height, but he was strongly built with wide shoulders, firm muscles, and a narrow waist. His dark hair had gone almost completely white, but his face was younger than his sixty years. His eyes were Ryan's own color—a steel gray. The shock came because Ryan knew he was looking into his own face in thirty years. Except he hoped—he prayed—that his face would not be so stern and that he would not exact the fear and frustration in his children's heart that his father always did in his.

While Willard, the firstborn, had been named after their revered grandfather, who had controlled the family fortune at the time of his birth, Ryan had been named for his father, Sterling Ryan Oakman, though they'd ended up calling him by his middle name to avoid confusion. Ryan had wondered countless times if his name was part of why his father was so disappointed in his choice not to follow his own career in law. Maybe if they'd named him Joe or Tom or even Willard, he wouldn't have cared so much.

At least today Ryan was dressed like his father—and so was Willard, of course. But Sundays were the only days he wore suit pants and a dress shirt.

"Ryan." His father nodded and crossed the room. He took Ryan's hand and shook it, his other hand coming up to pat his back. "You look well. All but the beard, of course. Another play?"

"I'm thinking of keeping it," he said, just to be stubborn. "It suits me."

"I don't agree, but it's your face." His father waved a hand in dismissal. "Come here, children." He shook their hands gravely. "It's good to see you."

"Hi, Grandpa." Ria was chewing on her lips, and next to her, Tiger shifted nervously. To Ryan's relief, his mother clapped her hands for attention.

"Come on, let's sit down. Dinner's long been ready. Oh, I'd better get Tiger a bib."

"Aw, Grandma, I don't need a bib anymore. I'm not a baby."

Elizabeth smiled. "Okay, then. If you say so." She was rewarded by a sincere grin.

Sterling studied his grandson. "If he spills, I don't suppose it'll hurt that shirt."

He was right. Tiger was wearing his favorite Spiderman shirt, and since he wore it every day after school except when Ryan could wrest it away for laundering, it was dingy and had a few tiny holes in it. Tiger loved the shirt so much that Ryan didn't have the heart to throw it away.

"Spidey doesn't care," Tiger agreed.

"That's right." Ryan squeezed his shoulder before looking his father in the eye, almost expecting him to say something more, but Sterling avoided Ryan's gaze.

"Willard," Sterling said, "will you offer the blessing on the food?"

Ryan bent his head with the others. He should have been grateful his family actually said prayers, not irritated that Willard was always the one asked. Next to him, Tiger put his hand out to touch Ryan's leg, and Ryan covered it with his larger one. *I will never make you doubt your worth,* he promised silently.

The meal began in near silence, with everyone passing food around the table. Elizabeth helped Ria, while Ryan filled Tiger's plate, making sure to avoid the green beans. Thankfully, there was corn as well, which Tiger adored. As Ryan cut the pot roast into small bites, Tiger promptly took one with his fingers and stuck it in his mouth.

"Use your fork," admonished his grandfather.

With a wary look in his direction, Tiger found his fork and, grabbing it in his fist, jabbed it into a piece of meat. Sterling sighed and looked away.

He's only four! Ryan wanted to protest. But Tiger hadn't noticed anything, so it was better left unsaid. Out of the corner of his eye, he caught his mother watching him worriedly. Ryan wished it was time to leave.

"Aren't you going to ask what we learned in church today?" Ria asked. That was their routine at home while they ate. "I learned about Jesus getting baptized. He left us a perfect example."

"I learned about families!" Tiger yelled. He always yelled when he got excited. Ryan saw his father flinch.

"It's not your turn. It's Grandma's." Ria looked at Elizabeth. "What did you learn?"

"In Relief Society, we talked about testimonies."

"You went to church?" Ryan didn't think about the words before they slipped out.

"Don't sound so surprised," his father said. "We go every week."

"You didn't use to."

"Well, we do now."

That was it. No stories of conversion or spiritual revelation. Nothing but the cut and dried declaration.

"Well, that's good, I guess."

His father's eyes settled on him for a few minutes before he turned to Willard. "So, tell me what's going on at work?" In the space of a heartbeat the two of them were in their own world, discussing legal cases, business mergers, and whatever else successful, workaholic lawyers liked to talk about. For an instant, Ryan was cast back into the role he'd played as a child, knowing his brother was his father's favorite but helpless to do anything about it. He hadn't liked sports like they did, and money had never been important to him. Was that because his parents had taken care of all his needs?

Money was certainly important to him now that he had children. Yet not important enough to take him away from them. After Tiger had been born, he'd seriously thought about changing careers but had stayed with the post office. His job, though he did enjoy working the route, was first and foremost a way to earn sufficient money and keep the schedule he required. His life was his kids. He'd always felt that the freedom to be with his children was far more important than a fat bank account. If he'd received a dollar for every hour his father had worked overtime while he was growing up, Ryan would be a wealthy man right now. If he'd had a dollar for every time his father had played with him, he wouldn't be able to pay a month's mortgage.

His mother made small talk to cover the fact that his father and brother ignored him. Ryan tried not to care. He regaled her with back-stage stories which had her and the children laughing. At one point he stopped to see that his father and Willard were also listening.

At last dinner was over, but not the end of his torture. "Come sit in the green room," his mother said, leading the way. The green room was a large patio that had been encased in glass to form a showcase for his mother's plants. The floor was lined with beautiful hand-painted tiles and large cream-colored throw rugs that were the thickest, softest rugs he'd ever seen. The upscale, olive-colored, wrought iron patio furniture was comfortable but not meant for children to jump on, though to Elizabeth's dismay, the cushions made decidedly good oversized Frisbees. After the second warning to Tiger, Ryan asked his mother desperately, "Don't you have a ball or something they could take outside and throw around?" It wasn't a normal Sunday activity for them, but it was that or leave immediately—which would make things even worse with his parents.

A light came to her eyes. "Good idea. I found a box of things a few months ago. I've been meaning to ask if you want them." She hurried away and returned with the children's jackets and a blue tote box of mitts, baseballs, and other sports paraphernalia that Ryan recognized as once belonging to him and Willard. Everything was in almost new condition. While his father and Willard had loved watching sports, their love had never extended to actually playing. As for Ryan, well, it was never much fun to play alone.

"Cool." Ria swept up a mitt and ball, and Tiger did the same. They raced to the door, forgetting the rules about running in their grandparents' house. To Ryan's complete and utter shock, his father took a large mitt from the bottom of the box and went after them. In less than a minute, he was lobbing a ball in Ria's direction. She caught each one and threw them right back with uncanny accuracy. Ria was good at any sport she tried. On the other hand, Tiger dropped most of the balls tossed his way, despite how often Ria practiced mercilessly with him at home.

"Look at that," Willard said, shaking his head. "Never thought I'd see the day."

Ryan stared at him. This was a Willard he didn't know. "You never liked to play," he said, half accusing.

"Dad never wanted to. He only liked to watch."

There was a silence for a long moment as Ryan considered the implications. He'd always thought his brother had been as caught up in watching sports as his father. Had he done that only to be close to him?

"Uh, boys." Their mother cleared her throat gently. "Some, uh, friends of your father's and mine are coming over for a short visit." She eyed her watch nervously and added, "In about ten minutes or so."

Willard nodded, but Ryan was immediately suspicious. "Friends? What friends?"

"Just a couple Sterling did work for a few years back. We go out with them sometimes. In fact, they have a lovely daughter about your age—well, maybe some years younger—and I believe she's bringing a friend tonight." She glanced pointedly at Willard, who suddenly sat up, looking more interested.

"I don't want to meet any young girls," Ryan said.

"I don't think she's that young."

Ryan should have known. Within six months of Laurie's death, his parents had come up with an abundance of suitable women for him to date. Unfortunately, not only were they barely out of their teens but they were from upper-class families who weren't excited about adding a lowly government employee to the family, especially when he showed no interest in their fathers' varied businesses. Ryan had found the women nice, sweet, and smart but not really interesting. There was so much they hadn't experienced! They had not yet formed opinions, desires, goals, or even really their personalities. They were too willing to agree with anything he said, making him feel more like a father than a date. He knew that most single men would jump at the chance of a young, beautiful wife they could mold into their lives, but Ryan hadn't been able to see any of them as Ria's mother. Tiger's, yes; he'd still been so young. But Ria needed more. Ryan needed more. For no reason at all he thought of Kerrianne, of her expression when she'd told him about her husband's death. Of how she twisted her wedding ring on her finger.

He didn't wear his ring anymore and hadn't since Laurie's death; that had been the agreement he'd made with her. She'd wanted him to take it off when she died. Before her death, he'd often removed it when he worked around the house, forgetting to wear it for days, but when it came down to taking it off for the rest of his life, he'd taken two months to work up the courage. Finally placing it in a box of her things had been almost as hard as burying her.

"Never mind him, Mom," Willard said. "I'm interested. I haven't been meeting any women in New York."

"You're still married, aren't you?" Ryan couldn't help asking.

"Actually, no. My divorce went through last week."

Ryan felt a stab of remorse. Cindy had been the one bright spot left in family gatherings, and he'd retained a secret hope that his brother would see the light once she'd gone and work to get her back.

"These girls are nice," Elizabeth said. "You boys both should give them a chance."

"But I already met a woman," Ryan said, surprising even himself.

His mother's eyes widened. "Oh?"

"She's a widow on my route, very nice. Has three children."

"How long have you known her?" There was no emotion in the words, but his mother's pursed lips weren't exactly a good sign. Willard just shook his head.

Ryan shrugged. "A long time. But I didn't know she was a widow until recently. She was at my play last night." His word choice seemed to indicate that they were together. The mistake was unintentional, but Ryan didn't feel the need to explain further.

"Three children, Ryan?" Elizabeth asked. "Isn't that a lot to take on?"

Ah, so that's her problem. All the women his parents had introduced to him had never been married and certainly had no children. Aloud he said, "Seem like nice kids. We play ball."

He was saved further questioning by the doorbell—a fortunate occurrence because he had no idea what to say next without making something up. As his mother went to answer, Ryan settled back in his chair, folded his arms across his chest, and stared outside through the glass, where the light was already beginning to fade. His father was smiling. Ria had backed up to the end of the yard, and she was still catching balls. Tiger was kicking a basketball around the yard; soccer hadn't been popular in Ryan's day, so he'd never owned a soccer ball.

In spite of everything, Ryan found himself eager to meet the women his mother talked about. Maybe one of them was the one he was looking for.

"Oh, my parents should be here any minute," came a voice through the door. "MaryAnn and I drove up from Salt Lake ourselves. We share an apartment there."

"I see." Elizabeth led the way into the green room. "Well, boys, I want you to meet—Colleen Dempsey and MaryAnn . . ."

"Turner," the girl supplied.

Ryan stood up to offer his hand. After an instant's delay, Willard followed suit.

Colleen was a shapely girl with beautiful long brown hair and eyes like a doe. Her makeup was heavily but artfully applied, making her face almost perfect except for a slightly wide nose. She was obviously the kind of girl that made men look twice. MaryAnn was less stunning with short brown hair and a slender build, but her pale blue eyes were lively and intelligent and her face more delicate. Both looked about twenty-five, which would make them nearly a decade younger than Ryan. A few years more than that for Willard. *Right up his alley,* Ryan thought unkindly.

Colleen immediately took center stage, telling all about her job as a secretary to some representative or other. He knew she had to be smart to hold such a job, but everything about her was superficial. No wonder Willard was immediately attracted to her. Unfortunately, Colleen didn't often look in his direction. Ryan felt a little sorry for his brother, a feeling he hadn't experienced in a long time. After all Willard must be lonely now that Cindy was gone, despite his infidelities. He didn't even have children to keep him company.

MaryAnn said little, except to confirm that she worked as a loan underwriter. Ryan got the sense that she was shy and a little embarrassed to be there. Every now and then, she met his eyes and glanced away.

"And so when I got the third call from this same woman," Colleen was saying, "demanding to speak with him immediately, I told her that I was the representative and please tell me the problem. And she did."

"She didn't notice that you were a woman?" Willard asked.

"Apparently not." Colleen gave an exaggerated shrug.

"And did you solve her problem?" MaryAnn asked.

"Lands, no! I don't even remember what it was. Besides, if she didn't know whether her representative was male or female, she likely didn't know enough of whatever issue it was to even talk to *me!*" She gave a derisive laugh, which Willard copied. The two seemed to be a match made in heaven.

Colleen apparently didn't think so. "So what do you do?" she asked Ryan, her face and posture inviting.

"I work for the post office."

"I see." She obviously didn't.

"It's a good job," Ryan said only to make polite conversation. "Keeps me fit, and on most days I can get home by four to be with my kids." He gestured out the window at Ria and Tiger.

Neither girl acted surprised or asked about his wife. His mother must have sent the word ahead.

"I'm an attorney in New York," Willard said to no one in particular. "But I'm considering moving back here to Utah. There's nothing really holding me there."

Ryan wasn't surprised to see Colleen finally focus her attention on Willard. Had she previously thought Willard was the mailman with the kids and Ryan the hotshot lawyer? Well, it made no difference. He'd never ask her out anyway. Unlike Willard, he had other people to think about. Colleen wouldn't be good for Ria. MaryAnn, maybe—under other circumstances that didn't involve his parents—but she was still very young. Why did he suddenly feel so old?

He stood abruptly, a plastic smile on his lips. "Well, it's been fun, but I'd better get home. I need to be at work early, and we've a long drive ahead." Mondays were always the worst days at the post office. After no delivery on Sunday, the mail stacked up. On some Mondays he was lucky to make it home by five or six, even when he hurried. Without waiting for a response, he strode to the far door, opened it, and stepped outside.

"Ria, Tiger, we're going."

"Aw, Dad," Ria whined.

Tiger hurried over to Ryan eagerly, his face red from the cold.

"I'm getting a little winded anyway," Sterling said.

Ria looked disappointed but obeyed. "Grandpa's pretty cool," she told Ryan. "I never knew he could throw a ball."

"Neither did I." His whole family was full of surprises today. At least his father's surprise had been welcome.

"Can we keep the mitts?" Ria asked.

"I think so. Go ask Grandma."

As the kids disappeared inside, his father came toward him, ball in hand. "Wait a minute, son," he said as Ryan reached for the doorknob.

Ryan dropped his hand. He felt cold from the collar of his white dress shirt to the tips of his toes. His heart was a block of ice.

"That Ria," Sterling continued, "she's really got a good arm, doesn't she?"

"Always has. Frankly, I'm surprised you noticed." Ryan knew he should keep his mouth shut, but it was hard to behave himself when he was around his father.

"I notice a lot of stuff."

"Oh?" Ryan let a challenge creep into his voice.

Sterling didn't take the bait. "I see you met the girl your mother brought around." He nodded through the glass toward Colleen, which told Ryan he had met her before.

"Yeah."

"Pretty, huh?"

"Beautiful."

Sterling nodded, a small smile coming to his mouth. "I thought you would like her. Hair reminds me of Laurie's."

"Laurie's hair was black, not brown." A lovely shining raven black that reflected the light as he held it between his fingers.

His father gave an impatient shake of his head. "I want you to seriously consider this girl."

"Why?" Ryan didn't have anything against Colleen, except that he didn't like her, but he wanted an explanation.

"Because your children dress like urchins, their manners are atrocious, and you need a wife."

"All that may be true, but I think I'm perfectly capable of finding someone on my own."

"Well, so far you've done a poor job of it. Look at you. With all your talents and abilities, and you're out putting letters in boxes."

"I like my job," Ryan said through gritted teeth. "I like my co-workers. They're good, hard-working people. And contrary to what you keep implying, I can support my family there. When I'm ready, there are administrative positions I can apply for. But right now I need to work certain hours. I need to be with my kids."

"What you need is ambition—like Willard." His father matched his angry tone.

Ryan rolled his eyes. "I'm supposed to look up to Willard? I'm sorry if I don't care about his success as a lawyer. What does that mean in the end? I would never treat a woman the way he treated Cindy, and certainly not my own wife. I adored her, and Willard should have adored Cindy. When he lost her, he lost everything, in my opinion." It hurt Ryan deeply that Willard had carelessly thrown away a precious relationship like the one that had been stolen from Ryan.

"He's a good provider."

Anger chipped away at the ice in Ryan's heart. "My children have food, they have clothes, and more important, I spend time with them every night. They know I love them."

The implication was clear, but would his father ignore it as he always had? Ryan held up his chin a bit more firmly.

"I've always loved you, son," Sterling said. "I may not have shown it, but I've always loved you."

Then let me be who I am! Ryan agonized silently. *I can't be Willard. I can't be Sterling Jr. I can only be Ryan. Just accept me as I am.* Why couldn't he say it aloud?

"Thank you for playing ball with Ria," he said instead. "She really had a good time." Leaving his father outside, Ryan went back in to say his farewells.

Chapter Six

On Monday morning there was a strange conflict within Kerrianne as she debated whether or not to go out and get the mail as always. The attraction she'd experienced for Ryan made her feel she was betraying Adam, and yet over the past years the mail had been such a stabilizing part of her life that she was reluctant to let it go. What if Ryan hadn't been so faithful and early over the years? What if there had been nothing to get her out of bed?

She dressed carefully—or tried to. Her sweats were out of the question, and her black pants too dressy for a Monday morning. She had to settle for her jeans that had to be held up with an old belt she hadn't used since before the children were born. She found a brown fitted top that was almost as ancient, but at least it didn't droop on her.

I'll just wait until he goes by, she thought as she made breakfast for the children. *And then run out and get the mail.*

"Mom!" Misty wailed from the top of the stairs. "I can't find my tan jeans. I wanted to wear them with the top that you got for my birthday."

"They're in the dryer," Kerrianne called. "They'll be a little wrinkled, but after an hour or so of wearing them, they'll straighten out. Then eat. I made oatmeal with raisins."

Misty appeared in the kitchen doorway, still wearing her pajama bottoms. "Can't I have regular cereal?"

"Sorry, all out. Better hurry before the boys eat it all."

Misty sighed loudly and plodded down the hall to get her jeans.

Kerrianne went into her living room and peered out the window into the gray-looking streets. Lots of clouds blowing in from the north, but no mail truck yet. She pulled away from the blinds and went to gather the backpacks.

The mail still hadn't arrived by the time Misty and Benjamin ran down the street to catch the school bus that had lumbered to a stop at the house on the other side of Maxine's. Kerrianne and Caleb stood on the porch and watched them climb inside. As the bus passed the house, Benjamin waved, and Kerrianne touched a hand to her mouth in their signal for "I love you." He waved again and was gone.

"Can I watch cartoons?" Caleb asked. He was holding his blue ball in the hopes of playing with Ryan but was already shivering.

"Sure." Kerrianne went inside with him.

When she peeked out her blinds a few minutes later, the mail truck was at her box. *I'm not going out while he's still there,* she thought. A part of her resented the fact that she'd met Ryan in a somewhat social situation and had been attracted enough that she was now self-conscious and worried about facing him again. *Why should I care what he thinks?*

She saw him put the mail in her box and then hesitate, looking up at the house. Before Kerrianne registered what she was doing, she'd slipped on old sandals and opened the door. *Keep walking,* she told herself. *Don't look unnatural.* She'd been going out to get the mail for four years, barely noticing the mailman's passing. Most days, he was onto the next box before she would even have to acknowledge him with a smile or a nod. Today was different.

He saw her coming. His smile warmed her bare arms, cold from the chill November morning. The truck rolled forward, and Kerrianne felt the sharp sting of disappointment. He was leaving like he had every other morning, as though they hadn't spoken so personally about their spouses or felt any connection. Then again, maybe he *hadn't* felt anything. She could have entirely imagined his appreciative stare Saturday night.

"Wait!" she called, sprinting down the crisp grass, her face flushing at how ungraceful she must look. "Uh, hi," she said, coming to a quick stop on the sidewalk.

He gave her a wide smile. "Good morning. What can I do for you?"

"Nothing. Uh . . ." She trailed off, feeling uncertain. Why *had* she stopped him? Surely she'd had some reason—she wasn't that far gone from sanity. She glanced back at the house, trying to remember.

"You have to get your kids ready for school?" he guessed.

"No, the older two are gone on the bus already."

"That's right, it's Monday. We had a lot of mail to sort this morning. Did you want to tell me something?"

"Uh, well, I . . ."

"Is it about the play?" He looked at her worriedly.

"No." She took a deep breath as her thoughts finally collected. "You may not remember, but that summer before . . . before my husband died, I was pregnant. I was out here a lot working on the yard in the early morning when it wasn't so hot."

His blue eyes quietly regarded her. "I remember," he said. "My wife was pregnant at the same time. She was so uncomfortable, and I remember feeling sorry for both of you and any other expectant mother I saw. She had Tiger in July." An expression of pain crossed his face, and Kerrianne wondered if it was around then that they learned of his wife's cancer.

Her next words spilled out of her in an effort to alleviate his pain—one she knew only too well. "You really helped me right after . . . you know . . . coming here every day, putting the mail in my box. If it snowed or rained or whatever, you were there. It gave me a reason to get up in the morning, something to do. I know that sounds silly, but it's true."

When he didn't reply right away, Kerrianne shifted on the sidewalk uneasily, clasping her hands behind her back and wishing she hadn't opened her mouth. She was normally more careful about exposing her feelings. Why did she have to be so impulsive today? "Well, um, I wanted to say thanks, that's all." She nodded at him and stepped away, her face flushing brighter still at his lack of response.

At last he cleared his throat and swallowed, as though doing so was difficult. "That means a lot," he said. "After my wife died, my son, he was only two. My daughter was so . . . well, strong and capable, but he needed me enough that I had to keep going forward. I understand better than anyone how important something simple can be after a tragedy." He smiled gently. "Whether it's getting the mail or changing a diaper."

Kerrianne felt the color and tenseness seep from her face. "I'm glad," she whispered. "Have a good day." With another nod, she turned and jogged up the walk. Inside the house, she stood with her back against the door, willing her heartbeat to slow. What was the big deal? She'd simply told the mailman what it had meant to her all these years to have something to get up for. Especially in the months directly following Adam's death—months that she might have spent entirely in bed. Instead, she had been sitting on the porch reading the mail by morning light. Or at least holding it and looking at the mountains.

"Mommy, are you okay?" Caleb came into the hall, carrying a book she'd told him she would read to him later. "Didn't we have mail?"

The mail! She'd completely forgotten to go to the box. She slowly opened the door and peered around it. The mail truck was nowhere to be seen. "I'll go get it now."

"I want to come."

They walked down to the curb together, only to discover two bills and a solicitation from a charity. Kerrianne wasn't surprised to find no personal letters. The only person she ever wrote was Adam's widowed mother in California, and she'd received a letter from her last week. Her other friends and family used e-mail.

She spent the morning reading to Caleb, tidying the house, and preparing for her preschool. She had started the school to help with the bills, wanting to save as much of Adam's life insurance as possible for the children's college. Adam had been a strong advocate of education, and she would see that their children had every opportunity in that respect.

Sometimes she pondered how strange it was that everything else proceeded onward when Adam's life had not. Each of her siblings was now married and had a family, all three having acquired a child or two at the time of their marriage. Amanda had gone on to have more children. Hurricanes and earthquakes still ravaged the world. People continued working. With the help of her brother, brother-in-law, and father, Kerrianne had finished a spacious room in her basement and started a preschool.

The funny thing was that sometimes she couldn't remember what Adam looked like. She'd take his picture and stare at it, but he would almost be a stranger. At other times, the picture brought back memories that made him seem so real she could reach out and touch his face.

When it was time for her afternoon classes, Kerrianne opened up her garage so the students could come in that way and down the stairs directly into the preschool. As the children arrived, Caleb was beside himself with excitement. "Look! We have new puzzles!" he shouted as the children gathered. "My mom opened the new ones."

The boys and girls worked at puzzles or played with toys as the others gathered. Kerrianne felt content as she helped each one feel comfortable. She loved teaching the children, and they loved her. They never looked at her as half of a couple.

The last child to arrive was accompanied by his grandmother, Bernice Stubbs, an older widow who lived two streets over. Bernice wore her gray hair proudly, and her face was thin and covered with what Kerrianne assumed must be all the wrong colors of makeup because she looked garish, pinched, and unhappy.

"Hello." Kerrianne gave her a smile.

"Would you mind if I picked Michael up ten minutes late today?" Bernice asked, smoothing her brown skirt. "I'm getting my hair done, and Maxine is also doing a facial for me afterwards. I just love her products. Pity they're so expensive."

Kerrianne nodded. "She only sells them to get a discount for herself. But they're good products. I'm thinking of buying a few things myself." She *had* felt pretty Saturday night.

"Oh?" Bernice's eyes dug into hers. "Makeup?"

"Yeah, I'm all out." No use in telling her how long she'd been out.

"You don't normally wear makeup, do you?" Bernice's voice was kind, but there was an underlying steel to her words.

Kerrianne made a face, remembering how Ryan hadn't recognized her at first on Saturday night. "I haven't for a while. I'm just ready for a change."

Bernice opened her mouth, hesitated a moment, and then replied, "Speaking of change, can you believe Maxine lately? I've seen her all over town with one gentleman or another. All the neighborhood is talking about it." She shook her head and tsked. "I know *I* couldn't do such a thing. It would be a betrayal to my poor, dear husband." She sighed loud and long. "You and I were lucky, Kerrianne. You can tell *we* really loved our husbands because of the way we act. Maxine must not have loved her husband nearly as much as we did ours or she would never be able to look at another man."

Kerrianne was confused for a moment because she knew Maxine had loved her husband deeply. "She should really stay home and knit or something," she declared flatly.

Kerrianne's sarcasm was lost on Bernice. "Exactly!" The older woman sniffed hard. "If she really loved her husband, she wouldn't need to go out. Before you know it, she'll get married. Humph! I would never get remarried. It would be a betrayal, I tell you."

Kerrianne didn't want to continue this conversation. It too closely mirrored the feelings in her own heart, though she certainly she didn't blame Maxine for wanting to have a bit of fun. And hadn't she herself agreed to get out and meet people? If Bernice found out, Kerrianne would be the talk of the neighborhood instead of Maxine.

That idea provoked Kerrianne to add somewhat nastily, "Maybe someone should tell the bishop." It was hard to say with a straight face, but she managed—barely.

Bernice looked at her, as though seriously considering her suggestion. "Well, you know what, you might be right. I think on Sunday I'll have a nice chat with the bishop about Maxine."

Kerrianne immediately felt guilty. "Bernice, no. I was just kid—"

"Don't worry about it. I won't mention your name. Really, it is for the best. Maxine has no idea what men can be like. They take advantage of widows all the time. It's for her own good."

Kerrianne couldn't imagine anyone taking advantage of Maxine.

"And the bishop will thank me, I'm sure."

Kerrianne gave up. This was not a conversation she could win. "I'm sure he'll be grateful," she lied. In reality, she bet the bishop ran the other way whenever he spotted Bernice. Or maybe he'd duck into the nursery to hide, knowing Bernice wouldn't likely be found there. The thought of their dignified ecclesiastical leader skulking in the nursery to keep away from Bernice cheered Kerrianne exceedingly. She may not have much of a social life, but at least her imagination was still working.

"Guess I'd better start class." Kerrianne gestured to the children. "How about I walk Michael over to Maxine's when we're finished?"

"Oh, that would be heavenly. Thanks so much." Bernice turned to Michael and to his disgust, smooched his cheek noisily. "Good-bye. Be a good boy." She stood up and turned so quickly that her high heel caught in the carpet, causing her to stumble up the first steps on the stairs. Pretending not to see, Kerrianne turned her back and began helping the children with the puzzle so Bernice wouldn't see her grin.

Old biddy. Kerrianne thought, surprising herself. It wasn't like her to be so unkind. But she suddenly found she was tired of being kind. Maxine was one of the most genuinely nice people Kerrianne had ever met. She didn't deserve to be gossiped about by a woman who apparently had nothing better to do than spy on her.

But was Bernice right? Was it impossible to enjoy the company of another man and still remain true to your husband? Well, it didn't matter because Kerrianne was perfectly happy with her life as it was. Even so, she was going to buy that makeup. She wanted to look good for herself, and that was that.

"Okay, children," she said, putting on a bright smile. "Let's practice phonics!"

❄ ❄ ❄

At ten minutes after two, Kerrianne walked down the street to Maxine's as Caleb and Michael skipped on ahead. The day had turned dull and gray, and the cloudy sky overhead looked threatening. Today was early out day, and Kerrianne hoped the children would be home from school before it began to pour.

She was surprised to see all the cars parked outside Maxine's, stretching past the neighboring houses on both sides. Apparently Bernice was not the only woman receiving a demonstration. There was a note on the door: *Come in, all ye who want to be more beautiful and look younger!*

"That's me all right," Kerrianne said aloud.

There was a burst of laughter as she stepped inside the house, accompanied by a flurry of excited voices. She followed the voices into Maxine's kitchen and adjoining sitting room. The couch, love seat, and kitchen chairs had all been pushed back against the walls, leaving the middle clear except for a coffee table filled with beauty products. The dozen women in attendance ranged in age from about forty to seventy, which meant that Kerrianne at nearly thirty-one was the youngest by almost a decade. Besides Maxine, she recognized only two women sitting on the raised hearth in front of the unlit gas fireplace. They lived in the neighborhood, though not close enough to attend the same ward on Sundays. She knew nothing else about them, not even their names, except that they were both divorced. Kerrianne wondered where Bernice was.

"Ah, Kerrianne," Maxine spied her as she entered the room. "Glad you're here. Bernice told me you were coming. Come and eat something." She gestured to her kitchen table that had been pushed against the wall, laden with goodies. Many of the women were eagerly filling their plates.

"Actually, I came to get a few things—makeup, I mean. If you don't mind. I didn't realize you were having a full-fledged party."

"I'm glad you came." Maxine leaned over and whispered. "For you everything is thirty-five percent off—that's my price. Most everyone else has to pay full price. Don't worry, they can afford it. They *need* to afford it." Her eyes fell on Caleb and Michael. "I bet you two would like some cookies," she said in a louder voice. "Go ahead. Help yourselves."

The boys shed their winter coats onto the floor and dug into the table of goodies with enthusiasm, never mind that Kerrianne had already given them snacks at preschool. Kerrianne picked up the coats as Maxine pulled her over to an empty chair straddling the line where the carpet met the ceramic floor tile. Kerrianne stuffed the boy's coats under the chair and sat.

"Everybody, this is Kerrianne," Maxine announced. "She's my neighbor and, of course, also in my ward."

"In our ward," said a woman on the couch across the room, punctuating her words with a sniff that sounded awfully familiar.

Bernice? Kerrianne gazed at the woman, blinking in complete surprise. What had happened to her? Her pinched, yellow look was gone, along with the bright blue eye makeup she'd sported earlier. These were replaced by muted shades that showcased her rather beautiful brown eyes. Her thin lips were emphasized by liner and lipstick, the colors more mauve and muted than the dark brown she usually wore.

Her hair was still gray and the hair permed in outdated ringlets, but the overall change was so dramatic that Kerrianne could only stare in wonder.

"You're gaping, dear," Maxine whispered in her ear before sweeping across the room to resume her work on a kindly woman with white hair and so many wrinkles that Kerrianne doubted any amount of cream could ever smooth her face.

Kerrianne clamped her mouth shut quickly. "You look great, Bernice." She'd been about to say "Wow, you don't look anything like yourself!" but bit her tongue just in time.

"Thanks. I do rather like it." Bernice looked at Maxine. "But isn't this rather expensive for eye shadow?"

"Not at all," Maxine said. "It's very concentrated and won't wear away like other eye shadows. Besides, it's made of all natural ingredients so you know you're protected from free radicals."

Kerrianne wasn't about to ask what those were. The last time she'd asked, the explanation had left her rather dazed but with an urgent desire to do anything to protect herself and her family from free radicals, which were apparently the cause of everything from mild bad breath to debilitating cancers.

"Welcome," said the woman seated next to Kerrianne. Her wavy hair was a strawberry blonde that attractively framed her heart-shaped face, and her makeup was applied with an expert hand, making it difficult to really pinpoint her age. Her figure was on the verge of being too thin inside her designer pantsuit. She held out a hand with a cheerful smile that lit up her hazel eyes. "I'm Tina. It's good to meet you!"

"I'm Kerrianne."

"I know, Maxine's told me about you. Isn't Maxine a hoot? I just love her."

"Yeah, she's great."

"You're younger than I expected, though. Too young for all this." Tina fluttered a hand.

"Too young for what—makeup?" Kerrianne motioned to the coffee table of beauty products.

She laughed. "You're *never* too young for that."

"Then what?"

She lowered her voice. "To be a part of the Independence Club. That's what I call this lot. In secret, of course. We're all widows or divorcees. So we're, well, a bit more independent than a lot of women we know. Meaning that we get out of the house alone more. We have a wonderful time together."

Kerrianne's smile froze on her face. "I—uh . . ." She didn't know what to say. Looking around the room, she did feel young. Way too young. Certainly too young to be part of any club that didn't include her husband, who had been her best friend almost since the day they'd met. She felt a driving urge to leap up and flee from the room. She needed chocolate, huge amounts of chocolate. Oh, why hadn't she made it to the store yet? She would have to go the instant the children arrived home.

Tina noticed the change in her expression. "Am I wrong? I'm sorry. I thought I heard Bernice and Maxine mention that your husband had passed away. Maybe they were talking about someone else."

"I am a widow." Kerrianne managed to say. "But I—I . . ."

"You miss him," Tina said, her thin arched eyebrows wrinkling with concern. "Of course you do! I bet you had one of those fairytale relationships. What a lucky girl! I bet you're grateful every day for the time you had."

She spoke brightly and with such enthusiasm that Kerrianne didn't have the heart to tell her on most days she wasn't grateful at all but instead spent her time mourning that her time with Adam had been so short. "Yes, I was lucky," she said to Tina. That much was true, whether or not she acknowledged it frequently.

"That's really great. The Lord certainly has a way of blessing us, doesn't He? Anyway, forgive me. I should be more careful when I speak."

"That's what you get for hanging around Maxine," Kerrianne muttered with a touch of asperity. "She always says what she thinks."

Tina laughed loudly, and to Kerrianne's surprise, she found herself smiling back.

"I've been taking lessons from her," Tina admitted. "She's a woman of many talents. But seriously, Kerrianne, life can be very rewarding even after . . . well, after such hard times. Look, I'm going to tell you the best-kept secret." She leaned over, placing a hand on Kerrianne's back, and Kerrianne leaned in closer to hear. "We never tell anyone unless they're single," she continued, grinning from ear to ear. "Here it is: Being single is *fun!* Really! You get to go out and laugh and enjoy yourself. You don't have to worry about cooking and cleaning for someone." She paused and brought her free hand to her chest, gazing beatifically up at the ceiling. "You get to be taken out and romanced. You get to dance and go to movies. Why, I receive flowers almost every day of the week! Plus, you can do anything you want without clearing it with someone. You don't have to feel bad if you're not home on time. You can take off to another state whenever you feel like it—provided you have the money, of course. Yep, it's the best-kept secret around . . . being single's a hoot! You'll see. Give yourself a few weeks."

A few weeks where? wondered Kerrianne, nodding politely. Who was this obscenely happy woman and where did she get these strange ideas? Everyone knew being single was fun, but that was before you settled down and had children. She couldn't believe it could ever be that way again. And yes, a large part of her didn't *want* it to be. She'd lost the love of her life—and she was supposed to find happiness in that? If a million men brought her flowers, it wouldn't make up for Adam not being able to do so himself.

Kerrianne looked across the room at Bernice, hoping to change the subject.

"She's so pretty," Tina whispered, following her gaze. "And what a sweet woman. I've really enjoyed getting to know her better today."

Kerrianne let out a loud snort, turning it into a hardy cough at the last moment. Sweet? When had anyone ever called Bernice sweet? She was a lot of things, but Kerrianne was absolutely sure sweet wasn't one of them. "You, uh, like Bernice?"

Tina nodded. "She has a lot of interesting ideas."

Interesting. That was one way of putting it.

"Oh, no! It's raining," exclaimed one of the women sitting on the ledge in front of the fireplace. She gave a careless toss of her head, and her short, stylish, black hair gleamed in the overhead light. "Drat, now I won't get to go on my walk." She looked down at her rotund figure in dismay.

"Do like I do and walk on the treadmill," said the pretty brunette next to her with a slight accent that signaled her Mexican decent. "I get more books read that way." She sighed. "I love to read."

"But, Rosalva, I get seasick if I read while I'm moving. It happens all the time in the car."

"It won't while you're walking," Rosalva said, pushing her long hair over her shoulder. "It's different. You'll see. I lost thirty pounds last year, reading and walking."

"I don't even have a treadmill."

Tina had stood up to look outside at the rain, her face still in its perpetual smile. "You can use my treadmill if you want, Evie. But come and look how pretty the rain is. And we do need it very badly since it was so dry last summer."

Evie came over to peer outside the window behind them, accompanied by her friend Rosalva and several other women. "It's gray and dull and ugly out there, Tina," Evie said with a little grimace of her shapely mouth. "But I'll come use your treadmill anyway, since you live so close." She smiled at Tina as the other women erupted in laughter. "Thanks for offering." Evie patted Tina's arm before returning to the fireplace.

"Anytime," Tina murmured happily.

Kerrianne took the opportunity to move to another seat, not being in the mood for Tina's brand of optimism. Unfortunately, the only seat open was on the couch next to Bernice. "I'm not sure this eye shadow really does my eyes justice," Bernice said to her in a loud whisper. She was holding up a small mirror and peering at her lids through one half-closed eye. "I think Maxine just wants to make money off me. Do you believe she only offered me thirty-five percent off?"

Kerrianne nearly choked on the drink someone had put in her hand. "Actually, that's her cost."

"Really?" Bernice looked thoughtful. "Well, maybe I'll take it after all. Or at least just this one. I can probably make do with my old lipstick."

"I think you really look great. Of course, I'm not sure your husband would approve. I mean, what if a whole bunch of widowers start asking you out?"

"I'd say no, of course," Bernice pursed her lips, looking like her sour old self. "Well, I guess it's not like I ever really spend anything on myself." She raised her voice. "Maxine, I'll take the lot of it. Write me up a bill, would you? I've got to get my grandson back home before my daughter comes to get him."

"Tina, would you write the orders?" Maxine asked, her hands still busy with the white-haired woman. "Tina's my upline," she explained to Kerrianne. "She's the one who got me started in all this."

"Oh, sure. I'd love to." Tina's voice changed to sing-song. "Come along, ladies. I'll take care of you."

Kerrianne watched as one woman after another made out an order and left. Soon even Tina was gone, after several annoyingly cheerful comments about the "wonderful day" they'd shared together. Briefly, Kerrianne realized she hadn't found much out about the woman except that she seemed to always find a positive side to everything. Had her husband died? Or was she divorced? Kerrianne made a mental note to ask Maxine sometime when she didn't look so tired.

Maxine turned on the TV above the fireplace for Caleb, put another drink in Kerrianne's hand, and sat down next to her, breathing a sigh of exhaustion. "I was beginning to think I'd have to pay Bernice to get that makeup," she grumbled.

"She looked great! But I'm surprised she could make a decision without her husband."

"That was part of the problem, I think. He must have died when that horrendous blue was in style." Maxine shook her head.

Kerrianne laughed but quickly found tears starting in her eyes. "Oh, Maxine, at least she's wearing makeup. I haven't bought any for almost four years. I'm such a hypocrite, aren't I? Poor Bernice."

"Yep, I definitely think you're going to burn in the afterlife. When you reach those pearly gates, they'll specifically ask you if you've been nice to Bernice. You, of course, will be honest and say no, so they'll send you down to shovel coal with me."

"Is that why you're trying so hard with her?" Kerrianne silently thanked Maxine for helping her to smile instead of weep.

"Probably. But I think it's a lost cause. I may as well give up now." She flexed her arms. "I've been working in my flower bed, so I know how to handle a shovel. Coal won't be too different from dirt."

"Bernice thinks you should be ashamed of yourself for flirting with men."

Maxine rolled her eyes. "Bernice thinks everyone should be ashamed. To her that's what it is to be religious. But she's wrong."

Kerrianne set down her glass. "I was having some fun with her this morning and told her maybe we should report you to the bishop."

Maxine groaned. "Don't tell me—she took you seriously!"

"'Fraid so. Sorry."

"Ah, for crying out loud, the poor bishop. Do you think if I bake him something he'll forgive me for Bernice cornering him?"

"Truthfully? It would have to be something big. Really, really big. Like maybe a dozen apple pies."

"I hate making apple pies," Maxine said morosely. "I swore I'd never make another one for any man."

An idea occurred to Kerrianne. "You know what? I think maybe Bernice might be jealous of you and Harold."

"Jealous? Of Harold?" Maxine was incredulous. "Whatever for? Why, take last night for instance. He went up on the stand to say the prayer at the single adult fireside, and he fell asleep in his seat." She paused before adding more thoughtfully, "At least I think he fell asleep. Anyway, he gave a loud snort when the bishop touched his shoulder to tell him it was his turn."

Kerrianne laughed. "At least it wasn't *during* the prayer. Who knows, maybe he was just thinking."

"Yeah, he's a deep thinker, all right. With all the thinking he does, he should have been able to figure out how to kiss a woman somewhere on the face instead of on the hand all the time. What is it about my hand anyway?" She held the offending body part out as though inspecting it for flaws.

Kerrianne giggled harder. "Maybe it's all that fancy lotion, you use."

"Speaking of which—" Maxine grabbed a bottle and squirted the contents on Kerrianne's hand. The faint smell of sweet apricots filled the air. "Try this."

"Nice," Kerrianne said, rubbing it in. "But after seeing these prices, I think just the eye shadow and liner, okay? I can do without the face creams, I think."

"Nonsense, we'll get it all or nothing. Look, I sold enough here to get a few extra things for a really deep discount, and since I don't need anything, you might as well get what you need. It'll cost a bit more than just the eye shadow, but you can get the whole face system as well. That's better than the cheap stuff you can get at the grocery store."

"But, Maxine—"

"No buts. Here's what I think we'll need. She began writing a list on a pad of paper while explaining the benefits of each product to Kerrianne. "I'll place the order tonight," she said when she finished. "I'll Fed-Ex it so it should be here before Friday. We want to look good for Friday."

Kerrianne's stomach was abruptly in knots. "About Friday, Maxine. I know I promised to go, but—"

"I said, No buts. I'm holding you to your promise." Maxine glanced at her grandfather clock, standing in the corner next to the couch. "Isn't the school bus due soon? I know you like to be home for your kids."

Kerrianne stood and gave Maxine a hug. "Thanks," she whispered. "I owe you one."

"You owe me Friday night."

"Okay. Friday." She held up a hand. "But only if that makeup is here. You've spoiled me. I'm not going out with that purple stuff on anymore."

"Well, there's always my samples," Maxine said airily. "Don't worry. I won't let you go anywhere looking like that." She pointed to the TV where a purple dinosaur was apparently exerting a magic hold over Caleb. Maxine leaned out and passed a hand between Caleb's face the TV. The child didn't look away or even appear to notice. Maxine looked again at the dinosaur and shuddered. "Now there's someone who could do with a good makeover. Couldn't they find a color other than purple?

Chapter Seven

The week passed in a haze for Ryan. Each morning at seven, almost without thinking, he sorted the mail, matching addresses in the order he would hit the houses on his route. After the Monday deluge, there was only the normal amount of mail, which he quickly dispatched with his own system. He was the quickest sorter in the entire office. The faster he went out on his route, the faster he could deliver the mail and get home to his children.

Sometimes the other workers called him Rapid Ryan and talked about him making them look bad. The comments were only half teasing. Despite this, they understood Ryan's family situation, and for the most part they respected him. His supervisor loved him, and that was what was important.

On Thursday morning he was out on the road at eight-thirty. As he put mail in the first two boxes, he kept glancing at Kerrianne's house. Was she waiting on the porch? Would she speak to him?

But she wasn't there, and he hadn't caught so much as a glimpse of her since Monday. He stared at the letters in his hand with frustration. There was nothing that would require him to go up the walk and ring the doorbell. Why hadn't someone sent her a lousy package? The morning skies were also clear, so there was no excuse to take the mail to her door, even on the pretense of a good deed. He was beginning to consider sending her a package himself just to see her.

Yesterday morning, he'd thrown the ball with her three children in front of the house, as the older ones waited for it to get late enough to run to the bus stop, but if she was aware of that, perhaps watching from inside the house, he couldn't tell. He'd delayed as long as he could but had to move on before the children's bus came.

Was something wrong with Kerrianne? He didn't think so. More likely she was embarrassed by what she'd told him on Monday and couldn't face him. He wished he could tell her how happy he was that he'd been a part of easing her hurt by delivering her mail. He couldn't begin to know where he'd be now if Tiger's constant needs hadn't seen him through those initial months after Laurie died.

The letters slipped from his hand back into the box on the next seat as memories of Laurie's last days flooded over him. Her sister had come to help out, and he wasn't really needed at home, but how could he stay away? He'd taken extended leave a month before her death when he simply couldn't bear to leave her anymore. Laurie had chided him about the decision because they'd needed the money—even now he was still paying medical bills—but he'd do it all again. He'd probably take the whole year off. How could he have known their time would be so short? If he could roll back the clock, he would. He'd change everything. He'd work the midnight shift when Laurie was sleeping so that they could spend every moment together during the day.

The memories faded, leaving as always the bittersweet mixture of love and pain. If he told the entire truth, it hadn't only been Tiger who'd helped him go on but the knowledge that his job was waiting. Part of that was the eagerness with which Kerrianne had awaited her mail. Why hadn't he told her that she'd helped him as well? Maybe if he'd told her the full truth, she'd still be there waiting for it. Waiting for him.

He rolled his eyes at his thoughts. "You are losing it, Ryan boy." He put the mail in her box and slammed the door shut.

As he began driving to the next house, he saw movement at the door and looked up eagerly. Kerrianne came onto the porch wearing loose jeans and a long-sleeved blue shirt that emphasized the color of her eyes. Her hair was attractively styled, but as on Monday she wasn't wearing makeup, which made her look different from the strong, composed woman of Saturday night. Not bad, just different. Younger. More vulnerable. How could he not have noticed just how vulnerable she'd looked each morning for nearly four years? Had he been so involved with his own sorrows that he'd failed to notice even a hint of hers? He shook his head, experiencing an odd, swelling sadness in his chest, one that made him want to hold her. Anyone should have been able to tell that she'd suffered a tragedy and wasn't simply a crazy woman obsessed with the mail.

She moved gracefully down the walk, and he let the truck roll forward a bit to where her driveway met the sidewalk. Her hair, a dark blonde bordering on brown, glinted in the sunlight. "Hello," she called. Her smile did funny things to his stomach.

Ryan stopped and stepped from the truck. This wasn't protocol, and his boss wouldn't be pleased that he was attending to his personal life during work hours, but he'd made a promise to Laurie. He'd been too rash when he'd vowed to give up the dating scene last Saturday. Maybe the woman he was supposed to meet had been in front of him all along.

"Hi," he said. "I was hoping to see you."

"Oh, do you have a package?" She craned her neck to look around him at the mail filling the inside of his vehicle. Ryan noticed the curve of her white throat and wondered if it was as soft as it looked.

"Uh, no. That's not it. I wanted to know if you'd like to go to a dance tonight." He'd become quite adept at asking women out in the past year. In fact, not one had turned him down. And why not? He was relatively young and nice-looking. He had a steady job and no vices to speak of except his acting, which wasn't really a vice at all. Why, then, was he suddenly nervous as he waited for her response?

Because I didn't really care if the others said no.

Shaking the thought away, Ryan waited expectantly. There was a tightening feeling in his stomach as he noticed that all the color had left her face. She looked ready to faint. "I, uh . . ."

"Ryan," he supplied, thinking she'd forgotten his name. "Ryan Oakman."

"I can't go out with you." She stared down at her hand, twisting her wedding ring. "I'm married."

With that, she turned and ran up the steps. Ryan watched her go. Strangely, he didn't feel rejected or upset that she hadn't said good-bye. He felt only the same swelling sadness that had made him want to hold her earlier. "I understand," he said to Kerrianne, though she was beyond hearing. "Part of me is still married, too." As he climbed back into the truck, he added to himself, "Too fast, Ryan. Way too fast."

Laurie had always said he moved too fast in everything he did. She'd made him wait a whole month before agreeing to marry him and another three until the wedding—months that had been torture for Ryan. But she'd been worth fighting for. Even knowing the ending, the horrible, heart-wrenching agony of losing her, he'd do it all again.

He believed Kerrianne was also worth fighting for. There was something special about her, something that went beyond the desire he had to comfort her. Or the smoothness of her white throat.

Instead of asking her out, he should have asked about letting Tiger play with her son. Or if she'd had a sudden opening in her preschool. After all, Tiger had been bugging him all week about coming over here. A smile came to Ryan's face as he thought of his small son. That was Tiger. Once he got something in his head, it was difficult to make him forget.

Should he ask her now? Ryan brought a hand up to scratch at his bearded cheek, almost surprised to remember he hadn't yet shaved it off. Kerrianne's house sat blankly and unwelcoming before him. No, he couldn't face it today. One rejection would have to tide him over. Forcing a grin of defeat, however temporary, he drove to the next house.

Though Ryan finished his route in the usual time, the day had gone by way too slowly. At last he arrived at his baby-sitter's, a small brick rambler several streets from his own house, to find Ria in front sitting on the cement stairs. Her glum face was red with cold, and her short black hair hung limply and rather too slick against the sides of her face. That meant she needed to wash it. What was it with his daughter any-way? A year ago he hadn't been able to get her out of the bath; now he had to remind her to take one.

Ria stared at him morosely. "Hi, Dad."

"What, no hug? No smile?"

"I hate school," she returned, clenching her small fists. "And I hate coming here after school. Jenny hates me." Jenny was the baby-sitter's daughter, and she often caused Ria of a lot of grief.

"Jenny doesn't hate you. It's just all the kids her mother watches, you know? She worries about them taking up all her time."

"She doesn't like to share anything," Ria said. "But I don't care, 'cause I hate her too."

Ryan blinked. Ria was often passionate, but she didn't usually claim to hate people. He sat beside her on the step. "Did something happen at school today?"

She shook her head, staring down at her hands. "Everything's fine. Are we going to see Sam tonight?"

"You know we won't be starting on the new play until after Christmas. Besides, tonight's Thursday. You have basketball practice."

Ria brightened. "Oh, yeah."

"Go get into the truck, okay? I'll get Tiger." He stood up and rang the bell.

Susan, his sitter, let him into the house, wiping her hands on a dishtowel. "Hi," she greeted him cheerily. "Come on in. Tiger's in the family room."

Sure enough, Ryan found Tiger watching television as usual, eyes glued to the cartoon figures. "Hey, Tiger," Ryan called.

"Hi, Dad." Tiger didn't so much as glance in his direction.

"Did you see Ria?" Susan asked, sitting on the edge of a worn pink and white sofa.

Ryan shifted his gaze to her. She wasn't an unattractive woman, but she looked as though she hadn't much time for herself. Her brown hair was pulled back into a ponytail, and her face showed traces of old makeup. She wore her customary jeans with the tight legs that had been popular years before and a T-shirt that barely stretched to cover her swelling midriff. Was she going to have a baby? Or had she put on weight like his mother? He didn't dare ask. He wondered when she found time to sleep.

"I saw her," he said, sitting on the opposite end of the sofa.

"She wouldn't come in," Susan continued. "She and Jenny were fighting when they got here." The light angling in from the side window made the freckles and blemishes in her skin stand out more clearly. "I had to send Jenny to her room."

"I'm sorry. What was the problem?" He hoped it wouldn't be too difficult to solve.

"It's the mother-daughter Thanksgiving tea party they're having at school next week. Apparently, the kids in several of the grades are planning a special day for their mothers or other guest."

Ryan's heart sank, knowing the "or other guest" part was mostly for Ria's benefit. These events were always hard on Ria, no matter how careful the teachers were not to single out her loss.

"The fight," Susan was saying, "was because Jenny told Ria she would have to find someone besides me to go with her." She gave him an apologetic look. "Do you have someone Ria could go with? Her grandmother maybe? Ordinarily, I'd volunteer, but Jenny's . . . well, she keeps begging me to quit baby-sitting as it is, and I feel she needs me to be there just for her."

"I'll take care of it," Ryan said shortly. Then, lest he'd hurt her feelings, he added, "Thanks, Susan—for telling me."

"You know, Ria's not happy here." Susan glanced at Tiger and two of her own towheaded sons. They were all engrossed in the cartoons and taking no notice of them. "I know it's been difficult since her mother . . . I've tried, but . . ." She shrugged. "Tiger's really no problem, but if you'd rather find another place for him so that Ria will be happier, I'd understand."

Ryan knew this wasn't easy for Susan to say. She needed the extra money baby-sitting brought to her family, and while Tiger's mind wasn't stretched or challenged at Susan's, he was always safe.

"I've been thinking about enrolling Tiger in a preschool in the afternoons," he said. "Just two or three times a week. I'd still pay as much as I do now if you'd see that he gets there and pick him up. Of course," he added hastily, seeing a tenseness come to her face, "if that's too much work, I might be able to work it out on my lunch hour or something."

"It's just with all the other kids, I'm pretty busy. I've got one-year-old twins I'm watching now."

Ryan nodded. He understood the complication of taking children anywhere. Asking Susan to bundle up one-year-old twins, her own three-year-old son, and the three other children she baby-sat would be simply too much to ask on a permanent basis. Then again, he didn't feel letting Tiger sit in front of the TV all day was a responsible thing to do. Tiger was ready to move on to something more challenging.

"When are you going to start him in school?" Susan asked.

"I don't really have it planned yet. I'm still looking for a teacher."

"Well, let me know." She tucked a frazzled wisp of hair that had strayed from her ponytail behind her ear and stood up.

"Come on, Tiger," Ryan said, rising from the sofa. "We need to go. Ria has practice, and we need to zip home and grab something to eat."

"Eat?" Tiger asked with interest, though his eyes didn't leave the cartoons.

Knowing it would be easier to physically move him than to entice him away from the TV, Ryan bent down and scooped up his little boy from the floor.

"Dad!" he protested.

Ignoring him, Ryan threw him over his shoulders. "Thanks for the sack of potatoes, Susan. I'll bring them back tomorrow."

Tiger giggled and beat on his back. "Dad, I'm not potatoes! I'm Tiger!"

"I think my potatoes are talking," Ryan said to no one in particular. "I guess they don't like the idea of becoming french fries."

"French fries? I want french fries!"

"Do you have to yell?" By this time they were out to the truck, and Ryan dumped Tiger unceremoniously inside next to Ria.

"We're going to have french fries tonight," Tiger was informing Ria as Ryan opened his own door and slid behind the wheel.

"No, we're not," Ryan said. "We're having whatever's in the freezer that we can warm up in the microwave."

"Aw, Dad."

"We've had enough french fries since I started in that play. We need something else. Something green." Ryan checked for traffic as he pulled from the curb.

"Yuck!" Ria and Tiger chimed together.

"Well, maybe not green, exactly, but healthier. You know what I mean."

"I had a green french fry once," Tiger said hopefully. "I found it under my bed."

Ria groaned, but Ryan laughed. "You mean you actually cleaned under it?"

"No, I was hiding Ria's doll."

"I don't have any dolls!" Ria's smile vanished. "I hate dolls."

Tiger was nonplussed. "I guess that's why you never came to look for it."

Ria folded her arms and gave an exaggerated sigh. "Anyway, we don't have any dinners in the freezer. I took out the last ones yesterday."

"You mean the Chinese bowls?" Ryan asked.

"Yeah. And there weren't any more at all. Well, there is that casserole, the one"—her voice suddenly sounded choked—"that Mom made."

Silence fell over them, as subtle as a ton of humongous green french fries. They all knew what Ria was talking about. When Laurie's illness had become pronounced, she'd made bunches of dinners whenever she had the energy, storing them in the freezer for nights when neither of them wanted to cook. After she'd taken to bed and her sister had come to help out, they hadn't used the dinners anymore. There'd been six left when Laurie died. He'd given one to the children every week or two, not eating any himself so the meal would last them several days. But he hadn't been able to cook the last one. It simply wasn't in him to have it all be over.

"Are we going to eat that?" Tiger looked at them with huge eyes.

"Do you want to?"

The kids thought for a moment, and then Ria shook her head. "No," she decided. "Let's save that for a special day. Maybe Christmas."

Ryan felt his face relax, though until that moment, he hadn't realized it had been frozen somewhere between a smile and a frown. "We'd better swing by the store then. We're almost home. You two stay in the truck while I run in and change. We still have time."

"We could get french fries instead," Tiger said, with his usual single-mindedness.

"Tiger!" Ria slugged him playfully in the shoulder, and he giggled.

Ryan pulled into their driveway and left them laughing while he hurried inside the house. He hated going in alone, even just for a minute. There was an abandoned air that he didn't know how to eliminate. Was it the dust on top of the picture frames that he never seemed to find time to clean? Was it the constant pile of dirty clothes in the laundry basket by the washer? Or perhaps Tiger's handprints on the walls? Saturday, he'd try to clean it all and see. Yet in his heart he knew it would still feel abandoned. Was this why Laurie had been so insistent on his remarrying? Did she understand the emptiness her leaving would create not only in his heart but in their home?

Shaking these thoughts from his mind, he pulled on jeans and a heavy flannel shirt. Then he traded his work boots for tennis shoes before hurrying out the door.

The children were still laughing, and he let them enjoy each other for a few minutes more before bringing up the problem at school. "So, I hear you're having a tea party," he said casually to Ria as they turned into Macey's parking lot. "It sounds really fun. Do I get to go?"

Ria's grin vanished instantly. "It's for moms."

"Or other guests."

"Yeah, so they say. But everyone will be bringing their moms, and you're not even a girl."

"Whew!" He pretended to wipe his brow. "That's a relief. It'd be pretty hard being a dad if I was a girl."

Tiger guffawed, slapping his leg, but Ria quelled him with a haughty glare. "If you're not a girl, you'll stand out. It'll be embarrassing."

"Not as embarrassing as if I were wearing a dress and a wig."

"Daaaaaad!" Ria's eyes glistened with tears, and Ryan knew he'd gone far enough. The Ria who would have giggled at imagining him wearing high heels was apparently long gone.

"What about Grandma?" he said more seriously.

Ria rolled her eyes. "Can't I just be sick that day?"

Ryan was tempted to say yes, but he knew that would make things worse the next time something similar came up. He found a parking place for the truck and turned toward her. "You can't stay home," he said quietly.

"Why not?" Her mouth trembled.

"Because it's not going away. All your life you're going to have to deal with events like this. We all will. And as much as we miss your mom, she wouldn't want us to hide at home when things get difficult."

"It wouldn't be a problem if you'd just marry Sam," came Ria's sullen retort.

"Sam's already married, and she loves her husband a lot."

"Well, he's stupid. He doesn't treat her right."

Sam's husband was a stubborn man, but not a bad one. "I think he'll change."

"Well, I hope he doesn't."

Ryan sighed. How could he explain to Ria that Sam was absolutely out of reach? Ryan could tell how much she still loved her husband even if she and everyone else was doubtful. He knew they'd work things out eventually. "Look, maybe I can ask Sam if she'll go with you," he said, deciding that compromise was the best solution.

That was the worst thing about single parenting—not having someone to bounce ideas off, to assure he was making the right decisions. What if something he chose now affected Ria's entire life negatively? There would only be himself to blame and no one to commiserate with or share the burden.

Ria smiled, though her eyes were still teary. "Thanks, Dad."

"Can we go in now?" Tiger said, pulling off his safety belt. He grinned at Ria. "I still think you should take Dad. He really could wear a dress, you know. Susan could give him one."

Ryan groaned. "Four years old and already a wise guy."

They had filled their shopping cart to the brim and were making a last dash for chocolate milk mix. He was surprised to see a boy Tiger's age waving at him with one hand, the other gripping a half-full cart of groceries.

Ryan immediately recognized the boy as Kerrianne Price's son—Caleb, if he remembered the name correctly. Sure enough, next to the cart, with her back toward him, was Kerrianne, reaching for what looked like an enormous slab of chocolate wrapped in cellophane. She wore the jeans and long-sleeved T-shirt of that morning, and her hair looked soft and freshly combed. From the side he could more clearly see her high cheekbones and fine pale skin. Her other two children, whom he also recognized but whose names he didn't know, were also with her: a boy with dark blond hair and the girl with the curly golden locks and smooth skin.

"Not that kind," Kerrianne was saying, bending closer to take a look at the labels. The two children leaned in with her. It was an oddly intimate moment, and though they were in the middle of a grocery store, Ryan had the distinct impression that he was intruding upon their privacy. Should he go back down the aisle? Or perhaps he should pass by her as though he hadn't seen them. Well, it was too late for that. Caleb was still waving with a bright grin on his face.

"Isn't that the lady from the other night?" Tiger asked, pointing at Kerrianne as she put something into her cart. "Is that her boy, the one I'm going to play with?"

Ryan knew he had no choice but to at least say a casual hello. He was both excited and nervous at the prospect. How would she react? Could it be any worse than that morning? Probably, but he found he was willing to take the chance.

Kerrianne was stretching now, reaching for something on a high shelf. In seconds she would turn and see him. A knot formed in Ryan's stomach.

That was when it began to rain chocolate.

Chapter Eight

Kerrianne couldn't believe the huge block of semisweet baking chocolate she'd bought on Monday after Maxine's makeup party was all gone. At the time she'd told herself there was no way she'd need more before her next shopping day, and as money was always tight, she'd decided against buying extra. Then Misty had volunteered to take a treat to her school class, and she'd chosen her favorite—homemade chocolate chip cookies. Since they were out of chocolate chips, they'd had to cut up a good portion of the baking chocolate to make the treats. Then Kerrianne had eaten the rest of it this morning after Ryan asked her out. Just the boost she'd needed before afternoon preschool.

Knowing she'd never make it through that night, much less the weekend without at least having a stash available in case of dire need, Kerrianne had hauled all the children to the store. It was going smoothly—or so she thought.

"We need the semisweet," she said. "We'll just get one." Then remembering the cookies, she decided to buy an extra for emergencies, even though she had two bags of chocolate chips already in the basket.

Benjamin had hold of the shelf that was even with his head and was pulling himself up to peer at the white chocolate. "Be careful," Kerrianne warned, eyes wandering over the many choices. Macey's had a great assortment of bulk baking chocolate this time of year since it was nearing the holidays. Some pieces were only as long as her hand, but others were almost double that size.

Misty grabbed onto the same shelf as Benjamin, trying to reach a slab on the shelf above. "I found a big one," she said, puffing a bit with effort.

"Mom," Caleb called. "Hey, Mom!"

"In a minute. Stay with the cart," Kerrianne was aware of someone moving down the aisle, passing several other customers near the middle of the row. She hoped they didn't need bulk chocolate. She liked taking time to choose the right pieces. "I'm almost finished," she told Caleb a little louder, in case the approaching customer was waiting for the chocolate. For some reason the cart had paused a few paces away.

She hurriedly put a second block of chocolate into her cart without glancing in the other shopper's direction. Would that be enough? Who knew with the evening Maxine had planned for her tomorrow night. Feeling a brief surge of panic, Kerrianne grabbed for another slab, almost losing her balance but catching herself with a hand on a shelf. Benjamin's shelf. The same one Misty was now practically climbing on in her efforts to reach the perfect piece of chocolate.

"Misty, get dow—"

The shelf gave a moan, and something broke with a sickening clang. Tilting downward, it disgorged its heavy load of chocolate. Kerrianne spread her hands, trying to catch the chocolate slabs as they fell, curling her body slightly to perhaps catch some on her knees. At the same time, she checked the children. Misty had fallen to the ground but was unhurt. Benjamin was holding a large block of chocolate and watching her with big eyes. "Ow!" he exclaimed, as a single remaining slab teetered and fell on his foot.

Kerrianne had managed to save four of the slabs but only just. One was balanced on her knee, and she had to carefully rescue it with her hands already full of chocolate. Her face was flushed, and she felt as hot as if she'd run five miles. She knew everyone in the aisle was staring at her. Someone laughed.

She reached up and righted the shelf, balancing on top of it the chocolate she'd saved before stooping down for more. The shelf promptly tilted, and the slabs fell toward Kerrianne's face at an alarming rate. She tried to bring up her hands, but they held more chocolate now and were too heavy to move quickly. A black eye was inevitable. Fleetingly, she wondered if this would finally cure her habit of emotional binging on chocolate.

A hand snatched the block of chocolate away before it slammed into her face. Kerrianne felt herself grow limp with relief. "Thanks," she murmured, catching sight of jeans and tennis shoes belonging to a man. She knew her face was bright red.

Too embarrassed to meet his gaze, she quickly began picking up the chocolate, stacking the good ones on the floor and placing all the damaged ones in her cart. Thankfully, there didn't seem to be too many as most of the slabs had kindly cushioned their fall by smacking into her arms and legs, though she'd certainly have to forget about a new outfit for tomorrow night. She would write a check and transfer the money from savings later.

"You don't have to buy it all," said a voice. "I'm sure the store will take care of it."

"I need it," she said loudly. "For the kids, I mean."

"We never get to eat that. Only you," Benjamin said helpfully, as though sure she'd forgotten.

"For cookies," she said, glaring at him. "You ate those, didn't you?"

"Mom, you never get this much." Misty stared with wide eyes.

Misty was right. Kerrianne stopped loading the chocolate into her cart, her eyes finally coming to rest on the man standing beside her. Her thanks froze on her tongue.

Ryan!

He looked more like he had as the Sheriff of Nottingham than when he delivered her mail. He wore his clothes as though they were comfortable, exuding a masculinity that made her feel lost. His face was still unshaven, and his gray eyes penetrating, causing that now-familiar warmth in her stomach.

"Hi," he said, his voice rich with amusement.

"Thanks," she managed, feeling a surge of resentment at Maxine. If it hadn't been for Maxine and that Saturday night play, she might not even have recognized him. *He certainly wouldn't have noticed me,* she thought with resentment. They could have passed like strangers without any awkwardness. Maybe he wouldn't even have stopped to help.

That seemed unfair. Even now, he was directing his daughter—Ria, Kerrianne remembered—to help pick up the remaining slabs while he held the broken shelf steady. Grinning, the girl did as her father instructed. Benjamin, too, was helping, but Misty was staring at Ryan's daughter, her blue eyes narrowed with concentration.

"I know you," Misty said. "You go to my school. You're in third grade, aren't you? In Mrs. McCoy's class."

Ria paused. "Yeah. I've seen you around. What grade are you in?"

"Second."

"Mrs. Jeppson's?"

"Yeah."

The conversation was cut short as a teenaged store employee with a spotty complexion came down the aisle. He looked at them accusingly. "What happened?"

"The shelf broke," Kerrianne said, unwilling to say anymore.

Ria pointed at Misty and Benjamin. "Those kids were climbing on it."

"It's my fault," Kerrianne said. "I steadied myself on the shelf."

With a disgruntled sigh and a cold stare that told her he thought she was insane, the teenager began fiddling with something under the shelf. Every so often he stopped to cast a venomous glance in Kerrianne's direction.

Probably interrupted his flirting with a checker, she thought.

Another store employee rounded the corner, coming toward them very fast. He was older with brown hair, and his short figure was rather stocky, looking strong enough to lift up all the shelves with only two fingers.

"Get a cart," he barked at the pimple-faced teen.

The boy obeyed immediately, his demeanor instantly changing. He dashed down the aisle and returned within seconds. The manager began placing the plastic-wrapped chocolate pieces in the cart. The teen helped, and so did Ryan. Kerrianne stood there, frozen, until they began unloading the chocolate from her own cart.

"Uh, I was going to buy those. They're damaged now."

The teen hesitated, holding a dented block of chocolate in his hands.

"You don't have to do that. We'll take care of it." The manager said airily, though Kerrianne could have sworn his eyes were telling her she most certainly should. Was it her imagination? He smiled at her but it looked more like a grimace.

The next thing she knew, they had completely emptied her cart of the chocolate. "Wait!" she said, her earlier panic returning. "I need one." She reached for the chocolate in the spotty teenager's hand, tugging on it.

He tugged back. "It's broken. You don't have to buy it."

"I need it!" Kerrianne felt close to tears. She gave a mighty tug. The package ripped as the chocolate snapped in two, the chipped pieces sprinkling to the floor like confetti.

The manager's face turned red, and the teen smirked at her. Ryan looked amused, while her children were watching with mouths ajar. Other customers in the aisle stifled their laughter.

"Well, it looks fresh," she said, examining the chocolate instead of all the staring faces. "That's good."

Mumbling something under his breath, the manager took an undamaged piece from the extra cart and handed it to Kerrianne, relieving her of the broken piece and giving it to the teenager. "Take the cart to the back." He glowered at the teen, who snapped his gum with apparent unconcern. "And in the future," the manager added in an icy tone, "please don't play tug-of-war with the customers."

The teen bobbed his head, carelessly tossed the broken chocolate slab on top of the pile, and wheeled off.

"But I need—" Kerrianne stopped short, staring at the block of chocolate the manager had given her. It was significantly smaller than either of the ones she'd originally chosen. She doubted it would last her until she arrived home, what with this horrible experience. When had her life spiraled so out of control?

"Let me walk you to the checkout," the manager said with a kind, weary smile. "Or did you need to get something else?"

Kerrianne knew he most certainly hoped she didn't want anything else. "Okay," she agreed meekly, grasping her cart and looking around for her children. For a moment she couldn't spot Caleb, and terror roared into her heart. It was a familiar sensation since Adam's death—one she often experienced in the dead of night when the phone rang and no one was on the other end or during a storm that awakened her with its ferocity. The feeling was the same as hearing that voice on the phone talking about Adam's car accident. "Caleb," she whispered.

Then her eyes fell on him near the end of the aisle, lying on the floor as he played cars with Ryan's son, Tiger. Her heartbeat slowed. She wiped her sweaty palms on the jacket she'd set over her purse in the cart and moved toward him. "Get off the floor, Caleb," she said automatically, fighting to keep her tone calm. "You'll get dirty."

"Boys are supposed to get dirty," he said, but he climbed to his feet. Kerrianne smiled, recognizing the phrase she'd said to her sister, Amanda, at least a hundred times as she learned to deal with her son, little Blakey, who seemed to have an unusual talent for attracting dirt, even for a boy.

"Let's go." She smiled vaguely in Ryan's direction without meeting his eyes and began walking to the checkout. The manager flanked her, as though determined to make sure she didn't damage his store further.

For an instant, Kerrianne envisioned him putting up her photograph and warning all the employees. The ridiculousness of the thought made her smile. The manager was just being helpful.

She was aware of being trailed by Ryan and his children. More aware than she wanted to be. The effort of keeping her gaze from his was taxing.

"Dad, he's my very best friend in the whole world," Tiger said behind them in a voice loud enough to be heard by everyone around them. "He said I could come over and play."

"Shhh, Tiger," Ria said. "You're yelling again. Sheesh!"

"Well, Dad?"

"We'll see."

Kerrianne walked faster to put some distance between them. She glanced down at Caleb, who was craning his neck to look around at Tiger. Caleb had a smug look on his face.

"I don't like that girl," Misty said in a whisper. "She's a mean tattle-tale."

"She doesn't seem mean to me," Benjamin said, overhearing them. "She only told what really happened."

The manager went to a register. "Let me help you here."

Kerrianne put her groceries on the counter. As he scanned the items, her eyes fell on the regular chocolate bars along the aisle. She reached for one and then for two more. It wasn't semisweet baking chocolate, but it would do in a pinch. Hm, maybe a few more would be a good idea.

"Dad, look how much chocolate she's buying," Ria said behind her.

Kerrianne clenched her jaw and with a defiant shake of her head added three more chocolate bars to the pile, followed by a pack of gum. Her children's eyes were huge, and Caleb actually licked his lips in anticipation. He turned to Tiger, who had come up next to him. "We must have been really, really good," he said in a loud whisper.

"Dad, I want a candy bar," Tiger yelled.

Kerrianne was glad when she'd paid for her groceries and was heading out the door. If she hurried, she wouldn't have to see Ryan again or face the conflicting emotions in her heart.

A rush of cold air hit her outside, but Kerrianne was still feeling sweaty so she didn't put her jacket on. The problem was, she couldn't seem to remember where she'd parked the van. She usually parked far away from the store, not only for the exercise but because then the van was easier to spot. Today, though, she'd parked closer. Where was it? There were dozens of gold vans, but none that had the same black trim across the door.

"Do you remember where we parked?" she asked the kids.

Benjamin shrugged, but Misty pointed, her finger barely emerging from the sleeve of her new coat. "I think down that way."

"Must be behind that green truck," Kerrianne hurried into the parking lot. Sure enough, now that she'd started toward the van, she could see the black trim on the end. "Here we go," she said, hurrying toward it.

"Whee!" screamed Caleb, who'd grabbed onto the back of the cart.

"Mom, slow down," complained Benjamin. Kerrianne grabbed his hand and helped him along.

While the kids scrambled inside the van, Kerrianne emptied the groceries into the back. Then she took her jacket and put it on, having finally cooled down. She spied one of the chocolate bars and opened one, breaking off a piece.

"Mom, I want some!" Caleb said.

"When we get home. I don't want chocolate all over the van."

"Aw. Can I hold it then?"

"Okay." Kerrianne leaned inside the back of the van and tossed each of the kids a chocolate bar. "Misty, put on Caleb's belt for me, all right?" She stood back and shut the hatch, taking another bite of chocolate. Not as comforting as semisweet, but it was calming all the same. She turned and nearly slammed into Tiger Oakman, his father standing behind him with a bag of groceries. Just her luck. All the empty spaces in the lot and he had to park near her.

"Hey, you guys are parked by us!" Tiger yelled.

Kerrianne opened her mouth to reply—and choked on her chocolate.

"Get in the truck, bud." Ryan spoke to the boy but was looking at Kerrianne.

She swallowed. Ryan was so handsome with his wavy hair and mysterious with that rugged, unshaven face. She wondered what the roughness would feel like against her skin if he kissed her—no, not her, but some other woman who was looking for a relationship. Not someone like her who'd already found and loved a soul mate.

Guiltily, she looked not at him but at a place near his left ear. "Thanks for helping me out in there."

"It's not every day I get to see chocolate fighting back." He glanced at the bar in her hand.

She laughed, feeling self-conscious. "Me either." For a moment, they were quiet, and Kerrianne wondered if he might ask her out again. She hoped not. She might not be able to say no.

"Well, good-bye," she said into the silence. With what she hoped was a nonchalant smile, she opened her door and climbed inside.

It wasn't until she was driving from the parking lot that she noticed the wide smear of chocolate on her chin.

She didn't feel like going home, so she drove to her parents' spacious house in Alpine. The children laughed with unconcealed joy as they ran into the garage and through the back door without knocking, opening their chocolate bars on the way. Kerrianne followed them more slowly, puzzling over the emotions in her heart. Instead of going into the house, she waded through the leaf-covered backyard where a swing set sat motionless in the cold air. Her parents had bought the swing set almost twenty years ago when Tyler was turning five. It'd seen a lot of use since then, especially with the growing number of grandchildren, and her father kept it in good repair.

Kerrianne sat on the closest swing. Adam had proposed to her in this very spot. Tears filled her eyes at the memory, and for a moment, she could almost sense him near. She grasped a handful of air, rubbing it between her fingers before holding it to her heart. There was a strange sort of peace with the moment, one that too often eluded her of late.

"I'd sit down if I thought the swing would hold me."

She looked up to see her father, Cameron Huntington, leaning against the pole of the swing set, the green eyes he had bestowed on Amanda and Tyler looking large behind his glasses.

"Hi, Dad."

He reached under his suit coat and pulled a Tootsie Roll from the pocket of his white dress shirt, handing it to her. He always carried the candies for his grandchildren or for whoever needed a lift.

"Thanks." She held the piece in her hand, feeling it as much as she had tried to feel the air a few seconds earlier.

"What's up?" Cameron gave her his sincere, irrepressible grin that had helped spiral him to success at the PR firm where he was an executive.

She looked away. "Nothing."

He squatted down in her line of sight, rubbing a thick hand over his round, balding head. "Are you all right?"

"I am . . . sometimes."

"Then what?"

"It's just . . ." She hesitated. Her father meant well and she loved him. She didn't want him to worry about her or to ache on her behalf. She ached enough for both of them. "Sometimes when people ask if I'm okay, I have this urge to scream and cry and tell them I'm not okay, that I'll never be okay again without Adam." Tears slipped from her eyes and rolled down her cheeks. "Sometimes I feel I'm just waiting for life to be over so I can see him again. But . . ." Now she looked up at the sky that was already darkening despite the early hour. "But sometimes I want to live and be happy. I get tired of being tired, of being lonely, of being scared." Her voice broke, and she was crying in earnest now.

Cameron put his arms around her, and Kerrianne was suddenly grateful for his comforting bulk. "I'm sorry, honey," he murmured. "I wish I could make it all better. I wish . . ." He suddenly didn't seem to know what he wished, or maybe thought better of what he'd been going to say. "I think Adam would want you to be happy," he said finally. "His time here on earth was over, but yours isn't. Your life goes on, and you must make the best of it."

Kerrianne nodded, too full of tears to speak. She knew all this, but saying it was oh so much easier than living it. And that's what she had to do—live it. If only she could find a way. Her father patted her back a few more times as her tears slowed.

"I am making progress," she said, wiping her face with her fingertips. "My two preschool classes are going well, and they keep me busy in the afternoons. Mornings, too, when I have to prepare crafts. I went to a play the other day, and I'm going somewhere with my friend Maxine tomorrow night." She shrugged. "I guess we're going to hang, or whatever it is they do these days."

Cameron faked an exaggerated grimace. "I always hated that term. Hang—hang where? Always seems to imply that you're doing nothing. Being lazy, unfocused."

"Maybe that's the point."

"Maybe." He gave her another of his engaging grins, as well as another Tootsie Roll. "Well, I hope this Maxine doesn't take you to a bar."

A laugh burst from Kerrianne. "Don't worry, Dad. It's probably a get-together of the Independence Club."

"What's that?"

Kerrianne thought of the ultra positive Tina, the rotund Evie, and the sour-faced Bernice and smiled. "Just some women I know." Thankfully, Bernice probably wouldn't be invited along, but with

Maxine, one never knew. "We'll probably get frozen yogurt and catch a movie."

"Sounds nice." Cameron stood and waited until she opened the second candy before tugging her to her feet. "Come on. Let's go see your mother before she calls for backup."

Knowing her mother, that was all too likely. They hurried across the brown leaves, cold and crisp beneath their feet.

In the spacious kitchen, Jessica Huntington had lined up her grandchildren at the counter on tall padded swivel chairs. They were eating their chocolate bars and twirling around on the seats like it was a playground. Kerrianne noticed her mother had also set freshly sliced fruit in front of the children, which had thus far been ignored. Their glasses of apple juice, however, set among scattered Tootsie Roll wrappers, showed signs of use.

Kerrianne's mother, the backbone of their family, was an elegant woman who paid close attention to her appearance. Her short blonde hair was stylish, reminding Kerrianne often of Maxine, though her mother was taller and not quite as thin. Jessica ran their family like a mother hen, always knowing what was going on in her four children's lives and never fearing to give advice when asked—and often when not. The siblings sometimes joked about her protectiveness, but they appreciated her more than they could ever say, especially now that they were older with families of their own. While Kerrianne was growing up, Jessica had been the rule giver, and though she'd had Cameron's full support with discipline, he had always followed her lead.

Jessica looked up, her frown causing the fine lines on her face to deepen. "Is everything okay?"

Kerrianne grinned at her father, glad that she no longer felt like screaming. That was how her emotions worked these days. Right after the accident, things were rockier longer and more often, but now she usually managed to steady herself after only a brief bout of self-pity.

"Fine," she said. "Well, we had an adventure shopping, but I think they'll be able to fix the shelf. The chocolate, however . . ." She trailed off.

"You should have seen it, Grandma!" Misty said, using her hands expressively as she talked. "There was chocolate everywhere! And there was this mean girl from school who said it was all our fault."

"I met my best friend," Caleb spoke up. "His dad's the mailman. He always plays ball with me."

"Oh, that's who he is." Misty only now made the connection.

"I didn't think that girl was mean," Benjamin said.

"Was too."

"Okay, whatever."

"Don't give in," Kerrianne told him. "You have to stick up for what you believe."

Misty shook her head. "Benjamin's my brother. He has to agree with me."

The adults laughed, causing Misty to pout. Kerrianne hugged her. "Oh, sweetie, you disagree with him sometimes. He's allowed to have an opinion, and it might not always be the same as yours."

Misty shrugged and picked up her juice, not deigning to answer her mother.

"Caleb has that kid's car," Benjamin said. "He should give it back."

Kerrianne looked at her youngest. No wonder he'd looked so smug at the store. "You have his car?"

"He let me keep it till he comes over," Caleb said. "Don't worry, Mom. He has lots of them. Like a hundred or a million or something."

Kerrianne sighed. Now she'd have to talk to Ryan again. She couldn't let Caleb keep the car. What if she put it in the mailbox with a note? Mentally she sighed and shook her head. Why was she afraid to face him? Was it because of the warmth that filled her every time those gray eyes lingered on her face?

"Will you stay for dinner?" her mother asked, cutting through Kerrianne's reverie.

"I was hoping you'd ask." Kerrianne gave a self-conscious laugh. "I love to cook, but these guys don't really appreciate my concoctions." She spun Benjamin around on his chair and then Caleb. They giggled loudly, grasping the armrests so they wouldn't fall. "I guess it's hardly worth it to make something elaborate for just me."

"Well, I'd love the company." Jessica glanced pointedly at Cameron. "He eats a lot, as you can plainly see, and he's appreciative as ever, but he's been rather too preoccupied to be good company."

Cameron came around the counter, giving his wife a good-natured hug. "Sorry about that, honey." To Kerrianne, he added. "I bought a stamp collection over the Internet from an estate sale in Missouri. The stamps arrived on Monday, and I've been organizing them after work." He kissed his wife's cheek. "I'll be done soon."

Jessica hit him playfully with the dishtowel in her hands. "Go on then. I've got Kerrianne and the kids to keep me company tonight."

With another kiss, Cameron winked at Kerrianne and escaped from the room. Jessica watched him leave, her blue eyes happy.

Kerrianne felt warmth seep into her heart. Some might think her parents mismatched, at least in appearance, but she had never doubted their love and commitment. They were the best example to Kerrianne of the beauty of marriage and family.

"That reminds me," Jessica said. "Do you have anything to wear tomorrow night?"

Kerrianne shrugged and shook her head. "Not particularly. I'll probably wear my black pants and that pink blouse Manda gave me."

"No, you won't. I was thinking about you going out with that friend of yours when I was shopping the other day. I saw this outfit that seemed to have your name on it. As soon as dinner's on, I'll show you."

"Mom, you didn't have to do—"

Jessica waved her protest aside. "Of course not. I wanted to."

"Twirl me again, Mommy," Caleb pleaded.

"And me!" Benjamin added.

Kerrianne obliged. Then she spun Misty as well, who had recovered from her pouting and was her normal sunshiny self. The moment was absolutely perfect. Kerrianne was in a safe, familiar house with parents who loved her and wonderful children who were the light of her life. Her mother had bought her an outfit that would take care of her wardrobe concerns for tomorrow without her having to think about it or gear up for a shopping trip—an outfit likely more in style and of better quality than Kerrianne herself would have chosen on her limited budget. Yes, the moment was perfect. There wasn't even room to miss Adam. Or was he here with her?

She sighed. "I wish we could keep this moment for always. It's so perfect. I wish we could stay right here and never go on."

Her mother gave a warm chuckle. "Oh, sweetheart, if we stayed right here, we wouldn't ever be able to experience all the other perfect moments ahead."

"Then let's go from perfect moment to perfect moment." She knew it sounded silly, but that was what she wanted.

"But then they wouldn't seem perfect anymore." Jessica came around the counter and put her arm around Kerrianne. "The sadness and the trials of those many unperfect moments is what makes us able to appreciate the perfect ones when they come along."

Her mother was right, and Kerrianne knew it. "Opposition in all things," she murmured somewhat resentfully. So much for her perfect moment.

"Something like that," Jessica said softly, her voice gentle and filled with understanding. "And I'm grateful. If there weren't opposition, I would never understand when the Lord is blessing me."

Kerrianne turned into her mother's arms and buried her face in her neck, fighting tears—of gratitude and pain, but most important of hope for the future. "I love you, Mom."

"I love you, too, Kerrianne. And I know there are many good things ahead for you. It's just a matter of time."

Chapter Nine

Kerrianne had more than her share of company as she dressed for her night out with Maxine. Her brother Mitch and his wife, Cory, had brought Lexi over to baby-sit again. They were also leaving their adopted three-year-old daughter, EmJay, to be watched by Lexi. Amanda and Blake, who had left their children home with a sitter, had come to pick up Mitch and Cory with the plan of catching a movie together. Kerrianne tried not to feel strange about them going out without her. Often she would accompany them, as they were really the only married couples she knew who still included her in their lives.

Cory and Amanda left the children with the men downstairs and waited in Kerrianne's room to see her new outfit. Maxine had come over earlier with Kerrianne's new makeup and helped her style her hair, so she was as ready as she was ever going to be. Her outfit consisted of wine-colored pants with black trim on the wide cuffed legs and around the faux pockets. The matching top was a fitted lightweight sweater accented by black fur trim around both the scooped neck and long sleeves.

"You look fabulous!" Cory said as she emerged from her small walk-in closet. "That wine color is really good on you. I could never wear it."

Kerrianne smiled at her red-haired sister-in-law, whose beautiful but unruly hair was one of her secret envies. "I hope I'm not over-dressed for wherever we're going. Maxine said this would be fine, but I wish she'd give me a little more detail. Apparently, we're going out to eat and then to some gathering at a church, but that's all I know."

"It's perfect for anywhere these days." Amanda held out high heels with thin straps. "When Mom told me about the outfit, I knew these would be just right."

"I have heels."

"Not like these. These'll make your ankles look knock-out fabu-lous. Besides, by the time my feet are back to normal size so I can wear them, probably a year with all the weight I've gained, they'll be out of style." Amanda smoothed her bulging stomach, covered in an obnox-iously bright pink maternity blouse, which exactly matched her per-sonality these days. "Someone might as well get some use from them."

"Thanks." Kerrianne was touched. Having her younger sister look out for her in this way was a little unsettling, but then Amanda had been doing that a lot in the past few years.

"Speaking of pregnancy . . ." Cory was seated next to Amanda on the queen-sized bed, but now she stood up awkwardly, uncharacteris-tically nervous. "I wanted you two to be the first to know that Mitch and I are beginning a round of fertilization attempts before we go on our next assignment. We've only been married fourteen months, so we're not really worried or anything, but we don't want to leave it too long. We're hoping to have good news before we go to Japan in February."

Amanda jumped to her feet and squealed with excitement. "Oh, Cory, that's wonderful! I'm so excited for you!"

"Me, too." Kerrianne hugged her.

Cory's freckled face was pale and her blue eyes washed with tears. "I've never wanted anything so much as I do this—except to marry

Mitch and adopt EmJay. Well, and maybe to be baptized. When I think that I might have a daughter and that she and EmJay will be raised as sisters as AshDee and I were . . ." She sighed longingly. AshDee was Cory's younger sister and also EmJay's birth mother, but she and her husband had drowned in a boating accident several years earlier. "It's all I could ever wish for, given the circumstances."

"AshDee's probably up there with your daughter now," Amanda said, "giving her pointers on how just how far a little sister can push an older sister." She smirked pointedly at Kerrianne.

Cory grinned. "I'm so glad to have you two. You're my sisters now." They laughed a little self-consciously, patting each other on the back and surreptitiously wiping their eyes with their fingertips.

"Look at the time," Amanda said. "We've got to get going. The movie starts at seven-thirty. I wish we could go out to dinner first instead of afterward."

"I've got some crackers in the car," Cory said. She looked at Kerrianne. "What time is your friend picking you up?"

"Any minute." Again, Kerrianne felt butterflies in her stomach. "Oh," she groaned, "I wish I were going with you guys instead."

"Well, you could, but the tickets are sold out," Amanda said. "Besides, you need to get out with people who aren't so boring."

"Hey, speak for yourself," Cory protested. "I'm not boring. And Mitch is never boring. By the way, I wouldn't get too close to him tonight. I'm not sure whether he has a gerbil in his pocket or that lizard he loves so much. Either way, it's bound to end up in someone's hair."

Amanda laughed. "Same old Mitch. But my point is, Why should Kerrianne hang out with married couples when there are more exciting people out there to meet?"

As one they looked Kerrianne, who sat on the bed and busied herself putting on Amanda's heels. They were becoming less and less subtle about their hints. Kerrianne had tried to explain that she was never going to remarry, but they simply didn't understand. Sometimes Kerrianne wondered if they didn't love their husbands as much as she loved Adam, but that sounded too much like Bernice and the way she had judged Maxine.

Maybe all her love for Adam was simply that old adage coming true: Absence makes the heart grow fonder. But did that mean the more time that passed, the more she would long for Adam? The more she would love him and yearn for his touch? Maybe by the time she finally went to meet him in heaven, she'd love him so much there would be no space for her at all. It would be Adam, Adam, and only Adam. That might bore him. After all, even in heaven they'd have separate callings and interests. She needed to remember not to lose sight of the part of her that made her unique. Loving Adam could not define all of who she was, even as much as she wanted it to.

"You're going to be late," she said, standing and walking to the door. There was silence behind her, but Kerrianne swept through the hall and down the stairs without looking back.

Her brother Mitch was seated on the floor with the children, allowing a gerbil to run around their knees, the smaller children squealing with joy when the animal crawled up into their laps. He looked up and whistled as he heard her come in. "You look fabulous!"

"Thank you," she replied breezily.

He glanced anxiously at the doorway, pushing back the long front strands of his brown hair. "Are they coming? We're going to be late if they don't hurry."

"Yes, I'm sure they'll be here shortly." Kerrianne reached down and scooped up the gerbil from Benjamin's lap. "They're discussing how boring married couples are. If I were you and Blake, I'd make tonight unusual." She plopped the gerbil into her brother's outstretched hands, ignoring the sighs of disappointment from the children.

"I see." Mitch grinned as he put the animal away in a little plastic ball he'd had especially made to carry the animal in his pocket.

Amanda and Cory entered the family room, and Mitch jumped to his feet to greet them, his thin frame taller than Kerrianne's by more than a head. "Blake went out to warm up the car. We'd better go."

Cory rushed to give little EmJay a hug, and there were a flurry of other good-byes before Kerrianne walked them to the door. Sure enough, Blake was outside, but he wasn't alone. Maxine had pulled up and the two of them were talking, Blake standing outside Maxine's car window.

Kerrianne's nervousness must have shown in her face because Mitch squeezed her arm and whispered. "You can go with us the next time."

"We'll see." She'd go if they arranged it, but she wasn't going to pester them. It was almost easier to stay home and wallow in self-pity than go with them and feel so strange without her other half. They missed Adam, too, she knew, but it wasn't the same thing. Not the same thing at all.

"Lock the door, Lexi," Kerrianne said as the other adults hurried outside in the darkening night. "And you have my number, don't you?"

"This time I memorized it," Lexi assured her.

Kerrianne grinned. "Thanks."

She pulled on her full-length black sweater. Though it was more than four years old, it looked almost brand new. There hadn't been many places to wear it. In the car Maxine's eyes flicked over her approvingly. "That almost hides how skinny you are."

"Look who's talking."

"Well, I'm short. And besides I wear at least two sizes larger than you do. Or three." Maxine began backing out of the driveway. "Still, I think you've actually gained a bit of weight this week, haven't you? Your face looks healthy."

Kerrianne decided to ignore the remark. With all the chocolate she'd inhaled this week, she'd gained a pound, and she was proud of it. But another ten and she'd start worrying in the other direction. She'd paid for her indulgence, though, by breaking out in a juvenile acne spree. Fortunately, all the worst blemishes were on her back or near her hairline. Not that it mattered—who was she trying to impress?

Myself, she said. *I'm going out with friends, and tonight I'm not going to think about Adam.*

Maxine herself looked dressed to kill in a form-fitting black outfit with elaborate gold embroidery. Tonight she wore dress boots instead of high heels.

"Who else is coming?" Kerrianne asked.

"Some of the girls." Maxine turned a corner. "They're meeting us at the restaurant. Except Bernice. She asked if she could get a ride."

"Probably to keep an eye on you. I bet she's gathering facts for another discussion with the bishop on Sunday."

Maxine gave a snort of disgust as Kerrianne dissolved into laughter. "Honestly," Kerrianne said, "you should have told her to get her own ride." Truthfully, she was glad Bernice was coming, not because she particularly enjoyed the woman's company, but that must mean there would be only women wherever they were going. Surely Bernice wouldn't stand for anything else.

"Her car is apparently in the shop," Maxine said with the air of a martyr. "But we all make our sacrifices. Besides, I'm interested to see how everyone reacts to her new look. If only I could get her to dye her hair a bit. That gray makes her too old." She had pulled up in front of Bernice's house. "Oh, look, there she is."

"I'll get in the back." Kerrianne reached for the door.

"Don't you dare!" Maxine gripped her arm. "I don't want to get stuck—"

"It's only polite." Kerrianne shook off Maxine's hand and pushed open the door. "She's older than me so she deserves the front." She lowered her voice. "Besides, it serves you right for all this secrecy about this so-called gathering and for inviting her in the first place. Ah, Bernice," she said to the woman who had reached the car, "please take the front."

Maxine threw an I'll-get-you-later look at Kerrianne, but she didn't make further protest, which worried Kerrianne. What did Maxine have in store for her?

Kerrianne slipped into the back and fastened her safety belt. "You look great, Bernice."

She did. Her makeup was the same muted style she'd been wearing at Maxine's after the makeover, which took years off her face. She wore a black skirt that was surprisingly in style and a pink zip-up sweater that made her look bright and cheerful—at least until she opened her mouth.

"Thank you, dear. I do try. Even though he's not here, I think my husband might be able to catch a glimpse of me and feel happy we'll be together again soon."

"Soon?" asked Maxine a little too hopefully. Kerrianne clamped her lips shut over a giggle.

"Relatively speaking," Bernice went on. "You know what they say—earth life is just a blink of an eye compared to eternity."

"Sure seems like an eternity sometimes," Maxine mumbled.

"What?" Bernice asked.

"I think we'll enjoy eternity when it's our time." Maxine flashed her a sweet grin that made Kerrianne rock with laughter, glad that she was in the back and could pretend to pick something off the floor to hide her giggles.

"Oh, yes, we most certainly will." Bernice smiled beatifically at the roof of the car.

Bernice kept up a steady conversation as Maxine drove to the American Fork border with Lehi where they were meeting the others at IHOP. She talked mostly about temple sealings and how important it was to her to remain faithful to her dead husband so that he would know how much she loved him.

"What if he was an abuser?" Maxine asked, never one to take a lecture without objecting to something.

Bernice gave a slight gasp. "Are you saying . . . Did your husband actually . . ."

"No," Maxine growled. "Not my husband, just any husband. And what if his dying was the best thing that ever happened to the woman?"

Bernice blinked several times. "You're talking about Tina, aren't you? I heard about that. Is it really true?"

Kerrianne's stomach clenched. Were they talking about the annoyingly positive Tina? Had her husband been that kind of monster?

"It's true," Maxine's voice was grim. An approaching car lit up her solemn face, turning her expression eerie. "He was awful to her, but she put on a good face. No one knew for a long time."

"Maybe he's changed now that he's dead," Bernice said.

"Maybe he hasn't." Maxine pulled into a parking lot and shut off the light. "The same spirit that possess our body now will possess it after death, right?" Without waiting for a reply, she opened her door and slid out of the car.

Bernice looked in the backseat at Kerrianne. "Well," she said. "Well."

Kerrianne shrugged, also at a loss. How horribly ironic that Tina's husband's death had freed her, while Adam's death had imprisoned Kerrianne. At least it felt that way. Imprisoned her in a life of longing and regret and loneliness.

As they entered the restaurant, Kerrianne could see two other women waiting for them. One was Tina and the other Evie, the large woman who complained about the rain. They were wearing jeans, but their blouses were dressy, and they both wore heels. Kerrianne didn't feel overdressed, though she did experience a twinge of nervousness when several approving male glances came her way.

"Oh, you're here!" Tina jumped up to meet them excitedly. "It's good to see you all. Bernice, I didn't expect you. You didn't seem like you enjoyed yourself much the last time we went to one of these things. But I'm so glad you came!"

"Yeah, uh, thanks," Bernice said awkwardly, and Kerrianne wondered if she was thinking about what Maxine had told them in the car. How had Tina remained positive when her life had been so hard?

"Isn't it a wonderful night?" Tina gushed on. "I just love it when the air is so crisp that it tingles when you breathe it in. It's like everything is clean and pure or something. It's a hoot."

"It's no fun to exercise in," complained Evie, casting them a cheerful smile that belied the comment. Kerrianne noticed again how beautiful her skin was and how shiny her short black hair.

"Is this all that's coming?" Maxine asked when they had ordered.

"Rosalva should be here soon," Evie answered. "Didn't you hear me order for her? I hope the waiter didn't think I was ordering two meals for myself." She laughed. "That would be just my luck. Oh, look, there Rosalva is now."

Kerrianne saw the brown-skinned, dark-haired woman coming toward them. She looked better than good in black pants, a red long-sleeved blouse with a loosely knitted black sweater on top. She was short but teetered on very high heels. Kerrianne thought with envy that this was one woman who had her figure under control—unlike Kerrianne and Tina, who were too thin, and Evie and Bernice who had gained too much weight. Only Maxine was as fit as Rosalva, though the twenty years between them was noticeable.

"You look smashing," Evie exclaimed.

"You think?" Rosalva sighed. "I worry these pants make me look too fat."

Evie rolled her eyes. "Why is it always the thin ones who complain about being fat? You wanna see fat, look at this." She slapped her ample thigh.

"You are exercising, aren't you?" Rosalva asked. "Did you read the books I gave you?"

"One of them," Evie said grudgingly.

Tina voice shook with eagerness. "She's been using my treadmill. She's lost three pounds already! Isn't she wonderful?"

The group congratulated Evie, while she looked embarrassed but pleased.

"What about you, Kerrianne?" Evie asked. "Do you exercise? You look like you do."

Kerrianne felt all eyes turn toward her. "I work in my yard a lot. Especially in the mornings now that the kids are in school."

"In this weather?" Evie's tone was admiring.

"I love working in my yard any time I can."

That wasn't quite true. After Adam died, there had been a time when she hadn't cared about the yard at all. She'd let it go horribly, the only work being done by Mitch, Tyler, and her father in their spare time. But last year she'd started taking interest again. Now she went out several times a week to work. There wasn't much to do in the winter, but she did what she could, making sure the leaves were raked and the flower beds free of old growth. Now she dreamed about creating a greenhouse in the corner of her yard but worried where she'd find the money. She was fairly sure she could put it together herself—and she'd enjoy doing so. Even if Adam had been alive, it would have been her project. He hadn't had much use for the yard and hated even mowing the grass. In fact, now that she thought about it, the yard had been a point of contention between them. Strange how she hadn't remembered that until now. The remembrance unsettled her. What else had she forgotten?

"Kerrianne?" Maxine's strident voice came into her thoughts. "Rosalva was asking you what you knew about apple trees. Do you have to spray them? Hers had worms this year."

"Yeah, you do. I actually spray mine twice."

"Can my teenagers do it?" Rosalva asked. "I've got two boys. One's going on a mission next year—if my ex doesn't talk him out of it." She heaved a great sigh.

"Aren't exes great?" Evie echoed her sigh. "I'm glad my children were grown before my husband left me. At least they're mostly safe from his influence." Then, for a moment, her pretty face turned bleak. "Stupid thing is, I still wish he hadn't gone. I wish we could have worked things out."

Her words made Kerrianne sadly aware that not all the members of the Independence Club were as carefree as Tina would like to believe. Everyone seemed to have regrets—everyone but Tina, and Kerrianne couldn't really fault her for that.

"Goodness," Tina said, staring in the direction of the waiter who was bringing out their food, "doesn't that look wonderful? I've never seen anything look so delicious."

The mood turned lighter after that, and Kerrianne was grateful for Tina's cheerfulness and ability to steer the conversation to positive thoughts. She had the strangest feeling of a clock turning back in time, as though suddenly she was a teenager once more, out with a group of friends. Of course, beneath the carefree talk and hearty laughter, there was always the knowledge that they were different from the young women they'd once been. Evie and Rosalva's difficult marriages had dissolved because of their husbands' infidelity. Tina, Maxine, Bernice, and Kerrianne were widows. Tina, Rosalva, and Kerrianne now had to deal with single parenthood. But even these differences managed to fade into the background, almost as though the night were borrowed from the past, before all the rest had happened. Kerrianne was determined to enjoy it.

Maxine caught her eyes and smiled. "Thanks," Kerrianne mouthed. Maxine was right about this being exactly what Kerrianne needed. She was glad she hadn't let her guilt over Benjamin getting sick the last time keep her at home.

"So," Kerrianne asked, fishing for more information about Maxine's plan, "are all the people at this gathering tonight divorced or widowed?"

Evie laughed. "Oh, no. Some have never been married. Younger ones don't come for long, though. Seems they always end up married." She laughed again, and the others joined her.

"He'll have to be really something for me to get married again," Rosalva said, her Spanish accent heavy with meaning. "I'm not going to make another mistake."

Evie lifted her glass of water. "I'll drink to that." They all did, but Tina choked on her water and sputtered it all over the table.

"Sorry, girls," she said, mopping up. There was a glittering drop on Tina's strawberry-blonde hair, but Maxine dabbed it with a napkin.

After the meal and much laughter, the women went out to their cars and drove to the church building. Kerrianne heard the music as she entered the doors and recognized the tune immediately.

Tina saw her mouthing the words. "That's what's so great about these things," she said. "They play music we loved growing up."

"I hope we're late enough," Evie said, checking her watch. "It's never good until it's been going on for a while."

After paying at a table, Maxine put an arm around Kerrianne and led her into the gym. Kerrianne took in the decorations, the disc jockey at the front of the room, the multicolored lights cutting into the dim room, and the couples rapidly filling up the floor space. Her chest tightened.

"A dance," she whispered, leaning toward Maxine. "You brought me to a dance?" Turning on her foot, she decided the only sane thing to do was to flee.

Chapter Ten

W hen she turned, the other women were standing in a solid line behind her, looking determined. Or was that her imagination?

Kerrianne whirled back to Maxine. "Why didn't you tell me it was a dance?" She tried to say the words forcefully, but they emerged in a pathetic whisper.

"Because you wouldn't have come if I had." Maxine tone was exasperated. "Come on, trust me. You need this. It's been okay so far, hasn't it?"

Kerrianne opened her mouth to protest, but before she could, a man appeared in front of her and asked her to dance. "I, uh, well . . ." When she'd attended dances without a date before her marriage, she'd made a rule never to turn down someone who asked her to dance. But that was before Adam.

This man was definitely not her type. He wore too-tight pants that hadn't been in style since the 80s, and though he wore no tie, his shirt was buttoned clear to the top. His mouse-colored hair was cut in a bowl shape above his round face, his bangs falling into smallish eyes of indefinable color. He was also at least twenty years older than she was.

"Not yet, Reuben." Evie pushed her bulk around Kerrianne. "She just got here. Give her a minute to get used to everything. Come on, I'll dance with you."

Reuben inclined his head, giving Kerrianne a shy smile. Then he went off with Evie. Kerrianne felt relieved.

"He's harmless," Maxine whispered. "He's not all quite there, if you know what I mean. A child, really. He'll ask you to dance again in a while. He always asks everyone who's not with a date."

"And sometimes even then," Bernice said with her customary sniff. "I told him that I was taken several times, but he doesn't listen."

"Probably having a hard time seeing your husband," Rosalva said in a too-innocent tone that went right over Bernice's head.

"It's an over-thirty dance," Maxine informed Kerrianne as she guided her to some chairs by the side of the room. "This is the best place to start since you're thirty. They have other dances where the top age is thirty-five, but I couldn't take you to one of those since I don't qualify."

Rosalva clicked her tongue and made a face. "You don't want to go to one of those. At least not until you're ready. Younger men don't know how to treat a woman. You should hear some of the things they say!"

"That's what you get for sneaking in," Bernice said. "You haven't seen thirty-five in more than five years."

Rosalva's eyes narrowed. She opened her mouth to say something, but Tina jumped in brightly. "All the dances I've gone to are a lot of fun, though I do agree that the older men know how to make a woman feel special. They always bring flowers."

Kerrianne was starting to breathe more normally now. *I can do this,* she thought. Now that the initial shock was over, she was actually anticipating the evening. Dancing was something she and Adam had loved to do together. Of course, they hadn't gone as much since the children were born, but they'd made it a point to get out every so often.

Adam had always sung softly in her ear on the slow dances, serenading her.

Maxine nudged her arm, and Kerrianne was startled to see a handsome older gentleman standing in front of her. He was probably older than her father, though he looked in better shape. "May I have this dance?" he asked.

Kerrianne stood up and let him lead her onto the floor. She was glad he was so much older. It didn't make her feel nervous at all but rather like a little girl dancing with her daddy.

"First time here?" He moved too slowly for the music, as though he couldn't quite catch the beat or was perhaps unable to keep up with it.

"It shows?"

He shook his head. "Maxine told me. My name is Harold, by the way. Harold Parry."

Harold? This was the man Maxine had been dating? Kerrianne looked at him more closely. He was nice-looking, arresting even, with his salt-and-pepper hair, thick gray eyebrows that framed curiously colorless eyes. He was a full foot taller than Kerrianne, which would make him heads above Maxine, and as broad-shouldered as any woman could want. He was wearing a suit that looked new and in style.

"I wore it for Maxine," he said with a gentle smile. "We older men like to dress up for the ladies." Not everyone was dressed up, however. Plenty of the men wore jeans, especially the younger ones.

Kerrianne let herself sway into the music, enjoying the beat, the movement, and the casual air of the dancers. When the song ended, she put her hand on Harold's arm. "Thanks," she said. "It's nice to finally meet you."

He placed his hand over hers and patted it in exactly the way her father would have. "The pleasure is all mine." They walked back to the place where Maxine and Bernice waited. Evie, Tina, and Rosalva were out on the floor dancing.

Harold bowed to Bernice. "Would you like to dance?"

"No, thank you," she said, her lips pursed in disapproval.

"But if you're not going to dance, why do you . . ." Maxine trailed off as Bernice glowered at her.

"If you change your mind," Harold said, "please let me know." His eyes were twinkling, and Kerrianne had the distinct feeling that he was holding in laughter. She grinned at him, and he winked back. He offered an arm to Maxine. "I think I have enough energy for another one, if you will do me the honor."

"Okay. But try to keep up, would you?" Her words were light and caused a chuckle from Harold.

Bernice shook her head as they moved away. "Disgraceful," she muttered.

Kerrianne's heart began thundering in her chest as a sudden, white-hot anger pulsed through her. What gave Bernice the right to judge? Her fists clenched in her lap.

"I can see why Evie and Rosalva are looking," Bernice continued. "Their husbands were jerks, so they need to find an eternal partner. And Tina, too, I suppose. But Maxine . . . I just don't see how—I mean, she was happily married. Just because he's gone doesn't mean she should forget him."

She was talking about Maxine, but the comment jabbed at Kerrianne, as though warning her to not follow the same path. Words of anger and despair boiled inside Kerrianne, and even if she'd wanted, there would have been no way to stop them from spewing forth. "Bernice, don't you get it? We have the rest of our lives to live without our husbands. For you that may not seem like a long time, but what about someone like me? It's more than half my whole life! Do you know how incredibly long that seems right now?" Tears threatened to fall, and her voice was choked. "I try to hold onto him, but you know what? He's not there tucking in my kids at night. He's not there to help pick up their toys or to worry when they're sick. He's not there to take me dancing. He isn't even around so I can beg him for three days to cut the stupid lawn." Kerrianne sucked in a deep breath, shaking her head. "How many years am I going to have to cut that lawn all by myself? Or all the other stuff? I tell you what. Right now, seeing it that way—your way—maybe I'd be better off dead."

Bernice's eyes widened, and her mouth worked, though no sound emerged. Without waiting for a reply, Kerrianne sprang to her feet and headed to the refreshment table at the back of the gym.

She hated the way Bernice judged Maxine. She hated being at a dance without Adam. But even more she hated feeling guilty. Maxine was right. Kerrianne needed to learn how to live again, to be herself. She needed to learn how to laugh and sing and, yes, dance without Adam.

"Hi, do you want to dance now?" Reuben was at her side now, his expression that of an anxious boy, belying the crow's feet around his eyes.

"Sure!" Kerrianne drank the rest of the punch she didn't really want and tossed the cup into the trash. She followed him into the middle of the dancers.

"So, do you like to dance?" Reuben asked after a minute. "I'm Reuben, by the way." He moved awkwardly, like a teen who'd never quite overcome his self-consciousness. His gaze was mostly on the ground, though he looked up every now and then at a space behind her right ear.

"Hi, Reuben. I'm Kerrianne, and I love to dance. Or used to. My kids keep me pretty busy right now."

He smiled a strangely beautiful smile. "You have kids?"

"Yes. Three."

"I don't have any kids. I've never been married."

"I see."

"My sister has kids, though. I like them." He looked up from the ground and actually met her gaze.

"That's nice."

"I come to a lot of dances. I like dancing." He did an ungraceful move with his hands and shoulders that Kerrianne thought he must have copied from a more experienced dancer.

"Well, this is the place for it," she said.

He nodded, apparently having reached the end of the topics in his repertoire.

Kerrianne used the lull in conversation to glance around at the other dancers. There were a lot of people, some who looked interesting. Again she had the feeling of being transported back in time. In high school, the more popular couples had also danced near the disk jockey and the loud speakers, and nothing seemed to have changed. Evie was in the midst of the current "in group," as was Rosalva, their faces alive and happy.

When the song came to an end, Reuben glanced up from the floor. "Would you like to dance again?"

Kerrianne was about to say yes—after all, she wanted to dance and Reuben certainly wasn't threatening—but a man appeared at her elbow. "May I please cut in, Reuben? You know what a hard time I have getting a partner. Not like you. Everyone dances with you."

Reuben grinned. "Okay." To Kerrianne, Reuben added, "I'll find you later." He glanced around, spied Bernice alone at the side of the room, and made a beeline for her.

"Good luck," the newcomer said under his breath. He was a handsome man of maybe forty with sand-colored hair that was slightly spiky on top. He wore blue jeans and a matching T-shirt, with a button-up shirt worn open like a jacket.

As they began moving to the music, the man leaned forward and said, "I'm Gunnar."

"I'm Kerrianne." His cologne was a bit strong that close, or at least seemed so to Kerrianne, who hadn't been that near a cologne-wearing man since her dating years. Adam had disdained the stuff.

"I've never seen you at any of the dances before."

"I've never been to any." They both smiled.

Behind him, Kerrianne caught a glimpse of Bernice dancing with Reuben. Apparently, not even she could turn down the childlike man.

After Gunnar, Kerrianne danced with three other men. Two were older, one with white hair who smelled like mint, and the other with graying hair who reeked with an unpleasant smell of body odor. With the vigorous way he danced, Kerrianne wasn't surprised, and she gave silent thanks that the song was a fast one so she wouldn't have to be too close. Both of the older men were polite and addressed her with respect. The other man was near her own age and seemed nice, except that he kept telling her how pretty she was, which made her mentally roll her eyes.

Then the blond Gunnar returned for a second dance. Kerrianne was feeling a little breathless and was glad it was a slow song. Gunnar's cologne was no longer so strong—either that or she'd become accustomed to it. "So, are you having fun?"

"Yes, actually."

He pulled her slightly closer—or was she imagining it?

"So, what's your story?" he asked.

"You first." She didn't feel like discussing her life with a near stranger.

"I'm divorced. I have four daughters with my ex. They live with her, but I see them every other weekend."

Kerrianne felt an ache in her heart. In a way, she was lucky. At least she wasn't forced to watch her children leave every other weekend. Not being with them . . . well, she couldn't imagine it, though surely there must be some way to muddle through such a situation, as Evie and Rosalva had done.

"Hello?" Gunnar waved a hand in the air by her face. "Is everything okay?"

"Sorry. I was thinking. It must be a challenge sharing custody like that. I have three children."

"You don't share custody?" He was holding her too tightly, so she stepped purposefully away.

"No." She could tell he was curious but had enough control not to probe. Instead, he looked at her expectantly, though she had no intention of elaborating yet. And why was he trying to hold her so close again? Or was it just her? Maybe she couldn't remember how this slow-dancing thing was supposed to go.

Kerrianne was thinking so hard about this and trying to extricate herself from Gunnar's grasp that she almost didn't catch the movement of a solitary figure watching them from the sidelines. He seemed familiar, and yet she couldn't place him. Then he saw her gaze and smiled.

Ryan, she thought. He'd shaved, and his hair was several inches shorter than the day before, which apparently brought out more of the curl, making it attractively messy. She could imagine that if it were any shorter, the curls might be out of control. *No wonder he keeps it that length,* she mused. He looked handsome in dark dress pants and a long-sleeve button-up shirt with multicolored vertical stripes. There was a wine color, and black, and two shades of green, and yellow. He wasn't wearing a tie, and the first button was open, giving a more casual air to the outfit. His smile made her forget all about Gunnar and her worry about dancing too close.

The music ended, but Gunnar kept holding her arm. "How about another one?"

"I think I'm ready for a drink," she said, still thinking about Ryan. Had he been planning to take her to this dance when he'd asked her out? She wondered if she'd ever know. He was hidden from her sight now. Could he be dancing? Why did that thought bother her?

Gunnar went with her to the refreshment table, offering her a drink of punch and then snagging a couple cookies for himself. They were silent as they watched the dancers. More people had arrived, and the place was beginning to seem almost crowded.

"Are there always so many people?" she asked.

"It really depends on the night and what else is going on."

"What else is going on? What do you mean?"

"Some nights there are more activities."

"I see." It was a whole community, then. One she hadn't realized existed. Well, at least not for people her age.

"So what's your last name?" Gunnar asked.

"Price."

"And you have three children?"

"Yes. A girl and two boys. The oldest is eight. They keep me busy." She almost hoped that fact would drive him away. The older men had chuckled when she told them about the kids, and she'd had the impression that her lifestyle was not something they were looking to share. She couldn't blame them; they'd already raised their families.

"I'd like to see you again. Could I call?"

Kerrianne bit her lip. "I don't know," she said finally. "Don't take this wrong, but I didn't even know I was coming here tonight. Some friends made me. I'm not sure I'm ready for dating."

"How long has it been?"

Been what? she wondered. Since she'd been divorced? Been dancing? Been in mourning? Should she tell him that four years ago everything in her life had stopped? No, it wouldn't be true. After all, here she was. And the children were waiting for her at home.

The music ended while she pondered her response. Why did she have to tell him anything? She suddenly felt like a package in a marketplace and Gunnar was checking the contents label to be sure she was to his liking.

Strains of "All Out of Love," by Air Supply, made Kerrianne freeze. Adam had loved this old song and had often performed it for her with his guitar. She was immediately swept into the past with the music, which feeling only intensified when the words started.

"Are you okay?" Gunnar asked, concern in his voice.

He was faceless to her, as though he didn't exist. There was only her and the music. And Adam. She thrust her cup unsteadily in his direction. "Excuse me. I have to go."

She fled toward the upright rectangle of light that marked the entrance. Someone, not Gunnar, called out her name, but she didn't stop.

The singer crooned on.

Blindly, Kerrianne passed the two women at the entry table and made for the foyer. There were people there, so she turned to the right, trying to open the door to the chapel overflow. It was locked. She went farther down the hall, but all the doors were locked. Finally, she found an open door that led into a tiny, dark room where the boys prepared the sacrament. She went inside, telling herself to breathe, that it was okay. She could still hear the music, though it was much fainter now. Any words that were obscured were immediately filled in by her memory. Almost she felt as if Adam were singing the song to her.

She leaned against the tiny counter and hoped no one would open the door. Was Gunnar still standing by the refreshment table? Wondering, perhaps, why she'd deserted him? And who had called her name? She didn't think it was Maxine.

The song wound down to the end. Still Kerrianne stayed where she was. Finally, she could breathe normally again. This had happened to her a great many times in the beginning, but not as much now. Probably the fact that she was dancing with other men had triggered this reaction. Did Adam think her unfaithful? No, she couldn't believe that.

At last she left the room and went outside into the dark night, shivering because her sweater jacket was still hanging near the entrance to the gym. The frosty air made her lungs hurt if she breathed too deeply, but she didn't mind. It also made her feel alive.

Ryan watched Kerrianne near the refreshment table with Gunnar, annoyed at the man, though he supposed he had no right to feel that way. Abruptly, she shoved her cup at Gunnar and started across the room, leaving Gunnar with mouth agape. Had the man said something inappropriate?

"Kerrianne!" He called, wanting to help.

She took no notice of him, apparently blind to everything but her destination. Either that or the music drowned out his call. Should he follow her and ask what had happened?

Maxine appeared at his elbow. "Stupid song. And things were going so well."

"The song?" he asked. Kerrianne had nearly reached the door to the gym.

"Her husband played the guitar. This song is on one of the tapes. She plays it a lot for the children." Maxine blinked up at him, appearing to notice his face for the first time. "I think I like you better the other way after all. You looked more dashing—dangerous."

He made a face. "Not a good thing when you're visiting houses of strangers every day."

"Nonsense. You have honest eyes." Her own eyes delved into his.

"What?" he asked.

"Why don't you go after her?"

Ryan looked longingly at the door. He didn't want to intrude where he wasn't wanted. "Maybe she wants to be left alone."

"She's been alone enough these past four years."

Maxine had a point. Ryan started across the room without another word. He emerged from the gym in time to see Kerrianne disappear into a room at the end of the hall. He debated within himself what to do, but there was no real choice. Maxine or no, he didn't have the right to barge in on a woman seeking solace—he wasn't close enough to her for that. He had to respect her privacy, knowing only too well that some things needed to be conquered alone. He waited in the hallway, talking with two nice women he'd met at other dances.

At last, from the corner of his eye, he saw Kerrianne leave the room. She didn't come his way but rather went out the far door. Ryan extricated himself from the women and sprinted after her.

Kerrianne had circled the church once when a voice stopped her. "Oh, there you are."

She glanced behind her, expecting to see Maxine or one her friends, but it was Ryan. "Hi," she said, glad she hadn't let her tears fall.

"I wondered where you went. Is everything all right?"

She nodded. "Just needed some air."

"That makes sense."

"It does?" She looked at him and saw his amused expression.

"Yeah, you were with Gunnar. It's no wonder you needed space . . . uh, air."

"He is a little too familiar, but I thought it might be just me."

"It's not."

She shivered. "I think I'm cold now."

"We'll have to go to the other door. They keep most of them locked."

They walked in silence for a space of a few heartbeats, and then Ryan said, "You like to dance, don't you? I can tell."

So he'd been watching her. "I love to dance. My . . . husband and I danced a lot."

Ryan laughed. "Laurie and I did, too, before we were married. We didn't after, though. Mostly because of me. I regret that now."

"There's too much to regret, isn't there?"

He gave her a wry grin. "Yeah."

"Adam loved music. He loved to sing." Kerrianne didn't know why she said this. Was it to put space between them? Or was it simply because she wanted someone to share the memory with?

"It's hard hearing a song they liked. Or that you liked with them." His gray eyes looked black in the darkness.

He knew. She didn't know how, but he knew why she'd left the dance. Or at least guessed at the cause. He opened the door for her and followed her inside. The music burst in on them, though they were still around the corner from the gym doors.

"Would you like to dance?" His expression was guarded, as though half expecting her to refuse.

Kerrianne smiled. "Yes, I think I would."

Chapter Eleven

Ryan led Kerrianne onto the floor. The music was fast, but he
figured it was probably better this way. She needed some time
to recover. She smiled at him and instead of the knots her smile
usually caused in his stomach, he simply felt content to be with her.

"So," she said now, raising her voice to be heard over the music,
"you come here a lot?"

He shrugged. "I used to. Not so much anymore. You see, I asked
this really gorgeous woman out tonight, and she said no. I needed
something to boost my spirits." He spoke teasingly and saw that she
was pleased with his lighthearted approach. They danced in compan-
ionable silence until the end of the song. He saw both Gunnar and a
solid block of a man making their way toward them, but he took her
arm and steered her around a clump of people.

"Another dance?" he asked.

She nodded mutely, almost shyly.

The music began, soft and slow. Sending a silent thanks heavenward, he put his arms around her, keeping a respectful distance
between them, though it took a lot of effort.

"So," she said after a minute, "is this where you were going to take that gorgeous woman?"

He laughed. "Not on your life. I would have taken her to a place where there were only married couples. I can't take the competition."

"Competition?"

He tilted his head toward the side where Gunnar was watching them. "I keep having to steer you away from him and another fellow."

She was grinning. "You mean Reuben?"

"No, that solid-looking guy over there by that blonde lady. He must have played football."

"You're imagining things. I don't know him. We haven't even danced."

"See what I mean? Competition." The playfulness of their words made Ryan feel young and foolish but also like laughing.

"Well, what about *her*?" Kerrianne indicated a woman who was dancing with a partner but staring soulfully at Ryan.

"Michelle," he said. "We went out a few times. She's a nice woman, but . . ."

"She has six children?"

"No. At least not that she told me, anyway. It just wasn't right."

"Is that what you want? Something that's right?"

"Don't you?"

She seemed to freeze in his arms but almost immediately relaxed. "To tell the truth, I thought I'd only have to look for something right just once in my life. I never thought I'd need to find it again." She gave him a wistful smile that made him feel protective.

"I know what you mean."

"That's what I like about you. You've been there." She spread her fingers, indicating the other dancers. "All the others I've danced with so far don't quite understand. Their spouses didn't die." Her voice was matter-of-fact. "Well, except for one of the older gentlemen. Oh, and Harold."

"Harold? Wait, I've heard that name before. You mean Maxine's

Harold?" When she nodded, he continued, "Where is he? I've got to meet this guy. I've seen them around, but I've never actually met him."

"I'll introduce you. He's a handsome guy. I think they're perfect together."

The light mood was back, and Ryan was grateful. After the song ended, Kerrianne took him to meet Harold, who was sitting on the chair by the wall looking rather winded. Maxine was dancing with Reuben.

"Harold, this is Ryan. He's the man who delivers our mail."

"The actor?" Harold stood and shook Ryan's hand. "Maxine's a big fan of yours. I tell you, the way she talks about you, I'm thinking about becoming a thespian myself. I never wanted to act, but if doing so helped me impress Maxine, it would be worth it."

"It's a lot of fun. We're having tryouts after Christmas for the next play. You should come."

"Maybe I will."

Probably he wouldn't, but Ryan had learned that you never knew who had a secret penchant for acting. As they talked, Gunnar suddenly appeared at Kerrianne's side. "Would you like to dance?"

Kerrianne shook her head. "I'm sorry, but I promised Ryan the next dance." She looked at Ryan, as though daring him to call her bluff. "Maybe the one after."

They danced two more fast dances and another slow one. This time Ryan dared to hold her a little closer. They were talking so much, they almost didn't notice the music had ended. Suddenly they were the only ones still holding each other in the whole room. Ryan was close enough to imagine the feel of the soft skin on her face and neck. She looked at him with wide blue eyes, and he wanted more than anything to kiss her.

Don't move too fast. The thought came out of nowhere.

Over her shoulder, he saw Gunnar making a beeline toward them. "Don't look now," he said, "but Gunnar's headed our way."

"I suppose I should dance with him."

"Not if you don't want to." He couldn't help the hopefulness in his tone.

She laughed. "Come on!" Grabbing his hand, she edged around a group of people who had now begun dancing again. Gunnar was lost to sight. Ryan felt heady with her impulsive action. They didn't stop walking until they were out in the foyer. Kerrianne sank down on an empty couch, and Ryan sat next to her.

"I haven't done anything like that since high school," she said, whispering so the couple on the couch opposite them wouldn't hear. "I almost feel sorry for him."

"Don't worry. He's a popular guy. He'll dance with someone else."

The talk drifted to the weather, their children, and finally to Ryan's upcoming play. "You should try out," he said. "It's only community theater, but we have some good talent."

"What's the play?"

"We're still haggling. Most of us want to do *A Midsummer Night's Dream,* but some don't want to because it won't be summer yet. If we did go ahead with it, you could try for the part of Titiana. Or maybe Hermia." For sure he'd love to play either Oberon or Lysander opposite her.

"Oh, I'm sure there are a lot of actresses who'd be better for the part."

"You never know. We have a lot of young actors and a lot of older ones, but not as many around your age." He hoped he'd phrased it inoffensively. Several women he'd dated had become quite angry whenever he'd mentioned age.

Kerrianne wasn't bothered. "That would take a lot of practicing, and I wouldn't know what to do with my kids."

"Bring 'em. I bring mine. They have a lot of fun."

She shook her head. "I haven't acted since high school. Besides, I've been thinking about starting a project that will take up my free time."

"Oh? Like what?"

"I want to build a greenhouse."

"A greenhouse?"

"Yeah. I love gardening, but there's not much to do during the winter." She frowned at the black night beyond the double set of glass doors to their right. The couple across from them arose and went outside, hand in hand.

"My mother has a kind of greenhouse." He regretted it almost the minute he said it.

"Oh, what's it like?"

"Well, it was actually a patio once, but then she had it enclosed with glass and put decorative tile on the floor. On top of those she has some rugs that your feet almost disappear into when you step on them. Since she has plants all along the windows, we call it the green room now. My mother tends to them like they were babies." He thought of how Ria had played catch with his father last Sunday. "It's a restful place if the kids are outside. Otherwise, I have to stop them from playing Frisbee with the cushions."

Kerrianne was silent, and he wondered if she was hoping for an invitation to see the green room. It was a natural progression of things, and he knew that if he had a real interest in furthering their relationship, he should jump at the opportunity to invite her. But he couldn't. He had once thought his parents might approve of a woman like Kerrianne, but at his last visit, they had made it clear they wanted him to marry a single woman—and not just any single woman but one with a college degree and an important family. A woman they considered an equal. Their equal. He had no idea where Kerrianne would fit in that scenario, but he wasn't willing to risk finding out. His parents were too unpredictable . . . and she was too fragile.

An uncomfortable silence grew between them, and then Kerrianne said with a stilted voice, "Well, I'm not thinking about building onto the house. I want to put my greenhouse in the corner of my backyard. It'll have a dirt floor, so basically it'll be a garden with a roof. I have a large garden area there now. I wouldn't take up the whole plot, though, just half."

"Must be a big plot."

"I used to plant a lot of stuff. I've only been using half since . . . well, lately. I planted the rest in pumpkins. We had a lot of pumpkins this year." She smiled. "Since the vines spread so much, it looked like I'd planted the whole thing."

"You did."

She laughed, and his heart constricted at how lovely she looked. "Pumpkins don't count," she said, "not really."

"They do to me. I love pumpkin pie—anything pumpkin. Unless you mix it with cheesecake. I hate cheesecake."

"No way. No one hates cheesecake."

"Well, I hate it. My children do, too." There was a pause, and then he asked, "So you're good at building things?"

She gave a delicate shrug. "I do some. I built a toddler bed once. I used to do crafts before I got tired of them. I put together a play set last summer for my children."

Ryan's jaw dropped. He'd never known a woman who could actually build things. Laurie had been afraid of most of his tools—especially his chainsaw. "Wasn't it heavy? The wood, I mean."

She shook her head and rolled her eyes. "It was a kit. It all came precut, so nothing was very heavy. Well, all but the sandbox. I did that myself. Wasn't too hard." She stopped talking and looked off into the distance, gone somewhere he couldn't go, and for a moment he was jealous of an experience that could take her from him so easily.

"The kits are kind of expensive," she added, focusing on him again, "so I may not be able to do a greenhouse right away. I've been saving up with the money I've earned from my preschool. I'm thinking of adding a morning class."

That was good news for him and Tiger. "How many classes do you have now?"

"Two—one from twelve to two on Mondays, Wednesdays, and Fridays, and the other on Tuesdays and Thursdays twelve to three."

"Six hours a week, eh?"

She grinned. "Believe me, it's enough. At this point some of the kids are too little to be away from their moms any longer."

Tiger was away from his mom a lot more than that, and as much as Ryan wished his son had his mother, there was nothing he could do to change things. Then again, Tiger didn't seem to mind being at his sitter's all day watching TV.

As though reading his mind, Kerrianne added, "Of course some of the kids could stay all day. They love the activities. They have a lot of energy."

"I know what you mean. My son—"

"Kerrianne!" interrupted a voice. "Oh, there you are!" Maxine appeared around the corner, followed by a gray-haired woman Ryan couldn't name, who gave Kerrianne an odd stare.

Kerrianne jumped to her feet almost guiltily, making Ryan smile. It wasn't as if they'd been caught kissing or something. He climbed slowly to his feet.

"The dance is over. Time to go home." Maxine looked from her to Ryan. "Unless you two are planning to get a drink or something."

Ryan wouldn't have minded, but Kerrianne shook her head. "I'd better get home to my kids. It's late."

Maxine sighed rather loudly, glancing at him as if to say, "Hey, you blew it, not me."

"Oh, I just remembered." Kerrianne turned toward him. "My son has one of your son's toy cars. Apparently, he got it from him at the grocery store." She turned pink, and he started grinning at the remembrance of her and all that chocolate.

He was about to say it didn't matter, that Tiger had more cars than he knew what to do with, but then he realized it was the perfect excuse. "We'll drop by and get it sometime."

"I could leave it in the mailbox."

He looked at her seriously, without allowing the slightest hint of a grin. "That's against the law. Only U.S. mail can go in the mailbox."

All three women stared at him for several seconds before Kerrianne started to laugh. Ryan joined her. Maxine looked annoyed, while the woman Ryan didn't know watched them in apparent confusion.

Maxine snorted, "Oh, brother. Come on." She tugged Kerrianne away from him and down the hall. Ryan watched them go, thinking that she hadn't exactly said no to his coming over to retrieve the toy. He would take the children to her house tomorrow.

Kerrianne glanced over her shoulder, and he again felt the pull he always seem to experience with her. Not everything had gone smoothly tonight, but he'd been at the right place at the right time, and she had appeared to enjoy his company. Ryan sent a silent thank-you heavenward. Someone knew what they were doing.

But who would be waiting for him tomorrow? Would it be the woman he was growing more and more attracted to or the woman who still lived in the past?

Whistling softly, Ryan went outside to his truck.

Chapter Twelve

Kerrianne left the temple Saturday morning feeling renewed and rested. From the driver's seat of her van, Amanda smiled at her. "It's a beautiful morning, isn't it?"

"Very. Thanks for going with me."

"My pleasure. Or at least it is if I'm driving." Amanda made a face. "Otherwise, I'd have lost my breakfast already."

Kerrianne remembered those days only vaguely. She remembered Adam bringing her dry toast on a plate as she lay in bed.

Amanda didn't notice Kerrianne's silence. She breezed on as she drove home, chatting about new clothes and a vacation to Hawaii to celebrate Kevin and Mara's sealing, which she and Blake planned for sometime in December. Kerrianne listened to her younger sister, glad for her happiness but only with half attention. She was thinking about Adam and the temple. Usually, she usually felt closer to him there than anywhere else, but today had been different. She hadn't sensed him at all.

"Is something wrong?" Amanda glanced over at her, finally noticing her absence from the conversation.

Kerrianne frowned. "It's just . . . well, I always considered Adam my soul mate, but I have to admit that I'm tired of being alone."

"That sounds pretty normal to me."

"Not really. If I married my soul mate, why would I ever want to be with anyone else? Even if he was stolen from me?" Kerrianne thought of Ryan and the warmth the sight of him evoked in her heart.

Amanda shook her head. "I don't believe in soul mates. What every relationship boils down to is hard work and sacrifice. I mean, I love Blake with all my heart, but sometimes I'd just as soon slap him as talk to him. But things always smooth over because we're both committed—to each other and the gospel. And after you face the trials together is when it gets good."

"Not if one of the people isn't there."

Compassion filled Amanda's eyes. "I'm sorry, Kerrianne. I'd give anything to change that. But what I'm trying to say is that there's no reason not to want another relationship."

"There's a woman in my ward who thinks if you truly loved your dead spouse, then you would never need to look at anyone else."

Amanda gave an exasperated sigh. "I don't know, Kerrianne. What do you think?"

"I told her that meant I had more than half my life to live alone." *And sometimes being alone feels worse than being dead.* But she didn't say this last bit aloud, not wanting to disturb her sister any more than she had. "Actually, I said rather more than that because she was talking about a friend of mine. I think I shocked her."

Amanda pulled into Kerrianne's driveway and left the van idling. She faced Kerrianne, the swell of her baby looking large in the cramped space. "Maybe she needed to be shocked. You know what I think?" She didn't wait for a reply. "I think that maybe the Lord is trying to tell you it's okay to go on with your life."

"I miss him." Kerrianne felt her jaw quiver, and she hated the weakness in herself. "I miss him every day. So much. So, so much. But then sometimes I don't even remember what he looks like." Her voice was scarcely a whisper.

Amanda's eyes reddened, but she smiled. "You remember *him,* though. That's what important, and for what it's worth, Kerrianne, I'm glad you're feeling . . . well, like you want more."

Is that what she was feeling? Maybe it was because suddenly she did want more: a companion, a father for her children, and someone to love.

"Anyway," Amanda went on, "you've spent a lot of years in a daze, letting life take you where it will. Maybe it's time you . . ." She trailed off.

"Get a life?" Kerrianne suggested bitterly. "Forget Adam? Stop wallowing in my misery?"

Amanda shook her head. "I was going to say, maybe it's time for you to get building that greenhouse you're always talking about."

They smiled at each other, followed by a burst of laughter. Kerrianne hugged her sister. "I love you, Manda."

Amanda grinned. "I love you, too. Now feel this." She grabbed Kerrianne's hand and put it on her stomach. Kerrianne felt the distinct kicking of her new little niece.

"Hi, baby," Kerrianne whispered. "We can't wait to see you."

Life went on, that was for sure, and Kerrianne was glad.

That afternoon Kerrianne had her children in the backyard pulling out dead pumpkin vines. The sun was shining overhead, but the cool nip in the air made coats, hats, and gloves a necessity. The boys loved tugging at the vines, but Misty, who was becoming fastidious as she grew older, was less than pleased at the dirt and grime. Kerrianne eventually let her rake the remaining leaves in the backyard, which was more to Misty's liking but which she had absolutely no skill at doing— especially since the lawn was still moist from the morning frost, making the leaves soggy and difficult to rake.

"Mommy, this one won't come out," Caleb said, grunting with effort as he tugged on a particularly stubborn vine.

"I'll help." Benjamin threw a vine into the garbage bin and rushed over, but even the two of them together couldn't budge the root.

Smiling, Kerrianne bent over and grasped the vine. "One, two, three!" she chanted. They tugged together, groaning with effort until *snap!* the vine broke and they tumbled backward onto the cold dirt. Caleb and Benjamin giggled and jumped on her, beginning a wrestling and tickling spree.

"Yuck!" Misty exclaimed. "You're getting all dirty!"

Soft chuckling came from another source, and Kerrianne looked up to see Ryan and his two children standing by her patio. "Hi," he called. "There was no answer so I figured we'd come around here."

With a yelp of delight, Caleb sprang from the ground and ran to hug his new best friend, Tiger, shedding his gloves on the way. Benjamin was not far behind. Kerrianne got up more slowly, dusting off as much of the dirt as she could. Her fingers felt cold even inside the gloves, but her heart was warm.

"You always seem to catch me at the best times." She let irony seep into her voice.

"Hey, I told you I'd come over today. You know, for the toy."

"Oh, right. Caleb? Where's the car you got from—" She stopped. Caleb and Benjamin had taken Ria and Tiger to the playhouse. Misty was there, too, but she didn't look happy. "Caleb can't hear me," she said unnecessarily.

Ryan shrugged. "That's okay. Tiger's got a hundred of those things. I'm always stepping on them. Look what I found." He came closer, holding out a sheaf of papers.

"What are they?"

"Look and see." His smile was amused.

She scanned the images. "Greenhouse kits?"

"Well, you sounded serious." He took the papers and shuffled through them. "Here's one that's a dome. Comes in all sizes. Kind of cool but not very space conscious. This one looks like a glass house. I like it, but it's costly. But this one . . . no . . . oh, here it is. This rectangle one with the curved roof is on some kind of sale. Almost a thirty percent discount. I like it as well as I like the house one. In fact, the top reminds me of a Russian church. It seems to be the best buy for the money. It's twelve by nine foot, instead of eight by six. Comes in green framing, if you'd like that. There's a lean-to as well, but I knew you didn't want to put it up against the house."

"So many choices." Kerrianne was touched. Narrowing down choices of greenhouses on an Internet search would have taken a lot of time. "When did you do all this?"

He shrugged. "Today was my day off, and I had some time on my hands. Anyway, the shipping is fairly even across the board. You might want to run down to the store here to see if they have anything so you can avoid shipping charges."

Kerrianne looked at the plans again. She really liked the rectangle one with the green frame. The price, even on sale, was steep, but she was already contemplating how she could swing the cost. She really wanted it.

"Maybe I will add another preschool class." She said this wistfully, though, not really wanting to give up the freedom of her mornings. That was the time she put her house to rights, went shopping, helped at the children's school, or prepared her lessons.

She walked over to the patio table and set the papers down, placing a garden trowel on top so the occasional puff of wind wouldn't send them flying. "I was clearing the spot," she told Ryan. "The vines are always easier to clear when they've died back, but we found a couple stubborn ones."

He grinned. "So I noticed."

Her face felt hot as she remembered her sprawled position when he'd arrived.

Ignoring her discomfort, Ryan glanced toward the playhouse. "Need a hand? Looks like you lost your helpers."

She was hesitant to accept. The last thing she needed was to start depending on someone again. One of the worst things about Adam's death was having no one to count on for little things she'd long taken for granted—putting a load of dishes in the dishwasher, changing the oil in the van, picking something up at the store on the way home from work, keeping the boys out of her hair while she made dinner. Yet she'd had to pressure him into mowing the lawn, pruning the trees, or helping her in the garden. It wasn't that he didn't want to help her but yard work was simply something he didn't enjoy, so Kerrianne had shouldered most of the work. With Adam doing so much else in their lives, it really hadn't been too heavy a load. She wished she'd realized that before instead of nagging him. Now, doing it all alone was next to impossible.

"Sure," she said, surprising herself. "But I don't have any gloves your size."

"That's okay. I'm used to it. Sometimes my hands are so cold when I deliver the mail in the winter that it's all I can do to separate the mail."

"You don't wear gloves?"

He shrugged. "They have to be a special kind or I can't grab the letters. Sometimes it's easier to go without."

Kerrianne nodded. They pulled vines in silence for a few minutes, and then she said, "You probably have enough of your own yard work to do at home."

"Not really. We're low maintenance at our house. There's just a lawn, and I pay Ria to mow that."

Kerrianne frowned. "But she's only, what, eight, nine?"

"Nine." He saw her aghast expression and said quickly, "She's a tomboy through and through. She loves tools and being independent. Unfortunately, it goes with the territory—not having a mother and all. Don't your kids have responsibility they wouldn't have if your husband were here?"

Kerrianne bent over a vine to hide her feelings. It was both strange and comforting to talk about Adam with Ryan. Aside from her family and Maxine, everyone else studiously avoided any reference to him. The vine came out easily—much more easily than her response.

"I guess they have more chores, things I used to have time to do for them. Folding and putting away their own clothes, getting their own lunch now and then, other household chores, but nothing dangerous."

Ryan tugged out the root of the vine that had sent Kerrianne and the boys to the ground. "Well, I did watch her the first few times."

"You don't even watch?" Kerrianne glared at him, hands on her hips.

He held up a hand to ward her off. "Kidding, kidding. Of course I watch." Under his breath he added, "Mostly."

Kerrianne began pulling up vines with more vigor. She was glad she hadn't gone out with him. He was seriously neglectful. Adam might not have been a great help in the yard, but he had certainly taken responsible care of the children.

"Give it back!" Misty yelled, breaking into Kerrianne's thoughts. "Now! It's mine!"

Kerrianne looked up to see Tiger and Caleb running around the backyard with one of Misty's Barbie dolls. They were giggling wildly, barely managing to keep a step ahead of Misty.

"Tiger!" Ryan said firmly. The boy ignored him and ducked around the swing set. Misty's normally pale, delicate face was red with fury, and tears were imminent.

Great, thought Kerrianne. *Not only is he negligent, but he has no clue about discipline. Tiger doesn't even hear him.*

Ria came to stand by them. "He'll never listen. Tiger, give it back!"

No reaction except that Tiger, who was holding the doll, tore off its clothes and threw them at Misty.

"No!" she shrieked dramatically.

Kerrianne thought things had gone far enough. She raised her voice. "Caleb Adam Price, you stop this instant or there will be serious consequences." Serious consequences meant no video games or movies, which Caleb loved more than anything. He faltered in his running, coming to a stop. "Aw, Mom, we were just having fun."

"At your sister's expense. That's not the sort of fun to have. Now you and Tiger give the doll back to Misty and say you're sorry."

Looking at the ground in shame, Tiger gave the doll to Caleb. Kerrianne started to congratulate herself on how well she'd handled things and hoping Ryan had taken notes when Caleb tucked the doll under his arm and darted past Misty, emitting an Indian war cry.

"Mom!" wailed Misty.

Kerrianne dropped the vine she was holding and took off after Caleb. She tackled him before he got to the front yard, her pants becoming damp from the grass, though her coat protected the rest of her. "You're busted, mister," she said, hauling her son to his feet.

Caleb handed over the doll, but he didn't look sorry. "This isn't like you, Caleb," she said in a low voice.

"Misty called us stupid heads."

"In that case it looks like both you and Misty are grounded—after we finish clearing the garden. Now get to back to work. No more play."

Hanging his head, Caleb plodded back to the garden.

Tiger met him there. "Your mom's a fast runner," he said in a loud whisper, his voice filled with awe. "I never saw a mom run like that before."

"She's good at everything," Caleb answered.

Kerrianne felt pleased, and she shot Ryan a smug glance. He just grinned.

"What about your dad?" Tiger asked Caleb.

"I don't have a dad."

Kerrianne's smile froze at her son's answer. He'd only been a few months old when Adam died and didn't remember him at all, which to a child was nearly the same as never having a father. She met Ryan's gaze again, wondering how Tiger would respond. Ryan's grin had disappeared, and he gave her a helpless half shrug.

Tiger paused less than the length of a heartbeat. "Did he die?"

"Yeah."

"So did my mom. Anyway, I think your mom runs faster than my dad."

Caleb nodded. "Probably."

As the words sank in, Kerrianne stifled a laugh, her concern dissipating with the boys' matter-of-fact attitude.

Ryan chuckled ruefully. "They might be right," he whispered.

Her annoyance at him was over, but Kerrianne thought it best to put distance between them. She was only too aware of how attractive he was to her. What would Adam say about that?

"Start pulling weeds, Tiger," Ryan said, pulling his grin under control. "No, don't ask me where the weeds are—they're everything."

"But I don't have any gloves."

Caleb held one out to him. "Take one of mine."

Kerrianne felt someone touch the sleeve of her coat. Ria stood there looking at her with a tight expression on her face. For the first time, Kerrianne noticed that her eyes weren't as dark as her brother's or even gray like her father's, but a lighter hazel. With her black hair and darker skin tone, she was pretty—or would be if she didn't keep stuffing her hair up under that cap and if she wore something other than boy clothes. Kerrianne thought her shirt closely resembled one she'd bought for Benjamin last month. Did Ryan shop for her in the boys' department?

"It was my fault," Ria said, oblivious to Kerrianne's thoughts. "I gave them the doll. It was in the playhouse." Then with a touch of disdain she added, "I didn't think anyone cared about it."

The truth was Misty probably hadn't cared—until the boys picked it up. "It's okay," Kerrianne assured her.

"Can I help?" Ria asked, her face relaxing into eagerness.

"Sure. You can pull vines with us. Or if you want, you can rake up those leaves." Kerrianne motioned to the abandoned rake. She doubted that Misty, who was sitting on the porch putting on her doll's clothes, would ever finish the job.

After another ten minutes, all the vines were in the garbage, no thanks to Caleb and Tiger who spent most of the time digging in the dirt with sticks. Benjamin had worked steadily by Ryan's side, and Ria had made good headway on the damp leaves. Misty stayed on the patio, watching Ria with a disgruntled expression on her face, and when Kerrianne motioned to her, she pretended not to see.

"That's good enough," Kerrianne said, pulling off her gloves. "My fingers are frozen."

"Mine, too." Ryan rubbed his bare hands together.

"Thanks for helping."

"It was fun. I like working outside."

He seemed to mean it. She'd become accustomed to the man in her life hating the hobby she loved best, and it was odd sharing this moment with Ryan. Very odd. But nice, too.

"Mom, let's get the hot chocolate," Benjamin said.

"Yeah, you promised." Caleb looked at Tiger. "You can have my other cup. I have two. Race ya." The boys ran to the back door leading into the garage, pulling at each other's coats along the way.

Ryan's gray eyes studied her, their color matching the dark, turgid clouds gathering in the distance.

"Would you like to come in?" she asked.

"I would." His voice was soft yet firm, and there was something in his expression that made Kerrianne's heart sing.

There's something here, she thought. The realization didn't come with fireworks or with mind-numbing speed. It just was. The something opened up all kinds of possibilities—Ryan as a boyfriend, as a husband, father, lover.

Feeling suddenly shy, she led the way into the garage where she pulled off her dirty shoes and gloves, leaving them at the door next to the boys' discarded sneakers. She was glad to see Ryan and the girls slip off their shoes before following her inside.

Kerrianne made hot chocolate while Ryan talked with the boys and Ria at the table.

"Where am I going to sit?" Misty complained, noting that all the chairs were taken.

"Go get one of the folding chairs from the garage," Kerrianne told her.

With a belabored sigh, Misty stomped from the room—and not in the direction of the garage.

Kerrianne wondered if Misty was still upset about the doll. Well, they'd work that out later. At that moment Ryan glanced up and met Kerrianne's gaze. She held his eyes boldly, not ashamed that he had caught her staring. She decided not to worry about anything right now except enjoying this moment with her children and a kind, good man who had helped her clear the pumpkin vines from her garden.

Chapter Thirteen

Several hours later, after drinking numerous mugs of what Ryan thought was the best hot chocolate he'd ever tasted, they were still at Kerrianne's table, poring over the greenhouse printouts. Ryan could see Kerrianne growing more and more excited about finally obtaining her dream.

"I'll help you build it," he said. "We could get some others here and get it up in a day or two."

"My brothers would help. And my dad."

Ryan wanted to meet her family. He wanted to know everything about her.

"Order it, then!" Ria was the only child still at the table with them, the boys having disappeared and Misty having never returned. Ryan had hoped the girls would get along, but instead of making friends with Misty, Ria had stayed at the table hanging on Kerrianne's every word the way she usually did with Sam. Ryan hoped he wasn't setting up his daughter for more heartache.

"I wish I could order it." Kerrianne bit her lower lip. "It's a nice size, not like those smaller ones. But it's almost two thousand dollars—still a bit steep for my budget." She sighed. "It's nice to dream about, though."

For the first time in his life Ryan wished he had a fancy job that would allow him to buy it for her. His brother Willard could have. Or his father. Of course they didn't have huge medical bills looming over them.

"We haven't called any stores yet," he suggested, covering his disappointment.

"Yeah! Let's try that!" Ria hopped up from her chair. "I'll get the phone book. Where is it?"

Kerrianne smiled at her enthusiasm. "In that drawer beneath the phone."

After calling several local stores, they hadn't found a better price, but Kerrianne wasn't discouraged. "It's okay," she said. "It'll happen. Something will come up."

Ryan didn't have her faith, and he felt deflated. Was there a way he could buy it for her? Would she accept it if he could?

"We should take Kerrianne to Grandma's," Ria said, startling him.

He gaped at his daughter, trying to hide his dismay. "You want to go to Grandma's?"

Ria fingered a houseplant that sat next to the phone. "I bet Kerrianne would like to see her plants." She looked at Kerrianne. "There are tons of them. The whole room is green."

"The green room," Kerrianne said. "Your father told me about it last night."

Ria wrinkled her brow, her eyes puzzled. "I though you went to a dance last night, Daddy."

"I did. Kerrianne was there."

"Did you dance with each other?"

Ryan nodded. "A few times."

Kerrianne laughed. "In fact, he rescued me from a rather . . ." She trailed off.

"Ardent admirer," Ryan finished, glad when she laughed again. He loved hearing her laugh.

"A handsome, ardent admirer," she corrected.

"How come you didn't tell me you were on a date?" Ria looked back and forth between them, as though unsure how to react to the news.

"It wasn't a date." Kerrianne looked around as though worried her children would hear, but the three boys were playing a loud game with cars in the family room and Misty was nowhere to be seen.

"Well, I did ask her for a date," Ryan said with a wink.

Ria started grinning. "Good! We can go to Grandma's for the date." She looked at Kerrianne and explained. "We go on Sundays sometimes. The last time my grandpa played ball with me. He's pretty good."

Kerrianne looked at Ryan expectantly. What could he do? "My parents aren't exactly . . . ," he began. "Well, they're kind of strange."

"Grandma's nice," Ria put in. "But you can't do anything in their house, so it's usually kind of boring. Except last time when Grandpa played ball with me." She paused, pondering for a moment that great occurrence. "Daddy doesn't like going there because they're always trying to find girls for him to marry."

Ryan groaned. "Ria."

"What? They do." Ria gave him a blank stare and scooted closer to Kerrianne. "So, do ya wanna come?"

"Well, I wouldn't want to get in the way of all those girls." Kerrianne's gaze on Ryan's face felt sharp.

"It's not really like that," he said.

She shrugged as if it didn't matter, and Ryan felt a flood of anxiety. If he was serious about her, and he was feeling more so every minute, then he would have to introduce his parents sooner or later. Perhaps it was better to get it over with before their relationship went any further. In all fairness, she should understand what she might be getting into. He took a deep breath. "I'd love to introduce you to my parents."

She blinked once, slowly. "Introduce?"

Ryan felt confused. Wasn't that was she wanted? But then, "introduce" was rather formal, wasn't it? The term implied there was something between them, which Ryan was willing to admit, but apparently Kerrianne wasn't. "I mean," he corrected smoothly, "to show you the green room. If you'd like to see it, that is. Just be aware that my parents are . . . well, rather different. Opinionated, you might say. My dad especially."

Kerrianne didn't speak. Her gaze went to the greenhouse printouts and beyond the sliding glass doors leading onto the patio, staring at something he couldn't see. Was she thinking about her husband? Adam seemed like a great guy, as great as Laurie had been. Could Ryan ever hope to measure up? If he pursued this relationship, would he always come in second best?

Regardless, it didn't matter, not now. One look in her eyes, one soft touch of her hand, and he was willing to risk his heart. Laurie would be pleased. "Well?" he pressed.

"Okay," she agreed slowly. "But what about my kids? I suppose I could drop them off at my sister's."

"That might be best."

Her forehead gathered as she frowned. "Your parents are that bad?" When he didn't answer, she added, "In that case, I think I'll take the kids along." She gave him a flat, challenging stare.

Ryan suddenly wanted to laugh. Why not? If he was taking Kerrianne to see his parents, why not bring the whole crowd? Watching his parents scramble might at least provide some amusement. He wasn't exactly trying to impress them or anything, though how Kerrianne could fail to impress them was beyond him. On the other hand, if they proved to be impossible, he would immediately get her out of there.

"Well, it's settled then," he said. "Would two o'clock be a good time to go tomorrow?"

"Perfect." Two spots of red appeared on her cheekbones—or had the rest of her face gone abruptly pale? Did that mean she was worried about something? He wished he could read her better.

"Thanks for your help today." She stood, signaling an end to their afternoon.

He arose, wanting to stay but not knowing how make it happen. "Yeah, it looks like it's time for me to go."

"Is it time for practice?" Ria asked. To Kerrianne, she added. "I always practice basketball on Saturdays. Do you like basketball? When I have a game, you can come and watch if you like." She shrugged and added quickly, "If you want to, I mean."

"Basketball is for boys." Misty had appeared in the kitchen doorway, dressed in a blue and white princess dress and wearing a tiara in her hair. She looked exactly like a little girl who'd just finished a photo shoot for an advertisement.

Ryan saw Ria's eyes widen with envy before her face hardened. "Well, I like boy stuff," she said. "Girl stuff is stupid and boring." Her gaze plainly said that she wouldn't be caught dead in a princess dress.

"Misty, you like basketball." Kerrianne crossed the room and made a bow with the ties in back of the dress.

"Not anymore. That's boy stuff, and I don't like boy stuff. Mom, do you think I can wear this dress to the tea party? All the girls can dress up if we want."

"You're going to the tea party, too?" Ria asked.

Kerrianne smiled at her. "I think all the second through fourth grades are involved."

"Oh." Ria's voice was dull, and in a rare moment of understanding, Ryan realized that she was worrying about what to wear. Ria was a tomboy, to be sure, but despite the attitude she was showing at the moment, she loved dressing up as much as the next girl. Maybe Sam would be willing to help him figure out what she should wear. With the way Ria and Misty were glaring at each other, asking Sam would be better than bringing it up now.

"Who's taking you?" Misty asked Ria.

Ria kept her face impassive. "A friend. Her name is Sam." And then as if she couldn't help herself, she added, "She's beautiful. You'll probably get to see her."

"Was that the lady from the other night at the play?" Kerrianne asked. When Ryan nodded, she added, "I thought I recognized her name."

No one spoke for a few seconds until Ryan said awkwardly, "I guess I should get our shoes from the garage."

Kerrianne nodded. "I'll go with you."

Before either of them could move, the doorbell rang. Misty ran to it excitedly, followed by the boys who came running from the family room. Kerrianne gave him a smile. "They always act like that," she said. "You'd think it was Santa Claus at the door."

He chuckled and followed her along the hallway, with Ria tagging behind. At the door stood a man with a large vase of flowers. "Delivery for Kerrianne Price," he announced, looking over the heads of the children.

"That's me. Those lilies are beautiful."

"Please sign here." He extended a clipboard with a paper attached.

She signed the paper, accepted the vase, and shut the door, her brow drawn in puzzlement. "I wonder who they're from." She looked at Ryan, but he shrugged.

"Read the card." Misty was already reaching for it.

Kerrianne grabbed it first. "Probably one of my brothers." She read the card silently, shaking her head. "It says, 'Enjoyed meeting you last night. Hope to see you again. Morgan.'"

She shook her head. "Must be a mistake. I don't know any Morgan. Oh, wait a minute. I think I might have danced with a Morgan last night. But I don't know if it was that older guy who smelled like mint, or that other guy who was my age. Or maybe it was . . ." She shrugged and trailed off.

"I don't know anyone named Morgan." Ryan was glad at least that the flowers were not from Gunnar.

"I didn't tell anyone my address, though."

Ryan smiled. "Believe me, that doesn't matter." He raised his eyebrows several times. "We have ways."

"Oh, I see. Hmm." Gently, she touched a white petal. "They're beautiful."

Just like you. But he couldn't say the words. They seemed too contrived.

She snapped her fingers. "I know who Morgan is. He was the guy about our age who kept telling me how pretty—" She broke off with an embarrassed shrug. "I'm sure he says it to everyone."

Ryan wasn't so sure, but he was glad he hadn't voiced his own thoughts along those lines. She would have thought it was a line.

She put the vase on the counter in the kitchen and led the way to the garage for the shoes. "Aw, do we have to go?" Tiger whined.

"Yes," Ryan said. "Ria has practice."

Tiger's eyes lit up. "Can we shoot hoops?"

Ryan thought of himself asking his father that same question many years earlier. "Of course we can. I'd like nothing better."

"I like basketball." Caleb was, in fact, holding his blue ball, the one he sometimes threw to Ryan in the mornings.

Ryan glanced at Kerrianne, wanting to invite the child but confused over the proper way to go about it. She shook her head almost imperceptibly. Apparently, she wasn't ready to trust him with her children—yet.

"We'll play sometime," he said instead.

"When?" Tiger asked—or yelled, as he always did. "And did you ask her again about school? I want to come here with Caleb. He's my best friend." The two boys linked arms over each other's shoulders, causing Caleb's ball to drop to the floor.

"She doesn't have any openings." Ryan scooped up the ball and handed it back to Caleb.

Kerrianne cleared her throat. "Actually, I do have space."

"What days?" Ryan couldn't believe his luck.

"Well, the Monday, Wednesday, and Friday class has fewer students, but I could squeeze him in on Tuesdays and Thursdays if you'd prefer."

He wondered briefly if she'd had the openings all along, or if a student had dropped out. If she'd had the openings all along, that meant she hadn't wanted Tiger in her class. Was it because of him? Had he made her nervous that night at the play? He couldn't decide if making her nervous was a good or a bad thing. Of course, it might have nothing to do with him at all or even a student dropping out. Perhaps her yearning for a greenhouse had encouraged her to enlarge the classes. He found he really didn't care what her reasons might be. Having Tiger at her house would allow him to see her more—a lot more.

"Okay," he said. "Let's do it." He was sure he could swing the price, but maybe this was one more reason to look into that management position down in Provo's East Bay location. If it meant more money, he might be able to handle the night shift. That would eliminate the need for a sitter during the day, though he'd have to find a college student to stay nights at the house with the kids.

The boys were jumping up and down and shouting with excitement, still clinging to each other. Benjamin and Ria looked on with indulgent smiles. Only Misty frowned, her arms folded across her middle. She caught Ryan watching her and quickly looked away.

Kerrianne smiled at the boys' excitement. "What days?"

Ryan considered a moment. "How about all of them? Tiger hasn't had any schooling at all. Where he is now, he mostly watches TV. I think he could use the extra time. I can swing by and drop him off on my lunch break, but I've got a little problem picking up at two or three. I don't get off until four, give or take a bit. But don't worry—I'll work it out. I know some people who can help." At least he hoped they would help. If Susan couldn't do it, he'd ask his neighbor, or maybe some of the women from the family ward he attended with the children. If worse came to worst, maybe Sam would pitch in a bit, provided her husband didn't object.

"Okay, then." Kerrianne was apparently unaware of his internal dilemma. Good. Just the way he wanted it.

Misty gave him a disgruntled look and stomped down the hall. Ryan knew he'd have to work on her, but if he couldn't understand the tomboy Ria half the time, how could he relate to a girl who was the image of a porcelain doll?

Later, as he started the truck, he realized he was thinking not only of having Kerrianne in his future but also her children.

"Dad, why are you stopping here?" Ria stared across him toward Maxine's house.

"Well, I know this lady, you see, and she owes me a favor."

"A favor?"

"Yeah. Come on." They trudged up to the front porch. The cold was biting now with the steady breeze, and Ryan felt a drop of icy rain on his cheek.

"I wanna push it!" Tiger stood on tiptoes to ring the doorbell.

Maxine opened the door, looking as trendy as ever in wide-legged dress pants and a patterned black and brown sweater with a waist tie. "Ryan? What are you doing here? I already got my mail this morning. Not delivered by you, I might add. You know, I don't like those other carriers as well. He left my mailbox half open, and in this weather!"

He chuckled. "I promise I'll talk to him. Look, I'm here for a favor, if you're willing."

She smiled and opened the door wider. "Why don't you all come in? I'm leaving for a date in a while, but you're welcome to sit for a minute."

"Actually, we have basketball practice so we'd better not come in," Ryan said. "Tiger's starting preschool at Kerrianne's next week, and I'm worried about finding someone to pick him up on time with so little notice. I think I'll be able to find someone, but if I can't, I was wondering if you'd let him come here on Monday for an hour or two until I can pick him up."

Her mouth fell open a little. "You want me to baby-sit?"

161

"Not really baby-sit. Just let him hang out until whoever picks him up. He's not a problem." Thankfully, Tiger was standing at Ryan's side on the porch looking angelic.

"What about me, Dad?" Ria asked, tugging on his sleeve.

"You'll walk to Susan's after school as usual."

Ria looked ready to cry at his answer.

Maxine swung her head back and forth. "Sounds to me like you're complicating things. Why don't you just ask Kerrianne to keep your son if there's ever a problem?"

"Because I think I just squeezed him in by the skin of his teeth, that's why. I don't want to give her a reason to change her mind."

Maxine snorted. "Oh, you're playing a game I see. When will you young people learn that games take too long? Just get to it!"

"To what?" asked Tiger, his head tilted back to see her better.

"To dating, to love, to life." Maxine emphasized each word with her slender hands.

Tiger scrunched up his mouth. "But I like games."

"Uh, never mind." Maxine shifted her gaze back to Ryan. "If you actually trust me with him, then yes, I'll stand in if you need me. Temporarily, of course, because I've been there, done that, you know? But you'd better call me as soon as you know you'll need me. I'll get my number." She was gone for a few minutes and then returned with a paper which she handed to Ryan. Then she smiled at Tiger. "Do you like exercise? I need a new walking partner."

"Don't you have a TV?"

"Not for you to watch. No, I think exercise is just what you need."

Tiger looked at her glumly while Ria smirked.

"You too, young lady." Maxine clicked her tongue.

Ria grinned at her. "I'm the best runner in my class." She thought a moment and then added, "I could be your walking partner. I could come every day after school." Her gaze was so hopeful that Ryan didn't have the heart to tell her Maxine usually had her walk in before he delivered the mail.

"All right, I'll try you out," Maxine said with a snap of her fingers. "You come on Monday. We'll pick up your brother and go for a walk."

"Uh, he'll get out at two on Monday," Ryan said. "Ria wouldn't get here until nearly four."

Ria shook her head. "Monday's an early day, remember? We get out an hour early."

"Oh, yeah. But you can't walk all the way here."

"I know which bus it is. Janelle goes on the same one. I've seen her get on a million times with Misty and Benjamin. I can go on the bus with Janelle and get off here." When she saw Ryan's doubtful face, she added. "Please, Dad. I know the way. You can even call Janelle's mom."

"I don't know."

"I think it's a great idea," Maxine said to Ryan. "Don't you worry one bit. We'll manage until you get here. Monday's your heavy day at the post office, isn't it?" She waggled a finger at him. "See? I pay attention. You're always late on Mondays so we won't expect you until four-thirty or five." She paused a minute before barreling on. "Never mind about calling me. Let's just plan on it. Monday is taken care of. No, come to think of it, they can come on Tuesday, too. Since next week is Thanksgiving and I bet Ria only has those two days at school. That will give you another week to make more permanent arrangements." She looked at him pointedly. "And that means finding another place for Ria after school. You can't expect her to go to this Susan's if she hates the place."

"That's easier said than done."

"Well, you'd better get to work finding something, then."

He didn't dare protest. At least he'd have time to work it out. He'd taken two vacation days next week so he could stay home and watch the children during their time out of school. With the holiday, that meant he'd only be working Monday and Tuesday. "Thanks, Maxine."

"Look, there's my date. See you on Monday." Maxine picked up her purse from somewhere near the door and pushed passed them, going down the steps at an alarming rate. Somewhat less quickly, Harold climbed from his car and met her on the walk, taking her hand and giving it a noisy kiss.

Maxine shook her head at him. "Goodness, Harold, what is this fascination you have with my hand?" Without waiting for an answer, she pulled open her own door and slid inside his car. Looking calm and unruffled, Harold trod slowly around to the other side.

Ryan grinned at Ria, who grinned back.

"She's weird, Dad," Tiger said in his loud kid whisper.

"Yeah," Ria agreed. "She's cool. I really like her."

Maxine waved to them as Harold's car drove away.

"So do I," Ryan said. He wondered what Kerrianne might do if he tried to kiss her hand.

Chapter Fourteen

Scarcely thirty minutes after Ryan left, the flowers from Morgan were followed by a dozen red roses from someone named Clark, who Kerrianne thought might have been one of the older men she'd danced with—hopefully the one who smelled like mint. She breathed in the intoxicating scent of the flowers and laughed. One had to admire the men's resourcefulness, especially as she hadn't given them any personal information except her name.

Though she felt a little foolish, she was enjoying the attention. Two bouquets in one day when she hadn't received flowers from a man not related to her in four long years. What an event! She hummed as she stood on a chair to unearth another vase from the small cupboard over her refrigerator. The green glass was slightly dusty, though she had cleaned out the space regularly. She had a lot of time to clean when the children were in bed.

"Are these from that guy who was here earlier?" Misty climbed up on a kitchen stool to better view the roses, her lips pursed in suspicion, though she usually loved flowers of every kind.

Kerrianne jumped down from her chair. "His name is Ryan. But no, sweetie, these came from someone else I danced with last night. Here, smell." She pulled a rose from the bunch and handed it to Misty.

"Was the dance fun?" Misty sniffed the rose.

Kerrianne grinned. "Yeah, it was."

"You and Daddy used to go dancing." Misty's blue eyes grew large. "Benjamin and I'd stay with Aunt Manda."

"I remember." Adam would sing in her ear all night until his voice was hoarse and she was so full of love for him that she couldn't speak. After coming home, they'd put the children to bed and dance on in their bedroom, all alone. He'd kiss her—oh, how he'd kiss her! And then finally, much later, he would bring out his guitar and play until she fell asleep, curled up next to him.

Tears filled Kerrianne's eyes, and her heart was full, as full as it had always been with love for Adam. There was no room for the pain, at the moment, or the longing for him. No room for regret or bitterness. There was only space for the love. It filled her up like water filled a stream, flowing with clear, vivid memories.

She reached out to smooth a curly lock of her daughter's blonde hair. "I loved to dance with your daddy."

"Better than Ryan?" Misty wrinkled her nose as if smelling something bad.

"Better than anyone. But that doesn't mean I'm never going to dance again." Once, she thought it might mean just that, but not after last night. Her experience was proof that she needed to dance, that she should go on with her life.

Misty considered the implication. "Oh. Well, it doesn't have to be with Ryan, does it?"

"No. But I do like him." Kerrianne picked up the vase and rinsed it under the tap.

"Are you going to marry him?"

"Heavens no! What made you ask that?"

Misty shrugged. "I don't like that girl."

"Why not? She seemed nice to me."

"I just don't!" Misty dropped the rose and folded her white, slightly chubby arms, so different from Ria's lean brown ones.

"I didn't notice her being mean."

"She said my doll was stupid!"

"Was that before or after she found out it was yours?"

Misty didn't answer.

"So it was before."

Misty touched a thorn on her fallen rose. "It's like she hangs on you—practically. I don't like her."

Kerrianne leaned over close to her daughter's face. "Why, Misty, I do believe your eyes are turning green."

"No, they're not. They're blue. They're always blue."

Kerrianne began to arrange the roses in the green vase. "Well, it sounds to me like you're a little jealous."

"Of her?" The scorn in Misty's voice was clear.

Letting the rest of the roses slide into the vase, Kerrianne leaned her elbows on the counter so she could stare into Misty's face. "Honey, Ria lost her mother. You know how much losing your daddy hurt? Well, think of how she must feel to lose her mother. It's not like you to be so unkind."

Misty's eyes filled with tears. "But you're *my* mother."

The words said it all. Misty didn't want to lose her, not even in part, to anyone else.

Kerrianne went around the counter and hugged her daughter, who clung on tightly, more like a baby than an eight-year-old. "I will always be your mother," Kerrianne said, surprised at the fierceness of her feelings. "That's never going to change. And I'll always love you as much as I do right now."

"Do we really have to go to Ria's grandma's tomorrow?" Misty released her neck and slid back onto her stool.

"I'd like to. I'm curious to see their green room, and I'd hate to cancel after I already said I'd go. But if you feel uncomfortable, you could stay with your aunt."

Frowning, Misty shook her head. "No, I'd better come." There was a determination in the gathering of her forehead that didn't bode well for the trip.

"Okay, but try to be nice. Maybe Ria isn't so bad. You might even become friends."

Misty's flat, uncompromising stare showed her how much she thought of that idea.

"Why don't you take the boys out on the driveway and play ball with them so I can start dinner? It shouldn't be too cold if you keep moving."

Misty shook her head. "Playing ball is for boys."

"But you've always played with them."

Her chin rose. "I'm going to play with my Polly Pockets and my dollhouse."

"Well, okay, but don't blame me when the boys break their clothes." The plastic clothing sported by most of the mini dolls was part of their appeal, but once broken, could never be mended.

"They won't." Misty slipped off her stool just as the phone rang. She hesitated near the refrigerator.

Kerrianne picked up the phone. "Hello?"

"Kerrianne?"

"Yes. Who's speaking?"

"It's Gunnar. You know, from the dance last night."

"Oh, hi." Kerrianne stifled her laughter. So Gunnar had found her, too. Tina had been right about all the attention. "How are you?"

"I'm fine. Well, I've been thinking a lot about you, but other than that . . ." He trailed off, ending with a chuckle.

Kerrianne shook her head. Now that was a line if she'd ever heard one.

"Mom, who is it?" Misty asked, though her attention was on the stainless steel handle of the refrigerator where she appeared to be looking carefully at her eyes.

Gunnar was speaking again, but Kerrianne didn't hear what he said. "Can you hold on a minute?" she asked.

Covering the receiver, she stepped toward Misty. "It's a man I danced with last night."

"Did he send the roses?" Misty looked toward her.

"No, someone else."

Misty shook her head. "You must have danced with a lot of guys."

"Something like that. Now aren't you going to get your Polly Pockets?"

"Yeah, but just so you know, my eyes are still blue." With that pronouncement, Misty left the room in search of the boys. Kerrianne knew they'd fall into Misty's doll-playing plan. While they would prefer ball, playing with Misty was more exciting than playing on their own.

"Okay, I'm back." Kerrianne tucked the phone between her ear and shoulder and began to arrange the roses against the greenery and the tiny white babies' breath that had come with them. She toyed with the idea of mixing the roses with the lilies of earlier, but decided she liked the look of the individual arrangements. She had the lilies on the table; these she'd leave on the counter where she could smell them often as she made dinner.

"I was thinking we could go out tonight, if you're not busy," Gunnar was saying. His voice lowered. "Or we could stay in—maybe at your place."

Kerrianne felt immediately uncomfortable. "Uh, that's not a good idea. My kids are here, and I don't want to . . ." She didn't know what she was trying to say, but she suddenly understood the conversation she'd overheard Rosalva and Tina having about keeping their children away from their dates until it became necessary to introduce them. Misty was already feeling threatened by Ryan and Ria, and Kerrianne wasn't about to add Gunnar to her load.

"Oh, yeah, your kids. Mine are with my ex-wife this weekend, and I didn't think—sorry."

"That's okay. It's natural." Or was it?

"We could see a movie," Gunnar said.

"I really can't. I left my children last night, and I don't want to leave them again so soon. They're not used to me . . . you know, going out." The truth was Kerrianne wasn't used to it either. How she had gone from a mourning widow one day to a woman being sent flowers and asked out the next was unfathomable.

"Oh, I see." Gunnar's disappointment was all too apparent. "What about next week?"

"Well, I'm not sure what I'm doing yet. I think Maxine mentioned another, uh, dance." Kerrianne wondered if he felt she was trying to give him the runaround. She really wasn't, but dancing was one thing, and dating quite another.

"There's a couple of things going on next week," Gunnar said. "But I really hoped to see you before then." His voice grew huskier, and Kerrianne again felt a distinct desire to laugh. Was he for real?

"I'm a little new at all this," she said, schooling her voice to be properly serious. "I want to get back into things slowly."

"I understand." He sounded, in fact, extremely sympathetic. "Well, I'll go to whatever dance you'll be at. We can see about things then."

"I think that would be best," Kerrianne said.

"But can I call you?"

"Sure, why not?" After the children went to sleep, there was only her and the quiet, creaking house, and that big empty bed waiting. She liked to put off going to bed for as long as possible and having Gunnar to talk to—having anyone to talk to—would give her an excuse to stay up.

Gunnar launched into a story about his neighbor, a military man whose yard was not allowed to have one blade of grass out of place. He told the story with skill, and Kerrianne found herself relaxing. Before she knew it, she'd finished the chicken and rice she was making for dinner, and it was time to call the kids.

"Well, I have to go," she said. "It was fun talking to you. And I mean that."

"I enjoyed it too. I'll call you again."

"I'd like that."

Kerrianne hung up the cordless phone in its cradle. She looked at it for a moment, contemplating the sudden absurdity of her life. "Adam," she said, looking heavenward, "you'd better not be up there laughing at me. In fact, I hope you're jealous!"

With that, she called the children to dinner.

About halfway through the meal, Misty set down her fork and stared at her. "Mommy, you seem different."

"Oh? How?"

"You're smiling a lot," Benjamin said.

Kerrianne stopped chewing. "That's a good thing, right?"

Benjamin and Caleb nodded furiously, Misty with more reserve. Kerrianne wondered if her bitterness and longing for the past had affected her children more than she realized. *I have to be careful of that,* she thought. More than anything she wanted her children to grow up healthy and happy—despite Adam's not being there for them. Did that mean not only hiding her constant longing for him but actually trying to find happiness? She wondered also if she should be actively seeking a new father figure for them as Ryan seemed to be searching for a mother for his children. Could another man love her children enough to fill that spot?

Maybe it was time she found out.

After a quiet evening with her children, they piled in her bed and she put on one of Adam's CDs. Heat blasted down at them from the overhead vent as they cuddled like a litter of puppies, squashed against each other, limbs entwined or sprawling as comfort demanded. Kerrianne felt warm and happy and content.

As she drifted off she wasn't thinking about her children, or Adam, Gunnar, or the men who'd sent flowers. She was thinking of Ryan.

Chapter Fifteen

Ryan's parents' house in Ogden was larger than Kerrianne expected, bigger even than her parents' comfortable home in Alpine where they'd raised four children. She knew the Oakmans had only two children, both of whom were long gone, and she wondered what they did with all the extra space. The house was tall, gray-colored, and forbidding but immaculately landscaped with mature trees and generous flowerbeds. Only a scattered handful of leaves dotted the grass, and Kerrianne bet they'd blown over from the neighbor's yard. There was even a waterfall in the front, though there was no water in it at the moment—probably having been winterized.

She turned off the engine and pulled the keys from the ignition. They'd had to take her van, as Ryan's truck had only three safety belts. She hadn't minded, though it had been a little awkward. He'd offered to drive, but she hated it when guys assumed they should drive just because they were men, so she'd refused. She had driven herself around for four years and liked the control it gave her.

Ria jumped out of the van and headed up the walk that led to wide, decorative cement stairs. The rest followed her more slowly.

Caleb tugged on Kerrianne's hand. "Mom, it's frowning at me," he whispered, staring up at the house. "Tiger's right. It's scary."

Kerrianne knew all about Tiger's ideas, as the child had loudly voiced them during the hour drive. "It's just a house," she told Caleb. "And remember, Ryan promised there would be food."

"But you might not like it," Tiger put in. The boys shared a mournful look and went solemnly up the walk, their hands shoved deep in their pockets. Benjamin squeezed between them, setting a comforting hand on each of their shoulders. Misty followed behind, her pretty face drawn into what seemed a permanent pout.

Ryan chuckled, but there was uneasiness in his eyes. "I guess you've realized my parents don't inspire much trust from my children."

Kerrianne thought how different it would be if they were visiting her parents. Her children always ran to be the first one to hug Grandma or Grandpa. "What about their other grandparents?" she asked.

"Laurie's parents live in New York so we rarely see them. She came out to Brigham Young University and lived with her grandmother, and that's how we met. Some of her brothers and sisters came, too, but she was the only one to stay. Five of them live near her parents, so they keep busy with grandkids. We haven't actually seen them since the funeral, though Laurie's sister came to visit once or twice. She was close to Laurie, especially at the end."

Kerrianne nodded, knowing how difficult it was to stay in contact with in-laws once a spouse wasn't around to plan visits. Since her own mother-in-law's health had declined, the only time the children saw her now was when Kerrianne managed to take them to California. They'd made it only twice in four years.

The air was still crisp and clean smelling, but there was a bite to it that made Kerrianne hold her coat more tightly around her. Ryan's eyes followed the movement with a smile. "It's cold," he said unnecessarily. His gray eyes were dark and deep, and they held hers with an intensity that was common with him, as though he were searching out her innermost feelings. Her breath caught in her throat, and she almost forgot to take a step, which caused her to stumble.

Ryan caught her elbow, but her stumbling had broken the connection between their eyes and she no longer needed any help. She was both exhilarated by and frustrated with his touch. They were only friends—why did he affect her so? Had it been that long since she'd felt a man's touch?

Yes. Four long years.

A gentle smile came to his lips as he drew his hand back. He was still looking at her, but Kerrianne was careful not to get caught again in his stare, though she wondered what he was thinking.

The children had reached the door, so Kerrianne quickened her pace. Misty was behind the others, her foot tapping with impatience. Kerrianne heaved an inner sigh. Misty was usually bossy and sure of herself, but she was also kind and giving and loving—especially to someone she deemed was an underdog. This sulky, petulant creature simply couldn't be her daughter. Kerrianne had to use tremendous effort to remind herself that Misty was acting from fear of losing her place in Kerrianne's life more than from any desire to hurt others.

The tall door opened, revealing a plump woman of average height. She had straight brown hair drawn back in a clip at the nape of her neck and blue eyes that ran over the children with an air that already signaled defeat. "Hello," she said in a soft voice that didn't surprise Kerrianne. It completed the picture of who she was.

She hugged Ria and Tiger, which they bore stoically, without real enthusiasm. Then Ryan kissed her cheek and turned to introduce Kerrianne. "Mom, this is Kerrianne. Kerrianne, my mother Elizabeth. And these are Kerrianne's children, Misty, Benjamin, and . . . uh . . . let's see." He faltered, pointing at Caleb.

"Caleb!" The boy sounded outraged.

"That's right. It's Jarob."

"No, Caleb!" Both Tiger and Caleb yelled.

"Callen," Ryan said.

"Caleb!" The boys screamed. But they were laughing now, having realized it was all a joke.

Ryan snapped his fingers. "Of course, how could I forget. It's Raleb." Caleb giggled.

"Nice to meet you all," Elizabeth said with a half smile. "Come in. It's cold out there."

Once in the house, they hung their coats on a coatrack by the door, careful not to drop them on the highly polished wood floor. Then the children stood looking nervously back and forth, waiting for Elizabeth to give them directions. Again Kerrianne was struck by the difference between this house and her parents'. Nothing here bore the wear of children, and having seen Ryan playing with the kids, she couldn't see him growing up here, couldn't make it fit together in her mind.

"Let's go to the green room." Elizabeth smiled and her eyes met Kerrianne's, but not for long, and Kerrianne was aware that she was not welcome here. There would be no overtures of friendship. But why? Elizabeth seemed like a nice woman who loved her son and grandchildren. Why wouldn't she want what could make them happy? Did she suspect Kerrianne's motives?

Good thing I don't have any. But even as the thought came, she looked toward Ryan and felt a softening within her.

The green room was much more than its name implied. All but one wall was made of glass, angled upwards where it joined the main house, and the numerous plants grew with a vigor that told of careful tending. Kerrianne wasn't familiar with most of the houseplants as she was more of an outdoor gardener with a particular interest in plants that bore edible fruit, but she could appreciate the effort Elizabeth so obviously put forth. She loved the tiles on the floor, and though cream rugs seemed rather excessive, they did match nicely. The patio furniture was perfect, and so was the recessed lighting.

"It's very lovely," Kerrianne said. "I've never seen a room so lovely. Thanks for letting me come and take a peek."

Elizabeth warmed toward her slightly after that, and the two sat and chatted amicably about plants for a while. The boys began wrestling in the far corner, dangerously near a large potted plant sitting on an elaborate stand. Elizabeth began paying only partial attention to the conversation as her eyes were drawn time and time again back to the boys. Kerrianne looked at Ryan, expecting him to do something, but he sat obliviously at the oblong table next to Ria, who was pounding her fist into her mitt. Misty sat daintily on the edge of her chair, trying to ignore both of them.

"Boys!" Kerrianne used her kindest I-mean-business voice. "Come here. You're going to topple that plant. I've got something here for you." She reached into her purse and drew out several large plastic zip bags with puzzle pieces inside.

"So Ryan tells me you're looking to buy a greenhouse," Elizabeth said, relaxing now that the boys were away from her beloved plants.

Kerrianne laughed. "Yeah, someday. I want to see what kind of vegetables I can raise all year long. I'm thinking I'll try some flowers, too."

"How nice." Elizabeth smiled again, and this time it was wider.

"They're costly, though." Kerrianne gave a shrug. "But I think things will work out somehow."

"How do you think—" Elizabeth broke off.

Kerrianne followed her gaze and saw Ryan's father stride into the room. Sterling Oakman gave them all a courteous smile that did not reach his eyes. He resembled Ryan in the cut of his face and the gray eyes, making it apparent they were father and son, but Sterling's eyes were deeper set, and there was an austere edge to his expression that Ryan didn't have. Kerrianne hadn't thought Ryan looked anything like his mother, but he'd apparently received something from her in the shape of his face, and Kerrianne was glad. His was a face that could laugh. Sterling senior didn't look as though he'd spent much time laughing. His hair was also black like Ryan's but scattered with gray that matched the iron in his eyes.

Only as Elizabeth made the introductions did Kerrianne realize Sterling was not alone. "This is our older son, Willard," Elizabeth said.

"Hello. Nice to meet you." Willard held out a hand and shook hers vigorously.

"You, too." Kerrianne was grateful at least for his exuberance, though she couldn't help comparing the two brothers. Willard looked soft and weak by comparison, and his eyes held no power over her, though he stared at her overlong. Willard didn't resemble either of his parents to any degree, though there was a slight family resemblance, as though he were a cousin or a nephew. She remembered Ryan saying something about his being a lawyer.

"Well, now that we're all here, how about a snack?" Elizabeth glanced in her husband's direction, and Kerrianne wondered if she was checking to make sure he didn't object. There was no doubt about who was in control here.

After greeting his father and brother, Ryan had sat down on the floor with the boys and began helping them with their puzzles. Kerrianne saw Sterling glance his son's way and thought there was a tightening of his mouth, but she may have imagined it.

"Oh, please," Kerrianne said, "don't go to any trouble on our part. Really, it was nice of you to just let us come."

"No trouble at all," Sterling said, indicating to his wife that she should bring in the food. "You've driven an hour, haven't you? And it'll be another going back. You'll need refreshments."

Kerrianne didn't let his gruff manner put her off. She owed them nothing, wanted nothing from them. Besides, growing up in her bustling family everyone had learned to stick up for themselves, or get lost in the crowd. All the Huntingtons were fighters.

"Thank you," she said, giving him her best smile. "I'm sure the children would enjoy that. Do you need a hand, Elizabeth?"

Halfway to the door, Elizabeth darted another quick glance toward her husband. "No, but thank you. It's all ready. I'll just bring it in."

"You help your mother," Sterling told Willard.

Willard seemed momentarily disgruntled but jumped to do his father's bidding.

"So," Sterling fixed his steely eyes on her when they'd left, "how did you meet my son?"

It was as if he'd asked "What are your intentions?"

"He delivers my mail. But we didn't really start talking until I saw him in a play. He's a great actor."

There, that tightening of the mouth again, and this time she was sure it wasn't her imagination. "Well, I guess," Sterling said rather carelessly.

Ryan left the puzzles to come and sit by her, moving his chair until it touched hers.

Sterling's eyes narrowed. "So that's how it is," he seemed to say. Kerrianne didn't move away, though Misty was staring at her intently. So was Ria, her face stretched in a wide grin.

"Kerrianne used to act in high school. I'm trying to get her to try out for the next play."

"I see." Sterling obviously wasn't impressed.

Ryan raised his eyebrows a couple times. "I'm trying out for one of the leads, and I'm hoping she'll play opposite me. It's a romantic plot."

Ria giggled, and Kerrianne felt a hot flush sweep over her face. She fought it down. "*A Midsummer Night's Dream* really isn't that romantic," she said. "I mean, all the men are fickle."

"Only because of the magic," Ryan protested.

"I'm going to try out for Puck," Ria put in. She had stood up when her grandfather entered the room and hardly seemed to care when he chose to sit in her seat. Now she hovered near his elbow, slamming her fist into her glove.

Kerrianne gave her a big smile. "You'd make a wonderful Puck."

Sterling's face darkened further, and Kerrianne was glad to see Elizabeth and Willard coming back into the room. Willard carried a large silver tray of dishes and Elizabeth pushed a serving cart made of dark wood. Kerrianne saw plates of finger sandwiches, a variety of tiny cookies, a relish plate, and a tray of sliced fruits. It was a nice display, one similar to what she might have served. The only thing Elizabeth had omitted was fresh raspberries for the lemonade.

"Uh, Grandpa," Ria said hesitantly, as though it was a new thing for her to address him so boldly, "do you want to play catch?" Hope shown in her bright face, and Kerrianne's heart went out to her. She hated to think of Sterling disappointing her, as she was sure he would. No matter that Ria had mentioned something about playing ball with him before, Sterling simply wasn't the type of man to toss a ball with a child. That was another place he differed greatly from his son.

Sterling looked at Ria for a several seconds, as if trying to understand her request. Then he looked down at his dress slacks and white shirt but only fleetingly. With amazement Kerrianne watched his face soften. "Sure," he said. "After we eat something, we'll go outside. Did you bring the ball?"

She nodded. "Dad made me leave it in my coat pocket."

Kerrianne felt relieved, and she let go of the breath she hadn't realized she was holding. She glanced at Ryan and saw a longing on his face, as though he, too, wished he could play ball with his father.

Willard set down his tray. He pulled up a chair nearly as close to Kerrianne as Ryan was sitting. He turned his gaze on her face with an abruptness that startled her. "So," he said, "where are you from?"

She saw her first impression had been wrong. He did resemble Ryan more than she thought, but the heaviness in his face hid the similarities. Still, he was a washed-out version—his gray eyes were not as dark, nor his hair, and his skin was pasty from lack of exposure to the sun. He made up for his physical lack in witty conversation. Before Kerrianne knew what was happening, Willard's verbal gymnastics put all the adults as ease. Sterling entered the conversation, as did Elizabeth. The feeling in the air became more cordial.

Okay, so maybe his family isn't all that bad, Kerrianne thought. She bet Willard was a good lawyer.

The boys were so busy eating that they were quiet for a change. Elizabeth seemed impressed with Misty and her delicate manners as she sipped her lemonade without spilling and daintily nibbled at her cookies. Several times Kerrianne caught Elizabeth shaking her head as Ria stuffed cookies into her mouth exactly like the boys.

"Such a sweet little girl," Elizabeth said of Misty, who beamed at her praise.

The talk drifted to world events, where Kerrianne felt comfortable adding her opinion. This was similar to talk they'd have at her own parents' table, and she'd read up enough to not feel stupid with her comments. Sterling seemed to purposely set up the conversation to make her look like a fool, but Kerrianne sidestepped him every time with facts her brother had written in the newspaper. Ryan's grin grew wider with each attempt. When Willard and Sterling began talking business, she didn't mind because she'd watched enough lawyer shows to be familiar with the jargon. She actually asked a question or two—when she was sure it sounded reasonably intelligent.

Ryan was the only one who remained quiet throughout the meal, and at times there was a wariness in his eyes that unnerved her, as though he waited for something unpleasant to happen.

Eventually, Sterling steered the conversation back to Kerrianne. "So where did you go to college?"

"BYU. Well, for a year at least."

"Only one?" Sterling asked, his face unreadable.

The question surprised her. "What?" she asked, stalling for time.

"So you only attended one year of college."

"More or less." She felt nervous enough to offer an explanation, though it was really none of his business. "My husband and I got married, and he was working on his master's, so I decided to work to help ends meet. Besides, we wanted to have children right away." She didn't add that the real reason she'd quit was because she hated school. She'd wanted to be a mother, to make a home for her husband and children, though Misty hadn't come along for several years. By then Adam had a job as an assistant principal. After that, the boys had followed in two-year intervals. Quitting school was the one regret she didn't have. If they'd waited to have children, and she had taken as long as she had to conceive Misty, she might have had nothing left of Adam with her now. The thought was unbearable.

"I see," Sterling said. There was no inflection in the words, but Kerrianne saw him exchange a knowing look with Elizabeth and had the feeling she'd failed some sort of test.

"Ryan here went all the way," Willard said. "He graduated in general education, though. Couldn't decide what he wanted to do."

"Oh, I knew what I wanted to do." Ryan leaned back in his chair, eyes glittering and looking much like his father's steely stare. "Just because it wasn't what everyone else wanted . . ." He trailed off, almost a challenge.

"Boys," Elizabeth said without strength.

Sterling's brow furrowed. "Ria, let's go toss the ball." The way he said it was a dismissal—of them all, but mostly Kerrianne and Ryan.

Ria scrambled for her coat, which she had retrieved from the entry-way and placed near her chair. She followed her grandfather out the glass door in the outer wall of the green room. The boys saw them going and followed in a wave.

"Coats first," Kerrianne called.

They groaned, but all of them obeyed, even Tiger.

"Aren't you going with them?" Elizabeth asked Misty.

"I'd rather not, if that's okay."

Elizabeth smiled. "Perfectly okay. Would you like another cookie?"

"Yes, please." Misty took one from the proffered dish.

Once outside, the boys began a game of their own in the corner of the spacious yard. Kerrianne wasn't surprised; she didn't see Sterling as someone who could muster much patience for little boys. She wondered what kind of life Ryan and Willard had endured growing up.

"I guess you've heard by now that I'm a lawyer," Willard said when the boys were gone, as though there had been no interruption or cause for concern.

"Ryan told me. But I would have guessed anyway by the fast way you talk." Kerrianne hadn't meant to say the last sentence aloud. "I mean," she hurried to add, "that you have a way with words."

Next to her Ryan grinned, making her stomach warm. She wasn't fooling him. He knew Willard's glib manner didn't impress her.

"A lawyer like your father," she babbled, trying to cover her physical response to Ryan's grin. "I bet that takes a lot of schooling."

Willard smiled. "You can say that again. It took years. But that's nothing compared to the overtime I had to put in *after* I became a lawyer. Some weeks, I barely slept at home."

His comment reminded Kerrianne of how Adam had decided to earn his doctorate, and how she had hadn't been happy at the prospect of raising the children by herself while he lived evenings at the college campus. Strange how she hadn't recalled that until now. She remembered resenting his assumption that she'd be supportive, as she'd always had been. Wouldn't he have understood if she'd confided in him? He'd always listened to her and put their family first. Yet she doubted she would have ever told him of her concern. That wasn't who she'd been back then. Neither would she have confessed how worried she'd been at the possibility of his outgrowing her altogether.

"I knew that sacrifice would bring success," Willard continued. "Everyone knows that while education is the key, work is the vehicle. Of course, some have the key but choose to walk." He smirked at Ryan.

"As you can tell, we take education and work seriously in this family," Ryan said mockingly. He lounged in his seat, looking out between half-closed eyes, an amused expression on his face. But he was far from amused. Kerrianne didn't know how she knew that, but she did. She was glad. He obviously didn't like the tone of Willard's comments, either.

"Even Mom graduated in English, didn't you, Mom?" Willard's tone was patronizing.

Elizabeth nodded. She looked uncertainly from each of her sons and then outside the glass windows where her husband tossed the ball with Ria. She didn't speak.

Kerrianne felt an urge to tell them that her three siblings had graduated from college, that her mother had gone back for her degree after the children had left home, that her father held two degrees, and that Adam, if he'd lived, would have had his doctorate by now. Her family also placed a high value on education.

Yet none of that really mattered, and she refused to play whatever game they were playing. Her family would never use their education to inflate their own importance.

"So, are you married?" Kerrianne asked Willard, more to change the subject than for anything else.

There was a silence for the space of several heartbeats. "Willard is divorced," Ryan said, sitting up. "Recently."

"We'd been drifting apart for a long time." Willard's bored voice dismissed his ex-wife as nothing of consequence.

"She was a good woman," Ryan countered.

Willard bristled. "You don't know what it was like."

"I knew what it was like for her." Ryan met his brother's eyes as Elizabeth clenched her hands together on the table.

The drama was too much for Kerrianne. She was glad she'd come to see the green room because of the ideas it had given her for her own greenhouse, but she was not impressed by Ryan's family. That was too bad because she'd really hoped to like them—and to have them like her.

"Excuse me," she said, addressing Elizabeth. "Could I use your bathroom? It's going to be a long drive home." She wished she didn't have to ask, but after three children, her bladder wasn't what it had been.

"Yes, out the door and to your right."

Kerrianne looked at Ryan. "We have to make sure the kids use the bathroom before we leave."

"You want me to call them in now?"

Kerrianne was glad he'd understood the point of her comment—she'd like to leave as soon as possible. She glanced outside at the boys, squatting down and huddled together on the grass laughing, and her resolve softened. "They'll be in soon," she said. "It's really cold out there. And Ria looks like she's having too much fun."

"We'll let her have a few more minutes, then."

Kerrianne escaped, glad to get away from Willard and Elizabeth . . . and even Ryan.

A few minutes later she returned, but the green room was deserted except for Misty who was standing by a tall plant and looking outside at Ria and the boys.

"They're in the kitchen," Misty informed her. "Cleaning up."

The cart was gone, as was the silver tray. Only a few used glasses still littered the table. Kerrianne gathered them up and went to find the kitchen. "I'll be right back, sweetie."

Misty shrugged and turned again to watch the other children.

The house was even larger than it looked, and Kerrianne passed through several sitting rooms until she heard voices. Ryan's came first.

"I don't know why you guys can't be a little more . . . nice."

"We've been nice." Elizabeth's voice was still soft but had taken on an affronted edge. "Whatever are you talking about?"

"Oh, you're nice on the surface, but . . . I just wish you could . . ." He stopped, apparently unable to find the right words.

"Well, you can't be serious about her," Willard said. "She's got three kids."

"Three great kids." Ryan's retorted. "And in case you hadn't noticed, I have two of my own."

"Hey, go out, have a little fun with her, but why would you want to take on so much responsibility—especially on your salary?"

"It all boils down to that, doesn't it?" Ryan was angry now, and Kerrianne winced at the hurt in his voice. "When will you finally understand, Willard, that a man's value isn't related to an oversized paycheck? I can support my family very well, thank you very much. Maybe not in a house like this, but it's good enough. And meanwhile, I'll actually be around to raise *my* children."

"But Ryan, what about those girls I had here last week?" His mother said in a placating tone. "Colleen and MaryAnn are our kind of people, and I know they were interested in you."

"What do you mean 'our kind of people?' What's that? Rich people? Educated people? Single people? Intolerant people? And how do you know what kind of people Kerrianne is? She's smart, she's funny, and did you see the way she handles those kids?"

"I'm not saying anything bad about your friend, dear. I'm just saying what about those other girls? Your father particularly liked Colleen."

"He'd like Kerrianne if he'd let himself. Did you see the way she was part of the conversation while we were eating? She knows what's going on in the world and isn't afraid to voice her opinion. That is something you should admire, if nothing else."

Elizabeth didn't react to the pointed remark. "But Colleen's family is—" Elizabeth began again.

"I don't care a fig about Colleen's family!"

"I do," Willard said. "I'm glad you're staying away. I asked her out. She's beautiful."

Ryan gave a snort. "You're welcome to her. Once she heard I wasn't a lawyer, she wasn't interested in me anyway. Besides, she's not nearly as beautiful as Kerrianne."

"Maybe," Willard agreed, "but three kids?"

"What about MaryAnn?" Elizabeth pressed.

Ryan hesitated, and his next words dug deep into Kerrianne's heart. "She seemed like a nice girl." MaryAnn must have made a good impression upon him.

"Then you'll go out with her?" Elizabeth was breathless. "Your father will be so pleased. I can call her tonight. Maybe invite her to Thanksgiving."

It was the wrong thing to say. Ryan exploded. "Would you listen to what I'm trying to say! *I'm* the one making the decisions here. I can handle—"

Whistling loudly, Kerrianne forced herself through the door. "Hello," she said brightly, holding out the glasses. "I brought the rest of the dishes."

She met Elizabeth's gaze steadily, and it was Elizabeth who looked away, her face turning crimson. Willard stared at the floor.

Ryan gaped at her, but she just winked. "It's time to go. Let's get the kids."

Ten minutes later they were at the door with their coats on, ready to leave. Ryan opened the front door, and the children spilled out like prisoners escaping from a jail, the boys jumping and hooting in chorus.

Kerrianne offered her hand to Elizabeth. "Thank you for having us. It was . . . enlightening." She couldn't say "pleasure" because it certainly hadn't been one. She nodded at Willard and at Sterling, who seemed rather surprised they were leaving so quickly, though not unhappy at the prospect. "Nice to meet you," she said. One little white lie seemed to be in order here.

Kerrianne wanted to hate them all. Disliking Willard was easy—he was annoying, self-centered, and condescending. But what about Elizabeth and Sterling? Elizabeth had been so kind to Misty, and Kerrianne knew Ryan loved his mother. There must be some basis for that. Yet Elizabeth was also spineless and snobbish, qualities Kerrianne abhorred. As for Sterling, well, she found little to redeem that over-bearing man—except his playing ball with Ria. She couldn't forget he'd given Ria that much. Still, Kerrianne hoped she wouldn't have to see any of them again.

Yes, in all, the day had been enlightening. Seeing where he'd come from had taught her a lot about Ryan, and she admired him even more than she had before. He'd been raised by worldly parents but had the strength and the courage to follow his own dreams. To have values that weren't skewed by the world.

She liked that.

She liked him. Maybe too much.

She put the key in the ignition and started the car. Suddenly Ryan's hand covered hers on the steering wheel. Warmth tingled up her entire arm. "You want me to drive?" he asked.

"No," she said. "I'm too mad to let anyone drive."

He grinned. "Funny. That's the way I always feel when I leave here."

She laughed, feeling slightly better.

Better, that is, until she thought of the unknown MaryAnn, the nice girl who had the blessing of Ryan's difficult family.

Chapter Sixteen

R yan enjoyed watching Kerrianne drive, though he tried not to stare or let her know how her movements fascinated him. He loved how she checked the rearview mirror just before she whipped her head around to peek at her blind spot, hair fanning out over her shoulders. Her hands as they turned the wheel into traffic were graceful and sure, much like her entire attitude. When the kids became too noisy, she ordered them to a respectable level with a measured few sentences. He could learn a thing or two from her, that was sure.

He felt a keen disappointment that his family had not risen above his expectations, though why he should be disappointed he could hardly say. They'd acted exactly as he predicted—not one iota worse. If he'd been foolish enough to harbor any hope of his family helping him win Kerrianne over, that hope would have been in vain.

Kerrianne, on the other hand, had exceeded all his expectations. She hadn't been a fragile, wimpy creature but a strong, capable woman sure of her own ability. Her behavior compared with that of his family was almost noble. Now he understood more fully why he hadn't been able to stop thinking about her for one minute since the play.

He was glad he'd presented her as a friend. If he'd said instead, "This is the woman I'm falling in love with" his family's reaction might have been more pronounced—not to mention that he'd have risked scaring Kerrianne away. Because he didn't think she was ready to admit that they weren't friends, not in the real sense. There was an unspeakable knowledge between them that this was something more, possibly much, much more. He chafed at the restrictions he felt, yet at the same time he didn't want to do anything to ruin what their relationship might become.

"I'm sorry," he said when she had steered the van onto the freeway.

She glanced over at him. "For what?"

"For how they acted—all of it."

"You warned me." She smiled. "But I'll be honest with you. I can't see how you came from that family."

"I'm the black sheep."

She laughed. "Maybe in this case that's a good thing." She fell quiet, stretching her neck to check the children in the rearview mirror.

"They've been out of the Church for many years," he said, feeling somehow that he had to excuse them. "They're coming back now, I think."

"That's good. But that's still no excuse to—" She broke off.

"You can say it. Go ahead."

"I feel sad about them. Your brother particularly. He's really full of himself, isn't he? And you know what? I think it's only fair to tell you that the reason I didn't finish school wasn't because I didn't have the opportunity. Adam wanted me to finish." Her voice lowered so the children wouldn't hear. "I didn't finish because I hated it. I wasn't a very good reader, and it was hard to keep up."

Ryan considered her confession. "I didn't like school, either. Well, I loved learning, but I hated the classroom."

"Yeah, that was it, too."

"Some people learn in different ways."

"That's what my mother says." She changed lanes before adding,

"I've been thinking about going back, though. Maybe take an independent course or two. See how it is now. My mother said she liked it better the second time around."

"I did a course last year. Musical theater. It was fun."

"You sing, too?"

"Well, actually not too well. I barely passed the course."

They laughed, and afterward there was silence again, but it wasn't one of the uncomfortable silences that had fallen at his parents' house.

"I suppose you'll go to your parents for Thanksgiving," she said.

"Not if I can find a way out." He gave an exaggerated sigh.

"I don't know. There might be a cute girl or two in it for you."

He groaned, sending a thousand mental darts at his mother. "You can be sure I'm not going, then." He was half hoping Kerrianne would invite him to her family's party but hesitated to push her for an invitation. If his mother did decide to invite other families with eligible daughters, he'd simply stay home. He'd seen some TV turkey dinners that didn't look half bad. While they ate, they could watch sports on TV, and that would please Ria.

"Oh, that reminds me." He peeked around his seat to make sure Ria, way in the back, was engrossed in conversation. "About that Thanksgiving tea at the school. It's this Tuesday, right?" When she nodded, he continued, "I've been wondering. What do you think Ria should wear? If all the other girls are wearing dresses . . . I mean, she's always been a tomboy, but lately . . ." He shrugged. "Well, lately, I just don't understand her."

"She doesn't have any dresses?"

"Just a skirt she wears to church. She changes the minute she gets home."

"I see. Let me think about it a minute. I might have an idea."

The conversation moved on. All too soon they had arrived at Kerrianne's where Ryan's green truck was parked out front.

"Good!" Misty muttered. She jumped from the van as Kerrianne brought it to a halt in the garage and headed into the house.

Kerrianne's lips tightened. "Now I'm the one to apologize. She's not normally this way. I wish she and Ria could be friends."

"It's okay. Give them time."

Kerrianne looked at him, her movements stilling, her eyes staring into his, as though trying to understand what he'd said.

What had he said?

Give her time.

Then he knew. Time meant being around. Time indicated a type of permanence.

The boys had all scrambled from the car and followed Misty into the house. Ria was going after them, but more slowly.

For Ryan no one existed but Kerrianne. They sat there in the van, each searching the face of the other. His eyes fell to her lips.

She swallowed hard and pulled back, a movement so slow and smooth that he almost didn't see it. "I think," she said, in a low voice, "I might have something for Ria to wear to the tea party. I've gathered a bunch of costumes for my preschool, and a few are too big for my preschoolers. Ria's thin enough that a few adjustments might . . . well, I'll check tomorrow and let you know."

He nodded, but his thoughts were elsewhere. "Kerrianne," he said, his voice low.

Her eyes were large and luminous, deep blue in the dim light of the garage. Ryan moved closer. The widening of her eyes stopped him cold, and he knew without a doubt that she wasn't ready. He didn't know how long it would be before she would be—an hour, a day, a week, a month—but now wasn't the right time. Moving away and opening his door was one of the hardest things he'd done in a year.

"So, you guys have a good time?" he asked Ria and Tiger as they climbed into the truck a few minutes later.

"Great!" Tiger said. "I love Caleb and Benjamin. I didn't even care that we had to go to Grandma's house."

"Good. I'm glad."

"Caleb and I are going to play Indians at preschool tomorrow. He says we get a recess. We're going to be the Indians and scare all the girls." Tiger talked on, his loud voice filling the entire cab. Ria was noticeably quiet.

"What's wrong, honey?" Ryan asked her when Tiger finally paused for breath.

She shrugged. "Nothing."

"Did you have fun with Grandpa?"

Again, she shrugged, staring down at her lap where her fingers twisted together.

Ryan pulled to the curb and let the engine idle. "I can't try to fix it if you won't talk to me."

She mumbled something under her breath. Ryan caught the words "tea party."

"That reminds me," he said, guessing at her concern and praying he was right. "I was talking to Kerrianne and she said something about having some dress-up costumes that you might want to wear to the tea party." Then, in case that didn't sound good, he added quickly, "Or we could go pick out a dress, if you'd like."

Ria looked up at him, her hazel eyes bright. "She has a dress-up dress? Like a princess or something?" She looked away, lifting one shoulder in a careless gesture. "I'm not really into that, but I could look at them."

Tenderness welled up in Ryan's heart, and he had to fight tears. "When I pick you up from Maxine's, we'll go over and see what she has. And if you don't like it, we'll find something else. You'll be the prettiest girl at the tea party." That was her cue to snort and correct him, saying she'd be the fastest girl or the best at basketball, but this time there was no correction. Apparently being a girl was becoming more important to her. He'd have to take her shopping for clothes soon and see what he could do about that.

"Misty has a lot of dress-ups," Ria said. "She'll look pretty, too." The statement came without envy, for which Ryan was glad.

"Yeah, too bad she's so mean," Tiger grumbled.

"She's just worried," Ryan said. "I mean, Kerrianne likes you two a lot."

Tiger's eyes went wide. "Better than Misty?"

"No, but maybe that's what Misty's afraid of."

Ria leaned into him. "I feel sorry for her. She doesn't do anything that's fun. She doesn't like sports. Do you think that's because she doesn't have a dad?"

"I don't know. Maybe."

"You really like Kerrianne, don't you?" Ria looked up at him hopefully.

"Yeah. Does that bother you?"

"Not really. She's nice. I think I'm going to grow my hair out like hers."

"But you hate your hair long."

"Not anymore."

Will wonders never cease? Ryan thought as he reached for the steering wheel again. Apparently not. Because at that moment he saw something in the backyard of the house where they were parked. He knew the older couple who lived here since they were now only two streets from their own house.

"Look at that," he said, pointing.

"A greenhouse?" Ria asked.

"Yes. A greenhouse."

"I wanna see it!" Tiger climbed over Ria and into Ryan's lap for a better view.

"Come on," Ryan said, opening his door. "Let's go take a look." He whistled as they went up the walk. He might have found exactly what Kerrianne was looking for.

Chapter Seventeen

Kerrianne laid out the dresses on the table, looking them over. Some were worse for wear, but one or two held promise, though transforming them would take considerable sewing skills. Fortunately, she was up to the task. After the children left for school, she would start. There should be enough time to make over at least one of them before she had to teach preschool.

"Mom, what are you doing?" Misty asked, when she began laying out her sewing materials.

"Ria needs something to wear for the Thanksgiving tea party."

Misty frowned. "Can't she wear one of her own dresses?"

Kerrianne sat down next to her daughter. "That's the problem. She doesn't have any dresses. Just one skirt." She held a finger to her lips. "And that's between you and me. I don't want you to tell that to anyone else."

"But why doesn't she have any?"

"She's never liked them. But now she wants to fit in with the rest of the girls."

"Then she should stop acting like a boy!"

Kerrianne stared at Misty for a long moment. "Honey, this isn't like

194

you. How would you feel if you didn't have a dress to wear? Pretty awful, wouldn't you?"

Misty dropped her eyes to the costumes, nodding once.

"But you have a half dozen nice dresses up there in your closet to choose from. And you know what? I was going to ask if you'd lend Ria one for the day, but with the way you've been acting toward her, I knew that wasn't going to happen." She shook her head. "I'm surprised, because in the old days, the Misty I knew would have found out about her needing a dress and would have already lent her one."

Misty continued to stare at the costumes, a tear starting down her cheek.

"Oh, honey, don't cry." Kerrianne pulled Misty to her and hugged the girl tight. "I love you so much. That's why I can't stand to see you unhappy. Sweetie, don't you understand that we need to love everyone? Ria's a daughter of our Heavenly Father just like you and me, and that makes her our sister."

The boys chose that moment to tumble down the stairs where they'd been dressing. Misty wiped away her tears and walked to the counter where Kerrianne had laid the bowls for oatmeal. She was quiet as they ate, but the boys more than made up for her silence.

"Mom, what time is it?" Caleb asked, shoveling a loaded spoon into his mouth. "Iwannapaybulwidrhine."

"What?"

He swallowed. "I want to play ball with Ryan."

"No," she said. "You'll see him later. It's freezing out there. I don't want you sick." She herself had the beginnings of a cough, and she wasn't taking any chances with Caleb. The last thing she wanted was a whole preschool of sick children. Thank heaven she had only two days of class this week.

Popping a cough drop into her mouth, she helped Misty and Benjamin gather their things and get out to the bus, looking like round balls bundled up in their thick winter coats. The cold was so intense that it hurt Kerrianne's throat. Glancing at the mailbox she wondered how Ryan could stand being out in this weather all day. She was glad she only had to wait here until the bus picked up the kids. When they were gone, she went inside and made a mug of hot chocolate. Then she wrote a note.

Caleb stared with interest. "Mom, can I have some?"

"It's not for me."

Pulling on her long black sweater and her slippers, she walked out to the mailbox while Caleb watched from the window. She put the mug of chocolate into the box and then sprinted back up to the house.

The air was freezing, reminding Ryan more of a winter day in early February than November. His hands were still warm inside his gloves, but he knew in a few hours they'd be stiff with cold. The skin on one or both would eventually split, causing days of pain. Maybe it was time to apply for that night management position at East Bay. No more days in the cold, and he'd be home all day and evening in case the children needed him. The only drawback was that he didn't like the idea of leaving them all night with a sitter, though they'd be asleep and wouldn't know it. He shook his head. No, East Bay didn't feel right.

At the same time, he felt he should pursue some new avenue for work. But what? If he talked to Kerrianne about it, he bet she'd say the Lord would provide a way. Thinking of her greenhouse, he had to grin. The Lord had certainly provided there. He couldn't wait to surprise her.

He reached her house, a half hour later than normal, though he'd worked rapidly through Monday's deluge of mail. He looked instinctively toward the porch. She wasn't there, causing him a moment of stabbing disappointment. Well, he didn't blame her. It was really cold out.

Was that a movement at her window? No, just a trick of the light.

Her box wasn't shut tight, and it practically fell open as he brought up his hand. Surprise coursed through his veins, followed by a rush of giddiness he hadn't felt since he married Laurie. Inside the mailbox was a large mug of steaming hot chocolate, filled nearly to the brim. He was glad she hadn't shut the box tightly or the liquid might have sloshed over when he yanked it open. The mug was warm in his hands, and the chocolate heated him from the inside, staving off the cold.

There was also a note: *Hey, Mister Mailman. I confess. I've been using this mailbox for my own nefarious purposes. I know it's against the law. Haven't you got to turn me in?*

He laughed and stared up at the house again. He was filled with an irresistible desire to march up her steps, bang on her door until she opened it, and give her a great big kiss—whether or not she was ready for it!

He was halfway to the door before he came to his senses. He was at work, not on his own time, and he'd learned well through the years that neighbors were always watching. Besides, the way he was feeling, he'd probably do something stupid like propose to her, and she'd pack and move to Brazil.

Heart thudding in his chest, he forced himself back into the mail truck, and drove to the next house.

❄ ❄ ❄

Before preschool, Kerrianne managed to fix up not one but both dressups for Ria, using Misty's size as a guideline, except for the height, which she increased for Ria. The finished dresses really didn't look as good as she'd hoped, though she doubted Ria would notice. Still, maybe she'd tell Ryan to buy her one. With Christmas around the corner, there would likely be some available in the stores. Of course, one evening wasn't a lot of time to find something Ria might like. Too bad Ryan hadn't thought of it earlier.

"Mommy, Mommy, Tiger's here!" Caleb called from the front window where he'd been watching for his friend. "He's coming up the front walk!"

Tiger didn't know yet that the preschool children were supposed to walk in her garage door and go directly downstairs to the rooms she'd finished in the basement. She'd have to remember to tell him.

Kerrianne went to open the front door for Ryan and Tiger, who was jumping up and down with excitement. Caleb pulled him into the house and they disappeared.

"Come in." She shut the door as he entered.

"I won't stay long. I know the other kids'll be here soon. I'm sorry I'm a little early. I'm on my lunch break."

"That's fine—really."

His face sobered. "We have something serious to talk about."

"Oh?" Her heart thumped loudly in her chest. She wasn't sure she was ready to talk about their relationship. At the same time, she would be glad to have it all out in the open. He had to understand that there really wasn't room for him in her heart.

"Yes." His mouth twitched, but he maintained his grave expression. "Now, I know I've told you before that though you purchased your mailbox and put it up yourself, your mailbox is still the property of the U.S. Postal Service, and by law it can't be used for anything but official business."

She nearly laughed out loud, from both relief and amusement. "It can't?" she asked, matching his seriousness.

Again the twitch of his mouth as he fought a smile. His gray eyes were warm like metal baked in the sun. "I'm going to have to turn you in, ma'am."

"I see," she said. "That's too bad, because my hot chocolate really is the best. I have a secret ingredient, you know."

"I do know." He took a step closer. Kerrianne would have stepped back but she was already against the wall. "That's why I'm willing to make an exception in this case," he continued.

"I'm glad you see it that way."

He was very close now, and the energy between them was so strong that all her nerves hummed with tension, screamed out to *do* something. Anything.

A kiss?

No, I don't want to kiss anyone but Adam.

Liar.

"We're willing to let it go this time," Ryan said. "However, the U.S. Postal Service must receive something in return." His grin broke through now but only for an instant.

Kerrianne put her hands on her hips. "And what might that be?"

Ryan shook his head in an exaggerated motion. "I'm not sure. Do you have any suggestions?"

Kerrianne could think of only one at the moment, one Adam certainly wouldn't approve of. "No," she whispered. *Kiss me!* she thought.

As though reading the thought in her eyes, Ryan's head dipped and their lips met. Softly, ever so softly, and then with more firmness. Kerrianne's head swirled with emotion. His hand went to the back of her neck, pulling her closer. All she wanted was for the kiss to continue forever. But what about Adam? Guiltily, she broke away.

Ryan gave a soft whistle. "I don't know, ma'am. That could be misconstrued as bribery, plain and simple. But we could try again just to be sure."

She laughed, sidestepping him. "Come and see these costumes. I hope Ria will like them."

"I'm sure she will." Disappointment wreathed his voice. He wasn't looking at the costumes—his gaze was fixed on her face. Kerrianne blushed. She heard the strand of Christmas bells ring on the back door, the one she always put there before preschool so she'd know when the kids began arriving. "That's a student," she said.

"I'd better get going, then. See you tonight. In fact, I have a surprise for you." His voice was full of—what? Promise? Tenderness? Frustration? Maybe a little of all three. He left before she had time to ask him who would be coming for Tiger at two.

Blowing out a short breath, she headed for the freezer for just a bite of semisweet baking chocolate before going downstairs.

Bernice arrived five minutes after preschool let out, looking somber in her usual gray. All the children were gone except Tiger, Caleb, and

Bernice's grandson Michael. Bernice didn't leave immediately but hovered near Kerrianne. "Look," she began, "about the other night at the dance."

"It's okay. Really—it's forgotten." Kerrianne felt embarrassed about her outburst now. She'd meant every word at the time but everything seemed brighter today.

"Well, I still don't think we should forget our husbands," Bernice said, "but I didn't want to cause you any pain. I know what it's like to be lonely."

Kerrianne decided that was the best apology she'd ever get from Bernice.

"Hello, ladies." Maxine was coming down the stairs, looking chic in a purple designer jogging suit. Kerrianne wondered why Maxine had stopped in. Maybe she'd come for the Primary manual, since it was her turn to teach their shared class next week.

Bernice looked at Maxine. "So," she said.

"Hello, Bernice." Maxine's voice was pleasant. "Did you do something different with your hair? It looks lovely."

Preoccupied with her own life, Kerrianne hadn't even noticed. Bernice's tightly permed hair had been blown dry or curled in such a way that the gray locks were nearly straight, puffing up at the scalp and curving slightly under near the ends, a short version of Maxine's style. The effect with the lighter makeup she was wearing did wonders for her pinched look.

"It's great!" Kerrianne said. "Wow." She didn't add that it took at least five years off Bernice's age.

"Now about the color," Maxine started to say. "Coloring your hair makes you feel like a new person. I was telling Kerrianne here the other day that my hairdresser is positively the best—"

"I don't want to color my hair!" Kerrianne and Bernice spoke in unison and then laughed.

Kerrianne felt like someone new already. After all, she'd kissed a man today. She still couldn't believe she'd done it. *What do you think of that, Adam?*

She got the feeling Adam didn't care about her hair, but he might just care about her kissing Ryan. So why did she want to do it again? *Think of Ryan's parents,* she thought. She didn't want to ever have to deal with them again.

"Well, I'd better get going. I have an appointment." Bernice took Michael's coat from a hook. "Come on, Michael. Let's get you back to your mom."

"See ya," Michael mumbled to the boys, and followed his grandma up the stairs.

Kerrianne sat down in her chair and began gathering the puzzle Michael had been working on. She glanced up at Maxine, wondering again why she was here. Could she be planning to drag Kerrianne to another dance? She smiled at the prospect. "So, Maxine, what brings you here?"

"I'm here for Tiger," Maxine said, as if it were the most natural thing in the world.

"Tiger?" Kerrianne repeated.

"Ryan wasn't sure if he'd be able to find someone to pick him up, so he asked me."

"I see." Kerrianne was surprised at the sting she felt that Ryan hadn't asked her. Why would she care? She'd told him the preschool hours and hadn't offered anything more. In fact, in the handout she'd given him, she'd mentioned the rule that parents had to pick up their children by five minutes after the hour unless they wanted to be charged an extra fee. In the days before that rule parents would often come to get their children as much as half an hour late. She should be grateful he wasn't the kind of parent to take advantage of her.

The truth was she didn't mind having Tiger around. Once she'd become accustomed to the loud way he yelled practically everything he said, she'd discovered a sweet little boy who seemed to enjoy sitting at her side and asking questions as much as he loved wrestling with

Caleb. During preschool the boys had been inseparable. Caleb had helped Tiger with anything he needed—showing him where the crayon boxes were, explaining the sounds of the first ten letters, and saving him a place at the table. Together they had terrorized the girls at recess, to the girls' delight, and the other boys enjoyed the new games Tiger taught them. Academically, Tiger was far behind the others, but he had a quick mind and since he would be coming every day, Kerrianne knew he'd catch up soon.

"Is that okay?" Maxine asked, when she didn't reply.

"Of course. It's just that Ryan didn't mention it. He has to come over later today and—" She broke off, feeling Maxine's stare like a weight. "What?"

"Nothing. I'm just wondering how long it's going to be until the two of you arrive at the obvious conclusion."

"Obvious conclusion? Maxine, whatever are you talking about?"

Maxine snorted. "Games."

"What?"

"Oh, never mind, far be it from me to be a nosy busybody."

"Ha!" Kerrianne laughed.

Maxine ignored her, glancing over to where Tiger and Caleb were engrossed in some game that involved every action figure in the preschool toy box. "Tiger, are you ready? We should get in some walking practice before your sister gets here."

"Ria? She's coming, too?" Kerrianne didn't hide her surprise.

"Yeah." Maxine flashed her an annoying smile, and Kerrianne had the feeling that she was somehow being set up, that Maxine had purposely introduced Ria's name into the conversation. "Apparently, the poor girl has been going to the same woman who baby-sits Tiger, but she really hates it there. She's miserable."

"She fights with Jenny all the time," Tiger piped in.

Caleb's eyes opened wide. "What do they fight about?"

"I don't know." Tiger shrugged before adding, "Well, sometimes they fight about what they want to watch on TV."

"Ria asked me if she could come to my house after school," Maxine continued. "So we're going for a walk."

"But it's freezing out there."

Maxine shook her head. "Not anymore. Started warming up a few hours ago. It's quite pleasant now. The weather man says that means snow later this week."

Kerrianne was glad for the break in the biting cold but was not as excited about the snow.

"Would you like to go with us on our walk?" Maxine asked.

Kerrianne shook her head. "I have things to get done before Misty and Benjamin get home." In fact, she'd just had an idea to fix the hem on one of the princess dresses that might still be too short for Ria.

"Can Caleb go?" Tiger asked. The boys stood in front of Maxine, arms linked.

"It's okay with me, if it's okay with your mom," Maxine said.

"Please, Mom?"

"Fine, go ahead. But mind Maxine or you won't go ever again."

When they were gone, Kerrianne went upstairs and sat at her kitchen table. She fingered the princess dresses for a minute thinking of nothing but Ryan's kiss. With a sigh, she went out to the garage freezer and grabbed a chunk of baking chocolate, the cure for all illnesses.

Caleb still hadn't returned by the time Misty and Benjamin walked in from the bus. Kerrianne greeted them with warm cinnamon cider and a piece of toast with jam. They were always starving after school.

Benjamin chattered away about the day, but Misty was silent. "Are you feeling all right?" Kerrianne asked, noticing her repetitive glances at the princess dresses Kerrianne had laid across on end of the table.

Misty nodded and excused herself, her toast only half finished.

"Ria came home on our bus today," Benjamin told Kerrianne. "She waved at me and Misty, but she didn't sit by us. She was with some girl. I don't know her name."

"Did Misty and Ria talk?"

"No. She was in the front, and she got off on another street with that girl."

"I see."

Misty returned then, her arms overflowing with a soft yellow princess dress she'd received for her birthday a few weeks earlier. Though it was big for her, dragging on the ground when she tried it on, the dress was one of her favorites. "Here," she said, laying it on Kerrianne's lap. "Ria can have this. Keep it, I mean."

Kerrianne felt her mouth drop—and if the truth be told, she was as disconcerted as she was proud at the child's generosity. Amanda had spent good money on this dress and had picked it out especially for Misty. Kerrianne had half a mind to overrule the decision.

"You don't think Aunt Manda will mind, do you?" Misty asked, her blue eyes earnest. "I love it, but it's the only dress I haven't worn a lot, and I think Ria will like it the best. It's long enough for her."

Tears gathered in Kerrianne's eyes. "Oh, sweetie, Aunt Manda won't mind at all. Thank you for being so kind. I think that's exactly what Jesus would do."

Next to the new yellow gown, the remade dresses looked shabby and worn, and Kerrianne was glad she had something better to offer Ria. With her olive skin, the yellow would look striking on her. She hugged Misty, still blinking back tears.

"Does this mean you're going to be nice to her now?" Benjamin asked.

Misty buried her face in Kerrianne's embrace and said nothing. Kerrianne shook her head at Benjamin.

"Ria was supposed to go to Maxine's after school," Kerrianne said. "Tiger and Caleb are there too. When Ryan picks them up, they'll come here for the dress."

"Will Ryan play ball with us?" Benjamin asked.

"Maybe. With a jacket, it's warm enough. But I don't know if he'll have time." Kerrianne thought fleetingly of the surprise Ryan had promised her. What could it be? Her lips tingled, and she brought a hand to them, remembering.

"Mom, are you okay?" Benjamin asked. "You look a little red."

"I'm fine," she said. "Just fine."

Ryan finished delivering the mail on his route at four-thirty. He'd worked as fast as he could, especially once the sun had burned off the cold, and felt relieved that he'd made such good time. His supervisor pulled him aside and told him what a great job he was doing and that his efforts hadn't gone unnoticed. "There are some changes coming up in this department," he said. "I just wanted you to know."

"What do you mean?"

He shook his head. "I can't say more than that now, but there may be some advancement opportunities."

Ryan nodded and mentally dismissed his words. There were always advancement opportunities in the post office, but they were often in another city, and he wasn't in a position for a long commute or relocation. His children had stability in Pleasant Grove. They had friends at school, teachers they loved. While he had begun to think that maybe this phase of his job was through, he wasn't quite sure in what direction he would turn.

At Maxine's, the children were up to their arms in flour and cookie cutters. "Hey," he said. "I thought you were going to take a walk."

"We did," Ria said. "But now we're making cookies."

"Look!" yelled Tiger. "My cookie is a turkey."

"Mine's an Indian." Caleb held up the cookie for Ryan to see.

"That's really something."

Maxine was grinning at him. "We're about finished cutting them out," she said, tossing him a rag. "Why don't you start over there?"

Ryan helped Ria clean up while Maxine loaded a plate of finished cookies for Caleb to take home to Kerrianne. At the mention of her name, Ryan felt an odd tightness in his chest. He hurried to finish, feeling foolish at his desire to see her.

"Thanks for watching them," he told Maxine.

"It was fun." Her eyes narrowed. "But not something I'll be doing every day, mind you, though your Ria really is sweet girl."

Sweet girl? Ryan grimaced internally. She had once been his sweet little tomboy, but now? Well, *sweet* was hardly the word for her outbursts. Still, today she seemed all right—happy, even. Content. Maybe half the battle was getting her to a place after school where she felt welcome.

Ria balanced the plate of frosted cookies, while Caleb and Tiger ran on ahead down the sidewalk to Kerrianne's. They were singing the ABC song. For a second, Ryan compared this scenario with the one of Tiger in front of the TV at Susan's. No doubt that he had made the right choice.

Benjamin opened the door for them. "Cookies!" he shouted back into the house. "Thanks, Ria!"

"We made 'em at Maxine's," Caleb said.

They went into the kitchen, where half the cookies disappeared in less than a minute. "Come on," Benjamin said. "Let's go get a ball."

"Will you play with us, Dad?" Tiger asked.

"Sure, in a minute." Ryan was looking at Kerrianne as he spoke. If possible, she looked more beautiful than earlier when he had finagled that kiss.

The boys disappeared, leaving the kitchen suddenly quiet. Ryan wondered why Ria hadn't gone with them but then noticed her staring at the dresses on the table. Besides the two Kerrianne had shown him earlier, there was another new-looking one of pale yellow.

"Ria," Kerrianne said, "I'm glad you came over. I thought you might like to have these dresses."

"All of them?" Ria's voice was full of wonder and the look she cast at Kerrianne was the same one she'd given Ryan when he'd bought her that top-of-the-line basketball last summer. "But aren't they Misty's?"

Ryan saw Kerrianne glance at her daughter, who was sitting at the table with a book in one hand and a cookie in the other. She was only pretending to read, however, and her eyes locked with Kerrianne's, sharing a message Ryan couldn't interpret. "No, they aren't Misty's," Kerrianne said to Ria. "They were given to me. These two have been worn and I adjusted them so they'd fit you, but the yellow one is new. You can take your choice, or keep all three. You could wear one of them to the Thanksgiving tea party tomorrow."

Ria stepped forward and fingered the clothes awkwardly. "Thank you," she said softly.

"Aren't you going to try them on?" Misty asked, her nonchalance dropping away.

"I'd love to see you in one," Ryan added. Misty's gaze drifted to him, and for the first time Ryan didn't feel a chill in her eyes.

"Okay. I guess." Ria worked hard to contain her excitement, but when she came from the bathroom a few minutes later wearing the yellow dress, her face was flushed and happy. The color made a beautiful contrast to her olive skin and dark hair. She spun around, making the skirt go out.

"It's beautiful on you," Kerrianne said. Ria stopped spinning and hugged her. Then she hugged Ryan.

"You look nice," Misty said. Without another word, she popped the last of her cookie into her mouth, shut her book, and left the room.

"Is Misty all right?" Ryan asked Kerrianne when Ria was changing back into her jeans.

"What, because she's talking to Ria?"

"No, she just seems . . . different. I don't know."

"She's fine." Kerrianne smiled at him, and he forgot about Misty.

"So aren't you in the least curious?" he asked.

"About what?"

"Your surprise."

"Oh, that's right. You did mention something." She smiled again. "So what is it?"

"What, no bribery?"

Her eyes dropped. "No," she said quietly, firmly. Two bright spots appeared on her cheeks.

"Well, that's okay, because it's yours anyway." He drew out his digital camera from the pocket of his coat where he'd placed it before going to Maxine's. "Look." He scooted his chair closer to show her the greenhouse on the small screen.

"What's this?"

"It's yours, if you want it. Some people in my neighborhood are selling their house to their children. They're going on a mission and want to scale back. Thing is, their yard is really small, and the daughter wants them to get rid of the greenhouse so she can put up a swing set and sand box for her children. I was passing by their house yesterday and remembered hearing them say something about it at church. I had the impression it was a broken down old thing but when I saw it, I realized it's perfect for what you want. It's not new, but it's been taken care of. I checked into it, and as long as we get it out of there this week, it's ours for nothing. It'll take some work—we'll have to dismantle it and move it over—but it can be done. Well, what do you think?"

Kerrianne's eyes when they met his were wide with shock. "I never thought . . . I can't believe . . ."

"Hey, it was you who said the Lord would provide."

A tear dripped from the corner of her eye. He reached to catch it. With his other hand, he pulled her closer, watched her eyes shut. Neither spoke as he touched his lips to hers. It took all the effort Ryan could exert not to lift her from her chair and crush her in his arms. *Man, I'm gone,* he thought. *I love her so much.* He hadn't been sure such a thing was possible, not after the way he'd loved Laurie—still loved Laurie—but here it was.

A sound near the doorway sent them scattering apart. Ria stood there, her hazel eyes taking it all in. Ryan cleared his throat awkwardly, while Kerrianne moved to another chair and busied herself covering the rest of the cookies.

At least it was Ria, Ryan thought, *and not Misty.*

"Come on, Dad," Ria said. "Let's go play basketball with the boys." The tension dissolved as she turned to Kerrianne. "You want to play?"

"I don't know."

Ria took her hand and pulled her to her feet. "Come on. It's fun."

"I'll go get Misty."

Ryan watched her leave the room before following Ria outside.

❄ ❄ ❄

Kerrianne found Misty lying on her bed upstairs listening to the CD of her daddy's guitar music. "Hey," she said, sitting on the bed beside her daughter. "What's up?"

"I'm glad I gave her the dress," Misty said, "but I feel sad I don't have it anymore." She looked up at Kerrianne. "Does that mean I'm selfish like Benjamin said I was on the bus this morning?"

"No, Misty. If you were selfish, you wouldn't have given her the dress." She snuggled closer to her daughter. "And you know what? I think it was probably harder for you to give the dress to Ria than to a good friend."

"Way harder," Misty murmured.

"I'm proud of you, sweetie. Really proud."

Misty hugged her tightly and smiled.

"Now, how about we go out and play basketball with the boys before it gets dark."

"Are *they* still here?"

"Yes. The boys really wanted to play with Ryan. They miss having Uncle Tyler over here to play so much."

"Well, basketball is for boys," Misty said. "But I guess I can watch."

"That's my girl."

Hand in hand, they went outside together.

Chapter Eighteen

On Tuesday morning as Kerrianne drove to the grade school, the sun was shining brightly overhead and the day promised good weather. Kerrianne knew it wouldn't last this late in November, but she would enjoy it while it did. The school tea party was at eleven, so she'd left her mother at her house with Caleb awaiting her preschoolers. Earlier, Kerrianne had arranged Misty's hair high on her head, with loose curls everywhere. She'd been so excited. Kerrianne had dressed up, too, wearing a long multicolored gypsy skirt that she'd hidden away in the closet for years but was now back in style. When she twirled, it fanned out almost like a princess dress. Maybe she'd have to wear this to her next singles dance.

The tea party was in the cafeteria, where the delicious smell of baking rolls floated on the air. The room was a blur of bright colors with all the girls wearing costumes or their Sunday best. Kerrianne briefly wondered where all the boys were before she overheard someone mention an activity for the boys and their parents in another part of the school.

"Mom!" Misty ran up and hugged her, looking regal and dainty in her blue Cinderella dress and white gloves.

"How's your hair holding up?" Kerrianne asked. "I brought some pins and stuff just in case."

"I think it's fine." Misty spun around gently like a runway model.

"It's perfect," Kerrianne said, silently congratulating herself.

"Let's sit by my friends over there."

Kerrianne let herself be pulled along, smiling or waving at other mothers she recognized. There were a few grandmothers, as well, and girls who might be older sisters. Laughter filled the air.

There was a tug on her arm and Misty pointed to where Ria was standing near a window, looking out and twisting her hands nervously. She looked nice. The yellow dress was as good on her as the day before, but her hair was flat around her face and she was wearing black shoes that didn't go at all with the dress.

I didn't think about shoes, Kerrianne thought, glancing down at her own daughter's white shoes that went perfectly with the white trim on her blue dress.

"What's wrong with Ria, Mom?" Misty asked.

Kerrianne looked at Ria again just in time to see her glance at the door to the hall in pure misery. "I don't know. Maybe I should go see. You stay here with your friends, okay?"

Misty nodded. "She looks nice in the dress. I wonder why she's sad."

Kerrianne didn't wonder. All the girls here had mothers or someone else with them—all but Ria. Ryan had said their friend Sam would come to be with her but she was nowhere in sight. Where was she? The image of the woman evoked unwanted stirrings of jealousy which Kerrianne fought to ignore.

"Hi, Ria."

The girl started abruptly and turned from the window. "Oh, hi. I thought you were someone else."

"Is everything okay?"

"Sam's not here yet. I don't know where she is."

"Maybe she got held up. But, wow, you look great in that dress!"

Ria gave her a genuine smile. "I like it," she said. "But I couldn't get my hair to do anything. Neither could Dad. He says it's stubborn."

"I know that feeling. Hey, you know what? There's still a few minutes before they start. Why don't we go out in the hall and put up your hair? I've had a lot of practice."

"There's a bathroom out there." Ria's eyes lost their sadness.

Ria's hair was thick and sleek, but with a little water, some deft twists and pinning and a touch of hair spray, Kerrianne managed what she thought a passable look—one that absolutely thrilled Ria. "Oh, thank you," she breathed. "It's so . . . I look grown up."

"Yes, you do. You are certainly growing up."

"Dad doesn't think so. He's says I'm only nine."

"Nine's pretty old. It's almost ten."

Ria grinned. "And ten's almost eleven."

"And eleven's almost twelve."

"And then I'll be a teenager."

"I don't think your dad's ready for that."

Ria nodded. "You can say that again."

"Should we go see if Sam's here?"

"Okay."

They returned to the lunchroom, but there was still no sign of Sam. The teachers were calling people to sit so they could begin. Ria bit her bottom lip and looked miserable. Misty waved at Kerrianne from a table, but she couldn't leave Ria standing by the door alone.

"Ria!"

They turned and saw Ryan, still dressed in his postal uniform. His eyes met Kerrianne's, running appreciatively over her face but not lingering. His concern was for his daughter.

"Dad, what are you doing here?" Ria replied in a loud whisper.

"Sam can't make it after all," he said. "Something about her husband. It was important, I'm sure, or she wouldn't have canceled. My supervisor finally got me the message. But I'm here. Don't worry. I got permission from work to spend lunch with you."

Ria looked around at the room full of women. "You're the only dad." Her voice was dull and tight.

"I did my best, Ria." Ryan's eyes were beseeching. "I don't know what else to do."

"You don't have to stay. I'll be all right alone."

"I want to stay. I just didn't have time to put on my dress."

That elicited the smallest smile from Ria.

"You wouldn't look good in a dress anyway," Kerrianne said. "Your legs are too hairy."

He turned to her. "How do you know about my legs, huh?"

"You wear shorts during the summers, that's how." She made a chopping motion at her knee to show the length of his shorts.

"Oh, right." Ryan leaned closer to Ria. "I knew she was checking me out."

Ria managed a laugh, but she cast a nervous glance at the tables around them that were almost full.

"You know," Kerrianne said to her. "You're lucky to have a dad come. Real tea parties always have gentlemen present. Besides, he looks like a prince in that uniform. Or like a soldier. Misty would give anything to have her dad come. She was his little princess." The words slipped out before she thought about them. She had no idea they would choke up her voice and fill her eyes with tears.

"We'd better sit down," Ria said, touching her hand in comfort.

"Are you sure it's okay that I stay?" Ryan asked.

"I guess." Ria led the way.

"You did her hair?" Ryan asked.

"It took her mind off things."

"Thanks."

"You're welcome."

There was only one open seat near Misty, but when a lady saw them coming, she had her daughter get up and move to another table so Ria and Ryan could sit with Misty and Kerrianne. Misty frowned because the girl was one of her best school friends, but Kerrianne knew the mother had used the excuse to sit with her own friends at the next table.

To the girls' delight, Ryan fell into his role as a soldier prince, play-acting chivalry and making up odd tales to keep them entranced. "Mi'lady," Ryan would say, passing a plate of goodies to Misty with an elaborate gesture. "Will you not have another of the queen's delicious tarts? I am told they are without equal in this land. Each tart takes a forest fairy five days to stir before baking." And to Ria, "Allow me, fair maiden, to fill your goblet with this delicious mead touched by the horn of a unicorn. But keep in mind that it is only for the pure in heart. Others will not be able to drink it without a bitterness in their mouths that will last for twenty and seven days." Then to Kerrianne, "I hear that my cousin, the vile prince Edward, has been calling you on the magic device at your residence and one of his minions has even sent you roses. I fear they might be poisoned. You must be very careful, for it is a wicked plot."

He was equally amusing to the three other girls and their mothers, and Kerrianne knew they all ate much more than they would have just to see what new turn of phrase he would use. They laughed a great deal, and the girls at other tables stared enviously.

Misty and Ria seemed to have put aside their differences, and Kerrianne was happy about that, though she still didn't know what she was going to do about Ryan.

After the tea party, there were games for the girls. As they watched from the side, Ryan leaned over to Kerrianne. "They say there's going to be a big snowstorm for Thanksgiving, and it may last off and on all weekend."

"I'm not surprised."

"Well, I've been thinking about the greenhouse. We could begin tonight and I have tomorrow off, but I don't know if we'll be able to get it all done ourselves in less than a week. If it's going to snow, we don't have a week."

"I could call my family. They'll be glad to help. My family is a wonder in a pinch."

"Good idea." There was a wistfulness in his tone, and Kerrianne knew he was thinking of his own family. "I'd like to meet them."

She didn't pursue that vein of thought. She wasn't presenting him to her family for approval or anything. It was only for the greenhouse. "Thanks again for the greenhouse," she said. "But I really feel guilty for you spending your day off helping me."

"I like working outside."

"In November?"

He shrugged and gave her the grin that always sent heat to her stomach.

"At least let me pay you."

"I like being with you."

The simple phrase cut into her offer, making it feel cheap. "Well, then I'm not charging you Tiger's tuition—at least for a few months. I like being with *him*." She wrinkled her nose, and he laughed.

"If we weren't surrounded by more than a hundred people . . ." he threatened, his voice low.

"Well, we are." She smirked, understanding exactly what he implied.

"It's about time to leave anyway." He motioned his head toward the door. "We could go out there."

"The game's not over." Her heart beat faster at the thought of being alone with him.

"The game has just begun. And I don't mean their game."

Kerrianne laughed. She so enjoyed verbal sparring with him. It was one of the things she missed most about losing Adam. He had been the king of words and double meanings, though he'd never had Ryan's talent at acting.

That's when Misty's voice cut through all the rest. "You're a liar, a stupid, stupid liar! They weren't kissing, and they aren't getting married. I hate you, I hate you! I wish I'd never given you my beautiful dress! And those shoes look ugly!" With that pronouncement, Misty flounced across the room and out the door, her nose in the air and her hands holding her dress so she wouldn't trip on the hem.

"So much for their truce," Kerrianne muttered.

Misty's teacher was looking after her in dismay, but Kerrianne shot her an it's-okay smile and ran after her daughter. "Stop right there, young lady," she said in the hall. Misty stopped but didn't turn. Kerrianne walked around her and stood with her hands on her hips. "What was that all about?"

A fat tear rolled down Misty's cheek. "Ria was telling everybody that you were kissing her dad and that meant you'd be getting married and you'd be her mother. She was saying all sorts of stuff. She was lying, Mom. I hate her!"

Kerrianne rubbed her hand over her forehead, wondering what to say. Wondering how to break the news to her daughter. "Misty," she said calmly, quietly. "Ryan and I are becoming very good friends. Last night after he showed me the greenhouse pictures, I did kiss him."

Misty looked horrified. "Because of the greenhouse?"

"Maybe partly." Kerrianne paused, trying to sort out her own see-sawing feelings. "But most of all I think it's because I wanted to kiss him. I like Ryan."

"Are you going to marry him?" Misty said the word *marry* like it was a disease.

"Misty, it's too soon to think about that. I still miss your daddy so much, but I don't think I can be alone the rest of my life. I want to have friends and to date. I need to do that. Can you understand?"

"But you have us."

"I know. You and your brothers are the most important things in my life, I promise you that. But sometimes I need to talk to an adult who's my friend. Like you want to be with your friends and not with your little brothers all the time." Kerrianne wasn't sure it was a good analogy, but she hoped it would work.

Misty folded her arms. "I want you to leave now. Everyone's starting to go home." She glanced down the hall where people were exiting the cafeteria.

"Okay, but you think about what I said."

"I still hate Ria," Misty said in a small voice. "She just wants to steal you away."

Kerrianne sighed. "Oh, sweetie, it's not like that. There's enough to go around. Please try to remember that Ria doesn't have a mom."

"So what? I don't have a dad, and I don't go around trying to steal hers!" Misty turned on her heel and marched stiffly down the hall, joining a group of classmates. Kerrianne let her go.

Maybe Misty was right. Maybe Kerrianne should stop seeing Ryan. *But I'm not actually seeing him,* she thought.

She went back to the lunchroom to see if Ryan or Ria were still there, but they had left.

"Hey."

She turned to see Ryan behind her. "How's Ria?"

"Fine. She went back to class."

"Was she upset?"

"A little. It'll be okay, though."

"If they don't kill each other first. I'm sorry. It was Misty's fault."

"Ria's every bit as much at fault. She shouldn't be talking that way."

"What should we do? Oh, I can't believe I just said that." Kerrianne reached out to steady herself against the wall, letting her gaze drop from his.

"What do you mean?"

She lifted her eyes. "It's just . . . I haven't talked with anyone about what to do with my children—not since Adam died. I've been the one making all the decisions, every one, all by myself. But for a minute there . . . well, it was weird." She shrugged and looked away again, not wanting him to see how shaken she was. She'd become so accustomed to carrying the burden alone that she'd forgotten what it was like to share the load, how comforting it could be to consider the opinion of another adult who was as involved as she was in whatever problem had arisen.

"I know exactly what you mean." He gave her a tentative smile.

Suddenly Kerrianne needed to escape. "Look, I have to get back to the preschool—my mom's teaching for me—and I know you have to go back to work."

"Yeah, I'm late as it is." He glanced at his watch as they walked out the door together. As she angled toward her van, he called after her. "Hey, would you mind telling Maxine I'm sorry, but I'll probably be a half hour late tonight?"

Kerrianne paused. "She's watching the kids again?"

"Yeah. Tonight's the last time."

"Well, if there's a problem, they can stay at my house."

"Thanks. I appreciate it."

"See you tonight."

"We'll start on the greenhouse."

Kerrianne went one way, and he went the other. She sat in her van and watched him drive off, feeling silly and confused. What must Ryan think of her? "Adam," she said, looking up into the sky. "Where are you? Why aren't you here to tell me what you think I should do with Misty?"

There was no answer, no feeling of connection.

"Stop playing that stupid harp and listen to me!"

Well, if I were there, there wouldn't be a problem now, would there?

Kerrianne knew the thought wasn't from him but from her own mind. And she was right. If Adam were alive, Ria would never have said that Ryan was going to marry her. In fact, she wouldn't even know Ryan or Ria. Or Tiger.

Why did that thought make her feel sad? If she had a choice, she'd want Adam back, and yet, since she couldn't . . .

Sighing, Kerrianne started the van and drove home.

Ryan had apparently arranged for someone to drop off Tiger at preschool, because he was playing with all the rest of the children when Kerrianne arrived. Her mother looked up at her as she came out to the backyard where the children were playing. "It was time for a break," Jessica said with a grin. She was on the patio, bundled in a suede coat, her short blonde hair looking like she'd just stepped out of the beauty shop.

"Thanks, Mom. I really appreciate you coming here."

Jessica shrugged, implying that it was of no consequence. "How'd it go?"

"Great. We had a good time." Thinking back at how Ryan had entertained everyone, she smiled.

"That good, huh?" Jessica looked at her closely.

"Well, until Misty got in a screaming match with one of the other girls."

"That doesn't sound like Misty."

"Lately, it does." Kerrianne lowered her voice. "She's feeling a little insecure because I've sort have been . . . well, I met a guy."

Jessica's blue eyes went wide. "That's wonderful! When?"

"Funny thing, he was right under my nose all along." Kerrianne briefly explained about Ryan, the play, and the dance before adding, "I don't know where it's headed. Well, actually, I don't even know if I'm ready for anything. I still feel married—I still am married in an eternal sense. But I really like Ryan. It's not that I feel about him like I feel about Adam. It's just . . . I don't know." And she didn't. Adam was gone, busy strumming that harp or whatever, and she was left to muddle through alone. A rush of self-pity filled her. How dare he sit up in heaven and play a stupid harp when she was down here raising their children alone! Paying bills alone, cleaning the house alone, taking care of the yard alone. Getting the oil changed and taking the van for repairs—alone. She was tired of it. How wonderful it had felt today to talk about Misty with Ryan, to begin sharing concerns with a man who had a stake in the matter. Of course that wasn't enough to build a future on, was it?

"It's been four years," Jessica said, misreading her silence.

Kerrianne nodded. "I know."

"So when do I get to meet him?" Jessica grinned.

"Mom, you never change. Not ever." Her mother had pushed for each child in turn to get married to someone suitable since the day they reached adulthood. She'd been gently pushing Kerrianne to start getting out again for more than a year.

Jessica shrugged delicately. "I only want the best for you."

"I know. And you can meet him tonight if you want. Someone he knows is getting rid of a greenhouse, and I can have it if we move it this week."

"It's supposed to snow for Thanksgiving."

"Exactly. That's why we're going to start moving it tonight and hopefully get it up by tomorrow. We'll need help, though."

"Well, Mitch and Cory are nearly finished editing their documentary, so I bet they'd come. Your father can come after work. We'll have to ask about Tyler. I haven't seen him since he got back from his honeymoon."

Kerrianne had forgotten Tyler had returned at all. She'd been that preoccupied.

"I don't know about Blake and Amanda," her mother went on. "Oh, wait, I think I remember something about a gathering on Blake's side of the family. But maybe they can help tomorrow."

"If worse comes to worst, we can leave it unbuilt here at the house," Kerrianne said, hoping that wouldn't happen. Now that she almost had the greenhouse, she couldn't wait to get it put together and filled with plants. "Would you mind calling them? I'm going over there today after the children get home. I'll give you the address."

"Do you need a truck? I wish Tyler still had his."

Kerrianne shook her head. "Ryan's got one. I hope everything will fit." She avoided her mother's gaze and looked out at the children. "Hey, guys!" she called, standing and waving her arms. "Recess is over. We've got some fun things to do before snack time."

The children came running. They loved making the crafts she prepared for them, and while the weather was warmer today, it was still cold enough to get into the bones after a while. Caleb and Tiger, ever together, ran up to her and gave her big hugs. Some of the other children followed suit. Kerrianne laughed. "I missed you guys."

"Did you see my sister?" Tiger asked.

"I did. And your dad."

Tiger's jaw dropped. "Was he wearing a dress?"

Kerrianne laughed. "No. Just his uniform. Come on inside now."

"And his father is?" Jessica asked as they headed for the basement preschool via the garage.

"Ryan, the guy I was talking about."

Jessica looked thoughtful but didn't comment. "Well, I'll take off," she said. "I'll make a few calls for you and let you know. I'll call you later for the address."

"Thanks, Mom. For everything." Kerrianne went inside with Caleb and Tiger holding her hands.

Chapter Nineteen

Darkness had set in by the time Kerrianne's family arrived to help take down the greenhouse. She and Ryan had managed to remove the roof and were breaking it down, carefully labeling each piece so it would be easier to reassemble. Her mother had returned earlier to the house to watch the children—except for Ria, who had wanted to help, and Misty, who had apparently decided to keep an eye on them. The girls didn't speak to each other, though there seemed to be an uneasy truce for the moment.

Ryan worked steadily and thoroughly, taking no shortcuts that might mess things up later in the rebuilding. Kerrianne was glad for that. She herself was an advocate of doing things the right way the first time instead of wasting even more time fixing mistakes.

Her dad, Mitch, and Cory came into the yard shortly after five. Kerrianne thanked them for coming and made the introductions. "Everyone, this is Ryan Oakman," she said, not explaining further. "Ryan, this is my dad, Cameron Huntington, and my brother Mitch, and my sister-in-law Cory."

"Nice to meet you." Ryan shook everyone's hand.

"Well, where do we start?" Mitch scratched at his neck, eyeing the greenhouse.

"Honey, you should put on the ski mask." Cory's own thick red hair was mostly hidden under a hat. Mitch did as she suggested. Then he picked up a screwdriver and began working.

"Looks like you have it bright enough out here," Cameron said.

"Yes, thanks to Ryan. He brought the flood lights."

With her family working hard, they soon had two walls down and loaded into the truck. But Kerrianne was worried about Mitch. Despite his sweatshirt, coat, and ski mask, her brother's breathing was raspy.

"Are you all right?" she asked him. "Maybe you should wait in the truck. You could turn on the heat."

"I'm fine," he said shortly, squeezing her arm to lessen the sting of the words. He went to help Cameron with a panel.

"He'll be okay," Cory told her. "I'll watch him." In a moment, she was at her husband's side, leaving Ryan and Kerrianne alone.

Ryan wrinkled his brow. "Is something wrong with your brother? I've noticed everyone keeps checking up on him."

Kerrianne had forgotten that he didn't know. Ryan fit in so well with the group, it seemed he'd always belonged. "He has something called cold urticaria," she said, "which is basically an allergy to cold. Or rather, changes to colder temperatures. When he gets out in the cold he starts itching and then gets hives pretty badly. If it's bad enough, he'll have trouble breathing. But it usually doesn't get life-threatening unless he ends up in water or something."

"I've never heard of anything like that before."

"It's really rare. He can't even play basketball without discomfort because the sweat cools him enough to bring hives. It's limiting, but he gets kind of irritated when we baby him. He still hopes he'll get over it if he keeps exposing himself to cold." She didn't add that they'd come close to losing Mitch a few times over the years when he hadn't been as careful as he should have been.

When another wall was dismantled, Mitch tossed his screwdriver into the toolbox. "I'm going to sit in my car for a while," he said. Kerrianne wondered why he had to announce it, to make sure everyone knew that he wasn't pulling the same weight as the rest of the group. Besides, he was wrong. They all knew he was a hard worker and that being out there in the cold, struggling to breathe while he worked, exhausted him several times faster than someone without his disease. They admired his ability to endure as long as he did. She wished he could just slip away quietly, but something inside him wouldn't allow that. He had to make sure everyone knew he was "wimping out," as he called it.

"You know what?" Ryan said. "I could use a break, too. I don't think we're going to get this all over in one trip. Why don't you and I drive to Kerrianne's and unload the first half in her driveway? Meanwhile the rest of you can finish taking apart this last wall."

Kerrianne could have hugged him. The journey to her house would give Mitch time to warm up in the truck and still save face. "Drive slowly," she whispered to Ryan.

"Don't worry. I'll take the long way."

"I'll call my mom and make sure she calls you both in for hot chocolate."

He grinned. "Is it as good as yours?"

She welcomed the heat his grin brought to her heart. She grinned back. "She taught me everything I know about cooking. Well, almost."

Less than two hours later, they were all nursing steaming mugs of hot chocolate in Kerrianne's family room. Ria and Misty were still not talking, but everyone else was having a great time. The boys, thrilled with the prospect of no school in the morning, had built an expansive tent in the family room with stools and blankets and books, one Kerrianne had to partly dismantle so her family could sit down.

Mitch and Ryan were exchanging mission stories—Ryan having gone to England and Mitch to Brazil. Cory had also lived in the Amazon for more than a year and had interesting stories that often made Kerrianne shake her head at her sister-in-law's bravery.

As Cory began telling Ryan a story that involved a black jaguar and her two cubs, Kerrianne went into the kitchen to make more hot chocolate and check on the cookies her mother had made. She felt light, as though her feet weren't touching the ground. It had been a long time since she'd felt a part of a gathering this way, even one with her family. Since Adam's death, she had been half of a pair, a broken half of something that had once been whole and right. But with Ryan around, things were different, as though their two broken halves almost—almost—made a whole. He was fabulous with her family, and she was sure they were all won over.

Jessica came into the kitchen to help her with the drinks. "Well?" Kerrianne asked her mother, shaking in cinnamon, the secret ingredient. "What do you think of Ryan?" She half expected her mother to start hinting at possible wedding dates.

Jessica was quiet for a moment—too quiet. "I don't know," she said at last. "I mean, I like him. It's just . . . well, he's so different from Adam."

That was it, the nugget of truth Kerrianne herself had been searching for. Ryan *was* different from Adam—very different. Adam had been a refined, thoughtful, educated man who enjoyed wearing a suit to work. He hadn't liked yard work and wasn't handy around the house. He was a considerate husband and good father who was stern with discipline but also generous with love and praise. In contrast, Ryan was a rugged, hands-on, outdoors type, similar to Kerrianne herself. His life revolved around his children, though he seemed to have no clue how to discipline them. He didn't see work as a means to personal fulfillment but as a necessity to support a family. If she fell in love with Ryan, or someone equally different, of course it wouldn't be the same as it had been with Adam. Some things would be harder and some things would be easier. Different.

"I know," she said to her mother. "But maybe that's okay."

"Sure—it was unexpected, that's all. I guess I thought when you found someone else, he'd be more like Adam."

Kerrianne gave a short laugh that held no mirth. "Ryan may not go to an office each day, but I bet his wife never had to beg him to mow the lawn." Tears stung her eyes. What did she mean by that?

I'm sorry, Adam. She felt her words betrayed him. How could she be angry with Adam for his little faults when at the end of the day, she would give anything to have him here?

Tears shimmered in Jessica's eyes. "You spend years seeing your daughter with a man she loves and adjusting to that relationship, and then . . . well, it's going to take some getting used to, no matter what you choose, but I'll support you all the way. I think Ryan is a great father and would be a kind husband." Jessica gathered her in a hug.

Kerrianne returned her mother's embrace, but her mind raced ahead. If she let herself become involved with Ryan, would there still be room for Adam?

"You could invite him for Thanksgiving, if you want," Jessica said. "We've plenty of room."

"I think he has plans with his family." Kerrianne wondered if his mother had invited the suitable MaryAnn and if Ryan were looking forward to seeing her.

The women separated as Ryan sauntered into the kitchen. "Need any help?"

"I got the chocolate." Picking up the tray with a smile, Jessica left them alone.

"The cookies are about done." Kerrianne was feeling suddenly warm. Was it because of Ryan's proximity? What would she do if he tried to kiss her with her family here? Feeling distinctly uncomfortable, she turned and started rinsing the dishes in the sink before placing them in the dishwasher.

Ryan began helping her.

Kerrianne felt her heart shift. Some things would be different, and some things, like washing the dishes and talking about their children, would remain the same. She swallowed hard.

"You know," Ryan said, "I was thinking that your yard would look really great if you planted a row of lilac bushes along the right side. When they grew big, they'd shade the playhouse and sand box, plus you'd get to cut the blooms to bring in the house."

"That's a great idea." Kerrianne had been thinking along those same lines, but she hadn't considered lilacs. The more she thought about it, the more she liked the idea.

Then a realization hit her—hard. During the past few days she had begun to believe in her heart that it might be possible to love again, that maybe a relationship could even be as good as it had been with Adam. But after tonight, working side by side with Ryan doing something she loved, and after hearing his suggestion about the lilacs, she realized that it was entirely possible that another relationship might actually be better—at least in certain respects. Before now that thought had never crossed her mind. She supposed everyone would always be second-best to Adam.

"Your family is wonderful. Far cry from mine." Ryan frowned, but almost immediately replaced the expression with a more pleasant one. "I can't wait to see how the greenhouse looks here, all built."

She knew what he meant. They'd seen it together in the other yard, but this time it would belong to her. "Neither can I."

Their hands stopped moving, and for a moment they stared silently at each other. Kerrianne was acutely aware of him—the angular shape of his face, the intensity of his eyes, the strength of his body. She was also aware of her family in the other room, of her own children awaiting her return.

She moved back to the stove. "The cookies are ready," she said. "Could you get the spatula from that drawer?"

Ryan passed the rest of Tuesday night and most of Wednesday in a happy blur. He enjoyed working with Kerrianne's family and having the satisfaction of watching the greenhouse spring up before their eyes, but most of all he enjoyed being with Kerrianne. He loved seeing up close her ability with tools and her excitement over the greenhouse. She outworked everyone, all the while keeping a discerning eye on the children—hers and his—as they played in the yard.

Mitch and Cory came to help during the day Wednesday, as did Kerrianne's sister Amanda and her husband, Blake, who'd taken the day off to spend with his family. Like the others, Blake didn't seem to mind using his vacation day to help his sister-in-law, and Ryan marveled at how different her family was from his. His brother would have asked him how much he'd be paid and then would have refused anyway because that kind of work was beneath him. His father would have rolled his eyes and said that if Ryan would get a decent job, he could hire someone to do his menial labor. Thinking of the ambiance and the closeness he'd felt with Kerrianne's family, he wondered if that attitude wasn't a big part of what was wrong with his family. He knew enough about Kerrianne's family to know they were every bit as successful as his. So what made his family so arrogant?

Early that morning, his mother had called to make sure he was coming to Thanksgiving dinner. "MaryAnn couldn't come, but we've invited the Nelsons and Roberts," she'd said by way of enticement. Knowing each family had at least one "suitable" daughter of marrying age, Ryan hadn't given her an answer yet. He was hoping Kerrianne's family would invite him and the kids so he'd have an excuse not to go to Ogden. He'd much rather spend his time with the Huntingtons instead of making small talk with his family and people he didn't know. Why couldn't his family be more like the Huntingtons?

They had all but the roof on when Tyler, Kerrianne's youngest brother, appeared at five o'clock with his new bride, Savvy. Tyler looked a great deal like Mitch, though not quite as tall or lean and his eyes were green like Amanda's and their father's instead of blue. His bride was a curvaceous beauty with long white-blonde hair and smooth skin that reminded Ryan of Misty. The couple greeted him cordially but were so wrapped up in each other that he learned little more about them except that Tyler was a journalist and Savvy had only two more classes to finish before obtaining a degree in astronomy. They were utterly useless in helping with the greenhouse, though some of the younger children found them useful to run behind during a game of tag. They also provided comic relief as Mitch teased them mercilessly until Amanda countered with stories about when he and Cory had been newly married.

The day had been uncommonly warm, but now as darkness fell, the cold set in. They worked fervently to fix the roof in place. At one point Kerrianne asked her brother Mitch to test out the heating unit, and Ryan understood the request was to get him out of the cold. She sneezed twice as she put in the last screws. He hoped she wasn't getting sick.

"Mom!" Misty called from the house. "Grandma's on the phone. She says Grandpa just got home and wants to know if he should come over."

"No. We've got it done," Kerrianne called back. "Tell them we'll see them tomorrow."

Tyler and Savvy left, still with eyes only for each other, and the other couples began rounding up their children, all of whom were playing in the yard, after having warmed up inside the house. All but Misty, who'd never set foot outside, though Ryan was sure he'd seen her peering out an upstairs window.

He wished he knew how to encourage Misty to like him, to give him a chance. The child seemed intent on hating him—more so now since Ria's announcement at school.

When her siblings had gone, Kerrianne went inside the greenhouse, lit now by a single bulb. "Do you know about electricity?" she asked. "I'm not sure how much my brother knows, and I want to make sure—"

"It won't burn down?"

She grinned. "Well, it's mostly plastic and metal, so not burn exactly, but melt or something. I don't want to lose my greenhouse before I ever get to use it."

"You won't." He began checking the lines along the wall. He knew the ones running in the PVC piping to the house were fine because he'd done those himself earlier.

Kerrianne sneezed again.

"I hope you're not getting sick."

"I do feel a little hot."

"That's because your brother turned on the heat pretty high. Too high. I know it's insulated, but that's a little much." He adjusted the knob. "Even at this temperature, your electricity bill will be going up, you know."

Kerrianne turned around, surveying their handiwork. "It's worth it. Thank you so much, Ryan."

"It wasn't me. You said yourself the Lord would provide."

"I'll remember to thank Him, but you deserve credit, too. How can I ever repay you?"

He closed the space between them. "You could go out with me."

"All right," she said so readily that he felt dizzy. Euphoric and dizzy. "When?"

"Tomorrow, the next day, and the next day would be a good start."

Again the smile that made him want to hold her. "Tomorrow's Thanksgiving. You'll be with your family. But call me tomorrow and we'll plan something for the weekend. I think I may have promised Maxine that I'd go to another dance with her, so I'd better talk to her first. I'm too exhausted to remember what day we talked about." She sneezed twice and then a third time.

"You'd better get inside. Looks like you're getting a cold."

"You're right. Besides, I'd better go see how big the boys' tent is now."

The boys were still playing in the family room, their tent covering the entire area. The girls were absent, but their raised voices echoed throughout the house. Giving him a despairing look, Kerrianne started for the stairs. Ryan followed her.

"You're stupid, and I hate you!" Misty shouted.

"Well, you're dumb, and so are your dolls! I don't care if I broke their clothes."

They found the girls glaring at each other, Misty holding a broken doll dress in her hand.

"Ria," Ryan said sharply, "what's going on?"

"I was just looking at the dolls. I tried to put the clothes on, but they broke."

"You weren't careful," Misty said spitefully. "You're too rough."

Ria glared at her.

"Girls." Kerrianne's voice demanded attention. They looked at her. "I'm quite sure this was an accident. No, Misty"—she held up a hand—"I don't want to hear it. We'll buy a replacement dress later. Meanwhile, Ryan has spent his entire day off helping me build the greenhouse. I think I owe him dinner. We're too tired to take you all out, but maybe we could get pizza and watch a video." Kerrianne looked to Ryan for support, and he nodded quickly, happy to agree to any plan that kept them together. "But if you two are going to act like this, maybe we shouldn't do it at all."

"What movie?" Misty asked, mollified as much by the promise of the movie as by a new dress for her doll.

Kerrianne thought a moment. "How about *The Princess Bride?*"

"Okay," Misty agreed with only a touch of sullenness. "But I don't want pepperoni."

"Ria?" Ryan asked.

"*Princess Bride?* It sounds stupid," she muttered.

Misty gave her a black glare. "It's not stupid. It's really funny." She turned to her mother. "I'll go get it from the cupboard." With another dark look at Ria, she started down the stairs.

"It really is funny," Kerrianne said to Ria. "Well, at least all the kids think so. Do you think she'll like it, Ryan?"

He shrugged. "I never saw it."

"You're kidding!" She let her mouth fall open in exaggerated surprise. "I can't believe it. It was popular when we were kids."

"It always sounded kind of, well, girly." He winked at Ria, who was nodding vigorously.

"Don't worry. You'll both like it." Kerrianne turned. "Let's go downstairs, and I'll call for pizza."

"Can't we have something else?" Ria asked.

Kerrianne cast Ryan a smirk. "Bored with pizza, huh?"

"Kind of." Ria looked at her hopefully.

"I have some leftover tuna casserole in the fridge."

"I'll try it."

Ryan hoped he could get some, too.

Hours later, full of tasty casserole and belly laughs, Ryan knew it was time to leave for home. The thought made him feel bleak. There was nothing awaiting him there. Just a cold bed and dishes he'd left in the sink for two days. But he couldn't very well ask to stay here.

"I'll go start the truck and get it warm," he said. "Then I'll carry Tiger out." Tiger was sleeping between Benjamin and Caleb on the floor, their small heads peeking out of their blanket tent.

Kerrianne didn't respond immediately, and Ryan wondered if she was okay. She was no longer sneezing, but her face was flushed and slightly glistening. "You all right?" he asked.

She rubbed her forehead. "Just tired, I guess. I'd better carry these boys to bed. Better yet, maybe they can just sleep here." She yawned, covering her mouth with a hand.

Misty touched her arm. "Mom, you're boiling hot."

"I am? I feel kind of cold." She shivered.

Ryan stopped himself from feeling her forehead. She was a grown woman and could take care of herself. Yet later when he touched her hand in farewell at the door, not daring to steal another kiss with Ria and Misty watching so intently, her skin felt hot. "You'd better get to bed," he said gruffly to hide the tenderness he was feeling.

"I will. I'm really tired."

He wished he could stay and take care of her. He was good at that. Laurie always said he had a great bedside manner.

Sudden fear gripped him. What if Kerrianne had something serious? Something that would take her from him? *Ridiculous,* he told himself. *It's just a cold. She's been outside too much these past days.* With great
effort, he forced himself to leave.

On the drive home, Ria heaved a long sigh. "I wish Misty didn't
hate me so much."

"She doesn't hate you. She gave you that dress, remember?"

"I know. I thought it was Kerrianne until Misty yelled at me at the
school."

"Me too. It was a nice thing to do."

"She shouldn't have yelled."

"You shouldn't have told private things to your friends."

Ria looked down at her lap. "I'm sorry."

"That's okay."

"But you do like her, don't you?" Ria looked up, her face eager.
"Even better than Sam."

"I like her loads better than Sam." He stopped, not ready to tell his
daughter he was falling in love. How could you tell your child that you
loved a woman who was not her mother? It didn't make sense.

Unless her mother was dead.

"I don't know how things are going to play out," he told Ria. "So
maybe it's better to keep you and Misty apart until we figure it out."

"But I like the boys." In a smaller voice, she added, "I like
Kerrianne, too. So does Tiger. If you're going to keep me away, then are
you going to find a new teacher for Tiger?"

"No."

"That's not fair. I don't want to be the only one left out. I like being
with Kerrianne, even if I have to see Misty."

"I just don't want you to get your hopes up, that's all."

"I won't—I promise."

Ryan glanced at the sleeping Tiger, sitting between them with his
head on Ria's lap. He didn't know what to say. Maybe his parents were
right. Maybe getting involved with a woman who had three children

wasn't a good idea. Maybe he was putting his own children at risk by letting them love her. What if she turned away from them in the end? It was an entirely possible scenario.

No, he thought. *Even if she and I don't end up working out, she would still be Tiger's teacher, and she might even agree to let Ria hang around after school.* If they weren't involved romantically, he would have asked her already.

"Dad, do we have to go to Grandma's tomorrow?"

He sighed, pulling his mind away from Kerrianne. "I don't want to. She's having two other families there."

"With women for you to date?" Ria giggled.

"Something like that."

"Well, I don't want to go, not even if Grandpa plays ball with me. You know what I think?"

"No. What?"

"I think we should stay home and cook Mom's casserole."

The casserole. The last casserole.

His throat felt dry. "Didn't you have enough casserole tonight? Between you and Tiger and me, we finished off every last drop, more than half the pan."

"That's what made me think of it. I bet Mom's chicken casserole is just as good—better than turkey any old day."

Ryan grinned. "Okay, it's a deal. Tomorrow, we'll stay home and have the casserole all by ourselves." Maybe with Kerrianne in his life it would be possible to cook the last meal Laurie had made.

"What are you going to tell Grandma?"

"I'll tell her that I'm having Thanksgiving with the most beautiful girl in the world, and it'll be the truth."

Ria smiled shyly. "Thanks, Dad."

"I love you, Ria."

"I love you, too."

Chapter Twenty

Kerrianne awoke to a pounding headache, fever, chills, and aches everywhere that had little to do with her physical exertions in building the greenhouse. She either had one whopping cold or the flu—it was hard to tell which. Groaning, she put her head under the pillow and tried to block out the light. At least there was no mail to worry about. In the past that had meant holidays were always worse for her. There had been no reason to get out of bed until the very last moment—and then only because her family expected her.

Today, on the first holiday she hadn't woken up from a dream about Adam, she would have loved to jump from bed, singing at the top of her lungs, and eagerly await a call from Ryan. Instead, she was sick.

The heater was on, triggered by a timing switch she'd put in last year, but she still felt cold. She kept her head under the pillow, shivering under a pile of blankets she'd torn off the boys' tent in the family room last night.

The children wandered in some time later. "What time are we going to Grandma's?" Misty asked.

"At noon," Kerrianne said with a groan.

"Are you sick?" Misty's face creased with concern.

Kerrianne nodded.

Benjamin tried to climb up on the bed, but Kerrianne waved him off. "You might get sick, sweetie. Look, Misty, can you get the boys breakfast? We have cold cereal in the cupboard."

"Yay!" The boys were out the door before she'd finished speaking, and Kerrianne stifled the urge to yell after them, "Hey, what's wrong with my oatmeal?" She was really too sick to be worrying what they ate for breakfast.

If Adam were here, he would take care of . . . She stopped the unexpected thought. In the beginning she'd always thought that way. Once or twice, she'd actually called Adam's work to ask him to pick up some items from the store on his way home. She'd hung up when a voice she didn't recognize answered—and then she spent the rest of the day crying and eating baking chocolate.

Not anymore.

She groaned again and replaced the pillow. At least she wasn't throwing up. That was good news.

By eleven she showed no signs of improvement and decided to call her sister. "Hi," she said.

"Is something wrong? You sound terrible."

"I'm sick. I can't go to Mom's today. I can't even get out of bed."

"Oh no! What do you have?"

"A cold, the flu. I don't know. Whatever it is, it's terrible."

Amanda thought a moment. "I know, we'll move Thanksgiving to your house. Mom's got most of the food, but it shouldn't be too hard."

The idea of having a houseful of partying people made Kerrianne feel worse. Especially the idea of numerous children running wild without her to watch what they might do to her house. "No way," she said. "I won't be able to participate anyway, and I'll just sit up here and wonder what's going on."

"Are you sure?"

"Very. I really just want to sleep in peace. But I don't want to disappoint the children, so I was wondering if you'd come by for them. You wouldn't mind watching them at Mom's, would you? That way, I could get some sleep."

"I'd be glad to. And don't worry, we'll drive very carefully. Blake's good with snow."

"Snow?"

"Yeah. You probably haven't seen. It snowed early this morning. There's several inches out there on the ground. Even the road is patchy."

Kerrianne stifled a desire to tell Amanda not to come for the children after all. Since Adam's car accident, it had been difficult to allow her children to drive with anyone else, especially in the snow, but she knew she shouldn't permit herself to be ruled by fear. But what if something did happen? What if another truck barreled into Blake and Amanda's van? She shivered violently—with fever or fear she couldn't say. She took a deep breath and then another. "I know you'll be careful," she whispered. Amanda of all people knew what keeping her children safe meant to her.

"Of course. Look, we'll be over in a minute. I bet you haven't eaten or taken anything, have you?"

"I'm not hungry."

"But you could use some aspirin."

"I don't want you to get sick. Really, I'm fine."

Amanda laughed. "Yeah, that's what you always say. Remember how Adam said that the only time you didn't say you were fine was after you'd been in hard labor for five hours with Benjamin and they couldn't find the anesthesiologist to give you an epidural?"

Kerrianne smiled at the memory. Adam had said that a lot, though it wasn't exactly true. She'd liked being strong for him. Yet in the past four years there had been many times she hadn't been strong at all. Emotional anguish reached far deeper than any physical pain she'd experienced.

"Kerrianne, are you okay? Does my talking about Adam like that bother you?"

"No, I've told you a hundred times that I want you to talk about him. I was just remembering. Thank you."

There was a sniff on the other end of the line. "I'll be right there, okay? I just have to get Blakey some clean underwear. I hope he doesn't have a potty relapse when the baby comes."

Kerrianne said good-bye, leaving the phone next to her on the bed.

Less than an hour later, Amanda was forcing a few bites of oatmeal into Kerrianne's mouth. "Just a bit more," she said, "and I'll let you take the aspirin. You should never take aspirin on an empty stomach."

"Where's Blake?" Kerrianne asked.

"Getting your kids ready. Don't worry. We'll take good care of them."

"I know you will."

Even so, Kerrianne worried for a full fifteen minutes after they left, her head once again under the pillow. After that, she relaxed because there had been no phone call from her mother saying they hadn't arrived. She thought of her family around the table, each voicing a blessing they'd received the past year. The ritual was always hard for her because she so vividly remembered the last Thanksgiving she'd shared with Adam. He'd said how grateful he was for his testimony and for the Savior's sacrifice, how he felt he'd come to know the Savior and feel the love He had for him and his family. Mere weeks later, Adam had gone home to that Savior. The memory of his words had given Kerrianne great comfort, but it also carried its share of pain. After each Thanksgiving dinner, Adam would always pull out his guitar and the whole family would sing until they were hoarse. Now there was only conversation, which was good, but for her the day had always come up lacking.

On the whole, Thanksgiving was hard—too hard.

She drifted into sleep, hearing guitar music, though she hadn't put any on. Guitar, and maybe just a little bit of harp.

❄ ❄ ❄

A ringing pulled her from the music. Kerrianne was reluctant to leave the dream, but it was gone and she couldn't recapture the feeling. She felt for the phone that had become embedded in the blankets. "Hello?" she said, somewhat hoarsely.

"Kerrianne, is that you?"

She knew the voice immediately. "Hi, Ryan."

"I didn't know if you'd be home. I thought you were going to your parents."

"I thought you were going to yours."

"We decided to stay home." He laughed. "I wasn't up for match-making today."

Smiling, Kerrianne grabbed Adam's pillow and put it under her head.

"What about you?" Ryan asked.

"I woke up with a fever. But I'm feeling a little better now. My sister gave me some aspirin when she came to pick up the kids."

"You're there all alone?"

"I've been sleeping."

"That's good, I guess."

"It's great. They offered to move Thanksgiving here, but I declined."

"I don't blame you. Not very restful to have a houseful of people over when you're sick."

"Exactly."

"Have you eaten?"

Kerrianne grimaced. "Manda made me eat oatmeal, and I'm sure she'll bring back leftovers."

"I love leftovers."

"Well, I hope no one misses the pies I usually make," Kerrianne said.

He laughed. "I'm sure they'll muddle through. I took out a frozen pie from the freezer. They're really good—if you haven't had real pie in a while." They laughed at that.

"Well, I was going to ask about our date," he said, "but maybe we'd better see how you feel tomorrow."

"That's probably a good idea." Even so, Kerrianne felt deflated. Why'd she have to get sick now?

They talked a few minutes more, until Ria urgently called him away to check on a casserole. "I'll call you later," he promised.

The phone rang again almost immediately. This time it was Gunnar. So much had happened since the dance, Kerrianne could barely remember his face. "I tried to call you several times yesterday," he said.

"I was working on my greenhouse."

"Greenhouse?"

"Yeah. We put it up yesterday." She explained about the greenhouse, and he whistled with appreciation.

"All in one day, huh?"

"Basically."

The talk moved on to children and how his were in the other room driving him crazy. "Don't get me wrong, I love them, but they need a woman's touch. Hey, if you're not doing anything, maybe I could stop by."

"I'm in bed, sick." She'd already told him earlier.

"Oh, that's right."

"So are you coming to the dance? There's one on Saturday that's supposed to be good."

"I thought they were all on Fridays."

"No. It varies."

"I might be there. If I'm better."

"I hope so. I can't wait to see you there." His voice was low and promising, and Kerrianne felt a prickle of unease. She decided that maybe Gunnar was not her type after all. Ryan never made her feel strange with his tone or implications. What was Ryan doing now? Was he really having a casserole for Thanksgiving dinner?

"Kerrianne, are you there?"

She hadn't heard any of Gunnar's last few comments. "I think my aspirin is wearing off," she said. "I'd better go. Thanks for calling." With a few more comments, she deftly ended the conversation.

She wondered fleetingly if either of the men who'd sent her flowers had tried to call this week as well. She hadn't been home as much as normal. Well, it didn't matter. Neither of them had impressed her like Ryan.

She fell into a restless sleep, forgetting to take more pain reliever, and when she awoke, she was burning again and shivering with chills. There was a ringing in her head—or so she thought until she finally realized it was the doorbell. She groaned, hoping whoever it was would go away and leave her to suffer in peace. But the ringing continued. Pushing herself from bed, she stumbled to the window and saw Ryan's truck in the driveway. Tears of frustration came to her eyes. This was not how she wanted Ryan to see her.

RING!

He apparently wasn't giving up. Pulling one of the blankets from the bed, she wrapped it around her, shoved her feet into her slippers, and made her way slowly down the stairs. She opened the door, feeling flushed and dizzy.

Ryan's mouth dropped open. "I'm so sorry. I thought you were feeling better. You sounded better than this on the phone."

"Thanks," she said dryly.

"We brought you some casserole," Ria held up a plate covered with tinfoil.

"Yeah," Tiger added. "We didn't want you to starve here all alone."

Kerrianne wished they had let her starve. "Well, come on in, I guess."

"We won't stay." Ryan eyed her uncertainly. "Look, can I get you some Tylenol or something?"

Kerrianne was feeling faint. "Will you help me to the couch?"

He did better than that. He swooped her up in his arms, blanket and all, and carried her to the family room. Kerrianne rested her head against his shoulder, feeling safe and protected. "Thanks," she muttered as he set her down gently on the couch.

Within minutes, Ryan had a glass of water and some pain reliever he'd found in a cupboard somewhere. Kerrianne took it gratefully.

"You shouldn't be alone," he said.

"I'm fine, really."

"I'm not leaving."

"Neither am I," Tiger said. "Can I watch TV?"

"No." Ryan said shortly in a voice that meant business. "Look, you and Ria fold up these blankets, okay? Then you can put all those books back on the shelf."

"But, Dad, that's our tent," Tiger protested. "Someone's already taken off some blankets." He looked pointedly at the blanket Kerrianne had wrapped around her.

"Now." Ryan boomed. "Or there will be no TV tonight at all. And I mean it this time." The children looked at him for a few seconds, as though trying to judge his sincerity, and then scurried to obey.

"I learned that from you," Ryan whispered, hiding a smile.

"So they can teach old dogs new tricks."

"Are you calling me a dog?"

She shook her head, too tired to spar even verbally. She closed her eyes and the next thing she knew Ryan had placed a cool rag on her forehead. "I think you dropped off there for a moment," he said. Sure enough, the family room was clean now and the children were putting a puzzle together near the TV.

"How do you feel?"

"My head's not pounding so much."

"Thank heaven for aspirin."

Her head might feel better, but her stomach was empty and complaining. Kerrianne didn't feel like eating, but she knew she should. "Do you think you could get me some toast?" she asked.

"Sure."

"What about the casserole!" Ria popped up from the floor, her face intent. "It's the best casserole in the whole world. Really." The intensity in the child's voice told Kerrianne this wasn't any ordinary casserole. She glanced at Ryan and saw his face unmoving and without expression—except for the eyes which were deep and sad.

"Okay," Kerrianne agreed. "Let's have the casserole then."

"We only brought some for you," Ria said. "We're saving the rest for leftovers."

"I see."

When Ryan went to heat up the casserole, Kerrianne asked Ria, "So did you make the casserole?"

"No. My mom did."

Her mom? That was something to digest.

"She left a lot of dinners," Tiger added. "This is the last one."

Kerrianne recognized the importance. She still had the Sunday School manual Adam had been teaching from a few days before he died. She'd read his last lesson, especially his scrawled notes, so many times that she'd memorized everything. But food couldn't be reused or replaced, and she knew their sharing of it was significant. "Thank you," she said solemnly. "I'm honored to taste your mother's casserole."

The casserole wasn't bad, though it had a slight taste of freezer burn that Ria had apparently not noticed. "Mmm, very nice. Your mother was a good cook."

"The best," Ria said. Then she added hastily, "You're good, too."

"Thank you. That's nice of you to say."

Ria seemed satisfied and went back to her puzzle. Tiger sat by Kerrianne and whispered. "I think you cook better, but don't tell Ria."

Kerrianne nodded gravely as he hopped down and joined his sister. She didn't expect Tiger to have the same loyalty to their mother that Ria did. After all, she'd been gone two years, and the four-year-old Tiger didn't remember her.

"I hope it tasted okay," Ryan said quietly, crouching down next to the couch. "When she heard you were sick here alone, Ria wanted to share it with you."

"Didn't you taste it?"

He shook his head. "Not yet."

Kerrianne thought this a little odd. "Well, it was nice of her. I'm glad you came over."

Ryan nodded absently, his mind apparently still on the casserole. "I didn't eat it . . . well . . . I wanted it to last for them. And it . . . it just brings it all back too much."

"I understand." Kerrianne did. In fact, she'd marveled at how he'd begun to date so early after his wife's death. She wanted to ask him why he had done it and how he'd done it, but she felt the question was too personal. Besides, her head hurt and she felt ill enough to want to close her eyes and sleep.

She must have dropped off again because when she woke up Caleb was home and hugging Tiger as though he hadn't seen him in a month.

"I'm glad you're here," Amanda was saying to Ryan. "I was a little worried when I called several times and no one answered."

"Must have been before I got here."

"You cleaned up the tent. I would have done it earlier, but Caleb begged me not to."

"Oh, sorry."

"Don't apologize. I'm glad you did. And see? He doesn't even remember they had a tent."

Sure enough, Caleb and Tiger had finished hugging and were talking animatedly with Benjamin and Ria. Misty sat stiffly on the end of the couch. When she felt Kerrianne's gaze, she asked, "Are you okay, Mom?"

"Yeah, I'm fine. Just fine."

Amanda sat down in the easy chair. "Well, I'm going to be here for a while, and then Mom's coming over. Says she's going to stay the night." She said more, and Kerrianne nodded, but she wasn't really listening. She was thinking how Ryan had carried her to the couch and tended her so lovingly. She was thinking about how much she was growing to care for him. How much she liked his children.

She fell into a dream. In the dream she and Ryan weren't alone. Adam was there, sitting in the easy chair watching them with eyes wide and knowing.

"I'm sorry, Adam," Kerrianne whispered. "You do understand, don't you?"

He didn't reply.

❄ ❄ ❄

Ryan didn't want to leave Kerrianne, but she had fallen asleep again and was in good hands. He'd call her tomorrow to see how she was doing. At least seeing her had softened the ache in his heart and let him feel hope for the future. Holidays were still so hard. He drove home silently.

"Dad, someone's here," Ria said, pointing to a sleek blue sedan parked in front of their house.

Ryan peered into the dusk and recognized one of his father's cars, an older model, not the new one he'd bought a few months ago. His stomach turned. His refusal to come to Thanksgiving dinner must have upset his father more than Ryan believed possible if he had come all this way. Ryan drove into the garage and set the parking brake with more force than necessary. *Why did he have to come now?* he thought bitterly. *Today of all days when we are the most vulnerable.*

Yet at the same time he hoped for something good to come of it. He hoped to finally talk with his father—not about his business or Ryan's failures as son but of the importance of family, of accepting one another as they were. Or perhaps about the gospel of Jesus Christ. Now that might be something on which they could find a meeting of the minds.

"Dad?" Ria's voice sounded worried.

"It's okay, honey. It's Grandpa's car." His mother's car was white. Of course, she may have ridden over with his father—it was too dark to see inside the sedan from this distance. He might have to face not only his father's stoic indifference but also his mother's tears at what she would surely deem his rejection. *Why did she have to invite those other families?*

Ryan went around the truck and scooped the sleeping Tiger off the seat. His eyelids fluttered, but his body remained limp. "I'll just get him into bed," he said more to himself than to Ria.

She wasn't paying attention. "Dad, look."

Ryan turned to see not his father but Willard coming up the walk. Sharp disappointment filled him for an instant until he battled it into a corner of his heart. *I should have known better.*

"Willard," he said when his brother had come into the garage. He shifted Tiger's weight against his chest.

His brother inclined his head. "Ryan." They weren't the type to hug and pound each other's back, and Ryan suddenly felt that loss. He remembered the hearty way Kerrianne's family greeted each other—as though they really loved.

"What brings you here?" His voice was more caustic than he'd intended, but he didn't know how to stop the pain from leaking into his conversation. Willard had never really been a big brother to him. Well, at least not since he was maybe Tiger's age. Every now and then, if he thought long and deep, a memory would emerge that didn't involve Willard putting Ryan down or hanging on their father's every word.

"Can we go inside?"

Ryan nodded, and motioned for Ria to open the door. In the kitchen he said, "I'm just going to put Tiger in bed."

When he returned, Willard was sitting at the kitchen table across from Ria. She gave him a look of utter relief and escaped from the room.

"So," Ryan said, seating himself. Then he remembered his manners. "You want anything to drink? We don't have much to eat. I can make you a sandwich." He wouldn't give Willard any of Laurie's casserole, no matter if he were starving.

Willard blew air from his mouth. "It's Thanksgiving. I ate more than enough, believe me." He patted the ample spare tire around his waist.

"Oh, yeah." Ryan didn't know why he was offering his brother anything. He didn't even want him here. But it had always been that way—inside where he didn't let it show, he'd always wanted his brother's approval. "So," he said again, "what's up?"

Willard stared at the table for a long time without speaking. Ryan's brow creased. *What is up with him?*

"I just," Willard began, then stopped. He sniffed loudly and drew a heavy finger over first one eye and then another. For the first time since he'd arrived, Ryan really looked at his brother. His straight brown hair was sticking up in places, looking more like Ryan's unruly curls, and his dress slacks and shirt were wrinkled. His flabby face looked haggard, and there were dark circles under his eyes—eyes that held an agony Ryan was stunned to see in his self-assured brother.

Willard's shoulders jerked with a sob. "I've lost it all," he said. "Cindy . . . it was all my fault. I can't believe I've been such an utter fool."

Ryan was glad he'd finally realized it. "Maybe it's not too late." He felt almost disloyal to Cindy as he said it because Willard really had been a jerk. He'd been the one to betray her; he'd let sin destroy the love they'd shared.

"She's met someone else," he said. "I always thought . . . Well, I don't know what I always thought, but it wasn't this. I've lost my wife, my home, my job—"

"Your job?" This was news to Ryan, but now it all made sense. This was why his brother was thinking of moving back to Utah. This was why he was still staying with his parents.

Willard nodded. "My fault. I made wrong choices, lost some good clients. The firm let me go. I just . . . it all spiraled out of control." He uttered an expletive, and Ryan was glad his children weren't in the room. "I can't even get a date."

"I thought you were—what about Colleen?"

"I'm not good enough. She saw right through me. Once, maybe, but not now. So here I am, a grown man, living on his parents' mercy."

"You told Dad?" Ryan asked in disbelief.

Willard nodded. "Not at first. Earlier this week."

"I'm sorry." Ryan could imagine what it must have been like. Their father wasn't the forgiving type.

"I thought he was going to throw me out in the street, he was so mad." Willard's jaw trembled. "I've never seen him that mad before." He uttered another word that grated on Ryan's soul.

"Please stop that," Ryan said. "Remember you're in my house."

"Sorry. I'm sorry. I really am. I just hate him so much."

Of all the things Willard could have said, this shocked Ryan the most. "You and Dad are tight," he said. "You've always been close— watching sports, talking shop."

"I hated it!" Willard slammed his fist on the table. "I only watched because he did. It made him happy. Just once I wanted him to throw a ball with me or take me fishing."

Ryan blinked back tears, but more took their place. "I felt the same way. I had no idea that you—"

"He pitted us against each other. I see that now." Willard looked at him, tears wetting his eyes. "But you never gave in. You never gave up what you wanted." His face crumpled. "I always admired you for that."

Ryan's tears fell, and for the first time in almost thirty years, the brothers hugged. "Will you help me?" Willard asked. "I don't know where to begin. I don't know what to do."

"Of course I'll help," Ryan said. "We'll sit and talk and decide where to start. If you want, you can stay here for a while."

Willard looked around the kitchen, and a touch of the old Willard was in his disdainful glance. "I think I'll stay with Mom. She takes good care of me. The place is big enough to avoid the old man for the time being."

Ryan was relieved. He had enough turmoil in his life without Willard coming to stay. "Okay, but let's talk about what you want to do."

They talked for three hours, and by the end of that time Willard seemed to be feeling more hopeful. "I guess I do want to keep being a lawyer," he said. "It's the other things in my life I want to change. Things like going to church, being honest at work, building meaningful relationships."

Ryan knew it wasn't going to be easy, but he would support Willard the best way he knew how.

Funny, it really does take a broken heart and a contrite spirit before a real change can be made. Ryan only wished it had happened to his brother before he'd ruined his marriage.

The hour was late, and Willard accepted Ryan's invitation to crash out on the couch. Before they retired, the brothers shared another hug. "I'm glad you came," Ryan told him. His voice felt choked, his chest tight with love he felt for his brother.

"Me too."

Then, as Ryan turned off the light and headed down the hall, Willard asked, "What about that woman you brought over on Sunday. Is that where you were today?"

Ryan stopped, his heartbeat sounding loud in the quiet. He prayed that Willard wouldn't say anything to mar their newfound friendship.

"Maybe you're right about her," Willard continued when Ryan didn't reply. "Maybe she's the kind of woman I should be looking for. Are you still seeing her, or can I have her number?"

Ryan relaxed and gave a short laugh. "Not on your life," he said. "She's had enough problems. Besides, she's the woman I'm going to marry."

Willard chuckled in the dark. "If you can talk her into it, you mean. Well, be careful, little brother, we Oakmans don't seem to have much luck with our women."

Ryan felt a shiver of unease work its way up his back. What did it mean? Surely it had nothing to do with him and Kerrianne.

"Good night, Willard." With that he stumbled down the hall to find his bed.

Chapter Twenty-One

Nearly three weeks after Thanksgiving, Kerrianne was sitting in the middle of her greenhouse on the dirt floor. The day was gray and dark though it wasn't yet four o'clock. The single bulb in the greenhouse did little to cut through the gloom both in the air and in her heart.

Kerrianne surveyed her tiny kingdom. She and Ryan had built wide shelves on one side of the greenhouse. These were covered with herbs—basil, parsley, dill, and thyme. In front of the shelf was a row of peas. Next to these, miniature lettuce, cucumber, and broccoli plants were peeking out in preparation to stretch toward the sun. At the far end she'd planted strawberries and artichokes. She was learning to make the best use of the space in her greenhouse, and part of each day she spent working in the soil. Though snow filled the yard, inside she was warm and her plants flourished. She didn't miss spring and long for the winter to end as she normally did. She felt at peace.

Except for today. This day would always be different.

Tears trickled down Kerrianne's face and fell to the dirt as she clutched her knees to her chest. These past weeks of dating Ryan had been the best she could remember for . . . well, forever. She and Ryan had laughed and danced and gardened and cooked together. He had taken her skiing, which she'd never done before but loved. This week Ria had begun coming to her house after school instead of Susan's in an unspoken agreement of how serious their relationship was becoming. There had even been a few more heart-racing kisses, shared out of sight of the children.

Yet when she'd woken up today and realized what day it was, she'd felt guilty and sad and mad and unworthy.

Another tear dripped and soaked into the dirt.

What was she doing dating Ryan?

The answer might have been clearer if her marriage had ended in divorce, but she and Adam had been in love. She'd promised to love him forever, not until death, but now the feelings she had for Ryan rivaled what she'd felt for Adam.

She hiccupped, and another tear wobbled down her chin.

"I thought I'd find you here."

She looked up, unsurprised to find Ryan towering over her. She'd tried to hold on until he'd come for his children, but when Ria and Misty had once again argued, Kerrianne had escaped from the house to find peace. But here, alone among her plants, thoughts of Adam assaulted her. More than anything, she needed to be alone to get this day over with, to maybe get Adam out of her system—or at least the guilt of wanting to go on without him. If only she could find a way to tell Ryan to leave without hurting his feelings.

She wiped at her face and swallowed her tears. She didn't like him seeing her this way.

"I know," he said, crouching next to her. "It's a hard day."

"People don't know what it's like." She hiccupped again, but this time no tear fell. "They're shocked to learn that we mark death dates just as they mark birthdays or anniversaries."

He settled onto the earth. There was only a narrow path without plants, but he was careful not to damage the new growth. "Tomorrow," he said. "Things will be better tomorrow."

"Better, maybe, but not all better." She met his gaze. "Even when Adam died, I didn't know the grief would own me forever. I learned that later."

He shook his head. "It doesn't own us, not really. It takes over for a while, but eventually it's only a part of who we are. That's life."

He was right. There were days now when Adam didn't enter her thoughts. "I was so angry with myself the first time I went a few hours without thinking about him," she said, dropping her gaze to the rich soil that she'd mixed with mulch from a bag. "And now, with you . . ."

He gave a dry laugh. "I know what you mean. Sometimes you can almost believe none of it ever happened, and then bang! it hits you—hard. Like today."

"It's been four years," Kerrianne said. "Getting to know some of the other young widows—well, many of them find new relationships really soon. What's wrong with me that it's taken so long? Why does it still hurt so bad?" She looked at him again. "How did you . . . ? I mean, you dated right away. I don't understand how." The knowledge continued to eat at her. Did men love their wives less? Or did they simply need companionship more than a woman did? If the situation had been reversed, would Adam have already met someone new? She felt almost certain he would have.

"Laurie was sick for two years," he said. "We had time to come to terms with what was going to happen. She made me promise to go on with my life." Tears gathered in his eyes and threatened to fall. "I had to separate myself emotionally long before she died, not in any big way, but kind of like putting your heart in a little box, locked out of the way so it wouldn't hurt so much when the end finally came."

"Did it work?"

He shrugged. "Didn't seem like it at the time, but I think it helped me recover faster. She was in a lot of pain, so there was some sense of relief when she didn't have to keep suffering."

"Maybe if I'd been able to say good-bye, it wouldn't have taken me so long to . . ."

"To live again?" Hope had replaced the tears in his eyes.

"I don't know, Ryan. Something's still holding me back. I've always felt Adam so close. Like he's been there these past years watching over us and cheering me on. I could talk to him and kind of feel him answer. It's only been about the last six months when he's suddenly not around anymore." Her voice shook, and she felt a little silly talking about it, but Ryan nodded for her to continue. "It's like he's found something more interesting to do, and we no longer matter."

"That can't be it. No one could ever forget you."

She smiled but was sure it looked more like a grimace. "Then maybe I'm forgetting him. That makes me feel like I've betrayed the promises I made to him when we got married." There, it was out in the open now. "But here you are, and I don't want to send you away." She was crying again in earnest. "I wish . . . I wish . . ."

"Shhhh." He put a finger on her lips. "It's okay. Look, I know you want to be alone, but I brought you something."

He picked up a grocery bag he'd set behind him. "I know you like chocolate. I wasn't sure what kind." The bag held ten kinds of chocolate bars and a sizeable chunk of semisweet baking chocolate.

Exactly what she needed. Kerrianne took the semisweet baking chocolate and handed back the rest. "Thank you," she muttered with a hearty sniff.

"Should I take the kids for a while? There's always McDonald's and ice cream."

Kerrianne nodded. "Okay."

He kissed his finger and set it briefly against her lips. "We'll be back soon."

Kerrianne was glad he had not tried to hold her. Today was Adam's day. "Take the van."

"I know where the keys are."

Kerrianne watched him go, waiting for the tears. But strangely, they would no longer come. After a while she managed to work up a few more drops and a stray sob or two, but it just wasn't the same. Ryan had somehow stopped her crying—and she wasn't all that unhappy about it. She gave in and opened the chocolate. If Adam could busy himself with the harp, she could certainly do the same with chocolate.

❄ ❄ ❄

When Ryan entered Kerrianne's house, Ria and Misty were having another shouting match, this time in the kitchen. He stifled a sigh. Ria loved coming here after school despite her differences with Misty, but something had to be done about the girls' relationship or he'd never win Kerrianne over. He knew how much their continued animosity worried her. That was one of the reasons she'd asked to have Ria and Tiger come here in the first place, hoping that daily proximity would help.

He passed the boys, who were engrossed in a car game in the family room.

"Why do you hate me so much!" Ria was yelling at Misty. "What did I ever do to you?"

"You told everybody they were kissing. Kissing!"

"They were. I saw them."

"My mom shouldn't kiss anyone but my dad!"

"Your dad's dead!"

"So, he's still my dad, and you're trying to steal my mom, just 'cause yours is dead."

"I am not! I only want to . . . I want to . . . You don't understand what it's like!" Ria was sobbing now and Ryan was ready to barrel into the kitchen to save her, but something stopped him in the hall.

"I don't know what to wear," Ria continued. "I don't know how to do my hair. I don't know how to cook, I can't fix my clothes when they have rips, and there's no one to do those things, not even my dad because he can't do everything either. We don't know anything unless it's baseball or basketball or soccer. The kids at school laugh at me. They say I'm a boy, and some say I don't take a bath or comb my hair, even when I do. And sometimes I miss my mom so much, and I think

254

that if I could just learn some things—girl things, I wouldn't miss her so bad. I wouldn't feel this big hole in my chest."

Tears came to Ryan's eyes. He had no idea Ria was feeling so insecure. How could he have let his preoccupation with his own life drown out his daughter's suffering? The changes in his daughter had been quite obvious.

There was a long silence, and then Misty spoke. "I don't hate you, Ria. And I'm sorry. I'm sorry I've been so mean. I just feel so mad and sad when you play with the boys and talk to my mom. It's like you're me, or something, taking my place. And then your dad—well, my dad used to play basketball outside with us. He was really bad." Misty gave a strangled laugh. "But he tried. Now the boys like your dad so much they've forgotten all about my dad. They don't even remember him at all. I was his special girl. Me. I was special, like you are to your dad. Now all I have is my mom. I don't hate you. I just want everything back the way it was. I want my mom *and* my dad."

Again there was a silence. "My dad's happier when he's with your mom." Ria's voice came more steadily now, and Ryan felt himself relax slightly.

"My mom laughs more," Misty admitted.

"Don't you want your mom to laugh?"

"I guess." Misty's reply was almost a whisper too soft to hear.

"I'm sorry for what I said at school. I haven't said it anymore. I think the kids have probably forgotten about it."

"They haven't."

"Well, we'll tell them to mind their own business."

"I guess we can try." Misty paused and then continued with more enthusiasm. "Hey, my mom knows how to cook really good and sew, too. She could teach you some stuff, I guess. Since you're coming here after school anyway."

"She makes great cookies."

"Let's ask her to teach us how."

"Okay, where is she?"

"We can't ask her today."

"Why not?"

Ryan thought now was the time to interrupt before they got on the subject of Adam's death. He knew Misty was aware of today's significance.

"Hey, girls!" He sailed into the kitchen, smiling. He looked at Misty. "Your mom's going to be out in the greenhouse for a while, and I asked if I could take you guys out for hamburgers."

"Yeah!" Ria looked at Misty. "That'll be fun, right?" Hope emanated from her in waves.

"Maybe another time," Misty said kindly. "I don't really feel like it right now." She stepped past Ryan, giving him a sullen glare. "You should know that I can't eat hamburgers today," she told him.

Ryan followed her to the base of the stairs. "It's okay to smile and be happy, Misty. Your father would want you to."

She whirled on him, venom arcing from her blue eyes. "How do you know what my father would like? You never knew him!" She stomped up the stairs.

Ryan didn't back down. "Because," he yelled after her, "I'm a father, and I know how I feel about my daughter. I'd want her to be happy, I'd want her to eat hamburgers, and I'd want her to play ball with another man if it made her happy. I'd want her to feel like it was okay to love another father."

Misty froze at the top of the staircase. Then her shoulders started shaking. Without looking around, she turned into her room.

Ryan raked his hand through his hair, his fingers tangling in the slightly longer curls in the back. Had he gone about it the wrong way? First Kerrianne and now Misty. This was turning out to be a pretty rotten day. At least he had Ria and the boys. But he'd told Kerrianne he'd take them all. He snapped his fingers. *Maxine. Maybe she can zip over.* She knew what day it was and only yesterday had hinted that she planned to be around in case Kerrianne needed her. *We both need you, Maxine.*

He found Maxine's number, and to his relief she was more than willing to watch Misty. "I went over once this morning and was on my way again when I saw your truck out front."

While he waited for Maxine, Ryan helped the boys dress in their coats and snow boots. To his surprise, Ria made no move to join them. "I'm staying with Misty," she announced and ran upstairs. Moments later, he heard a door slam.

Ryan blinked. What had just happened? He'd hoped to gain Misty, but had he instead lost Ria. *No,* he thought. *This is good. They need to bond. It's a first step.* At least he hoped. He didn't need Ria to start hating him, too. She already acted strange enough for three nine-year-olds.

Maxine arrived none too soon. He briefly explained the situation and then wished her good luck. "You're probably going to need it."

"No, I won't," Maxine said, removing her thick cream-color coat and matching boots. From a sack she pulled out fluffy slippers and let them drop to the floor. "I brought candy."

❄ ❄ ❄

"Do you like sleeping on the floor?" Benjamin asked Ryan as they walked out of McDonald's. It was still too early to head back to Kerrianne's, though that was where his heart wanted to be, so he figured he'd better take them to his place for an hour or so. He had video games he could play with them there.

"No, I'm too old for that," he said. "Unless I'm camping."

"Oh." Benjamin sounded disappointed.

Tiger looked at him wide-eyed. "But you could, right, Dad?"

Ryan suddenly understood that this conversation needed more attention than he was giving it. "I guess. If the situation called for it. Why?"

The boys whispered and nudged each other. Benjamin finally looked up. "I sometimes go into my mom's bed at night when I have a bad dream, and one time she said that even if she got married again, I still wouldn't have to sleep on the floor. So wouldn't that mean the other dad would have to?"

Ryan nearly laughed, but Benjamin's eyes were too somber to give in to the impulse. Strangely, he felt another presence with him, one he could not see. Was it the boy's father? All at once his chest felt tight with emotion. *I accept, Adam,* he thought. *If I'm allowed, I'll gladly accept the responsibility.*

"Benjamin," he said, leaning over to look into the child's face, "if I were ever lucky enough to marry your mother, I promise there would be room in that bed for all of us. Nobody would have to sleep on the floor."

Caleb and Tiger giggled. "I told you," Tiger said. "I always go in with Dad when I'm scared."

Benjamin smiled, and when Ryan offered his hand, the boy put his small one inside. The feeling that he wasn't acting alone persisted. He knew then that if Kerrianne would have him, he would spend the rest of his life being the best father he could to her children. He would be firm with discipline no matter how much the effort, he would be kind and always remember to give them an increase of love, and he would play with them every day so they would be glad he was there. He would do this not only for them and for himself, but because he'd promised their father, who had given him this trust.

Of course, he still had to convince Kerrianne. Much as he hated to admit it, Adam was coming between them much more than Ryan expected. He'd heard that it was hard to have a relationship with a widow who'd been happily married, but only now did he understand why. If Adam had been a jerk, maybe Kerrianne wouldn't feel so connected to him. Maybe she wouldn't compare them so much with equally positive results. Maybe she wouldn't still wish that Adam was alive.

The drive home went quickly, and with how most of the day had gone, he wasn't surprised to see his mother's white sedan waiting in his driveway, looking faded and gray in the darkening night. He parked

Kerrianne's van out front, glad the boys had boots on because they'd have to cross the snow-filled yard.

"Who's that, Dad?" Tiger asked.

"It's Grandma. Unless your uncle borrowed her car." At this thought, Ryan immediately felt better. His brother had come to see him three times in the past weeks, and their relationship was growing. Willard was still a spoiled, selfish man, but he was trying to break that mold. Trials had a way of doing that to people. Maybe, just maybe, Willard might have some advice to help him win Kerrianne. Maybe he knew how to compete with the memory of a perfect husband.

Yet it was Ryan's mother who stepped from the car. *Just my luck,* Ryan thought, though he did feel surprisingly happy to see her. He loved his mother, especially when she wasn't acting as his father's pawn or trying to match him up with a suitable girl.

"Mother," he said, bending to give her a kiss. "I hope you haven't been here long. It's cold."

"I had the heat on."

"Well, come inside. Boys, leave your boots at the back door, okay?"

"Can't we play in the backyard for a while?" Caleb asked.

"Yeah!" the other two chorused.

"All right. But keep your gloves on, and don't leave the backyard. I'll turn on the kitchen light so you can see."

The boys, full of energy as they always seemed to be, scrambled for the honor of being the first to reach the backyard.

In the kitchen, Ryan leaned against the counter. As his mother sat at the table and started to speak, he pondered at how cramped he felt here now that he'd been spending so much time at Kerrianne's. Her house had higher ceilings and a vaulted entryway, and the kitchen and family rooms had been designed in a wide, open fashion. His house, a simple rambler from an older generation, was tight everywhere and poorly designed. Besides that, the house was steeped in memories of Laurie. Everywhere he turned, something shouted her name—the framed prints on the wall, the wallpaper itself, the hot pads in the kitchen. None of these things had been his doing, and they brought poignant memories of his wife. The good ones he treasured, but the other ones, the ones where she lay on the bed dying, those sometimes tormented him until he had to leave, even if only for a walk around the block.

He much preferred Kerrianne's place, where mostly the bad memories could not enter. She and Adam had bought the house a year before he'd died. He'd asked her about memories last week, and she'd confessed to him, almost as though by a slip of the tongue, that she'd lived in the house far longer without Adam than with him and that sometimes she couldn't remember his ever being there. She'd looked sad when she'd said it, but he'd made her laugh soon after. She was beautiful when she laughed. He was glad her house didn't torment her as his did him.

"Aren't you going to answer?" his mother said with a touch of asperity.

Ryan pulled his thoughts back to the present. "I'm sorry. I was thinking of something. What did you say?"

"I was explaining why I came. I asked why you didn't tell us your friend was from such a fine family."

Ryan blinked, trying to understand her meaning. He didn't sit with her at the table but stayed leaning against the counter. "I assume you're talking about Kerrianne. What does her family matter? I would think a person should be judged by their own merits."

Elizabeth clicked her tongue impatiently. "Family always matters, dear."

He was about to protest, to tell her that Kerrianne still dated him *in spite of* his family, but hurting his mother would only make things worse between them.

Elizabeth fingered the plump flesh on her cheek. "You should have told us."

"I hadn't met her family," he said. "How do you know them, anyway?"

"I don't—exactly. Your father was contacted by a PR firm for representation. Cameron Huntington, your friend's father, came to conduct the interview. When Mr. Huntington learned your dad's name, he said he knew a Ryan Oakman, and that's how it came out. Your father was impressed with the man."

"So now you're going to roll out the red carpet?" Ryan didn't bother to keep the bitterness from his voice.

Elizabeth stared at her hands in her lap as though unable to meet his gaze. "Well, darling, I know we should have trusted you, but we worry as parents. It's only because we love you."

That might have worked when he was sixteen, but now he knew they acted more to protect their name and status than anything else.

"I should have known," Elizabeth added. "That little girl—Misty, wasn't it?—she was a complete little doll. So refined for such a young child."

"Oh, she can be unrefined, I guarantee it." Then he thought of how she had resolved her differences with Ria. "But she is a good kid. They all are."

"Well, I wanted to invite Kerrianne over again to make it up to her." Elizabeth looked at him now, her eyes pleading.

Ryan couldn't believe what she was asking. He didn't want to forgive them or to put Kerrianne in their path—even if they were suddenly being charming. "Why isn't Dad here?" he asked, stalling for time but also really wanting to know. His father had to be behind this visit because his father always pulled the strings.

"He knows I'm here, of course, but since I was the one she overheard in the kitchen, we thought—" She broke off delicately, her gaze falling again to her hands.

Despite his anger, Ryan felt his heart soften. "He should be here, Mom."

"He isn't good at this sort of thing."

Ryan laughed bitterly. "You mean family."

"I mean"—she met his eyes—"at being wrong."

"You need to stand up to him."

"Maybe."

It was likely all he'd ever get.

"So, will you do it? Willard tells me you're still dating her." There was a gleam of matchmaking in her eyes that would have made him laugh if it hadn't been so late.

What should he do? Kerrianne would forgive them—she was that way. For him it would be a little harder, but he'd try for her sake, knowing she'd want to smooth things over. What was it about women that made them so easily forgiving? Even his mother constantly forgave his father the control he maintained over her life. *Kerrianne wouldn't approve of that,* he thought. *She'd encourage Mom to make her own decisions and stand up to my father for what is right.* He smiled at the idea of Kerrianne and his mother as close friends. Maybe one day. It was a good dream. His father would have to watch out.

Elizabeth took his smile to mean something else. "Then you'll do it? How about this Sunday? Or we could wait until Christmas, though I suppose she'll want to spend that with her family." She looked at him expectantly.

"No." He shook his head. "I won't ask her to go to your house." Elizabeth looked crestfallen. He crossed the space between them and sat down, pulling his chair next to hers. "However," he amended, "I will ask her if she'll agree to have you and Dad over to her place." Her turf. That was the only way he'd agree to the meeting. "Then you can see who she really is, whether or not her family is in the picture."

His mother thought for a few moments. "That's fair, I suppose. But I'll have to discuss it with your father. I don't know if he'll come."

"I don't know if Kerrianne will agree, either."

"Do you think it would help if I went to see her? I could stop there now."

"Not tonight," he said shortly. When he saw the hurt in his mother's eyes, he explained. "Today is the fourth anniversary of her husband's death. It's a tough day for her."

"She loved him very much?" Elizabeth studied him.

He nodded. "Yes. Like I did—do—Laurie." Because he couldn't resist, he added, "You didn't like Laurie either because of her mixed blood. You don't know how much that hurt her."

Tears gleamed in Elizabeth's eyes. "I'm sorry, Ryan. I really am."

"Is he?"

Elizabeth nodded. "I believe he is."

"Then tell him to come because I won't let another wife of mine step into his house again until he wins her over."

"Wife?" Elizabeth said almost eagerly. "So it's really that serious?"

"On my part." He took a deep breath.

"And hers?"

He shrugged. "I don't know. I really don't know."

With that, he went to check on the boys.

Chapter Twenty-Two

She'd eaten enough chocolate to make herself sick and was well on her way to missing Ryan and the children when Maxine popped her head into the greenhouse.

"Nice setup," she said, whistling appreciatively. "Little dark, though. You need a better light."

Outside the greenhouse everything was black. How much time had passed since Ryan left? One hour? Two? Three?

Kerrianne stood to greet her friend because Maxine's beautiful off-white coat was not as conducive to sitting in the dirt as Ryan's jeans had been. Kerrianne brushed her own jeans clean—not from dirt but from bits of chocolate.

"Ryan called me a couple hours ago," Maxine went on. "He was taking the kids out, but Misty refused to go. Apparently, she and Ria were having a fight, and when that was taken care of, she wouldn't go out to eat because of what day it—"

"I'd better get in there." Kerrianne started to brush past Maxine, but Maxine reached out and held her in place.

"They're fine."

"They?" Kerrianne had been imagining Misty all alone, sobbing out her grief.

"Ria refused to go, too, and went up to Misty's room. I checked on them when I first got here, hands full of candy, of course, and they were laughing and talking on Misty's bed. They had some little dolls."

"They were playing? Together?"

"Yep. They've broken the proverbial ice. They went on and on about it, but truthfully, I sort of tuned them out after the fourth telling. You know how that goes."

Wonder filled Kerrianne's heart. "Does Ryan know?"

"Well, he saw Ria go into the room, so I'm thinking he does. I guess having both Ria and Tiger stay with you instead of that other baby-sitter paid off. I'm glad you're not playing games anymore."

Kerrianne chose to ignore that remark. "It hasn't been easy."

"I would say not." Maxine gave her a smile. "Just remember when you're mad at his kids that sometimes you don't like your own very much when they're naughty."

Kerrianne laughed. "It's not that, actually. I feel a little smothered is all. Ria follows me around a lot, but maybe that's because Misty's always pushing her away. Maybe now they'll keep each other occupied."

"I doubt it. In all the talking they mentioned something about you teaching them to sew and cook and about a dozen other things."

"I see."

They were quiet for a moment. Maxine studied a new sprout coming from a box on one of the shelves. "Why didn't you go with Ryan?"

Kerrianne looked at her. "You know what today is."

"So?"

"I don't know." Kerrianne resented her interference but couldn't exactly claim that Maxine had no idea how she felt. "Do you think I'll ever stop remembering this day? Do you think my life will ever be normal again?" She felt a little despairing as she said it. Four years was a long time—and yet perhaps not long enough.

"You want to know if you ever get used to them being gone, and the answer's no. But the missing them becomes okay after a while."

She was right. Some days missing Adam was okay. Especially now that Ryan had filled so much of her heart's emptiness. "But how," Kerrianne asked, "can I miss Adam and feel something for Ryan at the same time?"

Maxine turned from the new plants and put her hands on either side of Kerrianne's arms. "We can certainly mourn one spouse in the same heart that loves another. That's how we're made. Think of a mother who has lost a child. Does her grief and longing for that child mean that she can't love her other children? No, of course not. Adam is gone, Ryan is here, and that has to be okay."

"I wonder what Bernice would say about that," Kerrianne said dryly.

"She'd probably report us to the bishop." They both laughed.

Maxine took off her coat, unneeded in the heated greenhouse. "At the dance last week," she said casually, "a few of the guys asked me where you've been."

"They called me," Kerrianne said. "I said I was seeing someone." She'd told that to everyone, except for Gunnar. First she'd been sick, and then he'd been out of town. She'd never gotten around to it. Besides, she wasn't sure she wanted to tell him. Nothing was official between her and Ryan. They'd only dated a month, and she wasn't sure she was ready for a commitment. Sure, she'd dated Adam just two weeks before she'd known she loved him, but that was different, wasn't it?

"How many guys ended up sending flowers?" Maxine wanted to know. "Just those two?" At Kerrianne's nod she added, "There would have been more if you'd gone again. A lot more."

Kerrianne shrugged. "I'm still not sure who sent one of the bouquets. It was either the older gentleman who smelled like mint or the one who reeked of body odor."

"I know exactly who you're talking about!" Maxine said with a giggle. "They're both far too old for you. But that reminds me. It can't be the mint guy who sent the flowers. Rumor has it he's dating some-one."

"Good. I hope things work out for him."

Another brief pause, and then Maxine dropped a bomb. "Harold asked me to marry him."

"What? You're kidding!" Kerrianne grabbed Maxine's arm. "Oh, my goodness, that's wonderful—isn't it?" She wasn't sure by Maxine's expression. "Did you say yes?"

Maxine sniffed. "Of course not! I told you before that I'm not about to start washing a man's clothes again. Or feed him, for that matter. I have my freedom to think about."

"Well, you could make some agreement about that, couldn't you?"

She pursed her lips. "Besides, the old goat only kisses my hand. I may be old, but I'm not dead yet. I want romance—and I'm not just talking chocolates."

Kerrianne giggled. "I know what you mean."

"Oh?" Maxine said with a knowing smile. "Has Ryan kissed you?"

Blood rushed to Kerrianne's face. "I think it's time to look in on Misty and Ria."

❄ ❄ ❄

After saying good-bye to Maxine, Kerrianne found the girls seated companionably on the couch in the family room watching a video, right where Maxine had left them. Kerrianne was happy the two were finally getting along, but she didn't dare say anything that might break the truce.

"Mom?" Misty said as she entered. "Tomorrow will you teach Ria and me how to make snickerdoodles?"

Kerrianne was glad she'd asked for tomorrow. Snickerdoodles might push her over the edge on a day like today, and she'd spent too much time on the edge lately. "Sure, sweetie. We'll dust them with green and red sugar for Christmas."

The girls murmured happily and grinned at each other. Kerrianne noticed they were wearing some of Misty's dress-ups and play makeup. There was no trace of Ria the tomboy. Kerrianne hoped this meant Misty would play ball again with her brothers.

Kerrianne busied herself cleaning the kitchen until she heard the garage door opening and knew the boys were back. Ryan would be parking her van inside the garage and telling them to leave their boots outside by the door. She liked that he remembered, especially since she had barely mopped the kitchen floor. Setting the mop aside, she went into the family room. The outside door bumped a few times before it burst open to reveal Benjamin, Caleb, and Tiger. Ryan was behind them, grinning.

"We're back," he announced.

"I see. Come on in."

Ryan entered, keeping his hands behind his back. He glanced at the girls on the couch, his eyebrows raised in question. Kerrianne smiled and nodded.

"So, girls," he said with a satisfied grin. "Did you eat?"

Misty ignored him, but Ria nodded. "Yeah. Maxine helped us. Well, we didn't really need help, but she was here."

"Good, because guess what I brought?" Ryan pulled out the sack of candy bars he'd offered Kerrianne earlier.

"I want one! I want one!" the boys shouted, jumping for the sack.

"Wait." Ryan held it out of reach. "Princess Misty gets to pick first."

"Why?" Caleb complained. "I want the first one. I'm littlest."

"Misty picks first because she's had a difficult day. And because she's a girl and she's special."

"That's because she's wearing a princess dress," Caleb said.

"Nope. They're always princesses, and they always go first." Ryan walked around the couch and stood in front of the girls.

"Ria's a girl," Tiger said. "Why doesn't she pick first?"

"Misty's younger," Benjamin countered.

Ignoring them, Ryan went down on one knee with a flourish. "What about it, Lady Misty? Will you pick first?"

Kerrianne watched her daughter struggle with indecision. Not about what candy to choose but whether she should spurn Ryan altogether or give in to her desire for chocolate. Kerrianne knew what a hard decision it was—and not only because of the chocolate. One look into Ryan's pleading, intense eyes and Kerrianne would have given in immediately. Misty held out for a full fifteen seconds. Kerrianne counted them, marveling at the way Ryan didn't flinch.

"There's a Mounds," Ria whispered. "If you don't take it, Tiger will."

Misty could bear no more. Her hand shot out and closed around her favorite Mounds candy bar. Ryan didn't move but stayed in front of her waiting. "Thank you," she said finally.

"You are welcome, Princess." He passed the bag to Ria, and then to the boys, who were instructed to eat in the kitchen.

Misty bounced from the couch. "Mom, we're going to my room, okay?"

"Only for a minute," Kerrianne said. "We still have school tomorrow and it's bedtime."

Misty nodded and with a shy glance at Ryan, that held neither approval nor her usual disdain, she left the room with Ria tagging after.

"Whew!" Ryan drew his hand across his forehead. "She's a tough one."

"She was close to Adam. His little princess. She misses him."

"She's not the only one."

Kerrianne looked away. "No, she's not." She hoped he understood. After all, he knew what it was like to lose someone he loved.

Ryan took her hand and sat on the couch. Her hand tingled with his warmth, flooding her with confusion. She had never wanted and not wanted something so much. She took her hand away on the pretext of getting comfortable.

"My mother came to see me," he said. "We stopped by my place after dinner, and she was waiting there."

"What'd she want? Is she mad about Thanksgiving?"

"No, that wasn't it at all—though she probably is still upset about that. But what she came to do was apologize to you."

"What? Why?"

Ryan leaned back, looking handsomer than ever. She wanted to put her hands in the short curls in the nape of his neck. "Apparently, my dad is doing some legal work for the firm your father works for, and they got talking, and bingo."

"I thought they might change their minds about me if they knew my family, but I wasn't going to tell them." She wondered if she should be angry or amused at this turn of events.

"I'm sorry," he said.

"It's okay. I have too much to worry about to hold a grudge against them."

"They want to have us over for dinner again."

Kerrianne frowned. She didn't know if she was that bighearted. "Ryan, I know this means a lot to you, but—"

"I told her no."

"You did?" Kerrianne scooted closer to him on the couch.

"Yeah. Except that I did suggest that they come here instead. I was thinking you could meet them again on your turf, you know. But only if you want."

"That might be okay. Could I have some of my family here?"

He grinned, and her stomach flopped with the easiness of it. "It's your house. You can have anyone you want." He leaned forward abruptly and took her hands. "Kerrianne, I know this isn't the right time, but I think we have something good here, something lasting and powerful. Do you feel it?"

"Ryan, don't." She put a hand over his mouth to stop the flow of words, only to be startled when he kissed it. Unfortunately, it had the opposite effect from the one he'd intended. She started laughing.

"What?" he asked, sounding a little annoyed.

She giggled harder. "Maxine," she gasped. "When you did that I remembered her and Harold. He asked her to marry him, but she said no because he only kisses her hand."

"I can kiss you elsewhere," he threatened.

Kerrianne jumped up from the couch. "Not today, you won't."

"Not today. But maybe you should ask the Man Upstairs about us, okay?"

Her smile vanished. "Maybe. Right now I'm tired, and I want to go to bed." Tonight she'd put on Adam's music and think about him. She owed him that much.

Ryan capitulated with good grace. As she watched him drive down the road, piled on either side by frozen, dirt-stained snow, she wondered what she was going to do. Was it really possible, as Maxine had said, to love someone with the same heart that still mourned another?

Or did she have to choose?

For the next half hour Kerrianne busied herself getting the children ready for bed, beating their eight o'clock bedtime by twenty minutes.

"Mom," Misty said as she tucked her in, "Ria's actually kind of fun. She said she'd teach me how to play baseball in the summer. I can never hit the ball."

"I'm glad you two are getting along. I'm really proud of you for being nice. Ria needs a friend here."

"I still don't like Ryan." Misty's face turned bleak.

"Why?"

"I just don't. You're not going to marry him, are you? You love Daddy, not him."

Kerrianne sighed. She was having enough emotional turmoil without Misty adding to her guilt. "I'm not going to marry anyone right now. It's been a long day, sweetie. I need to go to bed."

"Are you going to listen to Daddy's music?"

"Yes."

"Turn it up high so I can hear, okay?"

Kerrianne kissed her daughter's forehead. "Okay."

She checked again on the boys, but they slept soundly, worn out by their busy day.

Kerrianne took her time getting ready for bed. Usually, she would hurry on a day like today so she could spend time with Adam's memory. But now her head was filled with Ryan, and because of that she doubted she would feel Adam's presence. She considered praying about their relationship, as Ryan had asked her to do, but the truth was she didn't want to drive Adam further away.

When she was in bed with the CD playing, she closed her eyes, willing herself to think and dream about Adam. As she suspected, she felt nothing of him. "Adam, I need you." His face was blurry in her mind, so she reached for his photograph by the bed. But this wasn't her Adam, not the way she wanted him. This Adam was a two-dimensional face instead of someone she had loved so very deeply.

Finally, she went downstairs to the TV and put in a video they'd taken five years ago on Christmas morning. There, she finally found the Adam she had loved. He tickled the boys and teased Misty, calling her princess. He played with their toys, making everyone laugh. Adam had delighted in Christmas even more than the children, and he'd been that way with every holiday. Always ready to hunt for eggs at Easter, the first to light fireworks on the Fourth of July, forever eager to show the children how the news programs tracked Santa's sleigh.

This was her Adam. No, it was the person he had been. What had he been doing these past four years in heaven? What was he like now?

"Where are you, Adam?" she whispered, reaching out to touch his face. The TV screen held no warmth of his flesh. "Can't you leave that stupid harp just for a minute? I miss you so much."

Except that wasn't as true as it had been last year and certainly not as true since she'd met Ryan. A cold sweat enveloped her body. She was losing even her tenuous connection with her husband. She'd never thought that could happen. Never. She'd felt him close for so long.

Then she knew. It was all because of Ryan. Maxine was wrong. She *had* to choose. And in that case there was really no choice at all.

"I love you," she whispered to the image on the screen.

There was no answer.

Chapter Twenty-Three

On Friday afternoon, two days after the anniversary of Adam's death, Kerrianne went to the temple for the sealing of Kevin and Mara to their parents, Amanda and Blake. Amanda, now six months along, was glowing with happiness. She and Blake stood together at the head of a table in the temple cafeteria where the family had come to eat after watching them be sealed as an eternal family.

"Thank you all for coming," Amanda said. "This is a day we've been waiting for, and we are so grateful."

Blake hugged his emotional wife and added with a grin, "Now, please, eat fast so we can get going. You may all have to stay in this frozen wasteland, but the surf and sand are awaiting us in Hawaii!"

"Your plane doesn't leave for hours," Mitch reminded him. He looked at Cory. "Honey, maybe we should set our next book in Hawaii. Think of all the beautiful photos you could take."

Cory smiled, looking happier than she had since their first attempt at in-vitro had failed earlier in the month. "We're going to China in February." Though they hadn't given up hope of having a child, they'd decided to adopt in the meantime, and China would be their first attempt. Cory was eager to get over there to see if there was any way she could expedite the long process.

"Right. How about after China?" Mitch said. "Maybe next year. We could adopt a baby in Hawaii, too. Then we'll go to India. Hey, we'll adopt a baby in every country."

"Whoa!" Cory said. "One at a time!"

The family laughed, and Kerrianne tried to laugh with them. She really was happy for all of them. So why did she want to cry?

I miss Ryan, she thought.

What about Adam? *I miss him, too.* It was all so confusing.

"Just so you'll be home before Christmas," Jessica said.

Amanda nodded. "We will, Mom. Don't worry."

Kerrianne suddenly felt teary about having her sister leave for a whole week. What if she needed someone to talk to? She looked down at her plate and concentrated on eating. This was Amanda's day, and she wasn't going to spoil it. She did wish she had someone to confide in about her decision regarding Ryan. Maybe it would help to have her choice validated. But she didn't dare tell any of them—she hadn't even figured out how to tell Ryan yet.

"Hey, sis."

She looked up at Tyler who was sitting next to her. He was almost back to normal, except when he glanced at his wife, and then the newlywed daze returned to his eyes.

"Hey," she replied.

Tyler put his arm around her. "Where's Ryan? I thought he might be here."

"He has work, you know." No need telling him she hadn't invited Ryan in the first place.

"Right. I'm glad you met him. Seems like a really nice guy."

Kerrianne schooled her face not to show any emotion, in case her brother was able to emerge from his bubble of happiness long enough to detect her unrest. "Yes, he's a really nice guy."

Tyler turned back to his food, and Kerrianne felt relieved. She didn't want him to see how desperately she wanted Ryan there by her side.

Ryan, not Adam.

That's only because you know Adam can't be here, she told herself. *There's nothing more to it than that.*

Tonight she'd agreed to go out with Ryan. Tonight she would tell him good-bye.

❄ ❄ ❄

"Are you sure this is a good idea?" Ryan asked Ria. They were standing in the kitchen waiting for the baby-sitter to arrive. Ryan hadn't felt this nervous since his first date when he was sixteen.

"I'm sure. Misty loves chocolate."

Tiger looked up from the drawing he was coloring. "Everybody loves chocolate."

"I still don't know why she hates me." Ryan wasn't used to kids reacting that way. He could usually charm them all.

Ria smiled and leaned her elbows on the table. "She doesn't exactly hate you. She talks nice about you sometimes. I tell her your good points."

"Oh?" This was interesting. He sat at the table next to his daughter.

"Yeah. Like how you don't make me do chores, and how I can watch TV after school and all day on Saturday if I want. And how we get to eat pizza all the time."

Ryan groaned. "Did you say these things in front of Kerrianne?"

"I don't know. Maybe."

"Never mind. Look, you sure you two are okay with all of this?"

"Really sure," Ria said.

Tiger nodded. "Me too. Caleb's my best friend. I want him to be my brother. But where would we live?"

Ryan couldn't answer. He'd been so sure even an hour ago that what he was planning to do was the right thing, but now he was having second thoughts—not about asking Kerrianne to marry him but worrying because she might say no.

She'd been more distant these past two days since the anniversary of Adam's death. When he'd dropped off Tiger or picked up the kids after work, she'd kept busy working on crafts for the next day's preschool activities or cleaning something. Though she was polite and friendly to him, and they shared a lot of laughs with the children, there seemed to be a growing expanse between them personally. Or was it all in his imagination? It was hard to know with Kerrianne. He'd learned that she kept a lot inside.

Today she hadn't even been there when he'd picked up the kids. Maxine was at the house baby-sitting and reminded him that she'd gone to the temple for her niece and nephew's sealing. Though he wouldn't have been able to get off for the event, he wished she'd at least asked him to attend. More than anything that signaled to him that all wasn't as it should be between them.

He'd bought the ring in the hopes that showing her how serious he was about them might change the tide. Earlier in the week, she'd agreed to go out with him, so he was taking her to The Roof restaurant at the top of the Joseph Smith Memorial Building in Salt Lake where he hoped to pop the question. It would be the first time in more than a week that they'd been alone for any length of time.

There was more to his excitement than his pending proposal. Today, he'd been offered a job as a supervisor at the post office. The offer included a nice raise and the same hours, so he could be with his kids as much as before, and he wouldn't have to move to another office. The new position meant no more cold days in the open or burning hot ones in the summer. He'd miss the nice days, of course, the exercise, and seeing the people on his route, but he was ready for the next challenge in his life. The mail, even Kerrianne's, didn't need him anymore, and he didn't need it.

The doorbell rang, signaling the baby-sitter's arrival from two houses down. "You guys be good now, okay?"

"Good luck, Dad!" Ria gave him a surprisingly strong punch to the arm.

"Yeah, good luck," echoed Tiger.

Minutes later, Ryan was inching at a snail's pace through the driving snow. He knew how Kerrianne felt about traveling in bad weather and hoped the snow would lighten up before they left her house, or the Point of the Mountain would be terrible to pass. He wondered if she always worried about car accidents the way he worried about going to the doctor.

Benjamin and Caleb opened the door, both giving him an exuberant hug. Ryan felt a rush of love for the boys. Neither could remember much about their father, and they'd accepted him practically without reservation. It was only Misty and Kerrianne he had to convince.

"Mom's still getting ready," Benjamin said, eyeing the sizeable box of wrapped chocolates in Ryan's hand.

"That's okay. Hey, is Misty here?"

Benjamin pointed vaguely. "She's with Lexi in the family room watching a video."

"Lexi's going to baby-sit us," Caleb told him. "She's spending the night."

"Look, you two run and ask Misty to come here for a minute, okay?"

"Wait," Ryan said as they started to leave. "I almost forgot. Look what Tiger and I found at the store today." He pulled a couple of miniature Matchbox cars from the pocket of his coat, still in their packaging.

"Wow!" Benjamin said. "Thanks, Ryan! I've been looking for this one. They're always sold out."

Caleb gripped his and jumped up and down. "Can we open them?"

"Sure, go ahead. But, quick, get your sister before your mom comes down. I'll wait right here."

Misty came to the entryway a few seconds later, a wary but expectant look in her eyes; she'd seen the boys' cars and knew he likely had something for her, too. It wasn't the first time. Only the day before he'd brought her new Polly Pocket doll clothes to finally replace the outfit Ria had ruined weeks ago. *This is bribery,* Ryan thought. *Plain and simple.* Well, he wasn't above bribery if it meant getting Misty to open up to him.

"I brought you something," he said, extending the box.

"Why?"

"Because I thought you might like it."

"Thank you."

"Aren't you going to open it?"

She ripped the paper with several delicate motions. Unlike Ria, she was always graceful—a lot like her mom.

"It's chocolates," she said, her voice sounding warmer.

"Three whole pounds."

"I never had a whole box before." She studied him a moment and then let her gaze drop again to the chocolates. "Thanks," her voice was quiet.

"I hope you enjoy them." His words were followed by a rather awkward silence. He wondered how to tell Misty it was okay to leave, that she didn't have to stand there thinking of things to say.

"I'm sorry I'm late." Kerrianne appeared in the entryway behind Misty.

Ryan was utterly relieved.

"What's this?" Kerrianne asked, seeing the box. "Chocolates?"

"They're for Misty." As he stared at Kerrianne, Ryan felt his heart in his throat. She was wearing wide, flowing black pants that looked like a skirt, topped by a blue metallic fitted top that emphasized her narrow waistline. Her hair was swept up on top, revealing her lovely neck and giving the outfit a sense of formalness. She was beautiful.

"The boys got a car," Misty said.

"You didn't need to bring them presents," Kerrianne chided gently, touching his arm and sending a warmth that traveled clear through his thick coat.

"It was nothing." He put a hand over hers, savoring the softness.

"We were at the store and saw the cars, that's all. I knew Benjamin had been searching for that particular one. They were less than a buck each."

Kerrianne grinned. "You mean you found *the car?* Oh, thank you! I was worried that I'd never find it."

Misty had been edging toward the far end of the entryway. Kerrianne walked over and gave her a kiss. "Let me just say good-bye to the boys. I'll be right back."

"That's okay," Ryan said, hoping the rest of the night went according to plan. "I'll wait."

Kerrianne was glad the snow had stopped coming down so furiously. The air felt heavy and almost warm, which Kerrianne suspected meant more snow coming later that night. Though the smaller roads were layered with tightly packed wet snow, the main roads had been cleared by a snowplow and gleamed a shiny black under the headlights. It really didn't matter. Kerrianne had no fear in Ryan's truck. Not only did it have four-wheel drive but it was large enough to withstand a lot of impact in case of an accident, unlike the compact car Adam had driven.

She shook the thoughts away. Tonight wasn't going to be easy, and she had to keep her wits about her. She had to convince Ryan that she wanted only to be friends.

She'd never been to The Roof before and was amazed at the lovely view of the Salt Lake Temple spires across from them and the formal atmosphere of the entire restaurant. Ryan had drinks brought to them in beautiful champagne glasses. There was crushed ice at the bottom and a fruity flavor that tickled her tongue. Though she was enjoying herself much more than she had a right to, she almost wished he hadn't brought her here. The meal was obviously expensive and what she had to say was better fitted for something less costly. She'd tried to tell him yesterday, and even today when he'd dropped off Tiger, but the words wouldn't leave her throat. With a sinking feeling she realized they probably wouldn't come tonight either. *But I have to stop leading him on,* she thought. *I have to tell him sometime.*

Ryan observed her with more than his usual intensity. She tried to breathe naturally, but her chest was suddenly so tight she felt like gasping for breath. Why was he acting so strangely? Kerrianne barely tasted the marvelous food as she wondered what was bothering him. Had he also realized it simply wouldn't work between them? Was this meant to be their farewell dinner? The thought brought an impossibly large lump to her throat. She could never remember afterward exactly what she had eaten.

Later in the truck, Ryan started the engine but made no effort to begin driving. The air was cold, but Kerrianne felt almost too warm in her coat.

"Kerrianne," he said, "I know I'm doing this all wrong. I'd planned to put it in your drink or something fancy like that. Or have the waiters present it and sing you a song, but I froze, and I feel—" He broke off but almost immediately continued. "From that very first night when you came to see my play—well, maybe not exactly that first night, though there was a certain chemistry between us even then. But I think I knew for sure that day at Macey's when you were surrounded by all that falling chocolate. That was when I knew I wanted to be with you." His voice deepened. "Kerrianne, I love you, and I want more than anything to marry you and take care of you and your kids. I want to make you happy."

He took his hand from his coat pocket and held out a box with a ring. "Will you marry me?"

Kerrianne didn't take the ring, though it was a beautiful piece with a unique square center diamond she had admired in a jewelry ad at some point in their relationship. She stared at it, wondering how she could possibly refuse. How easy it would be to fall into his arms and let her feelings for him take over the moment! But if she did that, she'd lose Adam for good. Ryan would fill up all the memories and cracks in her life until there would be no place for what had once been.

"Ryan, I can't." The words came out in a whisper, sounding harsh to her ears.

"I'm not Adam, and I don't want to replace him. I just want us to go on and be happy. To build a life together."

"Ryan, I know we've become good friends . . ." She trailed off.

"Friends?" He spat the word like a curse. "Friends don't feel about each other the way we feel."

She couldn't deny that. Her traitorous eyes caressed his face, her mind pondered how wonderful his lips would feel against hers.

"Is it Adam?" he asked gruffly. "Or you not being sure about us?"

She seized upon that as a way out of this difficult situation. "You're the first man I've dated since Adam. I don't really know if—if—if it's right."

"You're not sure about us." He said it as though he couldn't believe what he was hearing.

"And then there's Misty. She's really upset about everything."

"I'm working on that. I have some really great ideas I'm sure will work—eventually."

She shook her head and said softly, her heart aching, "I think we'd better back off."

"So you're not saying never, you're just saying not now."

That wasn't what she was saying. As much as she cared about Ryan, she wouldn't lose Adam for him. "I think we should date other people," she said firmly, not really caring if she ever dated anyone again, but understanding it was a way out. Tears threatened to fall, but she held them back, not looking at him so he wouldn't see the truth.

He slammed his hand against the steering wheel, but Kerrianne didn't feel in danger. She knew he was upset, but that he would quickly regain control. For a long moment, he didn't speak. Heat blasted out at them from the dash, like bad sound effects in a horror movie. After a moment, he seemed to make a decision. "I guess I misunderstood our relationship," he said evenly. "I can't force you to be a part of my life, but I would appreciate it if you would come with me somewhere for a moment so I can show you something."

She couldn't exactly refuse when he'd asked so nicely. Besides, she trusted him. "Okay."

Without another word, he put the truck in gear and began to drive.

Forty-five minutes later, they pulled into a church parking lot. He opened her door and helped her out of the truck, his hands gentle, though his face was stoic.

Inside, she could hear music. "Ryan, why are we here?"

"You haven't been in the singles scene long. I mean out there dating. You say you want to date, and I thought I'd show you what's available. Help you choose." His voice was steady but slightly pained, as though he wished he hadn't brought her here. They hadn't attended any singles events since they'd begun dating.

He paid the dance fee for both of them, and they went inside where people were already dancing. As they walked along the wall, Kerrianne regretted that they were not there on a regular date. She would have liked to dance with Ryan again.

"What about that guy right there?" He pointed to a blond man who was talking animatedly to a group of women. He reminded Kerrianne of Adam in his stance and the color of his hair.

At one time she'd been drawn to people who looked like Adam. She'd searched for him in the way people laughed, the way they talked or rested their chin on their hands. Maxine had told her that was how the heart kept the hope alive that he was still out there, that she would be with him again. But the similarities had always brought such a deep sadness that she'd stopped looking for that years ago.

"Handsome, huh?" Ryan asked.

Kerrianne had to nod, though the man was no temptation to her.

"Yeah? Well he just got out of prison. Tax evasion. Want to meet him? I guess the authorities could have been wrong."

"No, that's okay."

"What about him?" He pointed to a man with black hair the same color of Ryan's, though without curls. Kerrianne sort of liked his dark, dangerous looks. He was dancing with a blonde woman, and they seemed to be having a good time.

"Well?" Ryan asked.

"He looks nice."

"Nice?" Ryan snorted. "He beat his ex-wife and she finally divorced him. He's still in counseling, and we hope he'll be able to overcome his anger some day, but it's going to take awhile." He pointed to another handsome man with sandy blond hair. "That guy there has three ex-wives and pays alimony to all of them. That's okay if you plan to support yourself."

"Not everyone here's been married before."

"No, but the ones who haven't been married before tend to date others who haven't. A good thing, really. They deserve a chance to have what we had without the added complications."

Kerrianne hadn't thought of it that way.

Ryan looked around and spied another man, older and quite nice-looking, one Kerrianne faintly remembered dancing with. He whirled by with a dark-haired woman, leaving behind a vague aroma of body order. "That guy will never get married again," Ryan said. "He just comes to find new girlfriends to date. Always sends them flowers." Kerrianne swallowed hard.

"And he"—Ryan pointed to a man with brown hair that was so drop-dead gorgeous Kerrianne blinked when she looked at him—"used to be one of my good friends, until my children got in the way. He hasn't tried to see his own children in two years. Oh, and that red-haired guy? Well, he's still dating his ex."

Kerrianne was beginning to understand. He'd brought her here to show her that her choices were limited, that he was a good catch by comparison. "Are you saying all these men are jerks?"

"Not at all. I'm saying they all have issues and challenges far beyond what you might think, and it'll take more effort than you ever imagined to make a relationship with any of them work. Way more than the first time around. It's not impossible, but the odds are against you—especially for the women. And the guys who really want families, the ones with less hang-ups and baggage, are snatched up pretty quickly, usually within months. At least that's what I've seen."

Kerrianne had a terrible feeling he was right, but she wasn't willing to give in so easily. "So what does that say about you? If the good guys are snatched up so quickly, why aren't you married?"

He was silent for several long seconds before saying. "I've asked myself that same question many times, but now I know the answer. It's because I was waiting for you."

Kerrianne sucked in a breath. He was waiting for her. Her!

"Go ahead," he continued. "If you want to go out with any of these guys, I think you should. Maybe you're right. Maybe you'll find what you're looking for. Or maybe someone new will join the crowd. But maybe, just maybe, what you're looking for is right here in front of you. Then again, by the time you realize that, it'll be too late."

"Are you giving me an ultimatum?" Kerrianne was amazed. Hadn't she just turned down his marriage proposal?

The music changed at that moment, a soft crooning love song. "My children love you," Ryan said, his voice sounding suddenly loud. "I love you. I can't say it any better than that. We need you, too. And unless you're heading at least partly in that direction, then it's not fair for us to hang on the line while you date a million other guys. So, yes, I want an answer. Not meaning that you have to commit, but just that you'll give us a good shot. If you do, I'll try to be patient, which you know I don't do easily. On the other hand, I've been praying every day to find a partner to share my life with, and if you're not interested at all in being that person, if you're not praying to know if I'm the one, I have to keep searching. I owe that to myself, and to my children. And even to Laurie."

Kerrianne felt his words deeply. He'd been praying to find someone to build a future with, to find a mother for his children, a companion to love, while she had been praying only to feel the presence of her dead husband. What did that say about her? Didn't she care for her children? What about a father for them? What about someone to help her through life? To love her?

"Take me home, Ryan. I need to think."

He nodded, and they were moving toward the door when Maxine overtook them. "I didn't know you guys were coming. Come on. We're all over there." She pointed vaguely to the far side of the room.

"Not tonight, Maxine." To her chagrin, Kerrianne began to cry.

Maxine looked at her and then at Ryan. "What's going on? More games?"

"Maxine, will you take me home?" Kerrianne didn't look at Ryan, unwilling to see the hurt in his eyes—if it was there.

"Of course I will." Maxine hugged her, and the smell of her perfume was sweet and comforting. "Now, don't worry, Ryan. I'll get her home. You go on."

"But—"

"No buts. You can call her tomorrow."

Kerrianne knew he wouldn't, not after tonight.

Ryan still refused to leave, so Maxine settled Kerrianne on a chair and went to have a private talk with him.

Kerrianne had no sooner composed herself when a man asked her to dance. It was the guy who'd reminded her of Adam.

"I'm sorry," she said. "I'm waiting for someone." And then, because she'd seen that she'd hurt his feelings, she changed her mind. "Okay, let's dance."

Up close, he really wasn't like Adam as much as she'd thought. Adam had been a much better dancer, and Kerrianne was glad she'd agreed to the dance. *This is what I need,* she thought, trying to dismiss Ryan from her mind.

They exchanged basic information, which included her status as a widow, though she didn't go into details. The man's name was Ben, and he'd been divorced a year. He didn't mention tax fraud.

"It was nice meeting you," Kerrianne said when the music ended. She was glad he didn't ask for another dance.

The guy with body odor was heading her way, so Kerrianne turned around and ran smack into Gunnar. "Hey," he said, smiling. "You're here."

"Yes, I guess I am."

In minutes, Kerrianne was dancing with Gunnar, who could really be quite charming, though he still tried to hold her too closely. At one point, Kerrianne glanced toward the door and saw Ryan standing with Maxine. Their eyes met briefly. Ryan leaned over, whispered something to Maxine, and then turned and left the dance. Kerrianne bit her lip to stop from calling after him.

"Thanks," she said to Gunnar when the dance ended. "I have to go see Maxine for a minute."

"Wait." Gunnar led her to a chair away from the music. "I was hoping we could talk for a minute. Maybe make plans to go out."

Kerrianne thought about it. She'd told Ryan she wanted to date other people, and maybe she really should.

"Okay," she said, blinking hard in case the tears decided to return.

Gunnar shifted a little nervously. "There's only one thing I'd like to know," he said. "We haven't really talked about this yet, and I've been meaning to bring it up."

"What?" She was curious now.

"Well, are you sealed to your husband?"

"Of course we're sealed." What kind of question was that?

He sighed. "I was afraid you were." He stood up and brushed his hands on his pants. "I think it's better that we don't go out after all. I'm sure you understand. I want to find someone I can be sealed to forever. Thanks for the dance."

Kerrianne watched him go, too stunned to do anything but sit there. *Ryan's right,* she thought. *There's so much beneath the surface here that I didn't see. And I don't want to see—not any of it! I've got to get out of here.* Suddenly, she didn't care if she ever saw a man again—any man.

"There you are," Maxine slid into the seat Gunnar had vacated. "I wondered where you'd got to."

"Is Ryan okay?" Kerrianne asked.

"He'll live. He went home. I told him to give you some space."

"He told you?"

"That he asked you to marry him? Yes." She waited, but Kerrianne wasn't ready to talk about it.

"Did he tell you about his promotion?" Maxine asked. "They made him a supervisor."

"No. I guess there wasn't time." She felt even worse knowing he hadn't been able to share his good news. She knew how much it meant to him.

"There's always later."

Kerrianne wasn't so sure. "So has Harold kissed you yet?" she asked, determined to change the subject.

Maxine shook her head. "Probably give him a heart attack anyway. He makes me so mad I broke our date tonight and came here instead."

"Maybe Bernice is right. We loved our husbands. Maybe that's enough. Maybe we shouldn't even think about getting married again."

"Bernice? Ha, that old faker!" Maxine made a rude sound with her lips. "Didn't you hear? She's going out with someone, and rumor has it that things are getting serious."

Kerrianne blinked, feeling suddenly disoriented. "You've got to be kidding."

"Nope. I was just as shocked, believe me."

"But who's she's dating?"

"Remember that man about Harold's age who smells like mint all the time?"

"You said he was seeing someone."

"Yeah—Bernice. They met here at the dance that first night, and he's been courting her ever since."

"I can't believe it." Here Kerrianne was facing the prospect of living the rest of her life alone, and Bernice was cozying up with Mint Breath!

"Even Bernice knows when to admit she's wrong." Maxine looked at her pointedly.

Kerrianne sighed. "Maxine, I really need to go home."

"Okay, dear, let's go. I'm not having much fun here anyway."

When Kerrianne entered her family room a while later, her children eagerly jumped up from the couch to greet her. They were surprised to see her home alone, since Ryan always came in with her. "Where's Ryan?" Misty asked as they smothered her with exuberant hugs.

"We saved him some chocolates," Benjamin added.

Kerrianne looked into the faces of her children. "He went home." She could tell they were disappointed, even Misty.

"We can save them until tomorrow."

"I'm sure that'll be fine." Kerrianne looked at Lexi, who was watching her from the couch. "Lexi, will you put the kids to bed and everything? I'm really tired."

"Sure."

Nodding her thanks, Kerrianne swept past her children and up the stairs, feeling like a liar for not telling them they wouldn't be seeing Ryan tomorrow. For not admitting that they might never see him again.

Then again, there was always the mail, delivered by morning light—at least until Ryan's promotion kicked in. Now the waiting for it would hold an entirely new meaning. She only hoped she could live with her choice.

Chapter Twenty-Four

Kerrianne looked at herself in the bathroom mirror as she removed her makeup, her mind replaying the horrible evening that had started out like a fairytale in that beautiful restaurant.

"Is this what you wanted?" she whispered to herself. "To send Ryan away? To live the rest of your life alone?"

She had to admit that it wasn't. She'd been acting more from fear than from anything else. Worse, she hadn't even told Ryan the truth.

Yeah, right, she thought. *What could I say? Ryan, I'm afraid that if I let myself love you, I'll lose the tiny bit I have left of Adam.* What would he have said to that?

She already knew. He'd say, "But it's not me who's making that happen. You told me yourself you hadn't felt him much in the past six months. That's long before I came along."

So what was the truth? What did she want? What was best for her children?

She simply didn't know.

Pray. Ryan had asked her to pray.

After Adam's death, prayer had become a staple in Kerrianne's life, the only way to get from one day to the next. She had felt her Savior near, and at times His comfort had been the only thing standing between her and giving up. But she hadn't needed Him in that desperate way for more than a year now. She had slipped back into her old routine, forgetting how much He had supported her during the toughest time in her life.

Almost blindly, she stumbled into her walk-in closet, driven by a need for privacy, though Lexi would likely keep the children downstairs and quiet until their movie was over.

Not one of her clothes racks was empty. The place where Adam's clothes had been was now filled with outgrown clothing from the children or outfits bought on clearance that were still too big for them. She'd given most of Adam's things away, though she'd saved a few items for the children. She kept only his pajamas for herself in a plastic container on the top shelf out of sight.

Taking them from the shelf now, she sat on the floor and pressed her face into the flannel, glad to detect his smell, however faintly. How long had it been since she'd sat here with them in her hands?

A year. The last time had been on the third anniversary of his death.

Adam. She didn't cry. She just sat there, thinking. Finally, she began to pray.

She prayed long and hard until her knees grew weary, and she sat to rest. She closed her eyes for what seemed like only a moment. Then the dream came.

A blond man was standing far off, his back toward her. But Kerrianne knew who it was. She ran toward him. "Adam! Adam!"

He turned, looking surprised to see her. "Kerrianne." She was in his arms then, and the familiarity of it engulfed her with a deep, satisfying contentment.

"I've missed you so much," she said.

"I've missed you, too."

They hugged again and again. She wanted to stay here forever.

As if reading her thoughts, Adam said, "It's time to go."

"No! I want to stay here with you. I belong to you."

"I know, but you need to be with Ryan now. He loves you and the kids. He'll take care of you. You must go."

"But—"

He leaned down and brushed his lips against hers. "It's okay," he said, his breath warm on her skin. "I want you to be happy. I want you to love again."

"I love you!"

"I know that. But you love Ryan, too."

"I don't want to lose you."

"I'm not going anywhere." With that, he hugged her again, turned her around, and gave her a gentle push.

She awoke with tears in her eyes and Adam's pajamas wrapped around her neck like a scarf. *A dream,* she thought. *Only a dream.* And yet not just a dream, but her answer, sent in a way she could understand by a loving Heavenly Father.

All at once she understood. Her feeling of Adam, his presence, had gradually withdrawn until she was able to face life alone. Until she was ready to find happiness and love again. What's more, her children needed the stability. They needed a daddy. She and the children would always love Adam and cherish his memory, but they still needed help getting through the rest of their lives.

Ryan was her future. He had been prepared and waiting for her, sparing her more years of heartache and loneliness that at times was so profound she felt like the only person who had ever existed. She jumped from the closet floor, eager now to talk to Ryan, to tell him how she didn't want to live without him.

The clock by the bed read 4:00 AM, but now that it had been so long in coming, her love wouldn't wait. Rapidly, she dialed the number that was engraved upon her heart.

The phone by Ryan's bed rang, startling him from a sound sleep. He reached out, patting the objects on the nightstand until he found the phone. "Hello?" he asked, his voice groggy with sleep.

"Hi."

He recognized Kerrianne's voice immediately and wondered if he was dreaming. Why would she be calling at this hour? "Is everything all right? Is it one of the children?" He rubbed a heavy hand over his face, trying to focus his thoughts, trying to determine if this was for real.

"They're fine. Everything's fine." She laughed, a deep, throaty sound that made his heart pound. "More than fine."

"Well, then why—"

"I'm calling to tell you I've decided to try out for *A Midsummer Night's Dream*."

"*A Midsummer Night's Dream?*"

"I want to play opposite you, if I can."

"Really?" There was a meaning in her words, if only he could wrap his sleep-muddled head around it.

"Yes. I want to spend the rest of my life playing opposite you."

A rush of emotion fell over him as he understood what she was saying, and he was poorly prepared for the onslaught. His chest tightened, tears sprang to his eyes, and for a long moment he couldn't speak. This was no dream! Huskily, he said, "I thought I'd lost you."

"No. I'm still here. And I'm sorry."

"There's no need to be sorry. I love you, Kerrianne."

"I love you, too."

Much later, when he finally hung up the phone, he jumped from bed and punched his fists in the air. "Woohoo!" he shouted. "Yahoo!"

He didn't know for how long he yelled, but Ria soon came in, rubbing her eyes. "Dad? Are you okay? Should I call somebody?"

He covered the two steps between them, picked her up and whirled her around. She giggled and clung to him.

"She said yes! Kerrianne's going to marry me!"

"Yippee! I knew it! I knew she'd change her mind. When? When? Before Christmas? There's more than a week left."

He set her down. "No. Of course not before Christmas. Probably not until spring or even later."

"That's too long!"

"Well, we have to go slowly because we want to Misty to be okay with everything. Kerrianne's going to talk to her about it today, but she doesn't think Misty's going to take it well. At this rate, she might never actually marry us. So the way I see it, we need to win Misty over."

Ria rubbed her hands together conspiratorially. "Yeah."

"Come over here and sit on the bed," he said. "I think I know just the thing to do. Let me tell you all about it."

Kerrianne opened the door, glad to see Ryan and not his parents standing on her doorstep. She hadn't wanted to face his parents without him. Not that she would have been alone. Her mother was in the kitchen making sweet potatoes, while her father sat with the boys in the family room. Dinner was nearly ready, and the house smelled wonderful. Everything was clean and organized. Her house wasn't the size of the Oakmans', but Kerrianne had a talent for homemaking and believed Ryan's parents would be impressed. If they weren't, Ryan would still love her, and that was all that really mattered.

As Ria and Tiger ran past her in search of the other children, she went into Ryan's arms. He gave her a kiss that tingled to her very toes.

"Mmm," he said. "You smell good."

She laughed. "It's the food."

"They should bottle that smell. They'd make a million."

She noticed he had a tiny package in the palm of his hand. "What's this? Christmas is long over, Ryan."

"It's for Misty."

She sighed. In the month since his proposal, he'd been trying constantly with Misty, and while the child was being nicer, she was far from accepting him as a father. Last week Ryan had brought her a basketball and told her it was only for the two of them to play together. So far,

Misty had kept it under her bed unused. Kerrianne and Ryan had agreed they couldn't set a date until Misty felt better about everything. But sometimes Kerrianne despaired of ever becoming Ryan's wife and loving each other as they wanted to.

"It's the last present," he promised.

He was so earnest that Kerrianne didn't have the will to say anything negative. "Misty," she called. "Misty!"

Finally they found her up in her room with Ria. "Hey, princess," Ryan said. "I brought something for you."

"Give it to her, Dad!" Ria was bouncing from one foot to the other. "You're gonna love this, Misty. I helped pick it out!"

Misty eyed him warily as Ryan sat on the bed a few feet from her. Kerrianne folded her arms and watched from the door. She could tell, even if Ryan couldn't, that Misty's resolve was weakening. He held out the package.

She opened it slowly, revealing a ring nestled in a velvet box, and gasped.

"It's a ring, kind of like the one I gave your mother," Ryan told her. Kerrianne came forward and peered at it. The design was different from her engagement ring and much smaller, of course, but it was a beautiful piece of jewelry all the same. "That stone there is a diamond," Ryan went on. "And do you know why people buy them for wedding rings?"

"Why?" Misty asked, touching the diamond with a finger.

"Because it's such a hard stone. It sat under pressure for millions of years and that's how it was made. Diamonds last forever."

"Oh." Misty took the ring from the box, but she didn't put it on.

"The reason I'm giving this ring to you is because I know you're a little uncertain about things between your mom and me and that you miss your dad. This ring is a promise from me to you that I will take care of your mom and you and your brothers, that I'll love you, and that I'll always, always be here for you whenever you need me. I'm not saying it's going to be easy, but we'll be like that diamond and grow tough together until nothing can hurt us. We'll be a family, and we'll be very happy."

"What about my dad?" Misty asked in a whisper. She didn't look at any of them.

Ryan nodded, setting a hand on her back. "Think of me as just stepping in for a while until you can see him again. That's all. And your mom will do the same for Ria and Tiger. We'll all work for that. This ring is my promise to you. I know I'm not just marrying your mother, I'm marrying the whole family. I love you all, and I'm going to do everything I can to make you and your brothers happy, too."

A single tear ran down Misty's cheek. Without looking at him, she launched herself into his arms. Ryan held her tightly, looking up to meet Kerrianne's eyes. His jaw trembled, and she knew he was both stunned and deeply touched at Misty's reaction. She smiled at him, wiping her own tears.

Ria skipped over to Kerrianne and hugged her. "It worked," she whispered. "It worked!"

Kerrianne knew there would be more bumps along the road, but most certainly, Ryan had made some impressive headway.

Ryan picked up Misty and shared a group hug with Kerrianne and Ria. Then he helped Misty put on her new ring. "I have to go show Grandma!" she said excitedly. She and Ria ran from the room.

"That was perfect," Kerrianne said, wrapping her arms around him.

"For a minute I thought she was going to throw it at me."

She laughed. "Misty would never throw jewelry. She likes it too much."

"That's what Ria said." He leaned down to kiss her.

"As much as I'd like to stay here with you," she murmured, "we'd better go check on things before your parents get here."

"Okay, let's go." Instead, he kissed her one more time.

They eventually made it to the family room where Kerrianne's father, Cameron, kept slipping Tootsie Rolls from his shirt pocket to give to the kids. Kerrianne pretended not to see.

When the doorbell rang a short time later, Kerrianne looked at Ryan. "Must be your parents. Come with me, okay?"

"Thanks for doing this," he said to her as they walked into the entryway. "I know it's not going to be easy—it's never easy with my parents—but I have to admit that I'm really happy they've come around."

Kerrianne was too, and though she didn't hold the hope of ever having as close a relationship with his parents as she did her own, she was glad for Ryan's sake that his father had accepted her invitation. Yes, her own father's prestige had a lot to do with the Oakmans' turn-around, but she believed that in their hearts they wanted the best for their son. So did she.

She reached for the doorknob and had barely started to turn it when the door flung open and Maxine stepped into the entryway. "Good, you're home," she said.

Kerrianne blinked at her. "Of course, I'm home. I'm having a dinner party tonight, remember? I borrowed your crystal punch bowl."

"Oh, yeah. That's right." Maxine looked as elegant as ever, even if her hair was a little messy.

"You're welcome to stay, if you like," Kerrianne said.

"No, can't stay. Harold's waiting. But I had to come and tell you."

Kerrianne glanced at Ryan, but he shrugged, apparently as confused as she was by Maxine's pronouncement. "Tell me what?" Kerrianne asked. "Are you okay?"

"Okay?" Maxine repeated, her voice rising too high. "Okay? Well that's just it. I'm not okay. Not at all. It's all a disaster. And I'll tell you why. Harold's gone and done it."

"Done what?" Kerrianne hoped he hadn't suffered a heart attack. Despite her refusal to marry him, Maxine was fond of the man.

"He kissed me, that's what! The old fool's gone and kissed me. And now what? I ask you. Now what?"

Ryan chuckled, and Kerrianne clenched her lips together to stop from laughing out loud.

"I think," Kerrianne said, "that you're going to have do what I did—stop playing games, and tell the man you'll marry him."

Maxine blinked, her eyes showing surprise. "Oh." Then she seemed to recover her composure. "Maybe. Just maybe, mind you. But for crying out loud, I'm not washing his clothes. Or cooking either!" Without another word she turned around and hurried back outside, skirting an old pile of snow on the walk. Kerrianne saw Harold, bundled in an overcoat, waiting in the driveway next to his car. He waved, as patient and polite as ever, and opened the door for Maxine.

As they drove away, Kerrianne and Ryan fell into each other's arms and burst into laughter. Kerrianne thought how wonderful this moment was, shared with a man she loved.

"Ryan?" a hesitant voice asked behind them.

They turned to see Misty standing alone, holding the basketball Ryan had given her. "I was just wondering since your parents aren't here yet . . . Well, maybe there's enough time to play basketball."

Ryan grinned. "Misty, even if they come right now, I wouldn't miss playing with you for the world. It's cold, though. Better grab a coat, princess."

They ran outside, Misty smiling so broadly that it hurt Kerrianne's heart as she watched from the window, her fingers spread against the cold pane. *It's working, Adam,* she thought. *Our little girl is learning to love again.* The thought didn't come with heartache, sadness, or regret, but with the quiet knowledge that love would somehow find the way for all of them.

Ria came to stand beside her. "I'd go out there, but I think Daddy's going to pretend to lose, and I hate games like that."

"Would you like to help me whip the cream for the chocolate pie?" Kerrianne asked. "It's real cream, not the fake stuff."

Ria nodded eagerly. "Can I lick the beaters?"

"Of course you can."

With a hand on Ria's shoulder, Kerrianne took a confident step into her new life.

About the Author

Rachel Ann Nunes (pronounced noon-esh) learned to read when she was four, beginning a lifetime fascination with the written word. She began writing in the seventh grade and is now the author of two dozen published books, including the popular *Ariana* series and the picture book *Daughter of a King*, voted best children's book of the year in 2003 by the Association of Independent LDS Booksellers. Her newest picture book, *The Secret of the King*, was chosen by the Governor's Commission on Literacy to be awarded to all Utah grade schools as part of the "Read with a Child for 20 Minutes per Day" program.

Rachel served a mission to Portugal for The Church of Jesus Christ of Latter-day Saints and teaches Sunday School in her Utah ward. She and her husband, TJ, have six children. She loves camping with her family, traveling, meeting new people, and, of course, writing. She writes Monday through Friday in her home office, often with a child on her lap, taking frequent breaks to build Lego towers, practice phonics, or jump on the trampoline with the kids.

Rachel welcomes invitations to speak to church groups and schools. Write to her at Rachel@RachelAnnNunes.com or P.O. Box 353, American Fork, UT 84003–0353. You can also visit her website, www.RachelAnnNunes.com, to enjoy her monthly newsletter or sign up to hear about new releases.